TAITTIRIYA UPANISHAD

Self beyond Sheaths

Commentary by

Swami Chinmayananda

Central Chinmaya Mission Trust

First Edition 1955
Printed upto - October 2003 to February 2012 - 19,500 copies
Revised Edition - January 2014 to September 2023 - 10,300 copies
Reprint - May 2025 - 2,500 copies

Published by:
Chinmaya Prakashan
The Publications Division of
Central Chinmaya Mission Trust
Sandeepany Sadhanalaya
Saki Vihar Road, Powai, Mumbai - 400072, India
Tel.: +91-22-2803 4900
Email: ccmtpublications@chinmayamission.com
Website: www.chinmayamission.com

Distribution Centre in the USA:
Chinmaya Publications West
560 Bridgetown Pike
Feasterville, PA 19053-7240, USA
Tel.: (215) 396-0390, Fax: (215) 396-9710
Email: publications@chinmayamission.org
Website: www.chinmayapublications.com

Designed by: Chinmaya Kalpanam, Mumbai

Printed by: Usha Multigraphs Pvt. Ltd., Mumbai

ISBN 978-81-7597-622-1

Contents

S. No.	Subject Matter	Page No.
1.	**Preface to the Revised Edition**	i
2.	**Foreword**	vii
3.	**Introduction**	1
4.	**Chapter I : Śīkṣā-vallī**	
	Peace Invocation (Śāntipāṭha)	
	Section i : Propitiatory Chant to Cosmic Powers	11
	Section ii : Principles of Vaidika Phonetics	18
	Section iii : Meditation On Juxtaposition	22
	Section iv : Necessity of Intelligence and Wealth	38
	Section v : The Mystic Expression 'Mahaḥ'	55
	Section vi : Additional Details to Meditation	65
	Section vii : Some Helpful Thoughts to Educate The Mind In Philosophical Culture	75
	Section viii : Praṇava – The Highest Symbol of Meditation	79
	Section ix : Some Ethical Principles and Practices	89
	Section x : Sacred Recitation of Triśaṅku After Realisation	98
	Section xi : The Convocation Address – The Commandments of Hinduism	107
	Section xii : Concluding Śāntipāṭha	134

S. No.	Subject Matter	Page No.
5.	**Chapter II : Brahmānanda-vallī**	
	Peace Invocation (Śāntipāṭha)	137
	Section i : Brahman is Satyam, Jñānam, Anantam – Enunciation of The Doctrine of Sheaths	140
	Section ii : Food, The Universal Medicament	160
	Section iii : Prāṇa, The Universal Life – The Food Sheath and Prāṇa	169
	Section iv : The Knower of Eternal Truth Fears Not – The Mental Sheath	176
	Section v : The Intellectual Sheath – Individual Soul Is The Agent and Experiencer	186
	Section vi : Godhood – The Experience of Positive Existence	194
	Section vii : Brahman – Bliss By Nature – Source of Fearlessness and Cause For Fear	208
	Section viii : Brahmānanda – The Supreme Bliss	222
	Section ix : Knower of Brahman Is Fearless Concluding Śāntipāṭha	247

S. No.	Subject Matter	Page No.
6.	**Chapter III : Bhṛgu-vallī**	
	Introduction	257
	Peace Invocation (Śāntipāṭha)	259
	Section i : Bhṛgu Approaches His Father Varuṇa With A Request To Teach Him Brahman	261
	Section ii : Food Is Brahman	267
	Section iii : Prāṇa Is Brahman	271
	Section iv : Mind Is Brahman	274
	Section v : Knowledge Is Brahman	277
	Section vi : Bliss Is Brahman, Feels Bhṛgu	281
	Section vii : Food Is Brahman. Respect Food, Gather and Distribute Food	290
	Section viii : 'Do Not Reject Food'	297
	Section ix : Unity of Creation – Accumulate Food For Distribution	302
	Section x : 'Don't Turn Away Anyone Who Seeks Food and Shelter' – The Hindu Code of Dharma	307
	Concluding Śāntipāṭha	335
7.	**Alphabetical Index of Mantras**	338

Transliteration and Pronunciation Guide

In this book, Devanagari characters are transliterated according to the scheme adopted by the International Congress of Orientalists at Athens in 1912. In it one fixed pronunciation value is given to each letter; f, q, w, x and z are not called to use. According to this scheme:

Devanagari	Translit-eration	Sounds Like	Devanagari	Translit-eration	Sounds Like
अ	a	son	ढ्	ḍh	adhesive*
आ	ā	father	ण्	ṇ	under*
इ	i	different	त्	t	tabla
ई	ī	feel	थ्	th	thumb
उ	u	full	द्	d	this
ऊ	ū	boot	ध्	dh	Gandhi
ऋ	ṛ	rhythm*	न्	n	nose
ॠ	ṝ	**	प्	p	pen
ऌ	ḷ	**	फ्	ph	phantom*
ए	e	evade	ब्	b	boil
ऐ	ai	delight	भ्	bh	abhor
ओ	o	core	म्	m	mind
औ	au	now	य्	y	yes
क्	k	calm	र्	r	right
ख्	kh	khan	ल्	l	love
ग्	g	gate	व्	v	very
घ्	gh	ghost	श्	ś	shut
ङ्	ṅ	ankle*	ष्	ṣ	sugar
च्	c	chuckle	स्	s	simple
छ्	ch	witch*	ह्	h	happy
ज्	j	justice	ं	ṁ	improvise
झ्	jh	Jhansi	ः	ḥ	**
ञ्	ñ	banyan	क्ष्	kṣ	action
ट्	ṭ	tank	त्र्	tr	three*
ठ्	ṭh	**	ज्ञ्	jñ	gnosis
ड्	ḍ	dog	ऽ	'	a silent 'a'

* These letters don't have an exact English equivalent. An approximation is given here.
** These sounds cannot be approximated in English words.

Preface to the Revised Edition

We all know that much of our ancient literature is now extinct. There were as many as 1180 śākhās of Vaidika literature. It is believed that each school (śākhā) had one Upaniṣad attached to it. Of about 280 Upaniṣads unearthed so far, 108 have been generally accepted as authentic texts. Out of these, eleven, namely *Īśa, Kena, Kaṭha, Praśna, Muṇḍaka, Māṇḍūkya, Taittirīya, Aitareya, Chāndogya, Bṛhadāraṇyaka* and *Śvetāśvatara*, in that order, have been commented upon by recent Masters like Śaṅkarācārya, Rāmānujācārya and Madhvācārya and they are classified as 'major' or principal Upaniṣads. Some do not accept the commentary on the *Śvetāśvatara-upaniṣad* as that of Śaṅkarācārya and thus acknowledge only ten major Upaniṣads.

The other Upaniṣads are considered 'minor' – not on account of their contents or the depth of their thoughts or the completeness of their exposition but because no commentaries are available from the great Ācāryas. The new initiates are generally prescribed these minor Upaniṣads only after a thorough study of the exhaustive commentaries (bhāṣyas) by the great Masters on five or six of the major Upaniṣads. Thus, these became minor only with reference to the knowledge the students have already acquired as a result of their study of the main Upaniṣads and their reflection on these minor ones serves as an interesting revision of the knowledge already gathered.

All Upaniṣads – major or minor, enunciate the one goal which is Liberation and prescribe techniques of achieving that goal. Hence all are of equal importance and value. The classification – major or minor – is only to distinguish the well known ones commented upon by Śaṅkarācārya.

The superhuman genius Vedavyāsa, gathered for the first time, Vaidika mantras, recorded them in written language and classified the entire wealth of Vaidika knowledge into four volumes in a harmonious rhythm, both in the arrangement and in the classification of contents. Each Veda was further divided into three broad sections – mantras, brāhmaṇas and āraṇyakas.

The mantra portion contains expressions of wonderment, joy and ecstasy at the choking visions of beauty in nature's exuberance. The ṛṣis worshipped through the mantras, the dignity of the mountains, the majesty of the sunrise, the beauty of the moon, the grandeur of the ocean and other similar phenomena.

The second section, the brāhmaṇa portion, contains detailed and scientific descriptions of various rituals and methods to invoke the mighty powers of nature, to bless the devotees' desires into fulfilment. This section is further divided into two subsections – karma kāṇḍa and upāsanā kāṇḍa. The grosser rituals, their rules, prescriptions for various yajñas form the first subsection while comparatively subtler meditations, that are part and parcel of Vaidika ritualism, form the second subsection.

The last section is called āraṇyakas (āraṇya means forest) – that can be studied only in the quiet Himalayan valleys, in a mental climate of psychological and intellectual retirement from the stormy passions and desires. This section is also known as Upaniṣads or Vedānta (Veda + anta – that which is the end of the Vedas), and comprises of the philosophical portion of the Vedas.

Taittirīya-upaniṣad belongs to *Yajur-veda* which occupies an unrivalled place in the divine tradition of Hinduism. How it got its name from sparrow bird (tittiri), as narrated in the *Mahābhārata* (XII-319), has been explained in foreword. To a casual reader, different chapters and different sections within each chapter, nay, even the subject dealt within each section seems to have no interconnection. This Upaniṣad is couched in lucid language which provides an insight into the lofty Hindu philosophy. Importance of this Upaniṣad can very well be gauged from the fact that Śrī Śaṅkarācārya's first commentary was on this Upaniṣad; also in his bhāṣya on *Brahmasūtras*, he quoted this Upaniṣad 147 times!

The unique feature of this Upaniṣad is that it explains the subjective Reality in the seeker both by direct and indirect methods. A lucid description of the five sheaths is found for the first time, here in this Upaniṣad.

At the close of the first chapter Śīkṣā-vallī, on two occasions, a valedictory address and a convocation message is given. The teacher in the Upaniṣad declares a manifesto of the 'Hindu way of living.'

Says the ṛṣi: 'Speak the truth. Do your duty. Do not neglect the study of the scriptures. Do not cut the thread of progeny. Swerve not from truth. Deviate not from the path of good. Revere greatness.'

'Let your mother be a God to you; let your father be a God to you; let your teacher be a God to you; let your guest be a God to you. Do only actions which are blameless. Always show reverence to the great.'

'Whatever you give to others, give with love and reverence. Gifts must be given in abundance, with joy, humility and compassion.'

'If at any time there is a doubt with regard to good conduct, follow the practice of great souls.'

These commandments of Hinduism are not despotic – not 'thou shall' as in Christianity but 'You may do it.' This is the unique feature of Hindu philosophy.

The second chapter, Brahmānanda-vallī opens with a profound declaration:

'He who realises Brahman attains the supreme Brahman as Truth, Knowledge and Infinite.'

Before creation came into existence, Brahman existed as the unmanifest. From the unmanifest was created the manifest. From Himself He brought forth Himself. Hence He is known as the self-existent.

Through fear of Brahman, the wind blows and the sun shines, through fear of Him Indra, the god of rain,

Agni, the god of fire and Yama, the god of death, perform their tasks.

He who knows the joy of Brahman, which words cannot express and the mind cannot reach, is free from fear. Such thoughts as 'Why did I not do what is right? Why did I do what is wrong?' do not bother a man who knows the joy of Brahman.

In the third chapter, Bhṛgu-vallī, the father-teacher Varuṇa while teaching Brahman to his son-disciple states:

'He from whom all beings are born, having born in whom they live and to whom they return at death – seek to know Him. He is Brahman. Seek to know Brahman by meditation. Meditation is Brahman.' The preceptor-father leads his disciple-son Bhṛgu step by step through meditation from food to prāṇa, to mind, to intellect till he realises that joy is Brahman.

To say that in his commentary on this Upaniṣad, the journalist, the logician, the scholar and the master of English literature – Swami Chinmayananda – was at His best is only to limit the unlimited. His pen seems to dance in ecstasy and lifts the readers to utopian heights.

Repeated reprints has resulted in numerous inaccuracies rendering understanding difficult for new sādhakas. Besides, readability was poor in small print. Both these aspects are taken care of in the revised layout, the credit for which is due to Śrī Vishvamitra Puri who with consistent perseverance and devotion scrutinised the entire book very minutely to identify misprints, missing words and lines; added diacritical marks and pursued steadfastly, the suggested changes/ improvements, with the Ācārya of Sandeepany Sadhanalaya Mumbai for approval.

In this revised edition diacritical marks are used for transliteration of Sanskrit words in the verses as well as commentary.

To be true to the Sanskrit text in transliteration, we have used 'brāhmaṇa' for the first varṇa instead of the commonly used word 'brāhmin'; it need not be confused with the term 'Brahman' of the Vedāntins.

A key to the transliteration and pronunciation is added in the beginning of this text. The contents showing briefly the subject dealt with in each section are also given. Alphabetical index of mantras is also added at the end of the book. Some of the mantras are split in the commentary. To facilitate easy location of split portions as well as other important lines, quotable statements occurring in the Upaniṣad are included in the alphabetical index.

We are pleased to bring out the present revised edition of the original commentary given by H. H. Swami Chinmayananda whom we all reverentially refer to as Pūjya Gurudev. This is our humble offering at his holy feet with a prayer that may his words and guidance inspire us to carry on his work in all spheres of activities such as this publication of scriptural thoughts for the benefit of the society.

Sri Guru Purnima Day:
9th July, 1998 **Publishers**

Foreword

An attempt of the finite to explain the Infinite is the content and import of all the scriptures of the world. The Upaniṣads are no exceptions to it. To define the Infinite is impossible, although, through words we can certainly indicate the Truth to one, who is ready to recognise the indication, follow the directions and come to experience Godhood.

Any fact can ordinarily be indicated through two methods: one is the direct method of positive description and the other is the indirect method of indicating what the thing is not. Thus to indicate an ocean, we can directly explain it as an endless expanse of water surging and seething on its surface with its waves, but calm and tranquil in its unplumbed depths; indirectly it can be indicated as that which has no outgrowths on it, that which is not solid, that which is not motionless, that which can never float in the air.

Similarly, Truth also is directly indicated by attributing to it certain qualities and indirectly it is indicated through its own manifestations. The direct method is called in Sanskrit, as an explanation through svarūpa lakṣaṇa and the indirect method is called as the taṭastha lakṣaṇa.

For example, to indicate the house of Mr. Gupta in a street, we may directly do so by describing it as, 'that two-storeyed building with the porch and balcony, with decorations round the window sill,' or we may indirectly point it out as 'the house next to that mango tree' or as 'the house upon which that crow is sitting.' Here the mango tree and crow are something other than Mr. Gupta's house, but they are used to show through them ultimately Mr. Gupta's house.

In this Upaniṣad, unlike in any other scripture in the world, the subjective Reality in the seeker, is indicated both by the direct method of explanation and by the indirect method of indications. In the second chapter, there is a direct attempt at definition of the Truth as 'Satyam, Jñānam, Anantam' and the text contains in its bulk the indirect indication of the pure Consciousness through an elaborate description of the various matter envelopments and the personality layers in man.

Nowhere in the world do we get such a complete study of the human personality with all its exhaustive features as in the *Taittirīya-upaniṣad*. Even in the tradition of Vedānta, the only occasion where we get a clear description of the five sheaths (pañcakośas) is in this famous Upaniṣad; its fame rests mainly upon the extremely direct method of self-enquiry that it prescribes.

This Upaniṣad belongs to the *Kṛṣna-yajur-veda* and forms part of its Taittirīya-āraṇyaka. There is a beautiful story that traditionally describes the title 'Taittirīya.' It is said that this portion was taught to Yājñavalkya by his Guru but at the end of the studies the Guru got annoyed with the disciple and asked him to return all that he had learnt from the teacher. Yājñavalkya, it is said, 'vomited' out all that he had learnt, seeing which the Guru advised his disciples to turn themselves into tittirī-birds (sparrows) and consume the 'vomit'. They did so and thus they came to master this āraṇyaka.

This story need not give us any disgust at all if we understand it properly. Annoyed with the lesser students of the classroom, the teacher asked Yājñavalkya to repeat the lesson that he had taught and the genius in Yājñavalkya 'vomited' what was taught to him. When a student has absorbed any knowledge and when he gives it out, it becomes more palatable to the other students who did not understand it directly from the teacher's learned discourse. Seeing that the delivery of Yājñavalkya was masterly, the teacher in appreciation, asked the other students of the class to absorb it like 'sparrows', which they did.

Of all the birds, sparrows are most energetic and industrious; the two great qualities necessary for any diligent student of literature of Vedānta are indicated here.

The entire Upaniṣad is divided into three sections:

(a) Śīkṣā-vallī – A section containing instructions, in not only pronunciation etc. but also in the different types of upāsanās by which a student can purify and sharpen his inner equipment;

(b) Brahmānanda-vallī – A section in which the Truth is directly explained and indirectly indicated through a scientific analysis of personality construction in man; and

(c) Bhṛgu-vallī – A section in which we are shown the practical application of the philosophical theories propounded in the previous vallīs. The section emphasises the need for constant enquiry and consistent meditation if a student is to come to enjoy a guaranteed success in the path of Vedānta.

Apart from the philosophical interest, the Upaniṣad gives us a vivid picture of the exhaustive training that was given in the educational system of that day. This ensured the development, growth and healthy sustenance of the brilliant Hindu culture of the Vaidika period. The all comprehensive instructions and the definite advice on 'how to live Vedānta in life' are given by the teacher to the student, at the end of the first section in the valedictory address and in the convocation message.

Today, our country needs a special study of these two portions, which in clear terms, hoot down our impotent Hindu misconceptions of our 'Ideal life'. Reconstituted on the basis of these healthy suggestions, we can certainly rebuild a Hindu India of 'Spiritual Communism' based upon mutual love, reinforced with the cement of Hindu brotherhood.

In it, one can clearly see a healthy message for the war torn world labouring under its own misconceptions of what life is and its own wrong evaluations of the factors that constitute true living.

Publishers

Introduction

The attempt of the Upaniṣads is to express the inexpressible, to paint the formless and to sing the voiceless beauty and Bliss of the Absolute. The finite words are no instruments to echo the roaring silence of the all full spiritual perfection.

Even in our ordinary experience, when we have to voice forth our intimate subjective experiences, we know that language fails in its own limitations. It is only a superstitious belief that language can do wonders everywhere; except perhaps, in the market place and in the banker's office; everywhere else it must feel choked. Factual ideas directly perceived through the five sense organs can be expressed, to an extent, by means of sound symbols which have, by mutual consent, come to represent literally some uniform meaning. Thus, a botanist can, with ease and efficiency, describe a flower, part by part, but when the poet enters the field to express the message of the flower and the thrills of beauty it has produced in him, the trembling sentiments and the throbbing emotions must snap the silver strings of every language.

Even when such an ordinary experience as a taste or a touch or a vision cannot completely be explained or fully conveyed through words, we can easily understand how impossible it is for words to express the tranquil experience one gets when one has transcended oneself consciously the body, the mind and the intellect.

From this it should not be concluded that the experience of the Infinite cannot be conveyed and is not available for the teachers to teach.

From the above, we must only understand that a language, which is generally used to express finite experiences, is used in the scriptures in a different technique altogether. Thus, in objective descriptions, language is used in its direct import, but in expressing the subjective experiences the same words are used, but therein the ringing notes and suggestive imports of the words are employed. Every word has, in combination with others, a direct literal meaning and an indirect pregnant suggestion.

This suggestiveness implied in each word is often used in everyday life. 'See that the crows do not come into the dining room', does not mean that vultures and doves, dogs and cats, rats and cows can freely come and poison the food. Here, the word 'crow' no doubt means literally that black bird of harsh looks and ugly melodies, but in the content it indicates all the animals and undesirable intruders into the dining hall. Examples can be multiplied to prove thus that words have got not only their literal meaning but, by usage, they gather a suggestiveness of their own, stored up in themselves as their special flavour.

The inexpressible infinite Truth is thus indicated by the words of the scriptures but not openly and directly expressed. This is true in almost all other religions also when the prophets are in an ecstasy of their own mystical experiences. But, in Hinduism, we find that throughout the lore of Upaniṣads almost every word is used to express the suggestive sense.

This is the difficulty in reading and experiencing the Truth from the scriptures directly. The ṛṣis had, for this express purpose, prepared a handy language reinforced with suggestions and the language so purified for the purpose came to be called as Sanskrit (purified). Words can only bring about certain intended disturbances in the minds of the listeners. When I say 'cup', the word penetrates and falls into your mind and the disturbance so caused makes the mind ripple out into the remembered memory of the form and the use of a cup.

Thus, in transacting mutually known experiences, language can be a handy medium of sound. But when it is employed to convey the experiences of one to another who knows nothing similar to it, the conveyance becomes difficult. Therefore, it was insisted that the teacher and the taught should be fully attuned to each other before the Master's words could bring about the required emphasis of the goal to the disciples. Our initial discussions are mainly to set up this attunement between us.

These are the days of blind and unintelligent 'Guru worship' on one hand, and 'Guru damnation' on the other. Those who believe, do so like the dumb cattle driven in a herd and there is no active enthusiasm or diligent intellectual stock taking on their part when they hear an advice or follow a path; unfortunately, religion is not meant for the unintelligent or for the stupid.

On the other hand, there is now a growing majority of blasphemers who are to be congratulated, for, their calumny is rightly directed against the false pretenders and the 'professional priest' class. Gurudom has become, in this country of general ignorance and particular superstition, a very paying and safe business, wherein there need not be any investment and therefore, it is a safe activity of 'all gain and no loss!!'.

But between these two extremities of opinions somewhere lies the truth and the Hindu scriptures are amply clear in their definition of a true Guru. They are never tired of repeating that a Guru is not the one who has temporarily inspired an individual to live a nobler life, but a Guru in Brahmavidyā is one who is well-read in the śāstras and also well established in his experience of the Supreme. In short, he must be well versed in the theory of self-perfection and must equally be well grounded in the technical aspect of Self-discovery.

When we read these qualifications so palpably defined, we are apt to consider it as an exaggeration or an over-statement but we forget that in our workaday world, a final year medical college student getting a telegram that he has passed his examination, is not, we all know, yet a safe doctor to consult or to perform any operation. So too, a law graduate. Similar is the case of a boy who has finished the course in Bachelor of Engineering. No knowledge is complete by a mere study of the theory. Study of a cookery book does not make a dependable cook. In view of this understanding, when we reread the insistence of the scriptures, we are able to appreciate how a śāstrī who can quote all the scriptures or an illiterate saint in the cave, enjoying his 'Self-experience' cannot be a complete teacher and guide to any one, who wants to walk the path and reach the goal.

Not only is it sufficient that we discover a Guru with these qualifications, but we must be able to tune ourselves completely with that teacher. There are some unintelligent atheists who, in their haste, have come to wrong conclusions about the relationship between the teacher and the taught in ancient India. According to them, the complete surrender of the taught to his teacher is a convenience for the Guru and that, according to them, in these days there should be some sort of a 'union of disciples' guarding them from the tyrannies of the gurus!

Closer observation and examination of the working of the system will make it clear that in this relationship, instead of the Guru exploiting the disciple, it is the former that subjects himself to exploitation.

It is very well-known that we can appreciate only that art which is already in us and our capacity to appreciate the finer points in it depends upon our own growth and development in that line. A painter is no reviewer of poems; a sculptor is no judge of music. To enjoy music or painting, we must have in us the same art to some extent. The greater I can tune myself to the mental emotions of an artist, to that extent I can appreciate his art.

Similarly, the divine perfection experienced by the Master's mind can be relived by the disciple in himself only when the teacher and the taught have, to an extent, come to feel an inner identity, a divine attunement to each other; thereafter, the scintillating joys of the Master, symbolically represented by his gasping language, can enter the mind of the disciples in their echoing presence, a similar atmosphere of purity and divinity. Mere word meanings of the scriptures are not only half truths, but in many cases they prove to be positively dangerous. The suggestiveness of the words, like 'scent' in flowers, has a reach farther than the word and it is with this aura of the vocabulary that the Truth is illumined.

In order to raise the attunement to the necessary pitch, the methods of upāsanās are advised in all the Upaniṣads.

Upāsanā is an intellectual process of conscious thinking over a subtle object superimposed for the purpose by the mind, temporarily upon a grosser object. To have upon a lesser object (nikṛṣṭa vastu) a superimposition of a nobler ideal (utkṛṣṭa dṛṣṭi) is upāsanā. To superimpose the idea of the 'Goddess of Learning' and Her divinity upon the river Ganga and thereafter to worship its waters as sacred, and to offer to it with flowers and lights, milk and rice, is a typical example of upāsanā.

In the Upaniṣad under discussion, one-third of the portion deals with advising different details of upāsanās, which clearly shows how essential the preliminary technique of self-integration is for a seeker of knowledge.

The technique of upāsanā, as is met with in the Vedas, is adopted for a later generation, to suit the psychological demands of that age, in the bhakti cult or the bhāgavata cult. Śrī Vyāsa Bhagavāna is the master intellect that gave us the new adaptation of the method. To meditate upon a formless Power as it is advised in the Upaniṣads is essentially a dry and arid path over which the intellect strives forth in all its might and strength. The same path becomes a flower garden of scented beauty and soft pleasures when the formless God becomes the carved beauty of the paurāṇika age. In the garden of bhakti, the tender and the soft hearts dance in ecstasy among its arbours of music and joy.

Thus, it becomes clear that without a certain amount of positive ethical and moral living, a fair share of self-control (brahmacarya) and a lot of conscious and deliberate practices through devotion and selfless work, an individual student of philosophy will not have in himself the necessary amount of inner integration. Without the minimum amount of intellectual sharpness and mental tranquility, it is certainly impossible to understand the scriptures as they should be understood, if our studies were to fulfill themselves by bringing out the beauty that is now lying concealed within ourselves.

The entire opening chapter of this scripture contains different methods of upāsanās (meditations) which may sound to us as strange and meaningless, but we shall try to go through them as best as we can. In our examination, we shall try to get an idea of the old methods which were advised by those teachers for the developing of concentration and intellectual poise of the seekers of that time.

Taittirīya-upaniṣad

The *Taittirīya-upaniṣad* belongs to the *Kṛṣna-yajur-veda* and forms a part of its *Taittirīya-āraṇyaka.* There is an interesting tradition attached to the Taittirīya. It is said that Saint Vaiśampāyana got annoyed with a prominent disciple of his, Yājñavalkya and the Guru ordered the disciple to return all the knowledge so far taught to him. Yājñavalkya vomited the entire knowledge acquired seeing which Vaiśampāyana ordered his other disciples to take the form of partridges (tittirī birds) and consume the leavings. This is the reason, it seems, that this portion of the Veda was traditionally labelled as Taittirīya.

This story, if we understand it literally, may read as vulgar and abominable; but there are teachers who interpret it to mean that Yājñavalkya the genius that he was, was asked by his teacher to repeat what he had learnt and seeing that the prodigy had not only understood the true import of what the Master taught, but had in his own originality brought an independent charm into it that, the teacher asked his other disciples to consume it as best as they can. In this connection, it would be interesting to note that the tittirī birds, the partridges, though small in size are the most active and ever vigilant among the plumed variety. The story includes healthy instruction to the students of the Upaniṣads that they are to be intellectually as smart, as vigilant, and as active in their quest for knowledge as the tittirī birds are in their ordinary life.

All Upaniṣads start with a 'peace invocation', a prayer to the cosmic powers to ward off all obstacles on the path of study. This prayer is chanted daily together by the teacher and the taught. A prayer is an invocation and not a contract. Nowadays, we are misusing this technique of prayer in our own ignorance and therefore we find that our gods are deaf to our prayers. This is true today with all religions. The science of prayer explains that when an individual surrenders himself, meaning, all his identifications with his body, mind and intellect through devotion, reverence and understanding, he removes from himself all the causes for his limitations and what is thus left over is the absolute perfection which is the essence of his very being. Thus prayer is the active part of the divine action, while the final successful invocation is its fulfilment.

Here in the peace invocation, the thing desired or invoked is not something to satisfy the physical comfort or the mental desires of the students. He is no beggar even at the feet of the Lord! All that he demands of the cosmic powers, whom he is invoking, is that no obstacles shall come during the study of the śāstras at the feet of his Master. In this Upaniṣad, the very peace invocation is also repeated as the first 'section' of the opening vallī and hence we shall explain it as under the opening section.

Chapter I

Śīkṣā-vallī

Peace-invocation

(Śāntipāṭha)

Section i – अनुवाकः १

Propitiatory Chant to Cosmic Powers

ॐ शं नो मित्रः शं वरुणः। शं नो भवत्वर्यमा।
शं न इन्द्रो बृहस्पतिः। शं नो विष्णुरुरुक्रमः।
नमो ब्रह्मणे। नमस्ते वायो।
त्वमेव प्रत्यक्षं ब्रह्मासि।
त्वामेव प्रत्यक्षं ब्रह्म वदिष्यामि।
ऋतं वदिष्यामि। सत्यं वदिष्यामि।
तन्मामवतु तद्वक्तारमवतु।
अवतु माम्। अवतु वक्तारम्॥
ॐ शान्तिः शान्तिः शान्तिः ॥१॥

om śaṁ no mitraḥ śaṁ varuṇaḥ, śaṁ no bhavatvaryamā,
śaṁ na indro bṛhaspatiḥ, śaṁ no viṣṇururukramaḥ,
namo brahmaṇe, namaste vāyo,
tvameva pratyakṣaṁ brahmāsi,
tvāmeva pratyakṣaṁ brahma vadiṣyāmi,

ṛtaṁ vadiṣyāmi, satyaṁ vadiṣyāmi,
tanmāmavatu tadvaktāramavatu,
avatu mām, avatu vaktāram.
om śāntiḥ śāntiḥ śāntiḥ. (1)

ॐ – om; शम् – propitious; नः – to us; मित्रः – controller of day and prāṇa; शम् – propitious; वरुणः – controller of night and apāna; शम् – propitious; नः – to us; भवतु – may be; अर्यमा – controller of eyes and sun's orbit; शम् – propitious; नः – to us; इन्द्रः – controller of strength and arms; बृहस्पतिः – controller of speech and intellect; शम् – propitious; नः – to us; विष्णुः – controller of feet; उरुक्रमः – the all-pervading (wide-striding); नमः – salutation(s); ब्रह्मणे – unto Brahman; नमः – salutation; ते – unto thee; वायो – O vāyu; त्वम् – thou; एव – alone; प्रत्यक्षम् – perceivable; ब्रह्म – Brahman; असि – art; त्वाम् – thee; एव – alone; प्रत्यक्षम् – perceivable; ब्रह्म – Brahman; वदिष्यामि – I shall declare; ऋतम् – the right (controller of right); वदिष्यामि – I shall declare; सत्यम् – the good (controller of the good); वदिष्यामि – I shall declare; तत् – that (Brahman); माम् – me; अवतु – may protect; तत् – that (Brahman); वक्तारम् – the speaker; अवतु – may protect; अवतु – may protect; माम् – me; अवतु – may protect; वक्तारम् – the speaker

May Mitra be propitious to us. May Varuṇa bless us. May the blessings of Aryamā be with us. May the grace of Indra and Bṛhaspati be upon us. May Viṣṇu, the all-pervading (wide-striding) be propitious to us. Salutations to Brahman. Salutations to Thee, O Vāyu! Thou art the visible Brahman. Thee alone shall I consider as the visible Brahman. I shall declare: Thou art the 'Right'; Thou art the 'Good'. May That protect me; may That protect the speaker. Please protect me. Please protect the speaker.

Om Peace Peace Peace!

This peace chanting is sung by the teacher and the taught together and it is a prayer raised in devotion to the recognised gods of the Vaidika period, who were representations of the one divine cosmic power. The ideals of the Divine, such as Rāma, Kṛṣṇa and others are all a later development, being the products of the paurāṇika age. In early Hinduism, the devotees prayed at the feet of the one cosmic power recognised through its various representations as Mitra, Varuṇa, Aryamā, and so on. They are all, as the Veda declares, different names and expressions of the same one power that functions behind the entire phenomena of nature and presides over their destinies.

These deities invoked here, are all delegates representing in themselves one power or the other, given to them by the all powerful. Thus Mitra is the guardian spirit of the prāṇa and the day, since all energy and activity are expressed in full swing at the daytime. Varuṇa governs the 'outgoing breath' apāna and the night. Here it may be noted that whenever we call from ourselves any great exertion, such as lifting a weight, pushing a thing or expressing our thought; in all such moments of activity we have to breathe in hard and the activity ceases and exhausts at the expense of the outgoing breath; and with the completion of the apāna, the energy also exhausts.

Aryamā is the presiding deity of the sun and the eyes. The cosmic power identifed with the source of all energy and light, the sun, is called at that moment of identification, with reference to its particular conditioning, as Aryamā. If the sun were not there, sun, meaning the light principle, the objects and things of the world will not be illumined by the eyes, since, the sense organ, eyes can function only in the medium of light. Even the most powerful telescope or microscope cannot illumine an object in a dark room. In the medium of light alone can the eyes function and therefore, to consider the sun, the source of all light, as the presiding deity of the human eye, is quite reasonable and scientific.

To those who have been initiated into the secret of this conception, Indra is the governor of all might and the physical strength in an individual, though it cannot be located, we can at least say that its expression is generally through the instrument of the hands.

Bṛhaspati is again an expression of the Divine which controls intelligence and knowledge (speech and intellect). Viṣṇu, in his all-pervading nature, governs all movements and thus becomes the deity of the feet.

Thus, in invoking the blessings of Mitra, Varuṇa, Aryamā, Indra, Bṛhaspati and Viṣṇu, the Vaidika teachers and students were invoking healthy 'prāṇa', 'apāna', efficient eyesight, willing hands, wise speech and healthy limbs, so that day and night, with energy and strength, they may accomplish wise intellectual movement and fulfil the study in revolutionising the gross in them to become divine.

The word 'śaṁ' means 'well-being' and therefore, the entire invocation is a prayer to these forces for their grace, so that in their blessings, all the above mentioned instruments in us may be assured of their well-being. For a perfect and profitable 'listening' (śravaṇa) to the philosophical discourses and for the diligent pursuits in acquiring, maintaining and living the new values pointed out in the śāstra, it is amply self-evident that we want all these instruments and powers in full vigour and health.

To lift our eyes from the import and secret implications of this invocation to the society around and about us, crawling in disease and rotting in untimely deaths, is to understand how far we have ignored the spirit of our culture and have come to suffer. All that we can now claim of our great heritage is but a vain effort to give a gloss of philosophical neglect to our ignoble ignorance. Vedānta does not dole out any excuse for the society to ignore their health. Physical health is of consummate importance and it is so perfectly evident when we lift the veil of the words and understand the true import of this invocation.

So far, the invocation was dealing with the subjective individual himself and his anatomical and psychological parts. The prayer now becomes a direct call to the Supreme: 'Our salutations to Brahman', a name uniformly used in the entire Vaidika literature to address the infinite, supreme Truth, upon whom the pluralistic phenomena with their partial expressions of dynamism and energy are but an idle superimposition. 'Salutations unto Thee O Vāyu', meaning (here), the expression of life in and through the infinite variety of equipments which constitute the entire bulk and girth of the universe. This Vāyu is otherwise called in Vedānta as the Sūtrātmā, meaning, the 'evident expression of life' on the basis of which the entire kingdom of the living – the plant, the animal and the man – are wound together, as the different flowers are held together by the string to form a garland. The supreme Brahman is unmanifest and being all-pervading, is not available for our recognition either to the organs of knowledge, or to the mind or to the intellect. Vāyu represents the implicit expression of the infinite dynamism of the one Reality, as it is available for human cognition during a close observation of life and therefore, Vāyu represents the manifested Brahman (hiraṇyagarbha).

Ṛtam and satyam – Ṛtam is a technical term which, in its Vaidika usage, indicates the positive meaning of the śāstra when correctly understood through an intellectual appreciation of the spirit of the scriptures. Its practice in our day-to-day activities (ācāra) becomes the dharma and it is called satyam.

May 'That' (meaning the Supreme, the Essence of all such as the Vāyu) bless me, so that my studies are fruitful. This is sung, by a vidyārthī, meaning, one who demands (arthī) the blessing of brahmavidyā. The student prays to the Supreme that his teacher also be blessed so that no obstacles may come during this sacred transaction of the sacred study. The repetition is only for emphasis.

The invocation is rounded up with a thrice repeated 'call for peace'. This is to avert all possible obstacles. Obstacles are many and to exhaust all possibilities by name or label is impossible. But all obstacles can be classified under three heads with reference to the sources from which they arise. Thus, the sources of obstacles can be:

a) unseen,

b) seen and known,

c) subjective, within ourselves in our own mind.

In order to avert all obstacles arising from the above three types of causes, we have the thrice repeated peace call.

Section ii - अनुवाकः २

Principles of Vaidika Phonetics

ॐ शीक्षां व्याख्यास्यामः । वर्णः स्वरः ।
मात्रा बलम् । साम सन्तानः । इत्युक्तः शीक्षाध्यायः ॥१ ॥

om śīkṣāṁ vyākhyāsyāmaḥ, varṇaḥ svaraḥ,
mātrā balam, sāma santānaḥ, ityuktaḥ śīkṣādhyāyaḥ. (1)

ॐ – om; शीक्षाम् – the science of pronunciation; व्याख्यास्यामः – we shall explain; वर्णः – sound; स्वरः – accent or pitch; मात्रा – measure; बलम् – the effort employed in articulation; साम – uniformity; सन्तानः – continuity (in pronouncing the letters); इति – thus; उक्तः – has been explained; शीक्षाध्यायः – the chapter on pronunciation

1. We shall now explain the science of pronunciation. It consists of the sounds, accent or the pitch, quality or measure, the effort put in articulation, uniformity and continuity in pronouncing the letters. Thus has been explained the lesson on pronunciation.

In this section, we have the entire science of phonetics that goes under the name śīkṣā. Here the word śīkṣā, in which there is a lengthening of the first letter, is justified as grammatical peculiarity sanctioned in Vaidika usages. Before being instructed and initiated into the Vaidika study, the students had to go through a thorough schooling in the art and science of pronunciation. Unless a language codifies its rules of articulation and insists that every student must begin his education with a complete grounding in its rules, the chances are that, in a short time, the language will gain into its fold, local usages and wrong pronunciations.

A casual examination of all the existing languages today would give us an idea of this danger. The numberless dialects that are available from district to district in this vast country of ours, where, in many of them the mother language is almost forgotten, are instances in point. This is so not only in India; in Europe also the condition is the same. The telegraphic language adopted by the American press today is a living example of how the noble language of the eighteenth century, its dignity of diction, power of expression, rhythm and beauty of sounds used have all been lost in a vulgar slang wherein even vowels are totally swallowed or only partially gasped out.

Contrasted with this confusion in a spoken language as English brought about from place to place even within a couple of centuries, we have in the Vaidika lore, a language that has stood the test of thousands of years, and even today, except in rare cases, the pronunciation is uniform all over the country. It is so because the study of the science of pronunciation is insisted upon everywhere before the student is initiated into the Vedas.

The teacher here is addressing Vaidika students and by the time the student has come to the Upaniṣad class, he has, in his education, mastered the early lessons in the curriculum wherein he has already been initiated into these topics. Therefore, the teacher has only to remind the student of the importance of these topics and hence, in this section, we find only the enumeration of the various sub-headings. Maybe, the ṛṣi, at the time of his discourses, might have given exhaustive talks on these topics and the mantras, as they stand, only represent the points of the talk which the students were made to repeat as a help for them to remember the entire discourse.

The science of phonetics or orthography includes: varṇa (letter of sounds), svara (accent or pitch), mātrā (measure or length of time), balam (effort in pronouncing), sāma (pronouncing the letters of a word uniformly) and santāna (continuity of words). The letters fall under many groups; the guttural, the palatal, the dental, the labial and so on.

The 'accents' or tones that generally fall on the vowels in each word or syllable are of three kinds: udātta (the acute or high) anudātta (the low) and svarita (the grave or middle). The 'measure' or length of time required in pronouncing the short, the long and the lengthened vowels is also to be carefully noted by every student of phonetics. The correct time taken to pronounce a short vowel is considered as one P-instant (hrasva); to pronounce a long vowel is two P-instants (dīrgha); and a prolonged vowel is three P-instant (pluta).

The 'effort' in pronouncing is indicated by the exertion that the speaker has to put upon his vocal cords in bringing forth the right sound in the right way. The science explains these efforts under two different headings, the outer and the inner; and again, in its details divides the 'outer efforts' as of eleven kinds; and the 'inner' as of five kinds.

The rule of 'uniform' pronunciation is evidently most important or else the meaning can become totally different. 'Rāmaw ent tos chool' cannot be easily understood by anybody as 'Rāma went to school'. The 'regular blending' of sounds and words (santāna) is also as important in language, in order to elicit the correct meaning. 'Ajmer gayā' (gone to Ajmer) will become a statement of tragedy and bereavement if we disobey the rules of santāna and say, 'Āj mer (mar) gayā' (today he has died)!

Uktaḥ – 'has been explained'. This word indicates the end of the section and it clearly shows that the teacher must have given exhaustive discourses upon these six limbs of the science of pronunciation so that at the end of it all he concludes that the lesson on pronunciation 'has been explained.'

Section iii – अनुवाकः ३

Meditation On Juxtaposition

सह नौ यशः। सह नौ ब्रह्मवर्चसम् ।
अथातः सगुंहिताया उपनिषदं व्याख्यास्यामः।
पञ्चस्वधिकरणेषु।
अधिलोकमधिज्यौतिषमधिविद्यमधिप्रजमध्यात्मम्।
ता महासगुंहिता इत्याचक्षते ॥१॥

saha nau yaśaḥ, saha nau brahmavarcasam,
athātaḥ sagṁhitāyā upaniṣadaṁ vyākhyāsyāmaḥ,
pañcasvadhikaraṇeṣu,
adhilokamadhijyautiṣamadhividyamadhiprajamadhyātmam,
tā mahāsagṁhitā ityācakṣate. (1)

सह – together; नौ – for both of us; यशः – glory; सह – together; नौ – for both of us; ब्रह्मवर्चसम् – effulgence born of holy life and scriptural study; अथ – now; अतः – hereafter; सगुंहिताया – the teaching of conjunction; उपनिषदम् – sacred science; व्याख्यास्यामः – we shall explain; पञ्चसु – in five; अधिकरणेषु – perceptible objects; अधिलोकम् – concerning the universe; अधिज्यौतिषम् – concerning the luminaries; अधिविद्यम् – concerning learning; अधिप्रजम् – concerning progeny; अध्यात्मम् – concerning body; ता – they; महासगुंहिता – the great combinations; इति – thus; आचक्षते – they call, declare

1. The pupils say, 'May we both, teacher and disciple, have the glory and effulgence born of holy life and scriptural study'. The teacher says, 'Now we shall explain the secret of teaching of conjunction'. This teaching is based on five perceptible objects: a) Universe b) Luminaries c) Learning d) Progeny e) Body. These they call 'the great combinations' (or 'blendings').

The teacher and the taught, after the initial introductory talk on the science of pronunciation, they start the discussion on the Upaniṣad and the necessary upāsanās in making the mind and intellect perfectly sharp and sensitive for the full apprehension of the immortal Truth, the theme of the Upaniṣad. When the teacher has finished his previous talk and indicated it with the word 'uktaḥ', the student immediately raises a song of prayer inviting the glory of Brahman upon both the Master and himself. The prayer expresses a wish that both of them may be rendered shining with the joy of knowledge.

After this prayer, the teacher starts prescribing the various methods of upāsanās. We have already seen that upāsanā is a technique by which the entire dynamism of the mind is directed through a constant thought flow towards a defined goal through a well chalked out line of contemplation. For this, various instances are given and any one of them is as good as any other. Different types are given to suit, perhaps different entities, or may be, in his juvenile enthusiasm, a young boy's growing mind may get easily tired of one given method and may thirst to ramble into some novel methods of employing his surging mental dynamism. Therefore, it is perfectly justified if the ṛṣi gives a dozen different methods of meditations.

In the early stages, no student can attempt meditating upon a formless, nameless, attributeless Truth which is at once omniscient, omnipotent and infinite. As an elementary training, the mind needs some ideal or idea to fix its attention on and plough out all possibilities from it, in and around the central theme. Thus, in all upāsanās, the technique is to tie down the mind to a central idea – pivot, allowing the mind a limited movement, but with a full freedom to roam at will within those prescribed limitations. This scheme is well illustrated in the freedom of a cow on a pasture land when fixed to a peg with a long rope.

Rāma, Kṛṣṇa, Śiva are deities fashioned out for this purpose in the purāṇas, so that devotees will have some tangible divine personality upon whom they can fix the infinite qualities of Truth and have their elementary training in meditation. When the object or the support is thus a tangible and almost pulsating divine personality, the upāsanā becomes an emotional extravaganza and a love game in the garden of prema and bhakti. But in the days of the Vedas, the paurāṇika deities were not available; Vyāsa the author of purāṇas belonged to a much later date.

After planting a stone or a wooden cross, the devotee superimposes upon it the Śiva-tattva or the Christ-idea and meditates upon the Lord of his heart through this symbol. So too, the Vaidika ṛṣi had to supply a substratum, tangible and known to the students, before he could make them superimpose upon the provided symbol, the ideas of a vaster and an ampler Truth. Once this technique is understood, all upāsanās prescribed in the Vaidika lore become amply self-evident.

As students of Sanskrit, repeating daily Sanskrit statements and stanzas, they were familiar with the conjunction of syllables and joining of words. When two words are joined together, that compound word in Sanskrit invariably indicates the point of conjunction very clearly to the students who are literates in the language. During their chantings and in those days in their mutual conversations too they had been joining convenient words together and disjoining them when it suited their purpose and so they had a very clear idea of the construction of the 'compound word'. Therefore, the teacher intelligently took up a 'compound word' and its structure as a substratum for his students to superimpose certain prescribed ideas, so that they could meditate upon them. The rest of the technical tricks are all faithfully represented in the very well known bhakti mārga of our own times.

The superimpositions upon the 'combination of words' as advised here, fall under five headings. These represent the five different fields of independent thinking superimposed upon the limbs of the 'compound words.' For example, let us take a 'compound word' like Maheśvara, which is a word having for its limbs, an adjective and a noun: Mahā and Īśvara. The first word, Mahā is called the 'prior' and Īśvara that follows it is called the 'posterior'. The prior sound 'ā' with which the word Mahā ends, when it joins with the 'Ī' of the posterior word Īśvara, together they become 'ae' sound in conjunction. This is the clear form of the combination which is to serve as the substratum for the students' superimposition in upāsanā.

**अथाधिलोकम् । पृथिवी पूर्वरूपम् । द्यौरुत्तररूपम् ।
आकाशः सन्धिः । वायुः सन्धानम् । इत्यधिलोकम् ॥२॥**

*athādhilokam, pṛthivī pūrvarūpam, dyauruttararūpam,
ākāśaḥ sandhiḥ, vāyuḥ sandhānam, ityadhilokam. (2)*

अथ – now; **अधिलोकम्** – concerning the universe; **पृथिवी** – the earth; **पूर्वरूपम्** – prior form; **द्यौः** – the sky (firmament); **उत्तररूपम्** – posterior form; **आकाशः** – the atmosphere: **सन्धिः** – the junction; **वायुः** – the air; **सन्धानम्** – means of joining, connection; **इति** – thus; **अधिलोकम्** – on the universe; (**ध्यायेत्** – one should meditate)

2. The teaching concerning the universe is this: The earth is the prior form, the heaven (firmament) is the posterior form; the atmosphere is the junction, air is the connection. Thus one should meditate upon the universe.

On the familiar structure of the compound word, here is an idea to be superimposed by the upāsaka for the purpose of his contemplation. This treatment gives the student a chance to harness his naturally wandering mind into a subtle perception of the vastness of the cosmic and the interconnection between the perceived plurality in the phenomena. To any student, while reading or chanting, it is not possible to fix his entire mind upon the words of the text. The mind will naturally wander to the Guru's cowshed or to his half-ploughed fields; or, perhaps, into the jungle where he has to go in the afternoon to bring fuel for the āśrama kitchen.

In short, a large amount of the student's mental energy is always afloat, wandering in the other fields, except perhaps, for a short time during intervals, when he is focusing his entire attention on his studies. These wandering energies of the mind are being harnessed here for the purpose of concentration and the ideas upon which they are made to wander, in their very nature, give an expansion and a glorious reach for the mind and intellect of the upāsaka.

From the cowshed to the skies, from the jungle to the wide expanse of the world, from the clothes that had not been washed to the endless concept of space and from the unfinished ploughing to the concept of the atmospheric air – embracing at once, the heaven and the earth into its ample bosom – is indeed a glorious avenue through which the disciple's mind is made to expand into a thrilling freedom and exuberance.

अथाधिज्यौतिषम् । अग्निः पूर्वरूपम् ।
आदित्य उत्तररूपम् । आपः सन्धिः ।
वैद्युतः सन्धानम् । इत्यधिज्यौतिषम् ॥३॥

athādhijyautiṣam, agniḥ pūrvarūpam,
āditya uttararūpam, āpaḥ sandhiḥ,
vaidyutaḥ sandhānam, ityadhijyautiṣam. (3)

अथ – now; अधिज्यौतिषम् – concerning the luminaries; अग्निः – fire; पूर्वरूपम् – prior form; आदित्य – the sun; उत्तररूपम् – the posterior form; आपः – water; सन्धिः – the intermediate form; वैद्युतः – lightning; सन्धानम् – means of joining, the connection; इति – thus; अधिज्यौतिषम् – upon the light; (ध्यायेत् – one should meditate)

3. Now concerning the luminaries or meditations upon light; fire is the prior form, the sun is the posterior form; water is the intermediate form and lightning is the connection. Thus one should meditate upon light.

As explained above, upon the same substratum, here is another idea regarding luminaries which emit light. The source of light very well known to the student, is certainly fire which becomes the prior form and the posterior is represented by the sun which is the source of all life, meaning here, all energy. If two mutually unrelated objects are enumerated, no meditation upon them is possible unless we are told, or we come to discover, a relationship between them. That connection between the sun and the fire is explained here as water, meaning, the moisture in the atmosphere. Water can be converted into its vapour only through the application of heat energy. A certain amount of vapour is always present in the atmosophere, which is contributed by the heat energy from both, the fire and the sun. Thus we are told that vapour or moisture in the atmosphere is the connection between the sun and fire, which may also mean that one common factor in both of them, is heat.

If water vapour is thus the junction between the two, lightning is the means of joining them. When two things are amalgamated to become one homogeneous whole, there should be continuity in their quality throughout. Two samples of sugar, kept at a distance of a foot on the table, cannot be considered as one whole until they are brought together; when they are together, every part of it is sugar. Similarly, the heat and light energy in the sun and the heat and light energy in fire are separated from one another by an endless column of atmosphere. As a result of their heat, the atmosphere gets laden with moisture and the light and heat principle expressing themselves as streaks of lightning connect, in silvery threads, the sun above and his representative below! This beautiful picture not only smacks of science but, in its totality, provides a compelling but dreadful beauty expressing light and heat in all their might and intensity.

अथाधिविद्यम् । आचार्यः पूर्वरूपम् ।
अन्तेवास्युत्तररूपम् । विद्या सन्धिः ।
प्रवचनगं् सन्धानम् । इत्यधिविद्यम् ॥४ ॥

athādhividyam, ācāryaḥ pūrvarūpam,
antevāsyuttararūpam, vidyā sandhiḥ,
pravacanagṁ sandhānam, ityadhividyam. (4)

अथ – now; अधिविद्यम् – concerning learning; आचार्यः – the teacher; पूर्वरूपम् – the prior form; अन्तेवासी – the taught or pupil; उत्तररूपम् – the posterior form; विद्या – learning; सन्धिः – the intermediate form; प्रवचनम् – the instruction; सन्धानम् –

the connection, means of joining; इति – thus; अधिविद्यम् – upon learning; (ध्यायेत् – one should meditate)

4. Now concerning knowledge: The teacher is the prior form, the taught is the posterior form; learning is the intermediate form and the instruction is the means of joining. Thus one should meditate upon learning.

Using the same support for concentration (ālambanam) here the teacher is advising a new line of thought taken from the familiar field of the students' activity. It is a homely thing for every student and is very easy for him to understand when he is made to contemplate upon himself and his teacher and the relationship that exists between the two. The teacher and the students generally come to meet each other in a vibrant atmosphere of learning or studies, and the cord upon which the students and the teacher are strung together into a united whole is the cementing essence of the deep significance of the discourse given out by the teacher. The teacher invariably talks about the vision of Truth that he had gained within himself and the students are those who want to experience sympathetically the same vision, if not in actual experience, at least, for the time being, in an intellectual appreciation. Thus, a bristling atmosphere of mental unison is maintained in the halls of learning when the students crowd around the teacher and honestly strive to gather for themselves knowledge and wisdom from the teacher's mouth.

**अथाधिप्रजम् । माता पूर्वरूपम् । पितोत्तररूपम् ।
प्रजा सन्धिः । प्रजननगं् सन्धानम् । इत्यधिप्रजम् ॥५॥**

*athādhiprajam, mātā pūrvarūpam, pitottararūpam,
prajā sandhiḥ, prajananagṁ sandhānam, ityadhiprajam. (5)*

अथ – now; **अधिप्रजम्** – concerning progeny or birth; **माता** – mother; **पूर्वरूपम्** – the prior form; **पिता** – father; **उत्तररूपम्** – the posterior form; **प्रजा** – progeny; **सन्धिः** – the intermediate form, junction; **प्रजननम्** – procreation; **सन्धानम्** – the connection, means of joining; **इति** – thus; **अधिप्रजम्** – upon progeny; (**ध्यायेत्** – one should meditate)

5. Now concerning progeny: mother is the prior form, father is the posterior form; progeny is the junction and procreation is the connection. Thus one should meditate upon progeny.

In the days of yore, especially in the Vaidika period, the Upaniṣad had been freely taught to the deserving. But that did not mean that the study of the scriptures compelled or insisted or even prepared the ground for an immediate retirement from life into the jungles. The generation was taught these glorious secrets of life and trained in the art of living in complete unison with life and its circumstances before the members were sent to face the onslaughts of its day-to-day challenges. Therefore, instructions regarding the most vital urges in man, such as sex, were freely given out and, under healthy social conditions this cannot bring about any deterioration in the moral life of the people. It was only after Śaṅkarācārya's time that the tradition of young men taking to sannyāsa 'with a desire to learn the higher life and live the life divine' had come into vogue, since chances in society to learn the Upaniṣads had become almost little.

But the Upaniṣad studies have come to be recognised today as a special privilege of only sannyāsins and a corollary to this wrong impression is the superstitious belief, which frightens away the dull-witted, that the studies of the Upaniṣads will make a healthy man uninterested in life and ultimately it will abduct him away from the fields of activity to the dark caves of an impotent retirement!!

In the golden age of the Vaidika culture, the intelligent Hindus understood the value of the literature and the general curriculum in education included the study of the śruti. Under such a scheme of things, this meditation (upāsanā) advised, when viewed against the background of that age, need not give us the sense of outrageousness that we apt to feel at the first instance, during a hasty reading.

Again, unlike the suicidal belief in the Christian creed, we do not consider sex relationship as the first sin by which the God-man had come to fall to become the stupid, the deluded, the egocentric entity, rotting away in his own sorrows and sins! On the other hand, we believe that the relationship of man and woman is divine when rightly understood and wisely pursued. Progressive in thought, daring in planning the social welfare, the scientists of life, who gave us the immortal Sanātana Dharma through our scriptures, were not shy, sentimental, effeminate fools to fight shy of the great principle of life simply because of an idle misapprehension.

The unhealthy misunderstanding regarding the relationship of man and woman in life, I dare say, is the cause of almost all the terrible problems in the world today. Unhealthy intermingling, unintelligent compromises, misunderstood liberties and uncontrolled licentiousness have poisoned the lives of both the married and the unmarried, so that each new generation now finds itself the unclaimed child of its own past, not as an idol of the love lived, but as a caricature of the lust expressed.

This dreadful state of an orphan generation, untended and uncultivated, wrecking the entire destiny of the world, had been clearly visualised by the pure intellectuals of the Vaidika period and therefore, they thought it fit to give to their children, during their growing age of curiosity and nameless excitements, the correct scientific knowledge of true living in controlled indulgence. In the most sacred of their scriptures they incorporated chapters on sexology. On the walls of sanctum sanctorum in their temple, they sculptured the act of procreation. In the sacred books of their mythological stories, they painted naked, the gorgeous truths of balanced living in rationed revelry. In their literature they drenched their themes with pictures of beauty and showed the healthy way of enjoying them.

With this much of understanding of the views of the saints of that era, we can easily appreciate how the young brahmacārīs who had come to the teacher to learn the truth of the Absolute were made to meditate upon this line of thinking and yet, they were saved from all unhealthy mental depravity.

We had to go into this much in detail because of the condemning commentaries that are being made, most shamelessly, both the foreigners and the Indian converts, upon these glorious passages of such pregnant universal suggestions.

अथाध्यात्मम् । अधरा हनुः पूर्वरूपम् ।
उत्तरा हनुरुत्तररूपम् । वाक्सन्धिः ।
जिह्वा सन्धानम् । इत्यध्यात्मम् ॥६ ॥

athādhyātmam, adharā hanuḥ pūrvarūpam,
uttarā hanuruttararūpam, vāk-sandhiḥ,
jihvā sandhānam, ityadhyātmam. (6)

अथ – now; अध्यात्मम् – concerning the individual or the body; अधरा हनुः – the lower jaw; पूर्वरूपम् – the prior form; उत्तरा हनुः – the upper jaw; उत्तररूपम् – the posterior form; वाक् – speech; सन्धिः – the intermediate form; जिह्वा – tongue; सन्धानम् – the connection, means of union; इति – thus; अध्यात्मम् – upon the individual; (ध्यायेत् – one should meditate)

6. What follows is concerning the individual or the body. The lower jaw is the prior form, the upper jaw the posterior form, speech the conjunction, the tongue the means of union. Thus one should meditate upon oneself.

Those who have followed so far, the technique of superimposing a line of independent thinking upon the construction of a compound word must find it easy to understand this idea. To the student, this must be certainly a very easy thought to engage his mind upon, since he is all the time talking during his study hour or when he is in the field. The student is, therefore, made to maintain in his mind an undercurrent of meditative thoughts upon the significance of his own acts of articulation. Without the upper and the lower jaws and the vocal cords, no sound can be produced. Even when the sound is created, without the tongue coming into vigilant play in controlling and regulating the sounds, the various letters constituting the language, such as, guttural, palatal, dental or labial cannot be correctly or satisfactorily produced. With this much of understanding, it must be easy for any student to pursue this upāsanā.

इतीमा महासग्ंहिताः य एवमेता महासग्ंहिता
व्याख्याता वेद । सन्धीयते प्रजया पशुभिः ।
ब्रह्मवर्चसेनान्नाद्येन सुवर्ग्येण लोकेन ॥७॥

itīmā mahāsagṁhitā ya evametā mahāsagṁhitā
vyākhyātā veda, sandhīyate prajayā paśubhiḥ,
brahmavarcasenānnādyena suvargyeṇa lokena. (7)

इति – thus; इमा – these; महासग्ंहिताः – the great blendings; यः – he who; एवम् – thus; एता – these; महासग्ंहिताः – the great blendings; व्याख्याताः – expounded; वेद – understands; सन्धीयते – is united;

प्रजया – with progeny; **पशुभिः** – with cattle; **ब्रह्मवर्चसेन** – with the glory of the holy lustre; **अन्नाद्येन** – with food and the like; **सुवर्ग्येण लोकेन** – with joys of heavenly world

7. These are called 'the great blendings'; he who understands them as expounded here, becomes united with progeny, cattle, food and the like and with the glory of the holy lustre, wealth and heavenly joys.

Traditionally, a prescription for a karma or an upāsanā must have four limbs:

(a) A description of the presiding deity which indicates to us the nature of the karma (utpatti vidhi);

(b) A detailed instruction on all the acts that we have to do in the ritual (viniyoga vidhi);

(c) An exhaustive enumeration of the qualities necessary in making one fit to pursue the indicated ritualism (adhikāra vidhi); and

(d) The promise of the results that will be accrued when the ritualism is, with faith and devotion, diligently pursued (phala vidhi).

We now find that almost all these items are given here in this upāsanā upon the limbs of 'compound words'. Here, in this portion now under discussion, we read a complete description of the fruits that are gained by such a pursuit.

All karmas, sacred and secular, produce, in their reaction, some fruit or the other. In ritualism, when the divine acts are pursued with an intention to gain the fruits thereof, the individual, in proportion to his diligence and acquired mental strength, comes to enjoy the fruits but the same ritualisms, when pursued without a demand for the fruits thereof, result in an efficient integration of the upāsaka's inner personality.

Here this Upaniṣad, is an advice by the ṛṣis to their students, many of whom are yet to go back to a householder's life and live in society. Therefore, to show them the material gains that they can come to enjoy through a diligent pursuit of upāsanā, is certainly quite encouraging. They will be tempted to continue these exercises and thus slowly grow to a greater stature in their inner constitution of mind and intellect.

Section iv – अनुवाकः ४

Necessity of Intelligence and Wealth

यश्छन्दसामृषभो विश्वरूपः
छन्दोभ्योऽध्यमृतात् सम्बभूव ।
स मेन्द्रो मेधया स्पृणोतु ।
अमृतस्य देव धारणो भूयासम् ।
शरीरं मे विचर्षणम् । जिह्वा मे मधुमत्तमा ।
कर्णाभ्यां भूरि विश्रुवम् ।
ब्रह्मणः कोशोऽसि मेधया पिहितः ।
श्रुतं मे गोपाय ॥१ ॥

yaśchandasāmṛṣabho viśvarūpaḥ
chandobhyo'dhyamṛtāt sambabhūva,
sa mendro medhayā spṛṇotu,
amṛtasya deva dhāraṇo bhūyāsam,
śarīraṁ me vicarṣaṇam, jihvā me madhumattamā,
karṇābhyāṁ bhūri viśruvam,
brahmaṇaḥ kośo'si medhayā pihitaḥ,
śrutaṁ me gopāya. (1)

यः – he who; छन्दसाम् – among the sacred hymns of the Vedas; ऋषभः – pre-eminent; विश्वरूपः – manifold; छन्दोभ्यः – from the sacred hymns of the Vedas; अधि – above; अमृतात् – from the immortal; सम्बभूव – sprang up; सः – that; मा – to me; इन्द्रः – Indra; मेधया – with intellectual vigour; स्पृणोतु –

may fill, invigorate; अमृतस्य – of immortality; देव – O Lord; धारणः – possessor; भूयासम् – may I become; शरीरम् – body; मे – my; विचर्षणम् – able and active; जिह्वा – tongue; मे – my; मधुमत्तमा – sweet and agreeable to the utmost; (भूयात् – may become); कर्णाभ्याम् – with the ears; भूरि – abundantly; विश्रुवम् – may I listen; ब्रह्मणः – of Brahman; कोशः – sheath; असि – thou art; मेधया – by the intellect; पिहितः – covered; श्रुतम् – learning; मे – mine; गोपाय – may you preserve

1. He whose form is manifold, who is pre-eminent among the sacred hymns of the Vedas and who has sprung up from the sacred hymns which are immortal; that Indra (Omkāra) may fill me with intellectual vigour. O Lord, may I become the possessor of the immortal revelations. May my body become able and active, my speech sweet and agreeable to the utmost. May I listen abundantly with my ears. Thou art the sheath of Brahman. May you preserve my learning.

This section opens with a declaration of a mantra to be used by the students for daily repetition, a practice technically called japa. To keep the mind actively engaged in the repetition of a sacred hymn invoking divine ideas or ideals, which provides an infinite possibility for contemplation and intellectual flights, is japa. Here the japa advised is for the development of the intellect in a student.

For all serious students, there cannot be a greater ambition than that they should be able to shine in their class among others. In ancient days, the success of a student mainly depended upon his retentive capacity, since education started with memorising the Vaidika texts. Without an acute memory power (medhā-śakti), no student in those days could do well in his education. Here we have, therefore, a mantra for chanting, which when pursued properly with the necessary mental co-operation, can strengthen and purify the memory power in the student.

In this japa, the student is addressing Indra. Śrī Śaṅkarācārya in his commentary interprets rightly that Indra here means Omkāra. Etymologically, the word Indra is derived from a root, meaning 'to illuminate' (indhayati-iti-Indraḥ). The Om symbol indicating the Conscious Principle in man is the illuminator of all his faculties including his own intellect. The mantra, as it reads, is an invocation to Omkāra for a clearer consciousness or awareness in the student.

'He whose form is manifold' – The Awareness or Consciousness which is the supreme Reality, is the infinite substratum for all the finite names and forms which constitute the world as we perceive it. The waves and ripples, the bubbles and foam, the whirls and the dips that disturb the surface of the ocean are all, when analysed, found to be nothing but the manifold forms of the same ocean. The rings, the bangles and the innumerable varieties of ornaments, thin and thick, short and long, though different in shape, size and name, are all the manifold forms of the one and the same substance, gold. Similarly, the one infinite divine life spark expresses Itself through the endless forms and names that constitute the entire living world of beings and therefore, the Truth as expressed by its symbol Om is said to have manifold forms.

'Who is pre-eminent among the hymns of the Vedas' – Herein we have yet another clause qualifying the Om-symbol. The infinite and the immortal Truth, which is One without a second, all-pervading and perfect as indicated by the symbol Om, is the one common theme that is dealt with in all the hymns in the Vedas. Even in the mantra portion of the Vedas, the exclamations of the Āryans at the beauty of nature were but adorations of the Infinite; when the Hindus in the brāhmaṇa portion, entered into the scheme of ritualism, there too they invoked the same Truth, manifested for special purposes as Indra, Varuṇa and so on. Again in the Upaniṣads, when the great ṛṣis exploded in ecstasy and expressed their thrilling experiences of the 'end', and declared the path leading towards It, they again, with every mantra, indicated the same infinite Truth which, from behind the pluralistic world, lends Its vitality to nature. Therefore, the appellation given here is perfectly justified.

'Who has sprung up from the hymns' – This intellectual recognition of the all-pervading Reality is gained through a study of the Vedas. Thereafter, to a seeker, the same Veda prescribes the means by which he can pursue his pilgrimage towards this self-discovery. Again, the same Veda deals exhaustively with the methods of removing obstacles on the path of the seeker. Therefore, it is but a beautiful way of expression to declare the Truth symbolised by Om, as having 'sprung up from the hymns.'

Addressing this Om, the name of the Infinite, the student desires that he must be filled with intellectual vigour so that he may be able to understand, at least bring within his intellectual appreciation, the deep significances of the immortal revelations expounded in the Vaidika text. Not only is it sufficient that he is provided with a wonderful intellect capable of grasping and retaining the silent import of the pregnant Vaidika words, but also that the Āryan student is not satisfied without acquiring a healthy life in body and a sweet and agreeable way of expression in his speech. No student in the Vaidika period seems to have ever misappropriated knowledge with an intention to hoard. His charity is so divine and the theme of his study so inspiring that he feels himself fulfilled only when he has disseminated the knowledge he has acquired from his teacher, far and wide. Therefore, his request or demand is not only that he should become highly efficient in learning the Vedas, but also that he must have the physical abilities for continuous exertion in carrying out open propaganda with all the missionary zeal to spread the vital Truth and scatter the pearls of wisdom that form the very substance of his culture.

How different from what we understand today is the real declaration of our own sacred books! Here we are now trying to understand the words of a japa mantra advised by the ṛṣis for those students who are slightly dull, in order that they may become more efficient in their intellect. The great Masters of the Upaniṣads are not satisfied if their students are highly intellectual but weak and emaciated. Today, on the other hand, walk into any university hall and we can surely point out a first class student; for, he will invariably be a pale walking corpse which refuses to die, perhaps because he has not the vitality even to pack up his life and depart in peace! In the same university, the sportsman who is well built and beaming with health, is invariably marked out for a lucky third class or preferably a sure failure!

This state of affairs is certainly because of a very painful maladjustment in our educational system. This mantra by its suggestiveness gives us the hope that there can be a better system wherein physical health and intellectual accomplishments can go hand in hand and the vision of the educationists in any country should be to bring about this consummate happiness.

Just as a man of resounding knowledge, a genius of his age, is no more useful either to himself or to the society, but becomes only a liability if he be in a nursing home or an asylum; so too, a man with knowledge and health, again, is a living threat to his society and will bring ultimately a blot upon the fair face of the sacred culture, if he has not a sweet tongue to express his ideas in an attractive way. An individual becomes really a pest on the generation if he has not got the tolerance to give a patient hearing to others and does not try to digest and assimilate the best in them. Fanaticism and intolerance are the cankers that eat up the best blossom in any period of history. Not only is such a fanatic individual always unhappy in himself, but his mission also will always end in marching his generation into a chaotic state of mutual hatred and general unpleasantness.

The mantra is rounded up with an assertion that Om is 'the sheath of Brahman'. When we are invoking a power and requesting it to bless us with certain special strength and ability, we must know whether the invoked power has got the ability to fulfil our demand. Here it is said that Om is the very 'container' for the Supreme. The 'sheath' is invoked just as we do in our daily life when we actually mean the contained: "Bring the inkpot", "Pass me the cigarette case" and so on. In all such instances the request is not a direct demand merely for the bottle or for the case, but it is a demand for the ink in the bottle or the cigarettes in the case. The mantra here says that the Om-symbol is the sheath of Brahman and therefore, invoking Om is invoking the Supreme.

This mantra is repeated with extreme concentration regularly by the students who desired a more efficient memory and heightened intellectual capacity. In the very scheme of the different upāsanās narrated in the textbook, the ṛṣi declares how an individual should plan out his great career in order to live fully the entire implications of the inimitable Sanātana Dharma. When an intellect has fully developed and the individual has acquired sweet speech and a mental readiness to receive new ideas on every occasion, such an individual bubbling with health, is fit to pursue the 'ritual for wealth' which is to be prescribed now in order to acquire great wealth and rich fortune.

आवहन्ती वितन्वाना कुर्वाणाऽचीरमात्मनः ।
वासाग्ंसि मम गावश्च । अन्नपाने च सर्वदा ।
ततो मे श्रियमावह । लोमशां पशुभिः सह स्वाहा ।
आमायन्तु ब्रह्मचारिणः स्वाहा ।

विमायन्तु ब्रह्मचारिणः स्वाहा ।
प्रमायन्तु ब्रह्मचारिणः स्वाहा ।
दमायन्तु ब्रह्मचारिणः स्वाहा ।
शमायन्तु ब्रह्मचारिणः स्वाहा ॥२॥

āvahantī vitanvānā kurvāṇā'cīramātmanaḥ,
vāsāgṁsi mama gāvaśca, annapāne ca sarvadā,
tato me śriyamāvaha, lomaśāṁ paśubhiḥ saha svāhā,
āmāyantu brahmacāriṇaḥ svāhā,
vimāyantu brahmacāriṇaḥ svāhā,
pramāyantu brahmacāriṇaḥ svāhā,
damāyantu brahmacāriṇaḥ svāhā,
śamāyantu brahmacāriṇaḥ svāhā. (2)

आवहन्ती – bringing; वितन्वाना – multiplying; कुर्वाणा – producing; अचीरम् – without delay; आत्मनः – self; वासांग्सि – clothes; मम – my; गावः – cows ; च – and; अन्नपाने – food and drink; च – and; सर्वदा – for all time; ततः – afterwards; मे – for me; श्रियम् – prosperity; आवह – bring ; लोमशाम् – hairy animals; पशुभिः – cattle; सह – with; स्वाहा[1] – svāhā; आ – all along; मा – to me; यन्तु – may come; ब्रह्मचारिणः – celibate students of Brahmavidyā; स्वाहा – svāhā; वि – from various directions; मा – to me; यन्तु – may come; ब्रह्मचारिणः – celibate students; स्वाहा – svāhā; प्र – much (in large numbers); मा – to me; यन्तु – may come; ब्रह्मचारिणः – celibate students; स्वाहा – svāhā; दमायन्तु – be self-controlled; ब्रह्मचारिणः – celibate students; स्वाहा – svāhā; शमायन्तु – be peaceful; ब्रह्मचारिणः – celibate students; स्वाहा – svāhā

[1] Svāhā is an indeclinable word which marks the end of a formula and is repeated along with every oblation offered into the sacrificial fire.

2. O Lord, afterwards let prosperity be mine, consisting in hairy animals along with cattle. May fortune produce for me without delay and for all time, bringing continuously and in ever multiplying proportions, food and clothing and cattle. All along, may celibate students, thirsty to know, come to me. Svāhā! May they come to me from distant places and from all directions. May they come in large numbers. May the students, anxious to gain the knowledge of Brahman, control their senses. May the students, anxious to live the knowledge of Brahman, be peaceful. Svāhā!

Earlier, we were told of a mantra to be used in japa by which the discriminative intelligence and the retentive capacity of the student increases in greater proportions. Not only that he becomes intelligent, but we also saw that the meaning of the mantra provides the student with certain mental vision, physical strength and spiritual values. According to the śāstras, from the very order in which these upāsanās are laid, it is quite evident that such an individual alone is fit to claim prosperity and fortune. Here we have the prescription for a sacred ritualism which is performed by those who desire wealth.

Wealth in the hands of unprepared intellects and uncultured hearts is not only suicidal for themselves, but is a threat to the very stability of the society. In fact, in the world of ours, today, our political and economic problems can all be traced to the lack of character in the rich men. Materialism in our scientific world has created such an appeal wherein the good at heart and the pure in intellect have little scope to gain wealth, while the unscrupulous and the dishonest can easily court fortune. When such a heartless head comes to wealth, he becomes a miniature Nero setting fire to his society in order that he may enjoy his song in his own licentious freedom! The gunpowder kings cannot suffer for long their dull market and, therefore, they plan to bring about wars at every short interval! In all relationships between the landlord and the tenant, or the employer and the employee, the king and the people, the master and the servant, everywhere there is a growing discontentment because, in the scheme of things available today, the unprepared individuals can, and they do, come by great fortunes.

The Vaidika teachers have, therefore, indicated that desire for wealth can be a blessing only when the individual has been educated to entertain the noble qualities of the head and the heart and the enduring values of the spirit.

In this portion it is said: 'O Lord, afterwards' meaning, after having blessed me with full discrimination, good health, the spirit of tolerance and an irresistible impatience to serve others, 'confer on me good fortune'. Without these qualifications, wealth becomes as dangerous a weapon as a loaded pistol in the hands of an innocent child, a threat to itself and may be a threat to others around itself.

The fortune demanded is typical of the times; wealth was in those days, measured in terms of cattle and sheep. Wool was essential because of the climatic conditions of the North. In those days, when jungles were full of trees, and not as they are today, a mere story of historical tradition; when the Himalayas were not rendered bald by a caterpillar generation of profit hunting governments and gain-mad contractors, wool was, perhaps, a necessity of life.

Wealth was demanded not as fulfilment in itself, but they recognised that riches can be justified and enjoyed only by the mission that it fulfils. If wealth were to be idle and one knows only how to enjoy it as a dispenser of confidence and assurance of having a high bank balance, he knows not how to milk his wealth to yield a greater joy unto himself. Here the teacher is giving the right turn of mind to the growing disciples so that they may, when they are fit, desire for immense wealth for a great and noble cause, namely, for running universities where students are served and looked after. The rich are the trustees of the illiterate and the needy.

To say that Hinduism recognises no missionary zeal is to misread our sacred books. We may justify the statement inasmuch as Hinduism, the perfect science of peace and love, universal in its outlook, has for itself the goal of human evolution and therefore, it has no ugly proselytisation viewpoint in itself and so, compared with the mischief of such foreign institutions who are today making unhappy gashes on the national integrity and the cultural heritage of this sacred land, we may say that Hinduism is not missionary at all. But the sacred zeal with which the ṛṣis took upon themselves the noble cause in the spread of their sacred knowledge and the truths of their culture was nothing less than the zeal with which Saint Paul came to the East. Every student was charged with this divine duty of spreading the Hindu culture, in his own lifetime, among his own people and the foreigners who might reach them seeking the way.

The ambition of each student has been thus moulded by the teachers at the very time of their early initiation. They invoked the Lord through their rituals, and both the teacher and the taught demanded together that students of intelligence and self-control, of moral and ethical purity, of emotional stamina and psychological stability, should constantly reach them from all directions, from far and near. This healthy spirit of propagation got itself choked in the poisonous atmosphere of secularism and the criminal monopoly of knowledge that was practised by some erring generation somewhere in the near past. That suicidal policy has today brought the Hindus where they are and their scriptures have become a laughing stock for the whole world! Here we are discussing the very sacred book itself in which it is so clearly said that the goal and ambition of every student were to be that he would be able, in his lifetime, to get ample chances to train and perfect the next generation to carry on the torch of knowledge, trimmed and bright, as he himself got it from his own teacher.

Vedānta being not only a theory of perfect life, but also a technique of perfect living, the Hindu culture can be imparted efficiently and successfully only to those who are willing and ready to live these values. This is indicated by the demand of the worshipper that the students of Brahmavidyā, who reach the halls of study, must have ample self-control in the outward life and calmness in their inward living.

यशो जनेऽसानि स्वाहा । श्रेयान् वस्यसोऽसानि स्वाहा ।
तं त्वा भग प्रविशानि स्वाहा ।
स मा भग प्रविश स्वाहा ।
तस्मिन् सहस्रशाखे निभगाहं त्वयि मृजे स्वाहा ।
यथापः प्रवता यन्ति यथा मासा अहर्जरम् ।
एवं मां ब्रह्मचारिणः धातरायन्तु सर्वतः स्वाहा ।
प्रतिवेशोऽसि प्र मा भाहि प्र मा पद्यस्व ॥३॥

yaśo jane'sāni svāhā, śreyān vasyaso'sāni svāhā,
taṁ tvā bhaga praviśāni svāhā,
sa mā bhaga praviśa svāhā,
tasmin sahasraśākhe nibhagāhaṁ tvayi mṛje svāhā,
yathāpaḥ pravatā yanti yathā māsā aharjaram,
evaṁ māṁ brahmacāriṇaḥ dhātarāyantu sarvataḥ svāhā,
prativeśo'si pra mā bhāhi pra mā padyasva. (3)

यशः – successful; जने – among people; असानि – may I become; स्वाहा – svāhā; श्रेयान् – among the prosperous; वस्यसः – a superior; असानि – may I become; स्वाहा – svāhā; तम् – that; त्वा – thee; भग – O Lord of prosperity; प्रविशानि – may I enter into; स्वाहा – svāhā; सः – thou; मा – me; भग – the Lord of prosperity; प्रविशः – enter into; स्वाहा – svāhā; तस्मिन् सहस्रशाखे – in that (Self) of a thousand branches; भग – O Lord; अहम् – I; त्वयि – in thee; निमृजे – cleanse myself; स्वाहा – svāhā; यथा – as; आपः – water; प्रवता यन्ति – flows downwards; यथा – as; मासाः – months (fly into) ; अहर्जरम् – the year; एवम् – so too; माम् – me; ब्रह्मचारिणः – celibate students; धातः – O Lord; आयन्तु – may come; सर्वतः – from all places; स्वाहा – svāhā; प्रतिवेशः – refuge; असि – thou art; मा – me; प्र-भाहि – reveal yourself; मा – to me; प्र-पद्यस्व – come (possess)

3. May I become successful among the people. Svāhā! May I become superior among the rich. Svāhā! O Lord of prosperity, may I enter into Thee. Svāhā! Mayest Thou enter into me. In that Self of Thine with a thousand branches, O Lord, may I purify myself from all my sins. Svāhā! As water flows downwards, as months fly into years, so too, O Creator, may students of Brahmavidyā come to me from everywhere. Svāhā! Thou art the refuge! Beam upon me! Come to me!!

Continuing the ritual, the mantras reveal more and more the nobility of intentions and the purity of ambitions entertained by the upāsaka. The worshipper wants to become famous among men, in his knowledge and in his living, because in India, a philosopher never attracts any attention unless he lives up to the ideal of his philosophy. Thus, the renown meant here is not merely a popularity or a passing fame. This fame demanded is not for any self-aggrandisement or selfish gains but it is to assure that the best types of students will be constantly reaching from all directions and thus the upāsaka will gain in the days to come a greater field for his missionary activities.

This prayer that he should become famous, when read together with the previous demand for great fortunes, should give us the implication meant in: 'May I become superior among the rich'; meaning, let me not be a mere mule carrying the weight of gold, but an intelligent master of fortune who is able to bless the world with the riches that have come to me through the grace of the Lord. In doing so, he becomes, in fact, superior to those who are wealthier than himself. Wealth in itself is no mark of nobility or glory to man. It becomes so only when he comes to serve the society and thereby himself, with his wealth. Therefore, when a true Hindu acquires wealth to spend it in maintaining seekers during their stay with him; indeed, the wealth is spent in the right direction and the culture of the land is maintained and preserved thereby.

In order to become thus pure in living, the individual must gain a clean and divine heart. The method by which one can purify oneself and keep that bright shine in the inner world is now discussed. Sin is that which covers the true effulgence of the soul. In our śāstras, sin is not considered as some positive blemish, but only as a mistake in judgement; it is not a commission of an injustice, but an omission to do the right. Thus our scriptures forbid us from hating the sinner, but insist that we must hate the sins. This positive philosophy is the meaning of all scriptures in the world. 'Every saint has a past; every sinner a future'.

The moment we correct our thinking and redress the mistake in the evaluation of things in the world, we know how to redeem ourselves from the sins and walk the path of virtue.

But, the difficulty felt by practitioners is that they are not completely independent of the reactions of their past mistakes. Every action and every thought leaves its impression upon the mental world and every following thought and action has a tendency to repeat itself. Thus, having made one misjudgement, the flow of thoughts thereafter has an irresistible tendency and an irrepressible urge to flow in the same direction, pushing the injustice more and more into positive criminalities and low animalisms. The only way we can redeem ourselves from our mistakes is to correct our way of thinking and rewrite the entire pattern of thoughts within ourselves.

This erasing of the old wrong patterns and rewriting healthy lines of thinking are both accomplished by the same divine process which is prescribed in the sacred textbooks. The method advised is the constant and repeated chanting and japa of the sacred mantra of Praṇava, known as Omkāra. We have already seen how Om is the most excellent essence in all the Vedas. Since it represents the supreme Consciousness, it manifests itself into its manifold forms. This is indicated here in the term 'into a thousand branches'.

In our introductory talks, we had brought out the idea that the Āryan masters, soaked with the beauty of their native land, a wonderland of nature's exquisite excesses, were so moulded in their sentiments and emotions that they could not but think in metre and in rhyme. Even their subtlest philosophy is honeyed with poetry; even objective sciences like medicine, astronomy and so on have also been given out by them in majestic verses which often rise to the beauties of pure poetry in their style, diction, music and flow. This being the case, we find here in this mantra two brilliant flashes when the upāsaka requests the Lord to lead students to him from far and near. 'As water gushes downwards' is a simile that can compete only with the dynamic picture brought before us by 'as months flow into and merge with years'. In their expressiveness, grandeur and charm, they can stand a favourable comparison with the best in any literature. The rest is clear.

Section v – अनुवाकः ५

The Mystic Expression 'Mahaḥ'

भूर्भुवः सुवरिति वा एतास्तिस्रो व्याहृतयः ।
तासामु ह स्मैतां चतुर्थीं माहाचमस्यः प्रवेदयते ।
मह इति । तद् ब्रह्म ।
स आत्मा । अङ्गान्यन्या देवताः ॥१ ॥

bhūr-bhuvaḥ suvar-iti vā etās-tisro vyāhṛtayaḥ,
tāsāmu ha smaitāṁ caturthīṁ māhācamasyaḥ pravedayate,
maha iti, tad brahma,
sa ātmā aṅgānyanyā devatāḥ. (1)

भूः – world; भुवः – sky; सुवः – next world; इति – thus; वै – verily; एताः – these; तिस्रः – three; व्याहृतयः – the short utterances of mystical significances; तासाम् – of these; उ – in addition to; ह – of course; एताम् – this; चतुर्थीम् – the fourth; माहाचमस्यः – O Māhācamasya (the son of Mahācamasa); प्रवेदयते स्म[1] – knowing by intuition proclaimed; मह – Mahaḥ; इति – thus; तत् – that; ब्रह्म –Brahman; सः – he; आत्मा – the body (Self); अङ्गानि – the limbs; अन्या– other; देवताः – gods

1. Bhūḥ, bhuvaḥ, suvaḥ are the three short utterances of mystical significances. In addition to these, there is, the fourth

---

[1] 'स्म' 'Sma' is a particle added to the present tense of verbs (or to present particles) and giving them the sense of the past tense.

one, Mahaḥ, made known by the seer, Māhācamasya. That is Brahman. That is the body; other gods are its limbs.

This section opens out another method of meditation. The technique adopted has a direct bearing with things familiar for the students who had a thorough study earlier, of the brāhmaṇa portion of the Veda. Naturally, to them the 'short mystical utterances' (vyāhṛtis) are very familiar and full of import. But today, we find it difficult to enter into the very spirit of it because we are unable to appreciate or experience the import contained therein.

The terms bhūḥ, bhuvaḥ and so on indicate the various fields of experiences which the mind can indulge in, if it raises itself to be in unison with these realms of experience. Each one of them is considered to be subtler than the other. A subtler plane not only transcends the grosser but it is at once immanent in the grosser plane also. Compared with the most well known three fields, bhūḥ, bhuvaḥ and suvaḥ, the scripture says here, that there is yet another plane called Mahaḥ, which is subtler than the former three. This plane of experience, Mahaḥ, was first cognised by a great Ṛṣi called Māhācamasya and therefore, this world of experience is called 'Mahaḥ'.

Compared with the earlier three, the fourth is at once transcendent and immanent and therefore it is called 'Brahman'. The relationship between Mahaḥ and the other worlds is beautifully brought out in the declarations that Mahaḥ is the body and the others are but its limbs. We all know that limbs in themselves will not make the body, but the term 'body' includes and incorporates all the limbs in it. Having understood this much, we shall proceed further to examine the true import of what the Masters meant by demanding of their students to do certain types of superimpositions upon these terms for the purpose of meditation.

भूरिति वा अयं लोकः । भुव इत्यन्तरिक्षम् ।
सुवरित्यसौ लोकः । मह इत्यादित्यः ।
आदित्येन वाव सर्वे लोका महीयन्ते ॥२॥

bhūriti vā ayaṁ lokaḥ, bhuva ityantarikṣam,
suvarityasau lokaḥ, maha ityādityaḥ,
ādityena vāva sarve lokā mahīyante. (2)

भूः – earth; इति – thus; वै – verily; अयम् – this; लोकः – world; भुवः इति – what is known as bhuvaḥ (is); अन्तरिक्षम् – the sky; सुवः इति – what is known as suvaḥ (is); असौ – next (yonder) ; लोकः – world ; महः इति – what is known as Mahaḥ (is) ; आदित्यः – the sun; आदित्येन – by the sun; वाव – indeed; सर्वे – all; लोकाः – worlds; महीयन्ते – are nourished

2. Bhūḥ is this world. Bhuvaḥ is the sky. Suvaḥ is the next world. Mahaḥ is the sun. It is by the sun that all worlds are nourished.

Using the technique of upāsanā, which we have already found, is to superimpose the mighty upon the meagre, we have here various ideas superimposed on the three 'short mystic utterances' very familiar in the Veda, so that the student may understand that the fourth vyāhṛti, called Mahaḥ, represents in itself a factor subtler than all the other three. Indeed, we know that the sun, as the source of all energy and light, must be the nourisher of all the planes of experiences, described by the 'short utterances.'

भूरिति वा अग्निः । भुव इति वायुः ।
सुवरित्यादित्यः । मह इति चन्द्रमाः ।
चन्द्रमसा वाव सर्वाणि ज्योतीगंषि महीयन्ते ॥३ ॥

bhūriti vā agniḥ, bhuva iti vāyuḥ,
suvarityādityaḥ, maha iti candramāḥ,
candramasā vāva sarvāṇi jyotīgṁṣi mahīyante. (3)

भूः इति – what is known as bhūḥ (is); वै – verily; अग्निः – fire; भुवः इति – what is known as bhuvaḥ (is) ; वायुः – air; सुवः इति – what is known as suvaḥ (is); आदित्यः – the sun; महः इति – what is known as Mahaḥ (is); चन्द्रमाः – the moon; चन्द्रमसा – by the moon; वाव – indeed; सर्वाणि – all, ज्योतीगंषि – vitalities; महीयन्ते – thrive

3. Bhūḥ is fire. Bhuvaḥ is air. Suvaḥ is the sun. Mahaḥ is the moon. Indeed, it is by the moon that all vitalities thrive.

Giving another set of superimpositions, again the same truth that Mahaḥ transcends all the previous three and itself, forms the foundation for the previous ones, the ṛṣi here says that Mahaḥ is to be considered as the moon. The moon in Vedānta is the 'source of all essence' in the vegetable kingdom and the physical vitality in man. It is the moon again that is considered as the presiding deity of the mind. It is our experience that there is an intimate relationship between the moon and the mental conditions in man; if there is a doubt, watch the hysterical or the lunatic during the full moon!

The farmer prepares his seeds for the next crop not only by drying them in the sun, but he, though himself ignorant, is traditionally taught to leave the seeds exposed overnight to the moonlight. Collectors of honey certainly know that there is a lot of difference in the taste of the honey extracted during the wrong season.

In short, there seems to be an intimate connection between the vitamin contents and even caloric potential in the vegetables when not exposed to the moonlight. There are preparations in the Hindu system of medicine which are to be left exposed to the moonlight for a certain number of days before they can be given to the sick. Thus, we find enough data to justify the scientific belief of the Vaidika age that the moon is the nourisher of the world of matter.

भूरिति वा ऋचः । भुव इति सामानि ।
सुवरिति यजूग्ंषि । मह इति ब्रह्म ।
ब्रह्मणा वाव सर्वे वेदा महीयन्ते ॥४ ॥

bhūriti vā ṛcaḥ, bhuva iti sāmāni,
suvariti yajūgṁṣi, maha iti brahma,
brahmaṇā vāva sarve vedā mahīyante. (4)

भूः इति – what is known as bhūḥ (is); वै – verily; ऋचः – the Ṛk; भुवः इति – what is known as bhuvaḥ (is) ; सामानि – the hymns of *Sāma-veda*; सुवः इति – what is known as suvaḥ (is); यजूग्ंषि – the Yajus; महः इति – what is known as Mahaḥ (is); ब्रह्म – Brahman; ब्रह्मणा – by Brahman; वाव – indeed; सर्वे – all; वेदाः – Vedas; महीयन्ते – thrive

4. Bhūḥ is the Ṛk. Bhuvaḥ is the Sāman. Suvaḥ is the Yajus. Mahaḥ is the Brahman (as represented by the syllable Om). It is by the Brahman, indeed, that the Vedas thrive.

This set of superimpositons clearly indicates what we have been trying to feel in the other upāsanās. If the first three vyāhṛtis represent the mantras of *Ṛk, Sāma and Yajur-vedas*, then the ṛṣi declares, Mahaḥ is the Supreme, indicated by the symbol Om. We all know that in all the mantras of all the Vedas, they directly or indirectly point out to the one Supreme goal which is the theme of all our scriptural text books.

**भूरिति वै प्राणः। भुव इत्यपानः। सुवरिति व्यानः।
मह इत्यन्नम्। अन्नेन वाव सर्वे प्राणा महीयन्ते ॥५॥**

*bhūriti vai prāṇaḥ, bhuva ityapānaḥ, suvariti vyānaḥ,
maha ityannam, annena vāva sarve prāṇā mahīyante. (5)*

भूः इति – what is known as bhūḥ (is); वै – verily; प्राणः – prāṇa; भुवः इति – what is known as bhuvaḥ (is) ; अपानः – apāna; सुवः इति – what is known as suvaḥ (is); व्यानः – vyāna (circulation); महः इति – what is known as Mahaḥ (is); अन्नम् – food; अन्नेन – by food; वाव – indeed; सर्वे – all; प्राणाः – the prāṇas; महीयन्ते – thrive

5. Bhūḥ is prāṇa. Bhuvaḥ is apāna. Suvaḥ is vyāna. Mahaḥ is food. Indeed, it is by food that the prāṇas thrive.

Popularly it is understood that prāṇa is the breath. This is not scientifically quite appropriate since it has a subtler meaning in the śāstras. Prāṇa means the energy in man expressed through the different functions[1] and the vitality in man. The air that we breathe in and out through respiration feeds and maintains the vital energy in us. This energy generated within, expresses itself through five clear departments of activity. Thus we have the five different names to indicate the special activities performed by the one energy.

Thus, prāṇa is the energy that is expressed through the organs of knowledge; apāna is the energy that helps the body to throw out things from itself; samāna is the digestive vitality; vyāna is the circulatory force; udāna is the power by which, at the time of death, the mind and intellect of

[1] For more details read Swāmiji's Discourses on *Praśnopaniṣad*.

the individual are able to reject the present body and make their pilgrimage towards a new scheme of things and get themselves fixed in their identification with the required form conducive to fulfil their predominant desires.

Of these five departments of energy (pañcaprāṇas), three are taken here and superimposing them upon bhūḥ, bhuvaḥ and suvaḥ, the teacher concludes that Mahaḥ is food. We all know that the food is the source of all the energies within us.

ता वा एताश्चतस्रश्चतुर्धा ।
चतस्रश्चतस्रो व्याहृतयः । ता यो वेद ।
स वेद ब्रह्म । सर्वेऽस्मै देवा बलिमावहन्ति ॥६ ॥

tā vā etāścatasraś-caturdhā,
catasraścatasro vyāhṛtayaḥ, tā yo veda,
sa veda brahma, sarve'smai devā balimāvahanti. (6)

ताः – those; वै – verily; एताः – these; चतस्रः – four; चतुर्धा – fourfold; चतस्रः – four; चतस्रः – (and) four; व्याहृतयः – vyāhṛtis; ताः – them; यः – who; वेद – knows; सः – he; वेद – knows; ब्रह्म – Brahman; सर्वे – all; अस्मै – to him; देवाः – gods; बलिम् – offerings; आवहन्ति – carry

6. These above mentioned four are themselves fourfold and the four vyāhṛtis are each four in number. He, who

knows these, knows Brahman. All the devas carry offerings unto Him.

Vyāhṛtis	Meditation			
	No.1	No.2	No.3	No.4
Bhūḥ	World	Fire	Ṛk	Prāṇa
Bhuvaḥ	Sky	Air	Sāma	Apāna
Suvaḥ	Next world	Sun	Yajus	Vyāna
Mahaḥ	Sun	Moon	Om	Food

When all that has been described so far is represented in a mathematical table as above, it becomes clear that the four vyāhṛtis are each described in four different ways. For example: bhūḥ is described as world, fire, ṛk and prāṇa.

All these 16 items (4 x 4) together constitute the total universe, both the manifest and the unmanifest, the gross and the subtle, the matter and the energy-potentialities. This totality is represented by the term hiraṇyagarbha in the literature of Vedānta. We are told here that an upāsaka who is able to meditate upon the implications of these four groups of four each, becomes identified with the totality and, in his maturity, he will certainly come to experience, at once, all the joys of the world.

'All devas carry offerings unto Him' – The word 'deva' generally translated as God, comes from a root meaning 'to illumine' (dyotanāt deva). Thus in literature of Vedānta, deva is used to indicate the organs of perception which convey the impulses from the external world to the mind and intellect.

An upāsaka, who has become fully identified with the total mind and intellect (hiraṇyagarbha), naturally comes to experience all the joys of all individuals, who experience in their lives, a variety of happiness through their sense organs.

To express the idea of sense perceptions, as the sense organs carrying offerings from the external world, in the form of their experiences to the mind and intellect, has a beauty of gorgeous poetry at its best.

Section vi – अनुवाकः ६

Additional Details to Meditation

स य एषोऽन्तर्हृदय आकाशः।
तस्मिन्नयं पुरुषो मनोमयः।
अमृतो हिरण्मयः। अन्तरेण तालुके।
य एष स्तन इवावलम्बते। सेन्द्रयोनिः।
यत्रासौ केशान्तो विवर्तते। व्यपोह्य शीर्षकपाले ।१।

sa ya eṣo'ntarhṛdaya ākāśaḥ,
tasminnayaṁ puruṣo manomayaḥ,
amṛto hiraṇmayaḥ, antareṇa tāluke,
ya eṣa stana ivāvalambate, sendrayoniḥ,
yatrāsau keśānto vivartate, vyapohya śīrṣakapāle, (1)

सः – that; यः एषः – which is this; अन्तर्हृदये – within the heart; आकाशः – space; तस्मिन् – in it; अयम् – this; पुरुषः – puruṣaḥ (entity); मनोमयः – intelligent; अमृतः – imperishable; हिरण्मयः – effulgent; अन्तरेण – amidst, (between); तालुके – the palates; यः एषः – that which; स्तनः – nipple; इव – like ; अवलम्बते – hangs down; सा – that; इन्द्र योनिः – the birth place of Indra; यत्र – where; असौ – that; केशान्तः – root of hair; विवर्तते – is made of part; व्यपोह्य – opening; शीर्षकपाले – two sides of the skull

1. Here in this space within the heart resides the intelligent, imperishable, effulgent 'Puruṣa' or 'Entity'. Between the

palates, that which hangs like nipple (the uvula), that is the birthplace of Indra, where the root of hair is made to part, opening the skull in the centre.

भूरित्यग्नौ प्रतितिष्ठति । भुव इति वायौ ।
सुवरित्यादित्ये । मह इति ब्रह्मणि ।
आप्नोति स्वाराज्यम् । आप्नोति मनसस्पतिम् ।
वाक्पतिश्चक्षुष्पतिः । श्रोत्रपतिर्विज्ञानपतिः ।
एतत्ततो भवति । आकाशशरीरं ब्रह्म ।
सत्यात्म प्राणारामं मन आनन्दम् ।
शान्तिसमृद्धममृतम् । इति प्राचीनयोग्योपास्स्व ॥२॥

bhūrityagnau pratitiṣṭhati, bhuva iti vāyau,
suvarityāditye, maha iti brahmaṇi,
āpnoti svārājyam, āpnoti manasaspatim,
vākpatiścakṣuṣpatiḥ, śrotrapatirvijñānapatiḥ,
etattato bhavati, ākāśaśarīraṁ brahma,
satyātma prāṇārāmaṁ mana ānandam,
śāntisamṛddhamamṛtam, iti prācīnayogyopāssva. (2)

भूः इति – with the word bhūḥ; अग्नौ – in fire; प्रतितिष्ठति – stands; भुव इति – with the word bhuvaḥ; वायौ – in air; सुवः इति – with the word suvaḥ; आदित्ये – in the sun; मह इति – with the word Mahaḥ; ब्रह्मणि – in Brahman; आप्नोति – (he) obtains; स्वाराज्यम् – self-effulgence; आप्नोति – (he) obtains; मनसः पतिम् – Lordship over mind; वाक् पतिः – the Lord of speech; चक्षुष्पतिः – the Lord of the eyes; श्रोत्रपतिः – the Lord of the ears; विज्ञान-पतिः – the Lord of knowledge; एतत् – this; ततः – after that; भवति – becomes; आकाशशरीरम् – whose body is space; ब्रह्म – Brahman; सत्यात्म – (whose) nature is Truth; प्राणारामम् – who sports in dynamic life (prāṇa); मन आनन्दम् – whose mind is bliss; शान्तिसमृद्धम् – who is full of peace; अमृतम् – who is immortal; इति – thus; (हे) प्राचीनयोग्य – oh descendant of the ancient yoga culture; उपास्स्व– you meditate

2. With the word bhūḥ, he stands in fire; in the air in the shape of bhuvaḥ; as suvah in the sun; in the Brahman as Mahaḥ. He obtains self-effulgence. He obtains Lordship over minds; he becomes the Lord of speech, Lord of the eyes, Lord of the ears, the Lord of knowledge. Then he becomes this Brahman, whose body is space, whose nature is truth, who sports in dynamic life prāṇa, whose mind is bliss, who is full of peace, who is immortal. Thus, oh descendant of the ancient yoga culture, meditate.

In the last section, the meditation was upon the vyāhṛtis (which were regarded there as the worlds, the luminaries, the prāṇas and so on). Here, the object of contemplation is upon the intelligent, ever shining Soul. Earlier we were told that the meditator would, as a result of his upāsanā, become identified with the total mind, while here the very meditation is directly upon Brahman endowed with attributes (saguṇa Brahman). In the previous meditation, the fruit was described as 'the devas offer tribute', while here the meditator attains Lordship and independent sovereignty. He gets himself established in one or the other aspect of the total mind which he may happen to desire at the culmination of his existence in his present mortal coil. Thus, evidently, Section 5 and 6 together constitute one form of meditation whose various aspects have been dealt with in two stages in the two sections.

Since this section under discussion is a continuation of the previous one, the style becomes too cryptic. Therefore, it is not easy to coax words to yield their meaning directly to us. Even the Ācāryas who had brought into their discussions a vast amount of the subtlest intellect, could not give us a ready explanation of these mantras without supplementing words and ideas in filling, as it were, the blanks in this passage. Yawning gulfs separate idea from idea and within the section there seems to be many an unbridgeable gap which would have been better understood and would have been palatable had there been separate sections.

Now, we have to accept the section as it stands. It expresses:

(a) the object of meditation;

(b) the imaginary path of departure of the egocentric consciousness from one physical equipment to its own self-decided 'fresh woods and pastures new';

(c) the fruits of constant contemplation upon the different ideas prescribed in the earlier section; and lastly,

(d) the section is rounded up with a passionate call to the worthy descendant of hallowed Sanātana Dharma (prācīna yogya) to meditate continuously and thus grow in his mental amplitude and intellectual stature.

We shall try to go into these four ideas one by one:

(a) The object of contemplation – It is the conscious life principle which is described in this section as having its abode in the 'cave of the heart'. The educated young man is sure to protest against this crude statement of ignorance that the heart has got a cave, while the day's prophets of biology are daily opening up hearts with their scissors and scalpels to declare and to illustrate that there are no holes in the heart!

In the lyrical poetry which is the very language of the Āryan thought, they did not mean the pumping organ when they used the term 'heart' but what they meant by the term is the noble sentiments and the divine emotions which the humane in man is capable of expressing in its transactions with the world outside. The nobility of thought, the purity of emotions, the softness of sentiment, the glorious attributes of love, tolerance, mercy and kindness; these expressed by a man in his life constitute the 'heart' of his personality.

The tradition of Vedānta is that in this 'heart' there is a cave and in the cave is the seat of true intelligence. That is to say, in the poetic language of the Vedas, they only meant that a full man is he who discriminates and rationalises life and the happenings in it, through an intellect functioning in the fresh atmosphere of a 'pure heart'. A mere intellect is considered everywhere as an efficient annihilator of joy!

Rāvaṇa in the *Rāmāyaṇa* and the Hitlers and Mussolinis of our own days, are examples of the intellect divorced from the heart, emitting death and disaster to others, and ultimately bringing down fire and brimstone upon themselves. Such a crude intellect can serve us only in the fields of modern politics, economics and objective sciences. But the touch of the genius, the blessing of a divine glory can never be achieved by such activities of an intellect unless it is efficiently courted by a healthy and evolved heart. The glory of Buddha or Mahātmā Gandhi is that they could bring about a certain amount of social revival and political integrity in their own time, no doubt with well thought out and highly intellectual schemes and plans of activity. But their work seems to be more nobler and diviner than the achievements of the Napoleons and Hitlers inasmuch as the intellect in them functioned through the medium of a full-grown and evolved heart!!

Thus, it is only in the room of the skeleton that the physiologist comes to insist that the heart is the pumping organ in the bosom of living creatures. Even in our colleges, if we walk from the laboratory to the library, we can find that thinkers and writers have a separate connotation for the term 'heart'. Our ṛṣis, scientists of living as they were, when they declared that the seat of an evolved intellect is the heart, they only meant that an intellect functioning from the peaceful arbours of a fully grown 'love heart' alone can perceive the unifying cord of life that binds all the variegated plurality into one great garland of love. Truth is experienceable only with an intellect when it is analysing and observing, viewing and discriminating in the halls of the heart, where, in the clean aroma of love, the intellect seems to gather a greater subtlety to meditate and to realise.

(b) The imaginary path of departure – Every grown member of the present generation must have observed repeatedly the members of the last generation departing in peace; and necessarily, therefore, there can be no intelligent grown up man who has not, in himself, come to ask the why and the how and has not come to his own rough and ready explanation of this unavoidable and yet most painful of happenings known as death.

In his unscientific, rough and ready observations, he must have concluded that the dead body is the rejected covering of the dead one and that some 'vital thing', as it were, has left every dead body. The body, while living, was reacting to the impulses provided by the world outside. It used to entertain feelings. It had its own ideas and thoughts, and perhaps, it had some vague feelings or some prominent urgencies created by the restlessness of its soul. But the moment it is dead, it seems to function in none of these levels and therefore, any thinking person must have concluded that some essence or vitality has departed from that body.

This egocentric conscious living principle is the essence behind the sense organs, mind and intellect, the essence in whose divine presence the very matter made container, the body, resists nature's law of decay. It surrenders itself to that law, the moment this divine factor departs. If it thus gets itself divorced from one physical structure, then the layman would necessarily enquire to know which is the exit for the ego and life to pass out of the body.

When an uninitiated student reached the feet of the Master in the olden days for purposes of his studies in Vedānta, the teacher had certainly a very subtle job to do. Any student, when he entertains a doubt, cannot find the necessary mental peace and intellectual tranquillity for active study or vigilant pursuit of knowledge until the agitating doubt has been dispelled by some explanation or other. Masters of psychology as they were, the ṛṣis knew this and they invariably cleared all doubts with one myth or the other, which at that time would look seriously reasonable and fully explanatory to the student.

This technique is fully revealed in the explanations for the pluralistic creation that have been given by Masters in the various Upaniṣads. Here in the mantra, we have a very highly imaginative and serious looking explanation of the entire path by which the ego or the mind and intellect of the individual makes its exit from the physical body.

From the heart, which is the seat of the mind and intellect and therefore, of the ego, there is a subtle 'nerve' which runs up to the crown of the head along the uvula. The Sanskrit word 'nāḍī' had to be translated as 'nerve' in the absence of any better word, although this is not very correct. 'Nāḍī' in Sanskrit, as used in our śāstras, is only a direction along which life's energies flow. It is said here that through this vertical nāḍī, (called in the yoga śāstra as suṣumnā), the individual passes and escapes out of the physical structure at the crown.

(c) Fruits of constant contemplation – The third idea that seems to have been expounded in this section is a very familiar truth, perhaps very popular in the Vaidika days. This idea is accepted even now by modern psychology, namely, 'as you think, so you become'. We are all, at any moment, the product of our own thoughts. The criminal is he who entertains criminal thoughts constantly and a saint is he whose thoughts are saintly. If the thoughts are interchanged, the saint can sink into the sins of the former and the criminal can rise to the glories of the latter. The constant meditation upon bhūḥ, bhuvaḥ and suvaḥ leaves such a turn and character to the thought constitution in the individual that, at the time of his death, when the mind departs, it is propelled by its own thoughts to realise and live in the experience of the presiding deities of these vyāhṛtis. 'Such an upāsaka comes to reside in fire in the shape of bhūḥ, in the air in the shape of bhuvaḥ, in the sun as suvaḥ and in Brahman as Mahaḥ', explains Śaṅkarācārya.

Thus fulfilling its constant meditations, the ego of the upāsaka comes to realise and experience its identity with the total mind (hiraṇyagarbha). Naturally, he comes to experience the joys of the entire existence.

(d) The call to the Hindus to live the spiritual life – This section is rounded off with a passionate appeal to all Hindus to the life of purity, chastity and meditation, so that they may realise all the ampler possibilities that are now lying dormant in man. The term 'Prācīnayogya', a proper noun, is being translated by some as a mere proper noun, as the name of an individual student; but considering the word meaning, we would like to interpret it as the call of the ṛṣis to all 'worthy descendants of the ancients', men of the ancient yoga, or the worthy children of the hallowed Sanātana Dharma.

This section therefore concludes the instructions of the spiritual preceptor Māhācamasya, given out to Śrī Prācīnayogya or, through him, to the entire world of Hindus!!

Section vii – अनुवाकः ७

Some Helpful Thoughts to Educate The Mind In Philosophical Culture

पृथिव्यन्तरिक्षं द्यौर्दिशोऽवान्तरदिशः ।
अग्निर्वायुरादित्यश्चन्द्रमा नक्षत्राणि ।
आप ओषधयो वनस्पतय आकाश आत्मा ।
इत्यधिभूतम् । अथाध्यात्मम् ।
प्राणो व्यानोऽपान उदानः समानः ।
चक्षुः श्रोत्रं मनो वाक् त्वक् ।
चर्म मागंसगंस्नावास्थि मज्जा ।
एतदधिविधाय ऋषिरवोचत् ।
पाङ्क्तं वा इदगं सर्वम् ।
पाङ्क्तेनैव पाङ्क्तगं स्पृणोतीति ॥१॥

pṛthivyantarikṣaṁ dyaur-diśo'vāntaradiśaḥ,
agnirvāyurādityaścandramā nakṣatrāṇi,
āpa oṣadhayo vanaspataya ākāśa ātmā,
ityadhibhūtam, athādhyātmam,
prāṇo vyāno'pāna udānaḥ samānaḥ,
cakṣuḥ śrotraṁ mano vāk tvak,
carma māgṁsagṁsnāvāsthi majjā,
etadadhividhāya ṛṣiravocat,
pāṅktaṁ vā idagṁ sarvam,
pāṅktenaiva pāṅktagṁ spṛṇotīti. (1)

पृथिवी – the earth; अन्तरिक्षं – the interspace; द्यौ – the heaven; दिशः – the main quarters; अवान्तरदिशः – the intermediate quarters; अग्निः – the fire; वायुः – the air; आदित्यः – the sun; च – and; चन्द्रमा – the moon; नक्षत्राणि – the stars; आपः – the waters; ओषधयः – the herbs; वनस्पतयः – large trees; आकाशः – the space; आत्मा – the Ātman; इति – thus; अधिभूतम् – concerning all living creatures; अथ – then; अध्यात्मम् – upon the soul; प्राणः – the prāṇa; व्यानः – the vyāna; अपानः – the apāna; उदानः – the udāna; समानः – the samāna; चक्षुः – the eyes; श्रोत्रम् – the ears; मनः – the mind; वाक् – the speech; त्वक् – the touch; चर्म – the skin; मागंसगम् – the flesh; स्नावा – the muscles; अस्थि – the bones; मज्जा – the marrow; एतत् – this; अधिविधाय – analysing and determining; ऋषिः – the seer; अवोचत् – said; पाङ्क्तम् – five fold; वै – verily; इदगम् – this; सर्वम् – all; पाङ्क्तेन – by one set of five-fold grouping; एव – really; पाङ्क्तम् – the other set of pentadic grouping; स्पृणोति – (is) sustained; इति – thus

1. The earth, the sky, the interspace (antarikṣam), the heaven, the main quarters, the intermediate quarters; the fire, the air, the sun, the moon and the stars; the waters, the herbs, the forest trees, the space and Ātman – so far, regarding all living creatures and then come those regarding the Soul (adhyātmam) – the prāṇa, the vyāna, the apāna, the udāna and the samāna; the eyes, the ears, the mind, the speech and the touch; the skin, the flesh, the muscles, the bones and the marrow. After analysing and determining these, the seer said, 'All this is pāṅktam or five fold or pentadic. The one set of five fold grouping sustains the other pentadic grouping'.

A familiar Vaidika metre consisting of five pādas of five syllables each is technically called a paṅkti and the students of that age were extremely familiar with this pentadic sound arrangement in language. The attempt of the ṛṣi here is to prescribe a new method of meditation by which the attention of the student is brought to the fact that the world outside as well as the world within, are both arranged in groups of five. In thus showing that the world of matter (adhiloka), the world of elements (adhidaivika), the world of nature (adhihbhautika) and the world of the within (adhyātmika), are all constituted in themselves with a plurality that can be conveniently classified under five main headings. The ṛṣi is lending to the child a possibility to meditate upon an easily realisable oneness with the within and the without.

It is only a recent tragedy that has brought into the field of Indian thought a neglect of the outer world. And this tragedy becomes an abominable cruelty against our own culture when everybody, from the good for nothing saint to the complacent idler in the bazaar, glorifies his mental inertia and disgusting intellectual morbidity with the plumes of misquoted declarations of Vedānta. The ṛṣis must have felt that unless the students are well trained and educated with the idea of the sanctity of the whole, the chances are that the philosophy of Vedānta may give them a perversion in their evaluation of life. Certainly, no sage would have conceived a culture as acme if it were to yield to us only the present state of depravity, disintegration, devilry and diabolic decadence, which is now our lot as a community, inspite of all our learned śāstrīs, reliable paṇḍitas, divine saints and holy sages. The far sighted intelligence of the true Hindu had rightly foreseen this possibility and therefore, they prepared their children even in their early stages by instilling into them the idea of reverence and respect for the world without.

Concluding this grouping of the pentadic classification, the ṛṣi, standing on the high pedestal of his own realisation, declared with an authority and a power of assertion, born of his own experience of Truth, that the subjective world compliments the outer world as much as the outer fulfils itself in the inner. When the oneness of the supreme Self is ultimately realised, it is but logical that the outer is also to be experienced to be as much divine as the inner. The divinity which Vedānta respects is not a crystallised neutron like centre within, but it is an effulgence of divinity which pervades and sustains the entire universe of multiplicity, finitude and change. This idea of the oneness of the within and the without, is amply brought out in all our sacred books, in all the Upaniṣads and in almost all the chapters of the *Gītā*.

Section viii – अनुवाकः ८

Praṇava – The Highest Symbol of Meditation

ओमिति ब्रह्म । ओमितीदग्ं सर्वम् ॥१ ॥

omiti brahma, omitīdagm̐ sarvam. (1)

ओम् – Om; इति – thus; ब्रह्म – Brahman; ओम् – Om; इति – thus; इदग्म् – this (universe); सर्वम् – all

1. The sacred sound Om is Brahman. All this is the syllable Om.

The mystic syllable Om is the choiceless point of concentration prescribed for the benefit of the student of Vedānta, who is constitutionally more intellectual than emotional. In their early attempts at developing a highly concentrated mind and intellect, such students too need the help of a symbol or an idea which has infinite possibilities to entertain them with its inexhaustible contents. The genius in the Vaidika Masters gave us Om as an idea idol for the intellect to worship in the inner temple.

Life, we saw in our introductory talks, is a constant flow of experiences and these experiences when observed are found to fall into three layers, as the experiences of the waking state, of the dream state and of the deep sleep state. The life of everyone of us is certainly influenced by our experiences in all these three different planes of consciousness and they all have a totally positive influence in moulding our character and personality. This would read slightly strange to the modern young man because Western philosophy have all been so far striving to discover the fundamental in life by an analysis and close study of merely the life available for us in our waking state. It is indeed difficult, if not almost impossible, to come at a right evaluation of life and its meaning by observing only a third of its field.

When the ṛṣis, observed more and more closely these three fields of experiences, they discovered that an individual, identifying with his physical body, comes to live his waking state of outer gross objects as the 'waker'.

The same entity totally in oblivion of his body and the outer world, when gets exclusively identified with his mind and intellect, he comes to revel in an inner world of dreams, and experiences subtle objects of imagination as a 'dreamer'.

When the same entity becomes forgetful of the body and its outer world, the mind and intellect and their feelings and thoughts, he comes to enjoy a world of nothingness, no doubt peaceful and joyful, and yet, conscious of nothing but nothingness, he becomes the 'deep sleeper'.

The dreamer's experiences are totally different and sometimes even contrary to the waker's life and the experience of the 'deep sleeper' is common to all and seems to have no relationship with the waking and the dream conditions of experiences. Yet, it is the experience of all of us that we can remember, on our waking, all about our experiences during the last waking state, yester-night's early dreams and also the peaceful sleep that we had afterwards. From these observations the ṛṣis continued their bold and adventurous theory.

The law of memory is that one cannot oneself remember any experience of another; if one can remember anything at all, they are all actual experiences of the individual himself. That is to say, the law of memory enunciates that the rememberer and the experiencer must be one and the same individual, or else memory is impossible; I can never remember any one of your past experiences; nor can you remember any one of my experiences.

Applying this law of memory as a test, we find that, the 'waker', the 'dreamer' and the 'deep sleeper' are strangers among themselves, each living in its own world and seemingly having no passport to travel across its own frontiers. Since we can remember all our experiences in all three different planes, there must necessarily be a common factor which was a witness of all the happenings in all the three planes.

To make it clear, let us suppose that we have, on an idle afternoon, a friend in our drawing room, who starts revealing a slice of his biography in which he explains his despairing days in Madras, disastrous failure in Madurai and his glorious success in Delhi. Now, we all know that Madras is not Madurai, nor is Madurai one with Delhi. But our friend is describing his experiences of the three places from his own memory. Again, the despairs in Madras are different from the disasters in Madurai and both these sets of experiences are separate from the glorious successes in Delhi. But our friend is explaining all of them from his own memory. Under such circumstances, we instinctively understand that he, our friend, lived his despairing days in Madras and himself went to Madurai where he spent his days of failures and then he himself again left the Madurai-Madras zone to Delhi to reap his glorious successes.

Similarly, there must be some entity within ourselves who is present in the 'waking world', who moves to illumine the 'dreams', and who is a distant observer in the 'deep sleep world'; yet, all the same, it is not conditioned by any of these three realms. The entity is, as it were, conceived as the 'fourth', who is the Real, the Changeless and the intelligent Principle.

The sages of the Vedas, after indicating this much to the students of Vedānta, want them to experience the pure Subject, who in the waking world becomes the 'waker', in the dream becomes the 'dreamer' and in the sleep becomes the 'sleeper'.

The sound Om is constituted of three syllables[1], A, U and M. While chanting continuously the sound Om in the mind, the upāsaka is advised to superimpose upon these three sounds the three different planes of consciousness we have been describing so far, namely, the 'waking', the 'dream'

[1] For a more elaborate treatment of the subject see Swamiji's discourses on *Māṇḍūkyopaniṣad* with Gauḍapāda's *Kārikā*.

and the 'deep sleep'. The process of superimposition is the same as the principle underlying all idol worships. We have already discussed this technique by which the mighty is seen or imagined in the meagre: Śiva tattva in Śiva Liṅga; the divine Mother of Knowledge in the river Ganga, Śrī Nārāyaṇa in Śāligrāma and Christ on the Cross.

The practitioner, at his meditation, when he thus trains himself, consciously to superimpose the waker in him on the sound 'A'; and then, as the sound 'A' merges with the sound 'U', he gains a mental dexterity to forget totally his identity with the waking state experiences and to come to live consciously, in meditation, totally identified with the 'dreamer' in him. So too, when he comes to the sound 'M', he is able to blackout the entire state of plurality and arrive at a state of semi-conscious experience of all negation. Thereafter, his spiritual growth is assured in proportion to his intensity of pursuit, purity of life and intelligent sense of detachment.

Even this practice of getting oneself fully conscious of the sound 'A', 'U' and 'M', each marching into the other and getting telescoped in themselves, one into the other, is in itself a severe training for the mind at concentration. The conscious superimpositions unfolded and again folded up as explained above, is an equally all-absorbing occupation for the entire intellectual capacity in us, so that the true practitioner, if he be sincere and regular, gains, in a very short time, an infinite amount of integration both in his mind and in his intellect equipments.

Thereafter, the sensitised instruments of the within become subtle in him and dare to seek the pure Awareness which, in the three grosser planes, illumines the objects and sustains the mirage-personalities of the 'waker', the 'dreamer' and the 'deep sleeper'. The silence between two successive Oms is the point of concentration which the yogī attempts to merge with, and experience thereby in infinite contents of one split second, completely divorced from the past and entirely free from the mental slavery to the future. To live thus dynamically, free from within and from without, one second of human life is all that is needed to peep over the veils of ignorance and realise for ourselves, eternally thereafter, the true nature of the Self, the Godhood.

Here we need not have gone into such an exhaustive treatment since the reference in the text does not justify such a complete treatment; but we do so with the hope that it would help us all in our daily meditation class[1].

As we have explained above, Om represents a symbol of the waking, the dream and the deep sleep states of consciousness. Since our entire life is a sum total of different experiences in these three planes, Om, the symbol represents 'all this'. Om as the symbol of the infinite Reality that is behind the seeming multiplicity and the painful plurality, it becomes self-evident that the ṛṣis were not illogical or deliberately mystical when they declared this fact that Om is all this entire universe.

Mud is the reality; all pots of all colours, all shapes and all sizes, irrespective of their contents or condition, are all nothing but mud. Gold is the reality behind all ornaments,

[1] Swamiji's *Meditation and Life* is an exhausive treatment of the 'art of meditation.'

be they thin or thick, be they intricate or simple, be they for the neck or the legs, they are all nothing but gold. The ocean is the reality for all the waves, be they mountainous, be they small, be they frothy, be they naked, all of them are nothing but the very ocean itself. It is in this sense that Om, the idol of the Reality, has been explained in the mantra here as a symbol that represents 'the entire universe' experienced without as objects and within as thoughts and ideas.

ओमित्येतदनुकृतिर्ह स्म वा
अप्यो श्रावयेत्याश्रावयन्ति ।
ओमिति सामानि गायन्ति ।
ओगूंशोमिति शस्त्राणि शगूंसन्ति ।
ओमित्यध्वर्युः प्रतिगरं प्रतिगृणाति ।
ओमिति ब्रह्मा प्रसौति । ओमित्यग्निहोत्रमनुजानाति ।
ओमिति ब्राह्मणः प्रवक्ष्यन्नाह
ब्रह्मोपाप्नवानीति । ब्रह्मैवोपाप्नोति ॥२॥

omityetadanukṛtirha sma vā
apyo śrāvayetyāśrāvayanti,
omiti sāmāni gāyanti,
ogṁśomiti śastrāṇi śagṁsanti,
omityadhvaryuḥ pratigaraṁ pratigṛṇāti,
omiti brahmā prasauti, omityagnihotramanujānāti,
omiti brāhmaṇaḥ pravakṣyannāha
brahmopāpnavānīti, brahmaivopāpnoti. (2)

ओम् – Om; इति – thus; एतत् – this (syllable); अनुकृतिः – consent; ह स्म वै – is indeed widely known (famous); अपि – also; ओ श्रावय – O Śrāvaya; इति – thus; आश्रावयन्ति – they (the priests officiating at the sacrifice) encourage (their assistants); ओम् – Om; इति – thus; सामानि – the Sāma verses; गायन्ति – (they) sing; ओम् शोम् – Om śom; इति – thus; शस्त्राणि – invocation mantras; शगुंसन्ति – (they) recite; ओम् – Om; इति – thus; अध्वर्युः – the ṛtvik known as Adhvaryu; प्रतिगरम् – word of encouragement; प्रतिगृणाति – responds in recitation; ओम् – Om; इति – thus; ब्रह्मा – the chief priest (Brahmā), who sets right, possible mistakes; प्रसौति – expresses his assent; ओम् – Om; इति – thus; अग्निहोत्रम् – offering of oblation to the fire; अनुजानाति – permits; ओम् इति – with Om thus; ब्राह्मणः – the brāhmaṇa, one of the four varṇas – communicators of sacred knowledge; प्रवक्ष्यन् – beginning to recite the Veda; आह – says; ब्रह्म – the Brahman; उपाप्नवानि – may I obtain; इति – thus; ब्रह्म – Brahman; एव – surely; उपाप्नोति– (he) obtains

2. It is widely known that Om is uttered to indicate consent. The priest officiating at the sacrifice encourages his assistants with the words 'O Śrāvaya'. With the chanting of Om they start their singing of the Sāma verses; and with 'Om śom' they recite the śāstras; Adhvaryu answers with the syllable, 'Om'. With 'Om' the chief priest, Brahmā expresses his assent. One permits the offering of oblation to the fire with 'Om'. 'May I obtain the Brahman; with this determination, the brāhmaṇa says 'Om' before he begins to recite the Veda; and he does obtain the Brahman.

For the purpose of the upāsanā, it is necessary that the meditator (upāsaka) should be provided with some ideas of divinity and sanctity of his upāsanā, or else his mind cannot be persuaded to remain in a divine attitude of inspiration, attaching itself to the upāsya (the object of contemplation). Here the advice is given to meditate upon Om, and the teacher should provide the student with material to excite and sustain a spirit of inspiration in him.

The student is one who has reached the Master after years of devoted pursuit of the ritualistic portion of the Vedas. He is very familiar with the scene of sacrifice, the various priests and the words uttered by them and so on. No student of that time could have failed to feel divinely inspired when they were reminded of a yajñaśālā. Therefore, here we find the teacher is giving the student some definite ideas about the exact places in the rituals where the various priests and officials around the sacred fire familiarly chant Om with all the priestly dignity.

In the course of the ritualism when the subordinates ask, 'Shall I do the homa' or 'Shall I start chanting', the chief priest gives his consent by saying 'Om'. Again, when a ṛtivk is sleepy and misses chanting the mantras, in order to encourage him and bring his attention to the chanting, the elder priest would say, 'O Śrāvaya'. Thus Om is used by the chief priest not only for registering assent (anumati), but the same sound is used for encouragement (preraṇā).

The mantras of the *Sāma-veda* are sung to tune and the singers of the Sāman start their chanting with Om. Portions of *Sāma-veda*, not tuned to music, are called śastra and they too are recited with an invocation as 'Om śom'. The presiding priest of a yajña never talks during the yajña, and he sets the sacrifice in motion by saying 'Om'. The sacrificer authorises the priest to start the offering of oblations into the fire, again by uttering 'Om'. A brāhmaṇa with the desire 'Let me obtain the Vedas', starts chanting the Veda with a devoted 'Om'. Assuredly, he obtains Brahman, the theme of the Vedas.

By thus giving some hints of the sacred occasions when the sound Om is used in the divine atmosphere of the rituals, the meditator gets a mental attitude of godliness and sanctity; and the chances are that he will soon develop an amount of self-integration within himself as a result of his meditation on Om.

Section ix – अनुवाकः ९

Some Ethical Principles and Practices

ऋतं च स्वाध्यायप्रवचने च ।
सत्यं च स्वाध्यायप्रवचने च ।
तपश्च स्वाध्यायप्रवचने च ।
दमश्च स्वाध्यायप्रवचने च ।
शमश्च स्वाध्यायप्रवचने च ।
अग्नयश्च स्वाध्यायप्रवचने च ।
अग्निहोत्रं च स्वाध्यायप्रवचने च ।
अतिथयश्च स्वाध्यायप्रवचने च ।
मानुषं च स्वाध्यायप्रवचने च ।
प्रजा च स्वाध्यायप्रवचने च ।
प्रजनश्च स्वाध्यायप्रवचने च ।
प्रजातिश्च स्वाध्यायप्रवचने च ।
सत्यमिति सत्यवचा राथीतरः ।
तप इति तपोनित्यः पौरुशिष्टिः ।
स्वाध्यायप्रवचने एवेति नाको मौद्गल्यः ।
तद्धि तपस्तद्धि तपः ॥१॥

ṛtam ca svādhyāyapravacane ca,
satyam ca svādhyāyapravacane ca,
tapaśca svādhyāyapravacane ca,
damaśca svādhyāyapravacane ca,
śamaśca svādhyāyapravacane ca,

agnayaśca svādhyāyapravacane ca
agnihotram ca svādhyāyapravacane ca,
atithayaśca svādhyāyapravacane ca,
mānuṣaṁ ca svādhyāyapravacane ca,
prajā ca svādhyāyapravacane ca,
prajanaśca svādhyāyapravacane ca,
prajātiśca svādhyāyapravacane ca,
satyamiti satyavacā rāthītaraḥ,
tapa iti taponityaḥ pauruśiṣṭiḥ,
svādhyāyapravacane eveti nāko maudgalyaḥ,
taddhi tapastaddhi tapaḥ. (1)

ऋतम् – what is right and proper; च – and; स्वाध्यायप्रवचने च – study of the Vedas and propagation of the truth therein; सत्यम् – (intellectual) truthfulness; च – and; स्वाध्याय प्रवचने च – study of the Vedas and propagation of the truths therein; तपः – penance; च – and; स्वाध्यायप्रवचने च – study of the Vedas and propagation of the truths therein; दमः – control of the senses; च – and; स्वाध्यायप्रवचने च – study of the Vedas and propagation of the truths therein; शमः – tranquillity; च – and; स्वाध्यायप्रवचने च – study of the Vedas and propagation of the truths therein; अग्नयः – (maintenance of) fire; च – and; स्वाध्यायप्रवचने च – study of the Vedas and propagation of the truths therein; अग्निहोत्रम् – daily offering of the oblations in fire sacrifice; च – and; स्वाध्यायप्रवचने च – study of the Vedas and propagation of the truths therein; अतिथयः – guests; च – and; स्वाध्यायप्रवचने च – study of the Vedas and propagation of the truths therein; मानुषम् – what is good for human welfare; च – and; स्वाध्यायप्रवचने च – study of the Vedas and propagation of the truths therein; प्रजा – duties towards children; च – and;

स्वाध्यायप्रवचने च – study of the Vedas and propagation of the truths therein; प्रजनः – procreation; च – and; स्वाध्यायप्रवचने च – study of the Vedas and propagation of the truths therein; प्रजातिः – propagation of the race; च – and; स्वाध्यायप्रवचने च – study of the Vedas and propagation of the truths therein; (अनुष्ठेयानि – should be practised) सत्यम् इति – truth alone (is to be strictly practised); सत्यवचा – Satyavacā; राथीतरः – the son of Rāthītara; तपः इति – penance alone (is to be practised); तपोनित्यः – Taponitya (lit. constantly engaged in penance); पौरुशिष्टिः – son of Puruśiṣṭa; स्वाध्यायप्रवचने – study and teaching of the Vedas (are alone to be practised); एव – alone; इति – thus; नाकः – Nāka; मौद्गल्यः – the son of Mudgala; तत् – that; हि – verily; तपः – penance; तत् – that; हि – verily; तपः – penance

1. The practice of what is right and proper, as fixed by the scriptural texts, is to be done along with reading the texts oneself and propagating the truths of the same. 'Truth', meaning practising in life what is understood to be right and proper, is to be pursued along with regular studies and preaching. Penance, study and preaching; control of the senses, study and preaching; tranquillity, study and preaching; the 'maintenance of fire', study and preaching; offering of oblations in fire sacrifice, study and preaching of the Vedas; serving the guests, study and preaching; the performance of duties towards man, study and preaching; duties towards children, study and preaching of the Vedas; procreation, study and preaching; propagation of the race, study and preaching; all these are things to be practised sincerely. Satyavacā, son of Rāthītara, holds that truth alone is to be strictly practised. Taponitya, son of Puruśiṣṭa declares

that penance alone is to be practised. Nāka, son of Mudgala, holds the view that the study and preaching of the Vedas alone is to be practised; that verily, is penance; aye that is penance.

This portion represents the last concluding lecture given by the teacher to the students in their classroom. This almost represents the corresponding function that we have in our modern colleges, which goes by the term valedictory address. The students are told some main ideas as to how they should live, dedicated to their culture, and consistent with what has been taught to them as the goal and the way of life.

A careful analysis of the ideas here and a diligent inquiry into them, clearly gives us an insight into the special trait in our ancient generation which caused the whole world to stand aghast, lost in admiration and respect to the spiritual India! No doubt, the glory of India could not have been because of a few prophets or a handful of saints and sages, however great and divine they might have been. The admiration that historical figures could invoke in their limited lifetime could not be a sufficient theme to create the amount of awe at and reverence for India which the distant people of the world are paying even today.

From this portion it is clear that the present world's tribute to the glory that was India is not the adoration paid to a declared prophet or to some unknown saints, not to a philosophy or a science; it is a tribute paid to a generation that lived the enduring values of life in society, spreading more and more peace and tranquillity among men. It is not the compelling glory of some rare beings, mighty in their own perfection and glorious in their words, but it is the loving reverence that an age feels towards a past generation that knew how to live the right values of life and bring the entire generation to enjoy a greater quota of intellectual poise, mental stability, physical health, social happiness, communal growth and national well-being.

In order to create such a consummate scheme of things around and about us, among a people, it must be the duty of the educationists to see that they impart to the growing generation not merely some factual knowledge or some wondrous theories, but also instill into the growing generation ideals of pure living and train the children to live those ideals in their individual life. In short, the secret of our glory is crystallized in this valedictory address and we will find that this portion is more exhaustively amplified in the following section.

In this section, we find that twelve immortal ideas of living rules of conduct are given and on an equal number of times, it has been insisted that the student should continue his study of the scriptures and propagation of these immortal ideas of his glorious culture among the people all through his life. To believe that the Hindus are not missionary in their zeal for the propagation of their ideas in the world is not to understand at all the spirit of Hinduism. The ṛṣis themselves dedicated their entire life in spreading this culture and the entire educated community was commissioned to serve as preachers in the society.

Earlier also, we found that the teacher and the taught practised ritualism to invoke the grace of the Lord, demanding of Him infinite wealth for the purposes of opening universities and maintaining the same. Here, in the valedictory address, the teacher, addressing the students in the final class on the last day of their regular meetings, emphasises the need for continuing their studies till their death and making it a moral obligation on themselves to continuously preach the contents of the scriptures.

This glorious urge for a studious life bristling with the missionary zeal left us somewhere in the past, and from that cursed time onwards, the Hindu decadence has started its pernicious decay. The educated brāhmaṇas learned to misinterpret these words and arrogate to themselves a monopoly of knowledge. They viciously traded upon the cultural heritage of their noble land. Mainly guided by a misjudgement and mostly encouraged by the vicious charms of power and ambition, they felt it convenient to withdraw knowledge from the majority and share it among themselves. Thus they created an exclusive class of intelligensia blessed with special knowledge and therefore, with special patronage from the state.

This sad decadence, initiated then, came to roar its threats in the days of Buddha. By this time the sapless ritualistic excesses had made ugly gashes on the serene face of Mother India. Buddha, as a true son of this culture, rose in revolt at the existing imperfections and launched his campaign against it. Sadly enough, his followers misunderstood the message of the prophet of peace and misguided the generation. To retrieve the age back to the Sanātana Dharma, Śaṅkarācārya came and emphasised the essence of our religion in a language which that generation could understand then.

Reading the works of philosophers and the bibles of prophets without reference to their times, confuses every later generation and this tragedy happened to a large extent to the students of Śaṅkarācārya also. Thus, in slavery to words, we missed altogether their import and forgot to make restatements of the truths in the context of our time.

In these days, when Hinduism has sunk into the lowest ebb of its decadence, foreign ideas and ideologies are very systematically infiltrating into this country and taking hold of the people. These tragic ulcers are sure to end the individualistic glory of the Hindu culture. If we don't bring into the generation and the society the true vitality of the Truth of Upaniṣad with an urgency which the situation demands, unavoidable indeed is the Hindu disaster!

Our present idea that the spread of our culture and free discussions on the scriptures is the special right of a few and that it should be addressed to only a few specially selected individuals is an absurd notion which does not have the sanction of the ṛṣis, especially in our age. Here we find that the brilliant students are repeatedly commissioned to continue their study and to be preachers all their lifetime. The style of Upaniṣad is itself brevity. Even a syllable more than the minimum required, is considered as a great sin and yet, here we find in a small little section twelve repetitions of the same idea; study and discourse upon the Vedas (svādhyāya and pravacanam) with a view to make others understand and appreciate our culture.

For this missionary work, the Hindu ṛṣis never saw any necessity for organising a special class of teachers but it was made a duty of every householder. In the pursuit of his vocation, the householder was not asked to spare any special time or to sacrifice his duties either towards himself or his own children, or to the society or to the nation or to the world. But while emphasising the need for pursuing his duties on all these levels, he is asked to keep continuously in touch with the scriptures and to preach the same truth to others; both by his words and his actions.

The great qualities that have been insisted are:

a) Ṛtam—The practice of what is right and proper as indicated in the scriptures;

b) Satyam—Living up to the ideals that have been intellectually comprehended during their studies;

c) Tapas—Spirit of self-sacrifice and self-denial;

d) Dama—Control of the senses;

e) Śama—Tranquillity of the mind;

f) Agni—Maintenance of a charitable and ready kitchen at home in the sevā of all deserving hungry fellow beings;

g) Sacred Fires (of three kinds i.e., Gārhapatya, Āhavanīya, Dakṣiṇā) – Practice of concentration and ritualism through fire worship, as was in vogue in the society in those days; and

h) One's duty towards humanity, towards children, towards grand children and towards the society.

In the close of the section, three great Masters have been quoted. They had, in the past, declared the most important of the above qualities.The unavoidable quality to be cultivated according to each is either satyam or tapas or study of śāstras and its efficient spread in the society (svādhyāya-pravacanam).

In short, this section is as though a manifesto of the Hindu way of living in which every Hindu, striving to live up to his or her sacred culture, is charged to live true to his or her own intellectual convictions (satyam), in a spirit of self-denial (tapas), in the study of his sacred bible (svādhyāya) and spread his culture among the people of the world (pravacanam).

Section x – अनुवाकः १०

Sacred Recitation of Triśaṅku After Realisation

अहं वृक्षस्य रेरिवा । कीर्तिः पृष्ठं गिरेरिव ।
ऊर्ध्वपवित्रो वाजिनीव स्वमृतमस्मि ।
द्रविणग्ं सवर्चसम् । सुमेधा अमृतोक्षितः ।
इति त्रिशङ्कोर्वेदानुवचनम् ॥१ ॥

ahaṁ vṛkṣasya rerivā, kīrtiḥ pṛṣṭhaṁ gireriva,
ūrdhvapavitro vājinīva svamṛtamasmi,
draviṇagṁ savarcasam, sumedhā amṛtokṣitaḥ,
iti triśaṅkorvedānuvacanam. (1)

अहम् – I; वृक्षस्य – of the tree; रेरिवा – stimulator; कीर्तिः – fame (glory); पृष्ठम् – peak; गिरेः – of the mountain; इव – like; ऊर्ध्व-पवित्रः – high and pure (am I); वाजिनि – (the essence) in the sun; इव – like; स्वमृतम् – the excellent, immortal being; अस्मि – am I; द्रविणम् – power and wealth; सवर्चसम् – effulgent with intuition; सुमेधाः – intelligent; अमृतोक्षितः – the imperishable; the undecaying (am I); इति – thus; त्रिशङ्कोः – of the seer Triśaṅku; वेदानुवचनम् – the sacred recitation

1. 'I am the stimulator in the tree of universe. My fame (glory) is high as the peaks of the mountains. High and pure am I like the essence in the sun; I am the power and the wealth, effulgent with intuition. Intelligent, imperishable and

undecaying am I – this is the sacred recitation of Triśaṅku, after he realised the Truth.

This section has no direct bearing with what had preceded and, also as we shall find, no intimate bearing with what is to come. Śaṅkarācārya very intelligently interprets this section as a mantra for recitation just before the daily reading of scriptures (svādhyāya) which had been insisted upon twelve times in the previous section. This repeated insistence in the last section of both the study and the dissemination of the knowledge is termed by Śaṅkarācārya as Brahma-yajña.

Since the study of the Vedas is to be pursued by everyone all through one's life, and since the students are going out into the world commissioned to live as healthy social beings, they are soon to enter the householder's tribulations. Tossed by the daily circumstances of life, no individual human being can maintain his mental equipoise in life, which is so necessary for the study of the highly philosophical literature, without some special exercises in mental reconditioning.

As students, they can easily be kept in such an atmosphere where they can maintain this required inner poise; later on too, at the time of their retirement, the individuals can teach themselves to be in the same steady mental poise. But in the surging period of youth, chaotic with its physical appetites, mental commotions and intellectual ambitions; when the individual is fighting his lonely war in the field of life against a hosts of threatening circumstances, he will not ordinarily find that cool and calm spring season within.

In order that such a shattered mind be effectively brought to the seat of study daily, the ṛṣis of the scriptures had to find some secret method by which an individual devotee could discover in himself the necessary conditions for a profitable study. This mantra now under discussion is, according to Śaṅkarācārya, a formula for repetition, to be used by the householder before he starts his daily study of the scriptures. When we are introduced to the depths of significances of these words, we shall easily understand how, an individual, when with sincerity, faith and understanding repeats this stanza, can come to feel himself immediately wafted from his disturbing present into serener heights of a calm and tranquil divinity.

This mantra, therefore tunes up the students everyday by bringing out the song of the soul from the harp of the heart. The words here are the explosions of an unknown Ṛṣi, Triśaṅku by name, on his Self-discovery.

The words that express thoughts at the heights of their inspiration do not merely convey their literary meaning. Even in ordinary life it is evident from many passages in dramas when they come to the 'crisis'. Here also we find that the words in themselves do not, by their dictionary meaning, convey the full import.

Again, since we have now drifted away from the vast oceans of the resplendent Hindu culture to the straits of secularism and sectarian prejudices, we cannot understand very easily the implications of these words which have the flavour of the Vaidika tradition. There is nothing strange about it. If the great ṛṣis were to come down and move with us now, they too may not find it easy when we talk to them in our language and familiar expressions. Expressions like 'atom bombed the resolutions' or 'shelled with arguments', or 'met at tea', and so on would be confusing enough for them since they are uninitiated into the significance of 'atom bombed' or 'shelled' or 'at tea.' Similarly here, when we are reading some expressions of the ṛṣis which were, at that time very familiar to the students, we generally stand confused and lost.

'I am the stimulator of the tree' – If this be, according to Hinduism, the divine Self-realisation of the great sage, then surely there will be none here who would pride himself at being a Hindu; for to be a 'stimulator of a tree' is not quite satisfactory for us even if we are extremely imaginative. This confusion arises from our incapacity to understand what exactly is the connotation meant by the teachers when they used the term 'tree'. It is such expressions in our scriptures that confuse the West and confound the products of the West who have reached here to live in the East. We should certainly sympathise with them; they are disgustingly too low to deserve our hatred or wrath.

When we get more and more acquainted with the entire Vaidika literature, the scriptural connotation in which the term 'tree' is used becomes clear. It is the tradition of Hindu thought, from the early days of the Vedas, to consider the entire universe in the form of a tree. Not only in the Vedas, but we find the same tradition of referring to this universal symbol, both in its erect and inverted position, in Buddhistic,

Gnostic, Hermitic, Christian and Islamic religious books also. The *Maitreyopaniṣad* speaks of one Aśvattha tree identified with Om. The *Ṛg-veda* asks: 'What is that tree out of which heaven and earth are fashioned?' In *Muṇḍakopaniṣad*, again, there is the picture of the tree referred to. In the *Mahābhārata*, in its Aśvatthāmāparva, we find a full description of the Brahmavṛkṣa. In *Viṣṇu Sahasranāma* 'tree' is counted as one of the names of the supreme Lord. In the later literature, the conception changed and we find the same tree standing inverted, representing the entire finite world of plurality. The *Kaṭhopaniṣad*[1] conceives it, the *Śvetāśvataropaniṣad* refers to it and in the *Gītā* we find an exhaustive description of it.

The finite world of plurality is conceived of as an aśvattha tree because a banyan tree can be considered relatively immortal due to its long life. Again, there is no single tree which can be otherwise quoted which has such a large number of branches and leaves which are ever in a state of agitation, with so many adventitious roots flowing out of its branches to embrace the mother earth and make its shady grounds a thousand pillared hall of noisy confusion. The very name of the tree, aśvattha, also has, in the construction of its nomenclature, a meaning well suited for the purpose. Śvaḥ means 'tomorrow', 'ttha' means 'existence'; śvattha means, therefore, 'that which exists tomorrow also'. When the negative sense 'A' is prefixed, it becomes aśvattha, meaning, 'that which will not exist tomorrow', that which is finite.

This tree of universe, representing in itself the entire world of objects, is vitalised by the eternal, all-pervading

[1] Read Swāmiji's discourses on *Kaṭhopaniṣad*.

Consciousness which is the goal of ṛsis struggling on the path of Self-realisation. Ṛṣi Triśaṅku was successful in rediscovering himself to be this spiritual Perfection and the passage now under discussion is the song of ecstasy and joy that gurgled out from the blissful experience of this God-man.

He is here struggling to stammer out, in words, the divine inspiration that he has lived in his moment of realisation and therefore, we find that the mantra does not read as a statement of fact. The maimed words, broken and hesitating, though literally they express nothing in their voiceless significances, indicate an ocean of an extremely subjective experience. He cries, 'I, the pure Self, the conscious Principle, the infinite Reality, is the stimulator in the entire tree of universe; I am the sap of life, wherever it is manifest, from the lowest to the highest'.

Necessarily therefore, 'my glory is as high as the peaks of the mountains', inasmuch as wherever there is the thrilling glow of pulsating life felt, it is only the 'throb of my glory.' It is 'the song of my fame', in effect says the great ṛṣi.

The conscious life spark within ourselves or the purity of the individual concerned is untouched by animalism since Awareness, as such, is only the illuminating principle presiding within the being. Good and bad, sin and virtue, are conditions of the mind and the qualities of the thoughts. The Consciousness that illumines these conditions or qualities within ourselves should certainly be untouched by and separate from these objects illuminated; for, it is a law in nature that the illuminator is always separate from the illuminated.

The sun's rays may bless both a crime perpetrated and a divine ritualism performed; it may illuminate at once filth at one end and a pan of rose water at another place. The illuminator, the sun, being separate from these objects, none of them could condition the light or the source of light, the sun. Similarly, Consciousness illuminates the condition of mind of the individual, whether good or bad; the life spark in itself is ever the divine, the perfect and the blissful. It is in no way conditioned by the qualities or the textures of the passing thoughts or the entertained ideas.

Therefore, the great saint who comes to rediscover in himself that he is none but this Divine Centre in his real nature and thereby experiences himself to be the heart of the universe, cries from the balcony of his own experience, 'Pure am I, like the essence in the sun'.

The sceptic cannot and will not understand the benefits accrued by such a Self-realisation, since, to him, life without contentions is profitless. There are people amidst us, according to whom, life has a meaning and a purpose only so long as we have a fair chance of reaping our moans of the morning hours, hated thoughts of the midday hours and chances of fighting tooth and nail, all through the evenings. They cannot appreciate, nor can they live the quieter joys of the pregnant moments of peace the tranquillity of the inner poetry or of listening to the warbling notes of joy and cheer, that gurgle out from the bosom that is at rest, from a soul that is at peace with itself.

As an answer to such gross creatures who may suspect the futility of this consummation of evolution, Triśaṅku declares, 'I am the power and wealth'. Ordinarily, in life, man is constantly struggling to acquire wealth. Having become wealthy, we find that a rich man is not contented unless he can purchase power with his wealth. Understanding this fundamental weakness in man, Triśaṅku rightly declares that to know ourselves, to complete our rediscovery, to realise our divine nature, to live as the God in ourselves, is the only harbour wherein the frail mind shall no more be exposed to the storms of contentions and the surging waves of desires for wealth or temptations for power. To realise and live as the vitaliser behind the 'tree of the entire universe' is to realise at once the wealth, power, joy and perfection that is enjoyed and experienced by every living creature at all time (past, present and future) and at all places, all at once.

'Intelligent, imperishable, undecaying am I' – This is the final explosive expression by which the choking experience in the bosom of the great ṛṣi seems to burst out, expressing his lived bliss of Perfection. In order to show this Infinite, since language has no sway in that realm, all that the prophet or the saint can do is, as it were, to stand at the frontiers of the finite and with a pointing finger, indicate the Infinite in the language of contrast. To every one of us the finite alone is the land of our known experiences. We all know that the finite world of matter is inert, perishable and decaying and therefore, using opposite words, such as, intelligent, imperishable and undecaying, Triśanku is helping to convey to us the 'otherness' of the Infinite from what we know and experience in ourselves at present, in our egocentric misunderstandings.

To remember, thus, our Real Nature, as lived and experienced by Triśaṅku, is the most efficacious technique of turning ourselves to the highest purity and the greatest sense of detachment from our false values. When an individual recites this mantra daily, with sincerity, faith and conviction, it is evident that he will gain a sufficient amount of inward poise and tranquillity, which are surely necessary for a profitable study of the scriptures daily.

Section xi – अनुवाकः ११

The Convocation Address – The Commandments of Hinduism

वेदमनूच्याचार्योऽन्तेवासिनमनुशास्ति ।
सत्यं वद । धर्मं चर । स्वाध्यायान्मा प्रमदः ।
आचार्याय प्रियं धनमाहृत्य
प्रजातन्तुं मा व्यवच्छेत्सीः ।
सत्यान्न प्रमदितव्यम् । धर्मान्न प्रमदितव्यम् ।
कुशलान्न प्रमदितव्यम् । भूत्यै न प्रमदितव्यम् ।
स्वाध्यायप्रवचनाभ्यां न प्रमदितव्यम् ॥१ ॥

vedamanūcyācāryo'ntevāsinamanuśāsti,
satyaṁ vada, dharmaṁ cara, svādhyāyānmā pramadaḥ,
ācāryāya priyaṁ dhanamāhṛtya
prajātantuṁ mā vyavacchetsīḥ,
satyānna pramaditavyam, dharmānna pramaditavyam,
kuśalānna pramaditavyam, bhūtyai na pramaditavyam,
svādhyāyapravacanābhyāṁ na pramaditavyam. (1)

वेदम् – Veda; अनूच्य – having taught; आचार्यः – the teacher, preceptor; अन्तेवासिनम् – to the resident within the āśrama (disciple); अनुशास्ति – enjoins; सत्यम् – truth; वद – speak; धर्मम् – duty; चर – perform; स्वाध्यायात् – from the study of the Vedas; मा – never; प्रमदः – be heedless about (swerve); आचार्याय – for the teacher; प्रियम् – agreeable; धनम् – gift (fee);

आहृत्य – having given; प्रजातन्तुम् – line of descendents; मा – not; व्यवच्छेत्सीः – (you) sever; सत्यात् – from truth; न – never; प्रमदितव्यम् – fall; धर्मात् – from duty; न – never; प्रमदितव्यम् – fall; कुशलात् – from what is your own welfare; न – never; प्रमदितव्यम् – be indifferent; भूत्यै – (your) prosperity; न – never; प्रमदितव्यम् – neglect; स्वाध्याय-प्रवचनाभ्याम् – from the study of the Vedas and propagation of the truths therein; न – never; प्रमदितव्यम् – be indifferent

1. Having taught the Vedas, the preceptor enjoins the pupils – 'Speak the truth, do your duty, never swerve from the study of the Vedas, do not cut off the line of descendants in your family, after giving the preceptor the fee he desires. Never err from truth, never fall from duty, never overlook your own welfare, never neglect your prosperity and never neglect the study and the propagation of the Vedas'.

This chapter represents, we may say, the 'Convocation address' delivered to the students when they were returning home from the ancient gurukula-universities. This section represents the Hindu commandments, and the entire address systematically concludes in seven waves of thought, each following the other in a scientific rhythm which is the very melody of the Hindu thought.

This section can be considered subject-wise under seven sub-headings:

(1) Advices ruling one's own mode of living with reference to the society and oneself;

(2) Regulating one's relationship with the previous generation and the present elders;

(3) Relationship with oneself and one's teachers;

(4) One's attitude towards the learned and the wise in society;

(5) Charity and the 'laws of giving';

(6) Remedy for doubts regarding one's duty and conduct in life; and

(7) Doubts regarding one's relationship with others falsely accused in the world.

Concluding these seven specific waves of progressive thoughts, the teacher concludes that these commandments are to be strictly followed by every true Hindu, if he is worth the name. A careful study of the implications of these should give us an inkling of the secret by which we could maintain such subtle and divine culture amidst us so successfully for such a long period of unbroken history. Our covetable success in a competitive world, where ordinarily the devil governs more than God, must have been, again, because of these values of life upon which the society was taught to live.

After the studies, before the children are let out to meet their destinies in their independent individual lives as social beings, the teacher gives his exhortation which comprises in itself, we may say, 'Vedānta in practice'. The entire wealth of knowledge gained by the ṛṣis in their experiments with the world of objects, the world of thoughts and the world of ideas have been brought here from the temples and libraries to the homes and the fields. The modern half educated are tempted to cry down Vedānta as impracticable theory; this can only be the sad moaning of one who has not read this portion, the crystallized essence of Hinduism, with sufficient poise and peaceful thoughts.

Satyaṁ vada – In this exhortation the first wave of thoughts comprises the guru's advice to the students about their relationship with society. 'Speak the truth'. Truthfulness consists mainly in uttering a thought as it is actually perceived, without hypocrisy or any vulgar motive to do injury to others. Ordinarily, a liar is he who has not the moral courage to express what he sincerely feels. This disparity between thoughts and words creates in his mind a habit to entertain 'self-cancellation' of thoughts. This impoverishes the individual's mental strength, willpower and determinative dynamism. Such an exhausted mental character is too weak, thereafter, to make any progress in life's pilgrimage.

In fact, truthfulness in its essential meaning is not merely giving out one's honest feelings truly and effectively. In its deeper imports, it is the attunement of the mental thoughts with one's own intellectual convictions. Vedānta being the science of living, unless we are ready to discipline and marshal our thought forces to the unquestioning authority of our own reason chastened with knowledge, in the ensuing chaos within, we cannot grow to realise the fuller unfoldment of our truer and diviner nature.

Dharmaṁ cara: – Dharma is a word which has no corresponding word in English. Somebody in haste had translated it as 'righteousness' and those who had followed him had merely repeated the same word; thus, traditionally dharma is 'righteousness.' But it is too meagre a word to carry the load of meaning which is the contents of dharma. All those fundamental values of life which are universally good at all places and at all times; which form the foundation of all efforts at moral rearmament and all edifices of ethical perfection; which constitute the corner stones for all temples, churches, mosques, synagogues and gurudvārās; which are the eternal duties of every man who wants to live up to the full dignity of a human being and strive consistently to grow into his fullest stature as a God-man in this very life. In this ampler meaning, we may, for our convenience, and not with satisfaction, translate dharma as duty.

Hinduism is built upon duties and not on rights. The European way of thought has moulded itself upon the 'principle of rights' and they have been growing through arrows and boomerangs, bullets and shells to reach the present when they are threatening each other with atomic weapons and secret instruments of mutual slaughter, to demand and maintain the rights of each against the rights of the others. They are demanding rights: rights are to be taken; to be acquired; to be preserved. A civilisation that is based upon 'rights' must necessarily come to clamour and fight and the instincts of acquiring and hoarding, keeping and maintaining should develop in that society and should ultimately upset the peace.

On the other hand, the glorious Sanātana Dharma of the Hindus recognises his right 'to do his duties' as the fundamental privilege in life. When it is duty to be performed, a generation that has understood it, will be trained to demand of life only ample chances to fulfil their duty. Duty therefore develops the spirit of giving, the urge to be charitable rather than the lust to hoard or the anxiety to keep.

The growing buds of the generation, as they are leaving the teacher's presence, are advised to keep this glorious principle of fulfilling their duties towards the society, towards their relations and towards themselves.

The students were not asked to pay any fees before they entered the gurukula institution. That was not the rule in ancient India; education was free. A student entering the portals of education was a pleasant challenge, as it were, to the teacher who took up the challenge and saw to it that he made out of that raw material an efficient and independent earning member of the society.

After his education, the student was not thrown out into the world of tension and chaos from which he had been for so long and so efficiently kept away in the gurukula, as today we keep them in the libraries and laboratories. On the other hand, the educational system was so organised as to work perfectly in unison with the demands of the society and the needs of living at that time, so that a child who had walked out of his teacher's protection, from the day he reached his home, proved himself to be a fully trained soldier to fight the battle of his life.

The gurudakṣiṇā (the fee) was not even demanded of the boys when they were leaving the institution after their education. The gurukula system seemed not to justify itself to demand fees simply because they had educated the boys. The system was thorough and they were so confident of the results that they insisted that they would be receiving the payment only from the first independent income of the individual!

As soon as the student reached home, he plunged into work and his early savings that he could make entirely go towards the gurudakṣiṇā. And who among them could forget their own days of gurukula activities and the fact how, during their days, the old students had maintained the ṛṣi universities? Thus the boys of each generation continued subscribing towards the gurukula funds almost year after year or at least during the various stages of their life.

After paying the fees, the student is advised to enter the householder's life by marrying a fit lady and he is advised that he should live with her enjoying a perfectly controlled indulgence. It is one of the duties of the Hindu householder that he should not misunderstand his early education with its overemphasis on brahmacarya and practise sex control even in his householder's life, because such self-control may amount to sex suppression in the majority of cases. He is advised that he should not break the line of descendants.

The sequence of thoughts as expressed here: 'After giving the preceptor his fees, do not cut off the thread of progeny', implies a healthy suggestion for us how best to plan our life. After education, first of all, be economically independent, learn the trade, create a market, assure a comfortable income; and then, as the next duty in life, the scriptures say, marry and maintain the line of descendants in the family.

This is followed by a series of warnings not to swerve from truthfulness, duty, personal welfare and prosperity. If the Hindus had correctly understood this portion and pursued this most effective and necessary part, they would never have come to the plight to which they have today sunk. A devoted Hindu has come to express, nowadays, in the ways of his living and in his conduct in life, such a great amount of impotence, languor and dullness that he is no better than a walking corpse moving about with no self-assertion or personality. Like an idle dry leaf, kicked about here and there, according to the whims of the passing breeze, roams and exists the modern bhakta. This is against the principles and the theories propounded by seers and prophets. This idea is very well brought out by the irreplaceable commandment: 'Do not swerve from cleverness, nor from your prosperity.'

The above mentioned qualities like truthfulness and so on may become instead of creditable virtues, a liability for the devotee, especially in a world of criminals which recognises no higher values of existence. In our unintelligent insistence to follow these instructions blindly, we are apt to be made a fool of. Therefore, here the ṛṣis are advising the children of that age that a Hindu should not allow himself to be used as a cat's paw by others, nor should a Hindu permit others to trade upon his nobler virtues. Kuśalāt na pramaditavyam:

never swerve from cleverness, can be used as the watchword for the Hindu spirit of living!

'Never neglect your welfare' is the commandment and yet how differently we have understood our own sacred way of living! We have come to misunderstand our ethics and spiritual literature to be codes of behaviour by which we easily become a prey to every diplomacy and ultimately sink into wretched poverty and miserable destitution! This is exactly what we are seeing around us. On the other hand, the ṛṣi advised the students, as they went out to face their individual situations of life, that they should not on any score, neglect their welfare; not of course, for the purpose of self-aggrandisement, not to corner the entire wealth of the society creating unequal distribution of wealth and consequent poverty and sorrows for the country. They were asked to be prosperous so that they would be able to serve others in selfless charity; the rules of charity follow soon in this very section as the fourth wave of thoughts.

The above ideas of truthfulness, duty, cleverness and prosperity cannot be healthily developed and efficiently maintained unless we have the necessary spiritual stamina in ourselves and in the society. Therefore, it is reasserted that we must pursue the study of the scriptures and make it our life's mission to spread those truths among ourselves with a burning, irresistible missionary zeal.

देवपितृकार्याभ्यां न प्रमदितव्यम् ।
मातृदेवो भव । पितृदेवो भव ।
आचार्यदेवो भव । अतिथिदेवो भव ।२ ।

devapitṛkāryābhyāṁ na pramaditavyam,
mātṛdevo bhava, pitṛdevo bhava,
ācāryadevo bhava, atithidevo bhava, (2)

देव-पितृ-कार्याभ्याम् – from your duties towards gods and departed souls (ancestors); न – not; प्रमदितव्यम् – swerve; मातृ-देवः – he, to whom mother is a god; भव – you be; पितृ-देवः – he, to whom father is a god; भव – you be; आचार्य-देवः – he, to whom preceptor is a god; भव – you be; अतिथि-देवः – he, to whom a guest is a god; भव – you be

2. Never swerve from your duties towards gods and towards the departed 'souls' (manes). May the mother be, to thee, a god. May the father be, to thee, a god. May the preceptor be, to thee, a god. May the guest be, to thee, a god.

In those days of the Upaniṣads, the Vaidika literature did not give any method of worship upon a form. Their gods were, except fire, all conceptions of the unmanifest power of nature. The teachers of that era must have noticed the difficulties experienced by the beginners who, in their youthful days, waging their battle of life, could not find enough poise of mind or intellectual sharpness to devote themselves to subtle meditation upon the formless Truth. Some idol or living expression of divinity was to be supplied for their concentration, to serve them as a source of constant and unbroken inspiration.

The principle of idol worship, though not evolved as much as in later times, it is implicit in the principle of upāsanā where, as we have said earlier, the attempt is to see the mighty in the meagre. Thus, as a process of constant upāsanā, the student is told that he has to be, all through his life, one to whom his parents are expressions of godly qualities.

We need not necessarily take this idea only in its limited sense. In its ampler implications it can be an exhortation of the ṛṣis to the members of the present generation, that, in their youthful vigour, though they are inspired to dash forth into progressive plans for a greater future, they need not totally condemn and reject the last generation of elders in the society. The youth always have the urge to move forward and the energy to drag their present to the future; but, in so doing, they should respect and revere the wealth of experience that the old have with them as a result of their long life lived.

The last generation lingering with us need not be conceived as the authority and the only people who have the vision of the future but, at the same time, they need not be totally rejected, discarded or ridiculed. The ṛṣi means that the youth should be made to work, respecting the old.

यान्यनवद्यानि कर्माणि । तानि सेवितव्यानि ।
नो इतराणि । यान्यस्माकगंसुचरितानि ।
तानि त्वयोपास्यानि । नो इतराणि ॥३ ॥

yānyanavadyāni karmāṇi, tāni sevitavyāni,
no itarāṇi, yānyasmākagṁ-sucaritāni,
tāni tvayopāsyāni, no itarāṇi. (3)

यानि – such; अनवद्यानि – actions free from blemishes; कर्माणि – actions; तानि – those; सेवितव्यानि – must be done; नो (न + उ) – and not; इतराणि – others; यानि – which; अस्माकम् – pertaining to us; सुचरितानि – virtuous actions; तानि – those; त्वया – by you; उपास्यानि – must be followed; नो (न + उ) – and not; इतराणि – others

3. Let only the actions that are free from blemishes be done, and not others. You must follow only those virtuous actions which are irreproachable, and not others.

At the conclusion of this second thought wave, the declaration of the teacher gains for itself a roar of sincerity almost unequalled in any other religious literature in the world, both in its modesty and selfless dedication to Truth. Philosophy being a subjective science, its blessing can only be gained by us by actually living it. Apart from its logic and reason, the theory must have with it the dynamism of the teacher to inspire the student, at all times. Also, if reverence and respect for the teacher is not there, the moment suspicion and doubt creep into our minds regarding the purity and sincerity of the teacher, the philosophy that is declared, immediately becomes impotent in our hearts. Therefore, the teacher says, 'Follow only the irreproachable qualities in us'.

This does not mean that the teacher is full of vices, but the ṛṣi is extra careful to avoid all possibilities of any misjudgement. Even when an individual has no weakness, it is possible that an observer may project his own mental evaluations and come to criticise and condemn the other. As a remedy to all such mental mischiefs, the teacher, accepting this natural weakness in man, exhorts him to follow only those irreproachable qualities, habits and conduct noticed in the teacher: 'Not others', meanings, if there be any unhealthy trait, even though the teacher may practise it, on no score should it be copied and followed by a true student of this culture.

This portion clearly shows the attitude which the teacher maintained in the presence of the students. Neither did they, for a moment, pose as superhuman nor as colossuses of purity, strength or divinity. They behaved among the students as though they were mere mortals with all possible weaknesses, which a mortal is heir to.

Wearing this look of the ordinary, behaving as any ordinary mortal, these Men of Perfection faced their students. This, in fact, was the secret of their success in spreading this transcendental culture among people living the life's contentions in their day-to-day existence.

The greater the teacher and the firmer his realisation, easier he comes down to move shoulder to shoulder with the students in a spirit of camaraderie and unmistakable friendship. The formalities of distance between the teacher and the taught are insisted upon and maintained only by those uncertain masters who have not the confidence in their own knowledge nor the clarity to remember their own days of confusion to sympathise fully with their students.

This portion clearly shows again that whether it be an individual or an institution, they are not sanctioned by our śāstras to continue indulgence in any weakness even though their teacher had practised it. Smoking of tobacco, gānjā and so on, indulging in non-vegetarian diet, even drinking alcohol are being practised today in this country by individuals and institutions. Their justification seems to be that their teacher, once upon a time, did indulge in these. The portion now under discussion clearly dispels any doubt upon the point whether such indulgences are justifiable or not. A weakness is always a weakness and no seeker has a right to perpetuate it; no institution should entertain the audacity to argue for it.

ये के चास्मच्छ्रेयाग्ंसो ब्राह्मणाः ।
तेषां त्वयासनेन प्रश्वसितव्यम् ॥४ ॥

ye ke cāsmacchreyāgṁso brāhmaṇāḥ,
teṣāṁ tvayāsanena praśvasitavyam. (4)

ये के – those who are; च – and; अस्मत् – than us; श्रेयांसः – more distinguished; ब्राह्मणाः – brāhmaṇas; तेषाम् – of them; त्वया – by you; आसने – in discussion; न प्रश्वसितव्यम् – not even (a word) be breathed; (आसनेन – offering seat; प्रश्वसितव्यम् – should be worshipped)

4. You must not even breathe a word when those, who are more distinguished than you, are in discussion on spiritual

matters (or, you must offer a seat to superiors and worship them with acts of reverence and love).

In this fourth wave of thought, the teacher's declaration codifies the relationship of his students with other Gurus in the land, who are equal to, if not greater than, their own teachers. There was no spirit of rivalry between the teachers; in fact, they all worked as a team serving as preachers nourishing our culture and spreading the Hindu glory round the globe. But the students may, it is always natural, in their overenthusiasm and misunderstood devotion to their Guru, come to look down with contempt upon, other teachers in the land. This sectarian attitude and preferential reverence is looked down with a reproachful eye by the ṛṣis of old. They advised their students to follow a healthier and more tolerant attitude.

Tvayāsanena praśvasitavyam – The arrangement of words here is a masterly manipulation of sounds in such a way that in themselves they can be made to mean two ideas which are both instructions to the students. Tvayā + āsanena + praśvasitavyam is one way of dissolving the words, in which case it means that 'the master'. should be entertained with a seat and other things provided by you.

The same can, also, be dissolved as tvayā + āsane + na + praśvasitavyam, in which case it will mean that 'even a word should not be breathed by you when they are seated in their assembly for discussion'. In the former case it is an advice on how you should receive and entertain with respect and devotion all teachers; and in the latter case it is a prescription of the code of behaviour that one should observe in an assembly of teachers who are discussing philosophical matters among themselves. The idea is that you must be all ears and eyes when the wise talk and not full of noise and tongue. When such teachers discuss, there are plenty of ideas which one must try to absorb, later on to be discussed and assimilated properly. If one were to start a discussion and arguments in the very beginning, one is apt to lose oneself in a morass of words and get oneself perhaps choked and drowned in it.

श्रद्धया देयम्। अश्रद्धयाऽदेयम्।
श्रिया देयम्। ह्रिया देयम्।
भिया देयम्। संविदा देयम्॥५॥

śraddhayā deyam, aśraddhayā'deyam,
śriyā deyam, hriyā deyam,
bhiyā deyam, saṁvidā deyam. (5)

श्रद्धया – with faith, gladly and willingly; देयम् – (gifts) should be given; अश्रद्धया – without faith i.e. unwillingly; अदेयम् – (gifts) should not be given; श्रिया – in plenty (according to one's prosperity, capacity); देयम् – (gifts) should be given; ह्रिया – with modesty; देयम् – (they) should be given; भिया – with sympathy (lit. fear); देयम् – (they) should be given; संविदा – with friendliness (agreement in opinion); देयम् – (they) should be given

5. Gifts should be given with faith; they should never be given without faith; they should be given in plenty, with modesty and with sympathy. Let there be also agreement in opinion (or friendly feelings) when gifts are offered.

As we have noticed earlier, the Hindu culture is essentially based upon sacrifice implied in duty and not upon acquisition which is implied in rights. The very structure in Hinduism recognises the householder's existence only as a necessary training in curbing his animalism and purifying the greater heights of spiritualism. Cultural perfection was the goal. Every breath in the individual, every activity in his life, every thought in him, is marshalled and disciplined to bring out the symphony of the perfect Hindu Culture. As such, the householder is trained to live a life of earning and hoarding, mating and breeding, building and keeping, only as a field of activity for him to train himself in the values of love, kindness, service and charity. Ultimately, the individual is valued upon the spirit of sacrifice he could show towards the finite when the call of the Infinite reached to smother his bosom.

Naturally therefore, the teacher has to give some instruction as to how charity can best be practised. In the name of charity many a thing is ordinarily done in society which destroys both the giver and the recipient; the giver gains in his vanity, while the recipient becomes an irredeemable idler and a moral wreck. In order to avoid such a social suicide, the Master had to instruct the students on the 'laws of giving', lest it should kill the soul of this consummate social law.

Gifts should be given with faith – Faith is not what we generally understand it to mean. In society faith is generally understood as some idea to be swallowed without questioning, without enquiry. To be under the intellectual tyranny of an individual or a class is not faith according to Vedānta. This has been made clear in *Vivekacūḍāmaṇi* by Śrī Śaṅkarācārya. Śaṅkarācārya says that to judge and understand rightly the full import of the advices of the teachers, the depth of the declarations in the sacred textbooks and thereafter, to struggle in our thoughts and activities to attune ourselves constantly to these intellectual judgements, is called faith.

Therefore, charity is acceptable only when it toes the line of our own independent intellectual beliefs and convictions. Unless we are convinced of the nobility of the cause and unless we have come to a correct and independent judgement upon its worthiness, charity should not be practised. There is a school of intellectual idlers who believe that our charity must be as open and as free as the fruit trees in an orchard that give their fruits to all without questioning.

This is not acceptable to the science of Vedānta since it is not trying to cultivate fruit trees. Its aim is to cultivate the thinking animal called 'man'. Therefore, the ṛṣi pointedly condemns the opposite idea by the positive declaration that 'gifts should not be given without faith'. Every benefactor has the right, nay, has a duty to enquire into the bonafides of the cause which he is trying to patronise.

Again, a miserly giving will not benefit either the giver or the receiver and therefore, it is said that, having come to judge a cause to be deserving, give it your entire patronage: 'Give in plenty, with both hands give!'.

This very charity can bring into us feelings of egoism and vanity; and these are being avoided by instructing us to give with modesty. There are yet others who may have the intellectual vision to judge the cause he is patronising, the large-heartedness to give in plenty, with all modesty that has been required of him, and yet, he may not have the necessary love element to feel a deep sympathy for the cause he has come to patronise. The ṛṣi is advising here that we should not, on any score, ignore this most essential factor in all charities. To give without sympathy is to build a temple without an idol, and is as futile as to paint a picture with black ink on a blackboard!

Sympathy generates love in us and unless this love element comes to predominate in us, compelling us to seek an identity with the cause, we will not be spiritually evolving along the path of charity. Charity constricts the heart and obstructs the human growth, if it is not honeyed with the spirit of love and the joy of identification.

Hence we are warned against all charity without sympathy with the cause or the occasion. To throw 25 paisa to a helpless beggar and make him struggle to pick it up from the wayside dirt with his half eaten up leprous fingers is no charity at all, however thick the giver may wear his caste marks on his narrow forehead!!

अथ यदि ते कर्मविचिकित्सा वा वृत्तविचिकित्सा वा स्यात्।
ये तत्र ब्राह्मणाः सम्मर्शिनः। युक्ता आयुक्ताः।
अलूक्षा धर्मकामाः स्युः। यथा ते तत्र वर्तेरन्।
तथा तत्र वर्तेथाः ॥६ ॥

atha yadi te karmavicikitsā vā vṛttavicikitsā vā syāt,
ye tatra brāhmaṇāḥ sammarśinaḥ, yuktā āyuktāḥ,
alūkṣā dharmakāmāḥ syuḥ, yathā te tatra varteran,
tathā tatra vartethāḥ. (6)

अथ – now; **यदि** – if; **ते** – for you; **कर्म-विचिकित्सा** – any doubt regarding your acts; **वा** – or; **वृत्त-विचिकित्सा** – any uncertainty regarding your conduct in life; **वा** – or; **स्यात्** – should arise; **ये** – whoever; **तत्र** – there; **ब्राह्मणाः** – brāhmaṇas; **सम्मर्शिनः** – who are thoughtful, able to judge impartially; **युक्ताः** – religious (self-controlled, experienced); **आयुक्ताः** – independent; **अलूक्षाः** – not cruel; **धर्मकामाः** – devoted to dharma, lovers of law; **स्युः** – who are available, present; **यथा** – as ; **ते** – they ; **तत्र** – there; **वर्तेरन्** – would act; **तथा** – so too; **तत्र** – there; **वर्तेथाः** – (you) should act

6. Now, if there should arise any doubt regarding your acts or any uncertainty in respect of your conduct in life, you should act in those matters exactly as those brāhmaṇas who are present there, who are thoughtful, religious (experienced), not set on by others, not cruel (i.e. gentle) and are devoted to dharma.

अथाभ्याख्यातेषु । ये तत्र ब्राह्मणाः सम्मर्शिनः ।
युक्ता आयुक्ताः । अलूक्षा धर्मकामाः स्युः ।
यथा ते तेषु वर्तेरन् । तथा तेषु वर्तेथाः ॥७ ॥

athābhyākhyāteṣu, ye tatra brahmaṇāḥ sammarśinaḥ,
yuktā āyuktāḥ, alūkṣā dharmakāmāḥ syuḥ,
yathā te teṣu varteran, tathā teṣu vartethāḥ. (7)

अथ – now; **अभ्याख्यातेषु** – who are falsely accused of some crime; **ये** – whoever; **तत्र** – there; **ब्राह्मणाः** – brāhmaṇas; **सम्मर्शिनः** – thoughtful; **युक्ताः** – religious (self-controlled); **आयुक्ताः** – independent; **अलूक्षा** – not cruel; **धर्मकामाः** – devoted to dharma; **स्युः** – who are available; **यथा** – as; **ते** – they; **तेषु** – in such (situations); **वर्तेरन्** – would behave; **तथा** – so too; **तेषु** – in them; **वर्तेथाः** – (you) should act

7. And now with regard to those who are falsely accused of some crime; you should rule yourself exactly in the same manner as do the brāhmaṇas who are present there, who are thoughtful and religious, not set on by others, not cruel, and are devoted to dharma.

In the thick of this life's battle, there may arise situations in which there may be a doubt in your mind as to what is the ideal way to live. In all such cases, the Hindu youngster is advised to follow other elderly members of the society who are accredited champions of our culture.

These cultural perfections should not be, in themselves, the qualifications necessary to make a man perfect enough to be followed by others. He must be thoughtful – meaning one who is not blindly following the śāstras, but is one who is capable of independent thinking and correct judgement. He must not be one who is merely secular in his concept of things, but should have respect and reverence for the sanctity of the sacred.

A true brāhmaṇa is he, who is not only a man of independent judgement and truly religious, but he must also be a man with full freedom to express his ideas. This is exactly the quality absent in the present day brāhmaṇas of the world. The European philosophers and the Indian paṇḍitas including the president of the maṭhas, find themselves in an unenviable position, compelled to dilute their opinion to court the attitudes or even the prejudices of their patrons!!

Such ācāryas are not considered here as the ideal ones to be followed. An ideal brāhmaṇa should be one who is not set on by others. He must not be cruel. He must be a self-dedicated champion of the greater values of life as explained in the immortal scriptures of the Hindus. Such men of dedicated life firmly established in their ideas and stoutly independent, are the true sons of the Hindu culture and you have been asked to follow them whenever there is a doubt regarding either your action or your conduct.

Karmavicikitsā – Regarding ritualism there are some fundamental doubts upon the various rules, since we can meet with contradictory statements in the textbooks. Some branches believe that the fire worship should be before sunrise. Others insist that it should be after sunrise. Regarding the devatā also there are doubts; as to whether they are masculine or feminine, since both genders are found to be used in some cases in the purāṇas. In all such cases the boy is asked to follow what the ideal local brāhmaṇa pursues.

Vṛttavicikitsā – These represent certain doubts regarding man's conduct; for example, in a country like India, which incorporates in its vast embrace a variety of geographical conditions, habits and customs, flora and fauna, we find even contrary and opposite conducts are recognised as ethical and moral in different parts of the country. In Malabar, under the matriarchal system, the uncle's daughter can be married by the nephew, while in other parts of India it is tabooed. In one place the bridegroom is purchased by the father-in-law with a dowry for the sad privilege of accepting his daughter as wife, while in the Himalayan villages, the girl is purchased as cattle for agricultural purpose! In all other provinces of India, if one husband for a woman is considered as normal, among the paṭhāṇas, it is a code of morality that three or four brothers can together co-operatively maintain a single wife! In such circumstances it is possible that the student comes to doubt as to what is the right conduct; and he is directed in all such cases to follow the eminent men of culture in the district.

**एष आदेशः । एष उपदेशः । एषा वेदोपनिषत् ।
एतदनुशासनम् । एवमुपासितव्यम् ।
एवमु चैतदुपास्यम् ॥८ ॥**

*eṣa ādeśaḥ, eṣa upadeśaḥ, eṣā vedopaniṣat,
etadanuśāsanam, evamupāsitavyam,
evamu caitadupāsyam. (8)*

एषः – this; **आदेशः** – (is) the command; **एषः** – this; **उपदेशः** – (is) the teaching; **एषा** – this; **वेदोपनिषत्** – (is) the secret of the Vedas; **एतत्** – this; **अनुशासनम्** – (is) commandment; **एवम्** – in this way; **उपासितव्यम्** – one should live one's life; **एवम्** – thus; **उ** – verily; **च** – and; **एतत्** – this; **उपास्यम्** – one must act

8. This is the command. This is the teaching. This is the secret of the Vedas. This is the commandment. This should be observed. Verily, having understood this fully, one must act in the way taught above, continuously till the last and not otherwise.

With this seventh wave of thought this section concludes and the Master is here concluding his discourses. When we follow merely the word meaning we are apt to misjudge these words as a vain repetition of similar words already used, almost conveying the same sense. But on a closer analysis we can discover that in the dramatic layout of the Upanishad, as a conversation between the teacher and the taught, these words declare the character of the student as well as the temperament of the teacher.

Concluding his exhortation, the teacher declares that 'this is the command' (ādeśa). In the next sentence, he amends it by a much tamer term, such as, 'this is the advice' (upadeśa). In the dramatic situation here, it should be amply clear to any reader what exactly must have made the teacher amend his words. As soon as he declared that this is the 'command', in spite of their reverence to the Guru, the Hindu students, temperamentally not very willing to accept command on ethical and moral rules from anybody, even if it be from their own Guru, – unless he paused to explain and make them understand the logic of it – expressed a revolt in their looks. This attitude of intellectual dissatisfaction might have expressed itself in the sparkling eyes of the young students and so the Guru diluted his emphasis by his amendment.

Again the discriminative intellect of the Vaidika generation, even in their youthful days, was audacious enough to question the teacher until they got complete satisfaction; the teachers also never misunderstood their students. They, on the other hand, always expected and encouraged in their students all intellectual honesty and freedom. Seeing this healthy sign of revolt against an individual's intellectual dictatorship, especially in moral and ethical values, the teacher again appealed to them to accept what he said since his arguments were in no sense a mere intellectual hypothesis born of his own independent intellectual calculations, but it was he declared, the declarations of the Vedas (Vedopaniṣad).

Those who understand and enter into the spirit of the Vedas, know that declarations of the Vedas are no subject matter for doubt; they are all declarations of the saints and sages who reported their own transcendental experiences rather than enunciate with their finite and limited intellect.

Once the teacher remembers that what he had declared was the cream of Hinduism as declared by the endless hierarchy of divine Masters, then he gains a self-confidence as it were in himself and explodes, saying that this is the Commandment of the Lord, the very Creator of life (anuśāsanam).

The above passages starting with 'satyam vada', consisting of twenty five items and divisible into six waves of thoughts, constitute the sacred commandments in Hinduism. The waves of thoughts as indicated in this section are:

1) Advice regarding the individual himself;
2) His relationship with others;
3) His right action in the world;
4) His attitude towards the eminent men of culture;
5) The laws of charity; and
6) His duty to follow the eminent living men of his own times.

In the seventh wave of thought, the teacher concludes saying that these commandments are to be followed diligently by every intelligent seeker who lives his life for a higher cultural purpose, besides his worldly ambitions and secular activites. In short, over the shoulders of the students, as it were, the ṛṣi of *Taittirīya-upaniṣad* is addressing the entire Hindu community to follow these commandments.

Section xii – अनुवाकः १२

Concluding Śāntipāṭha

शं नो मित्रः शं वरुणः । शं नो भवत्वर्यमा ।
शं न इन्द्रो बृहस्पतिः । शं नो विष्णुरुरुक्रमः ।
नमो ब्रह्मणे । नमस्ते वायो ।
त्वमेव प्रत्यक्षं ब्रह्मासि ।
त्वामेव प्रत्यक्षं ब्रह्मावादिषम् ।
ऋतमवादिषम् । सत्यमवादिषम् । तन्मामावीत् ।
तद्वक्तारमावीत् । आवीन्माम् । आवीद्वक्तारम् ॥
ॐ शान्तिः शान्तिः शान्तिः ॥१ ॥

śaṁ no mitraḥ śaṁ varuṇaḥ śaṁ no bhavatvaryamā,
śaṁ na indro bṛhasaptiḥ, śaṁ no viṣṇururukramaḥ,
namo brahmaṇe, namaste vāyo,
tvameva pratyakṣaṁ brahmāsi,
tvāmeva pratyakṣaṁ brahmāvādiṣam,
ṛtamavādiṣam, satyamavādiṣam, tanmāmāvīt,
tadvaktāramāvīt, āvīnmām, āvīdvaktāram.
Oṁ Śāntiḥ, Śāntiḥ, Śāntiḥ. (1)

शम् – propitious; **नः** – to us; **मित्रः** – Mitra Devatā; **शम्** – propitious; **वरुणः** – Varuṇa; **शम्** – propitious; **नः** – to us; **भवतु** – may be; **अर्यमा** – Aryamā; **शम्** – propitious; **नः** – to us; **इन्द्रः** – Indra; **बृहस्पतिः** – Bṛhaspati; **शम्** – propitious; **नः** – to

us; विष्णुः – Viṣṇu; उरुक्रमः – the all-pervading (wide-striding); नमः – salutation(s); ब्रह्मणे – unto Brahman; नमः – salutations; ते – unto thee; वायो – O Vāyu; त्वम् – thou; एव – alone; प्रत्यक्षम् – perceivable; ब्रह्म – Brahman; असि – art; त्वाम् – thee; एव – alone; प्रत्यक्षम् – perceivable; ब्रह्म – Brahman; अवादिषम् – I have declared; ऋतम् – the right; अवादिषम् – I have declared; सत्यम् – the good; अवादिषम् – I have declared; तत् – that; माम् – me; आवीत् – has protected; तत् – that; वक्तारम् – the teacher; आवीत् – has protected; आवीत् – has protected; माम् – me; आवीत् – has protected; वक्तारम् – the teacher
ॐ – Om; शान्तिः – Peace; शान्तिः – Peace; शान्तिः – Peace

1. May the Mitra (Sun) be good to us. May Varuṇa be good to us. May Aryamā be good to us. May Indra and Bṛhaspati be good to us. May the all-pervading Viṣṇu be good to us. Prostrations to the Brahman. Prostration to thee, O Vāyu, Thou, indeed, art the visible Brahman. Thee I have declared the 'right'. Thee I have declared the 'good'. That has protected me. That has protected the teacher.

(Om Peace! Peace!! Peace!!!)

For the word meanings and the implications of this invocation,we may refer to the discourses reported on the same peace invocation at the opening of this chapter (Section i). But there is a difference in the tense of verbs used in the second half of this closing peace-invocation. While in the opening passage the invocation expressed a humble submission to the Supreme. Here it is the joy-cry of the devotee who feels himself the recipient of the grace. There, if it was a cry to be blessed, here it is the cry of satisfaction at having been blessed.

In short, the student feels here that the study all through this chapter has been fruitful and in this invocation he is expressing his gratitude for the blessings received from the cosmic powers, whom he had invoked at the beginning of the lessons.

Here Ends Śīkṣā-vallī

Chapter II

Brahmānanda-vallī

Peace-invocation
(Śāntipāṭha)

ॐ सह नाववतु । सह नौ भुनक्तु ।
सहवीर्यं करवावहै
तेजस्वि नावधीतमस्तु मा विद्विषावहै ॥
ॐ शान्तिः शान्तिः शान्तिः ॥१ ।

om saha nāvavatu, saha nau bhunaktu,
sahavīryaṁ karavāvahai
tejasvi nāvadhītamastu mā vidviṣāvahai.
om śāntiḥ śāntiḥ śāntiḥ. (1)

ॐ – symbol of the Para Brahman; सह – together; नौ – us both; अवतु – may He protect; सह – together; नौ – us both; भुनक्तु – may He help us enjoy (the fruits of scriptural study); सह – together; वीर्यम् – with enthusiasm; करवावहै – exert together (to find the true meaning of the sacred texts); तेजस्वि – brilliant; नौ – of both of us; अधीतम् – study; अस्तु – may be; मा – never; विद्विषावहै – (may we two) quarrel

Om. May He protect us both. May He help us both to enjoy the fruits of scriptural study. May we both exert together with enthusiasm to find the true meaning of the sacred texts. May our studies make us brilliant. May we never quarrel with each other.

(Om Peace! Peace!! Peace!!!)

This peace-invocation is chanted both by the teacher and the taught everyday during the study of the rest of the book. In thus reminding themselves, before their study each day, that they are to exert together in order to experience the Truth of the Upaniṣads, they get more and more tuned up with each other. This condition of perfect unison between the teacher and the taught is unavoidable in the study of the subjective science of Vedānta.

As in modern colleges, Vedānta cannot be learned merely from the bazaar notes. A deep and intimate personal experience is to be conveyed by the teacher in teaching the students. A transcendental experience that inspires the experiencer to a complete sublimation of his egocentric consciousness cannot become a theme that can be sung through the flimsy instrument of language. Therefore, the success in understanding the Vedas and ultimately gaining the experience of its Truth is dependent entirely upon the seeker's capacity to tune himself to the Master's own intimate experiences which are expressed vaguely in the intuitive song by him in the finite language of the text.

This perfect unison between the teacher and the taught generally gets molested by some misunderstanding between them. It may be either in the form of the teacher's dissatisfaction towards his students or it can be due to the student's misjudgement of the teacher's attitude or words. If either of them suffers from such a clogging of the heart, they become, as it were, 'short-circuited' and the transference of knowledge is immediately blocked. In order to avoid such a sad plight and assure a perfect tuning up both from the teacher to the taught and from the taught to the teacher, this stanza, with all sincerity is chanted daily by the preceptor and the disciple.

The thrice repeated peace chanting and their significances have already been explained at the end of the opening stanza of chapter I[1].

---

[1] Refer pages 16 and 17.

Section i – अनुवाकः १

Brahman is Satyam, Jñānam, Anantam – Enunciation of The Doctrine of Sheaths

ॐ ब्रह्मविदाप्नोति परम्। तदेषाऽभ्युक्ता।
सत्यं ज्ञानमनन्तं ब्रह्म।
यो वेद निहितं गुहायां परमे व्योमन्।
सोऽश्नुते सर्वान् कामान् सह ब्रह्मणा विपश्चितेति ॥१॥

om brahmavidāpnoti param, tadeṣā'bhyuktā,
satyaṁ jñānamanantaṁ brahma,
yo veda nihitaṁ guhāyāṁ parame vyoman,
so'śnute sarvān kamān saha brahmaṇā vipaściteti. (1)

ॐ – om; ब्रह्मवित् – the knower of Brahman; आप्नोति – attains; परम् – the Supreme; तत् एषा – with reference to that; अभ्युक्ता – is recited (the following hymns); सत्यम् – Truth; ज्ञानम् – Knowledge; अनन्तम् – Infinity; ब्रह्म – Brahman; यः – he who; वेद – knows (It); निहितम् – as existing; गुहायाम् – in the cave of the heart; परमे – in the transcendent; व्योमन् – ākāśa; सः – he; अश्नुते – realises; सर्वान् – all; कामान् – desires; सह – along with; ब्रह्मणा – as Brahman; विपश्चिता – omniscient; इति – thus

1. Om, the knower of Brahman attains the Supreme. With reference to that, is the following hymn recited: Brahman

is the Truth, Knowledge and Infinity. He who knows It as existing in the cave of the heart in the transcendent ākāśa, realises all his desires along with omniscient Brahman.

Sandwiched between the first and the last chapters, we have in this Brahmānanda-vallī, the philosophical essence of the Upaniṣad, described in the inimitable style of the *Taittirīya-upaniṣad.* Extremely scientific and incomparably analytical, the ṛṣi brings the wealth of this psychological understanding into the method of its exposition. Artistic in finish, the Master leaves no missing link in the chain of his arguments that the thesis, so complete and well rounded off, comes to stand out embossed attractively upon the background supplied by the earlier and the later chapters of the book. In the first chapter, the students were initiated into a series of different methods of concentration, so that, at the end of its practice, they may come to possess a more developed and better integrated mind and intellect so that they can much more easily journey themselves into the subtler heights of transcendental thoughts. After thus preparing the instruments of mind and intellect, the teacher here initiates the students into the great operation of Self-discovery.

In the *Taittirīya-upaniṣad* the goal is pointed out as the core of the individual seeker himself and, ultimately, this centre of the different concentric whirls of his own personality is brought within the cognition of the seeker by making him realise fully each of the outer layers of matters around him. One by one these outer layers are transcended and the individual is ultimately made to become fully aware of the innermost essence.

For the purposes of this scientific analysis, in this Upaniṣad, for the first time an individual is considered constituted of five different sheaths of matter, each covering the other with varying degree of grossness, the outermost being the grossest. Nowhere else in the literature of Vedānta do we get this analysis so completely and exhaustively. The theory of the five kośas has been sanctioned for the first time here, in this chapter.

The chapter opens with the declaration of the goal: ' The knower of Brahman reaches the Supreme'. The Upaniṣad is addressed to those seekers who are struggling to understand what is the goal of life and how to reach it. They were, first of all, assured that the goal is 'to know Brahman' and having known, 'the knower reaches the Supreme'. This reply to the seeker, though it is a declaration of the Truth, cannot be very satisfactory since it does not say anything about the goal. In other Upaniṣads too, similar assertions have been given, especially in the *Muṇḍaka-upaniṣad:* 'He who knows Brahman becomes Brahman'.[1]

These assertions are apt to be misunderstood or even criticised as impossible idealisms preached to canvas the beliefs of the unintelligent. The critics argue that by knowing a table we don't become a table, nor do we reach or come to possess the wealth of another by merely knowing his bank balance! 'If by knowing we were to come to possess and live our knowledge', laughs the hasty critic, 'in the world there would not have been, perhaps, a greater profession than to be a cashier in a state bank!'.

[1] Refer Swāmiji's discourses on *Muṇḍaka-upaniṣad* III-ii-9

This is exactly the mistake which one would naturally fall into when one tries to read and understand the Upaniṣads by the literary meaning of the words. In the literature of Upaniṣad, words borrowed from the finite language are being made use of for a higher and special purpose of indicating the Infinite. As such, these borrowed words are to be understood, in their special employment, to have gathered some special meaning and import. Thus the word 'knowing' here is not meant in the sense in which we generally 'know' things of the world, wherein the 'knower' is always different from the 'known' and the 'knowledge'. Here the word 'know' is used in the sense of discover or realise.

It often happens that we keep on desperately searching for a key or an important paper all over the room until somebody points it out to us; either the key is in our own hands or the paper is just in front of us on the table. The knowledge, that the key that I was searching for, is in my own hand, is a knowledge that gives me back the key that I had lost! Similarly, when we say that by 'knowing' the thing, we 'reach' the thing known, we only mean that the thing was already with us, and yet, it was screened off from us temporarily by our own ignorance of it. The ignorance of it is removed by our knowledge of it; and the thing that was already with us becomes available for our experience. Similarly, he who realises that divine Spark, the Self within himself, comes to know It, in the sense that he rediscovers that which was already within him, but It lay, unfortunately, veiled off from him by his own ignorance.

The students, to whom the Upaniṣad is declared are all great seekers wanting to know what life is, and whether there be any goal in life worth achieving. They are all great intellectual enquirers who have come to investigate upon the universal happenings in nature and come to question if there is any purpose to be gained or a goal that is to be reached in life. This question is answered completely here in this short and pithy declaration by the great ṛṣis. The goal is Brahman and one who realises it reaches the Supreme.

When the Guru has declared in one summary statement the goal of life, the Āryan students of the true Hindu stock, as we have found earlier, are not very ready to accept it immediately unless the statement is fully supported by the eternal Vaidika declarations. The teacher knew this tradition and therefore, he adds: 'In that sense is the following hymn recited'. He is quoting a Vaidika definition of Truth Absolute as indicated by the term Brahman.

The infinite Truth can, on no account, be fully defined in words; Infinite defined is finitude ill-expressed! And yet, we have here three words which, in their indicative meaning, completely give us an appreciable suggestions of what the Truth is.

Satyam – It is generally translated as Truth. In itself this translation is mum and does not express any idea. The words gather their momentum only in intellects that are familiar with the import of the words. In the tradition of Vedānta, 'Satyam' is that which is the changeless substratum for all changes and modification.

For example, the post is the 'truth' in the ghost vision; the rope is the 'truth' behind our misunderstanding that it is a serpent; or a dry twig or a crack on the surface of the earth or a streak of water. The idea is that, in all honest enquiries, ultimately the real substratum comes to be discovered; when we discover the post in the ghost, we all know how impermanent, relatively was the ghost. Therefore, the superimposition, the ghost and its ghastly grinnings, are all declared as 'false', while, relatively of course, the post is considered as 'Truth'.

In the life of plurality also we are watching an endless variety of change: time changes; seasons change; individuals keep on changing in their body, mind and intellect. Nothing is permanent even for a moment. In this general and continuous state of flux, there must be a changeless eternal factor that is the ground which makes changes possible upon it. That satyam is Brahman.

Without the steady, spotless screen behind the ever changing play of lights and shades, there cannot be the illusion of a thrilling film in the theatre; without its permanent and motionless bed, the waters of a river cannot maintain their endless flow; without the solid and inert rails, the flying wheels of the train cannot move on. The screen in the movie house, the river bed in the river, the rails in the railways, these are the changeless, the permanent, the 'truth'. That factor which is immutable, upon which the finite changes are rendered possible, is 'Satyam' – the Brahman of the literature of Upaniṣad.

Jñānam – This is generally translated as Knowledge. But, in order to warm ourselves up to the inspired meaning of the ṛṣis, we have to seek a fuller understanding of this term.

Knowledge is of two kinds (a) unconditioned knowledge, and (b) conditioned knowledge. We generally experience in the world only 'knowledge of' things. Herein knowledge is conditioned by the things known. These conditioned knowledge bits change from place to place and from time to time, since the objects that pure Knowledge happens to illumine are different from one another.

When Ganga water is poured into different types of bottles, the shapes of water conditioned by the different bottles should necessarily be different since the bottles are of different shapes. But this does not mean that water itself has any definite shape. Similarly, though the knowledge bits conditioned by different objects are seemingly different because of the plurality of the objects themselves, the Knowledge Absolute in its pure nature is unconditioned by any of the objects that it illuminates.

The term 'Jñānam' indicates this Knowledge Absolute which illuminates for us the objects of experiences in the outer and inner worlds. The conscious Principle, beaming out in its awareness, illuminates all objects that it comes across, just as the sunlight has no preference and blesses all objects with its light and grace irrespective of their nature and quality, when the objects come into the flood of the sun's light. By the word 'Jñānam', this Consciousness in us is indicated. We have already seen that it is this life spark that is the substratum, immutable and eternal, which makes the changes of the body, mind and intellect possible and realistic.

Anantam – It is translated as Infinity. Since by the word 'Satyam', Brahman was indicated as the real, the substratum from which the entire world of the finite had, as it were, emerged, it has become the cause of the phenomenal world. The cause from which effects arise (as pots or ornaments from mud or gold) is generally inert and inorganic and as such a doubt may arise that the Supreme is an inert and an unintelligent Principle (like mud or gold). To remove such a hasty conclusion, it is insisted that 'Satyam', though the cause of the world, is Intelligence itself.

This Consciousness that is the substratum of the created world may Itself end one day, is yet another doubt that can possibly come to the mind of the uninitiated. To refute this idea and to show that pure Awareness which is 'Satyam' is Itself not the effect of any other cause and as such, is infinite in nature, we have the term 'Anantam' used here. This term explains that though Truth be the cause of the pluralistic mutable world, in itself, It is the uncaused cause. Unborn and eternal, that Truth reveals Itself as infinite and conscious.

This is the core of man's own personality. Without this Consciousness or Awareness, however strong he may be physically, however noble in mind, however powerful in intellect; the individual will be considered dead by the world. Life means expression of awareful experiences. When an individual ceases to live his experiences, to live awareful of his outer and inner worlds, that mass of matter having the shape of a creature is considered as dead and the carcass is claimed by nature for reconversion into the five elements from which it had emerged!!

Thus, in this irrefutable definition made up by the inimitable usage of the pregnant suggestions contained in these three terms 'Satyam, Jñānam, Anantam', the immortal text of the Hindus, the Vedas, indicate the Absolute Reality which is at once immanent and transcendent. To seek this Truth within and to rediscover It is the divine unfoldment of the mortal to his own immortal stature; of the finite to the dignity of the Infinite; of the bound to the joys of freedom.

If there be thus a Truth as defined above, how do we reach that Brahman? The terms 'Satyam, Jñānam, Anantam' have a flavour as though they are expressing some definite qualities and in the ordinary usage of language, qualities qualify objects. As such, the students who are familiar with this word usage in language are apt to misunderstand from these qualifications that Truth is an object separate from the seeker.

He who rediscovers this conscious Principle within himself, is one who is considered as fully awakened to the divine nature in man. This awakening makes him drop, once and for ever, all his identifications with the false matter envelopments of his body, mind and intellect, and the choking world of plurality created from these three levels. Just as in any dream we, identifying ourselves with our mental creations, come to suffer dreadful sorrows within ourselves, so too, in the dream of plurality, our false identification with matter ends when we get ourselves awakened to our real divine nature.[1]

[1] For a closer study of the dream world see Swāmiji's discourses on *Māṇḍūkya-upaniṣad* with Gauḍapāda's *Kārikā*.

Practical minded as they all were, the children of the Āryan stock were not very much enamoured by the fact that the Vedas had thus declared a highly poetic and extremely consummate goal of life. They wanted to know how this great realisation of the Divine in them could facilitate the individual in living a more intelligent and healthy life. Theirs was a cry for a life of subtler joys; their demand was a complete freedom from the sorrows of the finite. However noble a goal the philosophy may point out, to the impatient seekers it is not acceptable unless it guides them to the goal that they wanted. The teacher knew this character and the healthy impatience of the students of that generation, and naturally therefore, he concludes in the same breath, as it were, that he, who realises this Conscious Principle in himself, 'enjoys all his desires, all at once, along with Brahman'.

The Consciousness in an individual being is the same as the one life factor in all the living world. It is the illuminator of all the joys enjoyed by everybody at all places and at all times. Therefore, in experiencing the spiritual centre in ourselves, we may say that we are at once experiencing thereby all joys experienced by all the living kingdom.

In Vedānta, the great scientists of life, the ṛṣis, had made an exhaustive study of the sources of joy in our ordinary life. The material preoccupation of the world today does not provide the required amount of intellectual poise for such a close study of life for the purposes of investigating into the mechanism of the joy transactions. Ordinarily nowadays, even the best of us feel that there is a joy when a desire is fulfilled, but we do not pause to make a scientific analysis nor investigate into the principles underlying and governing the sensuous joy.

Vedānta does not deny the fact that in our finite world there are joys. The flickering joys tantalizing man, with their flashy charms, are not a satisfying fulfilment to those who are really hungry to live fully. In their dissatisfaction the ṛṣis were goaded and encouraged to make exhaustive enquiries into the structure and composition of sensuous happiness.

No doubt, there is a joy when a desire is fulfilled; but it is enjoyable only by the one who entertains the desire. The joy that an object provides is, it is found, directly proportional to the intensity of desire with which the individual has struggled for it. We also find that a given object that gives joy to one, can itself dole out a measure of unhappiness to another! The same given cup of coffee, if it gives eighty units of happiness to a South Indian, it gives perhaps an equal amount of unhappiness to a Paṭhāṇa who is not familiar with the embittered Madrāsī coffee. A young lady, after days of struggling, at last fulfills her deep desire for a blue Mysore saree. It provides her with great satisfaction, while the same saree spells disastrous sorrow and a creeping sense of disgust in some of her dear friends!

If happiness were in the objects, the coffee or the saree should have given the same happiness to all of us; but it seems that the same object provides different units of happiness to different individuals and the same object graces the same individual with different textures of joy at different places and times. On the whole, we can say that the joy is not in the object, but the object is only an occasion when the required mental condition is gained by the individual, which provides him with a sense of joy that he experiences.

The seers of Vedānta explain this exhaustively. Their convincing arguments have in them a compelling force of persuasion and we are compelled to accept them. A desire is a torturous mental state wherein we fail to take our mind off a given thought disturbance. It demands an immediate satisfaction by physically possessing, mentally enjoying or intellectually appreciating some object or objects other than ourselves. Thus, the commotion desire creates is a mental disturbance and the thicker the desire, the more powerful is the commotion. At the satisfaction of the desire, the commotion ends and the peace in the mind allows the joy of the soul, as it were, to beam out undisturbed and unmolested.

The ṛṣis cry that the Self is the repository of all joy since pure Awareness or the Reality is itself Bliss Absolute. The mental thought disturbances, like thick monsoon clouds, veil the beam of joy. The attempt of an individual in procuring and keeping sensuous objects is an unconscious act of the individual to bring about the necessary condition in his mind so that the joyous soul may peep out shedding it's infinite joy.

Thus the ṛṣi declares that all joys come from the Self and the sensuous joys are all flickerings of the Self seen through the intervals of peace in the mind's natural state of thought chaos!

With this idea in mind, if we reread the declaration of Upaniṣad, it cannot be very difficult for us to understand how an individual, on realising his Self, comes to experience all the joys of every living creature – all at once.

तस्माद्वा एतस्मादात्मन आकाशः सम्भूतः ।
आकाशाद्वायुः । वायोरग्निः । अग्नेरापः ।
अद्भ्यः पृथिवी । पृथिव्या ओषधयः ।
ओषधीभ्योऽन्नम् । अन्नात्पुरुषः ॥२ ॥

tasmādvā etasmādātmana ākāśaḥ sambhūtaḥ,
ākāśādvāyuḥ, vāyoragniḥ, agnerāpaḥ,
adbhyaḥ pṛthivī, pṛthivyā oṣadhayaḥ,
oṣadhībhyo'nnam, annātpuruṣaḥ. (2)

तस्मात् – from that (Brahman); वै – verily; एतस्मात् – which is this; आत्मनः – Ātman; आकाशः – space; सम्भूतः – is born; आकाशात् – from space; वायुः – air; वायोः – from air; अग्निः – fire; अग्नेः – from fire; आपः – water; अद्भ्यः – from water; पृथिवी – the earth; पृथिव्याः – from the earth; ओषधयः – herbs; ओषधीभ्यः – from herbs; अन्नम् – food; अन्नात् – from food; पुरुषः – man

2. From that (which is) this Ātman, is space born; from ākāśa, air; from air, fire; from fire, water; from water, earth; from earth, herbs; from herbs, food; and from food, man.

Since, to the Hindu seekers, theology and philosophy are not in themselves a fulfilment, no true Āryan seeker feels happy or considers himself fulfilled at this. He demands out of philosophy a way of living by which he can actually come in contact with the Truth and raise himself to live on par with it. Self-experiencing and the consequent self-perfection alone satisfies the Hindu seeker.

Looking in and through the words of this passage, no ardent student can miss the picture of the salient beauty of the Himalayan valleys against which the āśrama nestles, swathed in divinity and comfort. In the open porch of it, sits the sacred Master instructing a gathering of his disciples! In this dramatic layout, the Master's declarations are all coloured by the appreciation and opinions expressed on the students' faces. When the teacher first declared that the Supreme is realised by those who know Brahman, the gurgling question in the heart of the student was: 'What is this Brahman?' The teacher defined that Brahman is Truth, Knowledge and Infinity. Even then the disciples were not satisfied; if there be an infinite Truth, they had not been told where exactly was this Truth to be contacted.

If, for my illness, the doctor says that there is a specific treatment and the medicine is 'Geolalopatte,' naturally, those who are ailing would (first) like to know what it is. On being told that it is a medicine to be taken orally twice a day, once after breakfast and again after dinner, the question arises as to where it can be procured. If at this juncture we are told that the original company is no longer preparing this medicine and that it is not available anywhere, then the medicine prescribed is not even worth the paper on which it is written.

Hence the doubt of the disciples. The teacher, therefore, explains further.

Here, we find that the Brahman defined can be realised in the innermost recesses of the seeker's own personality. The realm in which we can rediscover this Absolute Nature in us, explained here as the supreme sky, which is exactly what was meant by the term 'the cave of the heart' earlier.[1]

The pure Consciousness described at first objectively and later on indicated subjectively is one and the same. The Reality, being one, all-pervading and eternal, cannot be limited in any sense of the term and therefore, to assume that the Reality is not at once immanent and transcendent is to misjudge Its divine nature. To say that the Divine is yonder to be realised as the sulatāna of the skies is a terrible blasphemy, we will be attributing a limitation upon Its infinite and all-pervading nature. If Truth be within us also, then It is certainly realisable there in ourselves. It is to indicate this fact, that the Consciousness within and without is one unbroken homogeneous Truth, that in this section we are told, 'from That (which is) this Ātman'.

This idea is brought out fully and clearly in Vedānta through an analogy of the outer space and the room space or pot space. Space being a subtle, all-pervading element, it cannot be limited either by the walls of the room or the material of the pot. And yet, in our gross concept, we generally identify space with the four walls of the room or consider space as conditioned by the material of the pot

[1] Refer Swāmiji's discourses on *Kaṭhopaniṣad*.

and declare it as the 'room space' or the 'pot space'. Space, being homogeneous, is one and the same within and without. The very material of the pot or the walls of room are themselves standing in space and so space is not limited by the material walls.

Similarly, the cause of space, necessarily subtler than the space itself, the Reality, is One without a second both within the pluralistic world and without it. This oneness of the spiritual essence in man with the infinite Reality which is the substratum of the entire phenomenal world, is indicated here when the śāstras say, 'from That which is this Ātman.'

To every real seeker of Truth, there is a period in his intellectual quest when he comes to wonder at, and feels bewildered by, the why and the how of the universe. This doubt is to be first of all answered thoroughly by the teacher, or else the student will not be able to harness all his mental energies to the true scientific analysis of himself and through deeper meditation, reach the realm of the subjective experience of Truth.

Therefore, we find that all teachers have to give some explanation, which would suit the mental temperament of the student and give him the necessary satisfaction, at least temporarily. It is in this sense that we find in the literature of Upanisad varied explanations on how creation first came into being. One such explanation which can temporarily give a sense of satisfaction to the seeker is given here by the ṛṣi of the *Taittirīya-upaniṣad*. He narrates the story of how the five great elements have in an unbroken sequence emerged out of the Supreme.

First of all, the subtlest of the five elements, ākāśa emerged from Truth and from it a grosser element, the air, came; a grosser fire came from air; and still grosser element water, manifested itself from fire; the series ended with the grossest manifestation, the element earth. These five elements have been accepted as the fundamentals in the manifested world of matter, by almost all the philosophers and scientists of the world, according to whom the entire pluralistic phenomenon is an endless variety of combinations and manipulations of these five great elements.

These five elements are arranged in order of their relative subtlety, measured in terms of their qualities. Ākāśa considered to be the subtlest, has only one quality, sound; we know sound cannot be created where there is no space. Air has the quality of sound and also its own special quality; touch; therefore air is considered grosser than ākāśa. The next in the series, fire, has qualities of space and air apart from its own quality of form. Water, besides the qualities of all the previous ones, namely, sound, touch and form, has its own special quality of taste. And earth, the grossest of the lot, has all the four qualities described above, along with its own specific quality of smell.

Thus, we find that the great elements, each representing one or other of the sense objects cognisable by man through his sense organs, are described in the poetic language of the scriptures, as the deities of the five sense organs: ākāśa in the ears, air in the skin, fire in the eyes, water in the tongue and earth in the nose.

These concepts in Vedānta are explained in such detail here only to give an idea of how clearly and precisely the ancient students must have understood their teacher's words at the time of the delivery of the text, when the students were already familiar with this idea that the elements represent the sense organs. Therefore, though macrocosmically this portion reads as the story of the elements and their manifestation from the Supreme, microcosmically it at once expresses how, in the individual, the five great sense organs, the ears, the skin, the eyes, the tongue and the nose rose, as though a separate creation of the Ātman.

From earth, the food – Out of the gross earth arose the entire world of vegetation; the herbs, plants and trees are the food materials which can maintain the physical health and stamina of an individual. The food that is taken in large quantities by the father crystallises into its essence as the seeds in him and a seed, fertilising an ovum in the womb of the mother, grows into its full maturity, to be born as an individual called Puruṣa.

स वा एष पुरुषोऽन्नरसमयः ।
तस्येदमेव शिरः । अयं दक्षिणः पक्षः ।
अयमुत्तरः पक्षः । अयमात्मा ।
इदं पुच्छं प्रतिष्ठा । तदप्येष श्लोको भवति ॥ ३ ॥

sa vā eṣa puruṣo'nnarasamayaḥ,
tasyedameva śiraḥ, ayaṁ dakṣiṇaḥ pakṣaḥ,
ayamuttaraḥ pakṣaḥ, ayamātmā,
idam pucchaṁ pratiṣṭhā, tadapyeṣa śloko bhavati. (3)

स – he; वै – indeed; एषः – this; पुरुषः – man; अन्नरसमयः – consisting of the essence of food; तस्य – his; इदम् – this; एव – indeed; शिरः – head; अयम् – this; दक्षिणः – (his) right; पक्षः – wing; अयम् – this; उत्तरः – (his) left; पक्षः – wing; अयम् – this; आत्मा – (his) trunk; इदम् – this; पुच्छम् – hind part; प्रतिष्ठा – (his) support and foundation; तत् – (about) that; अपि – also; एषः – this; श्लोकः – verse; भवति – is there

3. He indeed is this man consisting of the essence of food. This is his head. This is his right wing. This is his left wing (side). This is his trunk. This is the hind part forming his support and foundation. About this also is the following Vaidika verse.

After describing the outer world and how it was caused, the teacher is slowly gliding his discourse to the subjective theme of self-analysis. The goal of spiritual quest is the Supreme and the subjective search is the technique adopted in Vedānta.

This physical body, born of food, is described here as the essence of food, anna-rasamayaḥ. When man is thus explained as made up of food, the students might misunderstand the theme indicated by the term to mean man with his physical, mental and intellectual personalities. The ṛṣi here is definitely guiding the student's attention to the purely physical structure of himself. He at present is talking merely of the physical sheath in man. To indicate exhaustively a physical sheath in all its entirety, the teacher is pointing out the five main parts of the body; as the head, the right and the left sides, the trunk and the lower limbs.

Sureśvarācārya, while commenting upon this portion, describes it as a metaphor drawn from the hawk like arrangement of the sacred fire in some special types of yajñas. Here the ṛṣi is dramatically pointing out to his own head, limbs and trunk, and is describing the parts constituting the annamaya kośa, the food sheath. The description indicates that what the ṛṣi meant by the food sheath is the physiological structure of man constituted of the head, the trunk and the limbs.

Strictly following the tradition of the Vaidika faith, the teacher, after making this bold assertion, immediately hastens to add that what he said was not a mere individualistic philosophy or a mere intellectual hypothesis, but that it is fully supported by the words of the Vedas. The Vaidika stanza is quoted in the next section.

Section ii – अनुवाकः २

Food, The Universal Medicament

अन्नाद्वै प्रजाः प्रजायन्ते ।
याः काश्च पृथिवीगूंश्रिताः ।
अथो अन्नेनैव जीवन्ति । अथैनदपि यन्त्यन्ततः ।
अन्नगूंहि भूतानां ज्येष्ठम् ।
तस्मात्सर्वौषधमुच्यते ।
सर्वं वै तेऽन्नमाप्नुवन्ति
येऽन्नं ब्रह्मोपासते ।
अन्नगूं हि भूतानां ज्येष्ठम् ।
तस्मात्सर्वौषधमुच्यते ।
अन्नाद्भूतानि जायन्ते । जातान्यन्नेन वर्धन्ते ।
अद्यतेऽत्ति च भूतानि । तस्मादन्नं तदुच्यत इति ॥१ ॥

annādvai prajāḥ prajāyante,
yāḥ kāśca pṛthivīgṁśritāḥ,
atho annenaiva jīvanti, athainadapi yantyantataḥ,
annagṁhi bhūtānāṁ jyeṣṭham,
tasmātsarvauṣadhamucyate,
sarvam vai te'nnamāpnuvanti
ye'nnaṁ brahmopāsate,
annagṁ hi bhūtānāṁ jyeṣṭham,
tasmātsarvauṣadhamucyate,
annādbhūtāni jāyante, jātānyannena vardhante,
adyate'tti ca bhūtāni, tasmādannaṁ taducyata iti. (1)

अन्नात् – from food; वै – indeed; प्रजाः – beings; प्रजायन्ते – are born; याः काः च – whichever and whoever; पृथिवीम् – on earth; श्रिताः – exist; अथो – thereafter; अन्नेन – by food; एव – alone; जीवन्ति – live; अथ – again; एनत् अपि – into (food) alone; यन्ति – (they) merge; अन्ततः – ultimately; अन्नम् – food; हि – verily; भूतानाम् – of all creatures; ज्येष्ठम् – the eldest; तस्मात् – on that ground; सर्वौषधम् – medicament for all; उच्यते – (it) is called; सर्वम् – all; वै – verily; ते – they; अन्नम् – food; आप्नुवन्ति – obtain; ये – those; अन्नम् – food; ब्रह्म – as Brahman; उपासते – meditate; अन्नम् – food; हि – indeed; भूतानाम् – of all creatures; ज्येष्ठम् – the eldest; तस्मात् – on that ground; सर्वौषधम् – medicament for all; उच्यते – (it) is called; अन्नात् – from food; भूतानि – all beings; जायन्ते – are born; जातानि – the born; अन्नेन – by food; वर्धन्ते – grow; अद्यते – it is eaten; अत्ति – eats; च – and; भूतानि – beings; तस्मात् – therefore; अन्नम् – as 'annam'; तत् – that; उच्यते – is called; इति – thus

1. All beings that exist on earth are born of food. They, thereafter, live by food; again, they ultimately go back to it and merge to become food. So, verily, food is the eldest of all the creatures. On that ground it is called the medicament for all. Those who meditate on Brahman as food, indeed obtain all food. From food all beings are born, having been born, they grow by (consuming) food. Food is that which is eaten by the beings and also that which in the end eats them; therefore, food is called annam.

A pot that is created from mud exists only in mud, for if we remove the mud, the pot cannot exist! Also, we know that when the pot is broken, it surrenders itself to become the mud! That is, an effect arising from the cause, exists in the cause, and ultimately merges back again, to become one with the cause. Therefore, the pot is called a mud pot.

Similarly, the physical body of man is born from the food taken by his father and maintained and nourished by the food consumed by him. Ultimately, since the physical body of everyone must go back to earth to fertilise it and become food for others, this physical structure also is called the 'food sheath'. This idea is indicated here by the Vaidika mantra which says: 'all living creatures of the world are born of food, live by food and at the end they go back to become food'. Therefore, says the ṛṣi, food is the first gross element which is self-evident without any special explanation.

The etymology of the word 'annam' is also given by Śruti to justify what she has already explained by the word. She says: 'That which is eaten (adyate) and that which eats (atti) is called food (annam)'. Medical science also explains that the general deterioration of health in the world today is because man is overeating. Overeating saps his vitality, ruins his health and in the end kills him. In small doses, even poison is a curative medicine! Similarly, food also, in right healthy proportions is a blessing to the body but when we begin to overeat and indulge in gluttony, we slowly deteriorate in our health and soon die away.

This idea is beautifully put in the words of the Śruti when she says that food is 'that which is eaten by the eater and which in the end eats the very eater'. Food is also called, therefore, a great universal medicine: in right doses it blesses; in overdose it kills. 'Those who worship food with this understanding will become,' declares the rsi, 'rich in food'.

This portion is generally passed over by merely declaring that this is a method of upāsanā or meditation. To understand it as a method of meditation which promises the meditator more and more wealth and food, is to almost insult the passage. Vedānta is a literature that is generally prescribed by the orthodox paṇḍitas only to those who are well suited for the same. These adhikārīs are men of detachment and renunciation. Therefore, it should sit ill upon the lips of paṇḍitas to translate the passage as a mere 'method of worship' (upāsanā) which would provide the seeker with a lot of material gains and food!

This seems to be a passage which justifies the Hindu attitude of sanctity for food. The portion now under discussion should be considered as a secret knowledge not only for the happiness of the individuals, but of the community, of the nation and even of the world.

The food problem of the world can directly be attributed, in almost a majority of cases, to the irreverence with which we handle the problem.

Food is insulted through overeating. Idlers, who have not contributed their share of 'upāsanā' in its cultivation, hoard the food. The honest upāsakas, who have done the sādhanā in the field, are in the end plundered. When in one part of the world there is scarcity, in another part we either find food insulted through bad storing or ignorant cultivation. Sometimes, through deliberate crimes, the entire crop is burnt or thrown into the sea with a view to raise its price in the world market. In our country, where famine is so natural and regular, we have learnt now to accept it with a philosophical resignation as a milestone down the road. Any average economist would declare from the housetops that famines in India are always due to our irreverence for food in the present and our long and continuous blasphemy against food in the past. Neglect of agricultural facilities like irrigation, livestock, implements and manure as also the irreligious ways in which the priests of the 'temple of food' are behaving or in the modern language, it is because of the ignorance of the cultivators themselves.

In case we know how to respect food, knowing fully well all its implications, that it is pre-eminent among all the beings and that it is the greatest medicament known to man, certainly that individual or community or nation can expect to gain more and more food for themselves.

तस्माद्वा एतस्मादन्नरसमयादन्योऽन्तर आत्मा प्राणमयः।
तेनैष पूर्णः।
स वा एष पुरुषविध एव। तस्य पुरुषविधतामन्वयं पुरुषविधः।
तस्य प्राण एव शिरः।
व्यानो दक्षिणः पक्षः। अपान उत्तरः पक्षः।
आकाश आत्मा। पृथिवी पुच्छं प्रतिष्ठा।
तदप्येष श्लोको भवति ॥२॥

tasmādvā etasmād-anna-rasamayādanyo'ntara ātmā prāṇa-mayaḥ,
tenaiṣa pūrṇaḥ,
sa vā eṣa puruṣavidha eva, tasya puruṣavidhatāmanvayaṁ puruṣa-

vidhaḥ, tasya prāṇa eva śiraḥ,
vyāno dakṣinaḥ pakṣaḥ, apāna uttaraḥ pakṣaḥ,
ākāśa ātmā, pṛthivī puccham pratiṣṭhā,
tadapyeṣa śloko bhavati. (2)

तस्मात् – other than that; वै – verily; एतस्मात् – than this; अन्न-रसमयात् – than the one made of the essence of food; अन्यः – other (there is); अन्तरः – inner; आत्मा – soul; प्राणमयः – of prāṇa; तेन – with it; एष – this; पूर्णः – is full; सः – he; वै – indeed; एष – this; पुरुषविधः – of the form of a person; एव – exactly; तस्य – his; पुरुषविधताम् – being in the form of a person; अनु – similarly; अयम् – this too; पुरुषविधः – of the shape of a person; तस्य – for that; प्राणः – prāṇa; एव – alone; शिरः – is head; व्यानः – vyāna; दक्षिणः पक्षः – is the right side; अपानः – apāna; उत्तरः पक्षः – is the left side; आकाशः – space; आत्मा – is the trunk (body); पृथिवी – the earth; पुच्छम् – the hind part; प्रतिष्ठा – as support (foundation); तत् – about that; अपि – also; एष – this; श्लोकः – verse; भवति – there is

2. Other than that (soul) made up of the essence of food there is an inner soul (sheath) made of the prāṇa. With it this is filled. This (prāṇamaya) is of the same form as the previous. Its human form is exactly as the human form of the former. Of that, prāṇa is the head, vyāna is the right side, apāna the left side, ākāśa is the trunk, earth is the tail or the support. About this also there is the following Vaidika verse.

In this portion the preceptor is guiding the attention of the disciple to a point interior to the gross physical structure which has been fully described already. The second sheath is constituted of the prāṇas. Here prāṇa is not air; this is generally the mistaken notion entertained by all hasty readers, who thereby come to misunderstand the entire śāstra. Prāṇa only means that vitality which expresses itself in a body when it is alive. This vitality of life expressing itself from various centres in the physical structure and pursuing different functions is together indicated by the term prāṇa in the Vedas.

The vital air sheath is described here as the one interior to the food sheath, forming, as it were, a silk lining to the outer sheath. Molten metal poured into a mould should necessarily take the shape of the mould; so too, the prāṇamaya is fully occupying the food sheath.

Vital activity of life is not centred at one special point, nor is it scattered at different points of the physical sheath. It, being the very nature of life, expresses its nature through every conceivable point in the body.

When, into a mould of a God form, molten metal is poured and in another mould of an animal form, a sample of the same molten metal is poured, it is very well known that on destroying the mould the shape within should exactly correspond with the shape of the mould. Similarly, the vital air sheath when it is full in the food sheath, must have the same shape as the physical body and therefore, the teacher goes on to describe the head, trunk and limbs of the prāṇamaya sheath.

The life's total vitality, as expressed through the physical body, has been very carefully noted for the purposes of scientific classification. Though life be one, it expresses itself in different departments of activities and therefore, the prāṇa is considered under five main classifications by the ancient teachers. To understand them as five distinct prāṇas will be a misreading of our scriptures; the prāṇa remaining one and the same, the five different names have been given to it to indicate the various departments of its activities.

Just as the same individual is a father at home, an officer in the office, a friend in the club, a mere devotee in the pilgrim centre; so too, the same prāṇa is known by the five different names to indicate its five different activities. Life's vitality functioning in the organs of perception is called prāṇa; the vitality that presides over the actions that throw out or reject the by-products from the physical body is called apāna; the strength in administering the department of digestion is called samāna; the energy behind the distribution of the assimilated food to the various corners of the body politic is called vyāna. The energy which helps the ego-centre to leave one physical structure at the time of its death, to pursue its transmigratory pilgrimage seeking 'fresh woods and pastures new' where it fulfils all its matured desires, is called udāna.

These five prāṇas together constitute life's vitality as exhibited in a living creature. Therefore, while considering the structure of the vital air sheath, the teacher explains that its anatomy is constituted of these five prāṇas. As before, the description explains that the prāṇa is the head. Vyāna and apāna are the right and left sides. The trunk is described as ākāśa (space). This is quite natural because energy or vitality can be expressed only in a fit field for its expression and therefore, space is considered as the very stay of the vital air sheath, inasmuch as no vitality can ever be expressed where there is no space!!

Its lower limbs are explained here as earth. This is very scientific and indeed acceptable to us since we are the children of the knowledge of Newton. The gravitational force is that which keeps us on to the surface of the earth; but for which we would have been all weightless things floating in the atmosphere like cotton! That we are able to live under the influence of prāṇa is due to the fact that we are planted on the surface of the earth, chained to its centre by the unseen forces of attraction called gravitation. Otherwise we would have been under the influence of udāna and floating about without any permanent mooring.

This idea is also fully endorsed by a Vaidika mantra which is given in the following section.

Section iii – अनुवाकः ३

Prāṇa, The Universal Life – The Food Sheath and Prāṇa

प्राणं देवा अनुप्राणन्ति । मनुष्याः पशवश्च ये ।
प्राणो हि भूतानामायुः । तस्मात्सर्वायुषमुच्यते ।
सर्वमेव त आयुर्यन्ति ये प्राणं ब्रह्मोपासते ।
प्राणो हि भूतानामायुः । तस्मात्सर्वायुषमुच्यत इति ॥१ ॥

prāṇaṁ devā anuprāṇanti, manuṣyāḥ paśavaśca ye,
prāṇo hi bhūtānāmāyuḥ, tasmātsarvāyuṣamucyate,
sarvameva ta āyuryanti ye prāṇaṁ brahmopāsate,
prāṇo hi bhūtānāmāyuḥ, tasmātsarvāyuṣamucyata iti. (1)

प्राणम् – prāṇa; देवा – gods (indriyas, senses); अनु – depending upon (prāṇa); प्राणन्ति – live; मनुष्याः – (so too) men; पशवः – animals; च – and; ये – whatever (beings); प्राणः – prāṇa; हि – indeed; भूतानाम् – of all beings; आयुः – (is) the life; तस्मात् – therefore; सर्वायुषम् – universal life; उच्यते – it (prāṇa) is called; सर्वम् – all; एव – verily; ते – they, those; आयुः – full span of life; यन्ति – reach; ये – those; प्राणम् – prāṇa; ब्रह्म – as Brahman; उपासते – meditate (worship); प्राणः – prāṇa; हि – verily; भूतानाम् – of beings; आयुः – the life; तस्मात् –therefore; सर्वायुषम् – universal life; उच्यते – it (prāṇa) is called; इति – thus

1. Through prāṇa, the gods (indriyas) live and so also do men and the animal kingdom. Prāṇa is verily the life of beings.

Therefore, it is called the universal life or the life of all. Those who meditate on Brahman as prāṇa come to live the full span of their life. Prāṇa verily is the life of beings. Therefore, it is called universal life or the life of all.

The translation itself is amply clear, especially to those who have been initiated into the special attitude in which similar ideas have been expressed in the earlier sections. Here also, there are paṇḍitas who believe that this (upāsanā) is a method of worshipping prāṇa as Brahman. To assume that it is only a method of worship, without having any implication of life, is to scandalise the wealth of import in our scriptures. From what we have already seen, it is evident that one who worships prāṇa in all its five fields of activities and lives in self-control and thus economises the expenditure of vitality, can certainly come to live the full span of human life – which is recognised by our śāstras as hundred and twenty smiling years.

Any doctor, who is not fully preoccupied with his own income and therefore not totally blind to the world and its health, would endorse the statement that the faster we live, the quicker does the generation get wiped out of the face of the world by the relentless Lord of justice, Lord Death.

Because the vitality in the individual is a sign of that subject's life, the total prāṇa is called total life. The Vaidika mantra thus describes all about the prāṇa in us and the infinite Reality. Therefore, the Veda says that he who realises this sacredness of the very vitality in him, comes to economise his physical expenditure and thus, by avoiding all foolish dissipations, comes to live the full span of his life.

तस्यैष एव शारीर आत्मा यः पूर्वस्य ।
तस्माद्वा एतस्मात्प्राणमयात्-
अन्योऽन्तर आत्मा मनोमयः । तेनैष पूर्णः ।
स वा एष पुरुषविध एव । तस्य पुरुषविधताम्-
अन्वयं पुरुषविधः । तस्य यजुरेव शिरः ।
ऋग्दक्षिणः पक्षः । सामोत्तरः पक्षः ।
आदेश आत्मा । अथर्वाङ्गिरसः पुच्छं प्रतिष्ठा ।
तदप्येष श्लोको भवति । २ ॥

tasyaiṣa eva śārīra ātmā yaḥ pūrvasya,
tasmādvā etasmātprāṇamayāt-
anyo'ntara ātmā manomayaḥ, tenaiṣa pūrṇaḥ,
sa vā eṣa puruṣavidha eva, tasya puruṣavidhatām-
anvayaṁ puruṣavidhaḥ, tasya yajureva śiraḥ,
ṛgdakṣiṇaḥ pakṣaḥ, sāmottaraḥ pakṣaḥ,
ādeśa ātmā, atharvāṅgirasaḥ pucchaṁ pratiṣṭhā,
tadapyeṣa śloko bhavati. (2)

तस्य – of that (annamaya); एषः – this; एव – verily; शारीर आत्मा – (is) the embodied Ātman; यः – who; पूर्वस्य – of the former; तस्मात् वा एतस्मात् – as already explained indeed, from that very; प्राणमयात् – consisting of prāṇa (Ātman); अन्यः – other than, different from; अन्तर आत्मा – inner self; मनोमयः – constituted of mind; तेन – with that (self); एषः – this one; पूर्णः – (is) full; सः – he; वा – verily; एषः – this; पुरुष विधः – in the form of a person; एव – only; तस्य – its; पुरुष विधताम् – human form; अनु – depending upon or according to; अयम् – this one (prāṇamaya); पुरुष विधः – of the shape of the person; तस्य – of it; यजुः – yajus; एव – only; शिरः – the head; ऋक् – Ṛk; दक्षिणः पक्षः – the right side;

साम – sāma; उत्तरः पक्षः – the left side; आदेशः – the scriptural injunctions; आत्मा – the trunk; अथर्वाङ्गिरसः – the hymns of *Atharva-veda*; पुच्छं प्रतिष्ठा – the hind part and the support; तत् – about that; अपि –also; एषः – this; श्लोकः – verse; भवति – there is

2. Of that former (annamaya), this prāṇamaya is the ātman. Different from this prāṇamaya – self made up of the prāṇas, there is another self constituted of the mind. With that self made of mind, the prāṇamaya is full. This also is of the form of man. Its human form is according to that of the former. Of it, Yajus is the head, Ṛk is the right side, Sāman is the left side, the scriptural injunction (ādeśa) is the trunk and the group of hymns of *Atharva-vada* is the tail and the support. There is the following Vaidika verse about it.

As described earlier, here also the mental sheath is described as filling the entire area of the vital air sheath, which in its turn fills up the form of the food sheath. For this manomaya kośa, the *Yajur-veda* mantras form the head and the *Ṛg-veda* and the *Sāma-veda* mantras form the right and left sides. The *Yajur-veda* contains mantras which have no strict rules regarding the number of letters in each line, nor is there any definite rule regarding the ending letter in each line. *Ṛg-veda* mantras are those that are strictly bound by the laws of metrical composition.

These Vaidika mantras are external sounds. How they can be considered as parts of the human mind is a doubt that can certainly come to an intelligent reader's alert mind. In all upāsanās, an individual is advised to superimpose certain desirable meanings upon a substratum for the purpose of invoking the greatest concentration. Ordinarily, no explanation can be expected in the prescription for upāsanās since the worshipper never comes to demand any explanation. One, training for good marksmanship will not question the why and the wherefore of the fixed point of concentration. However, here there seems to be a fairly good logic about it. The Vaidika mantras are in themselves impotent unless the practitioner is ready to approach them in a spirit of total co-operation, investing his entire intellect and mind. Mantra means that symbol upon which we do our reflection (manana). As such, to indicate to the students of the Vedas of those days, especially when they were pure brahmacārins, that the mental sheath is nothing but the Vedas, is quite striking and appropriate. This clearly shows how single pointed and truly devoted to Knowledge the students were rendered in those days, during their educational career.

The injunctions prescribed in the Vedas, which detail the rules of conduct during ritualism, constitutes the trunk of the manomaya kośa. The *Atharva-veda*, constituted of mantras 'seen' by Ṛṣi Atharvaṇa and Aṅgirasa, is considered as the foundation upon which the mind exists.

When we understand that the *Atharva-veda* contains (or contained) all the knowledge of the secular sciences, such as machines and charms (yantra, mantra, tantra, and so on), the statement that it is the foundation of the mind gains a deeper and irresistible significance. Unfortunately, today in this country, we have only a very scrappy skeletonal portion of the Veda available in the original manuscript.

In saying that the *Atharva-veda* is the stay of the mind and the entire edifice of the mind is built up with the other three Vedas, we understand with what sanctity of understanding and sympathy did the ṛṣis of old look upon the secular activities of the state and the society.

To say that Vedānta closed its eyes to the material side of life, is an undigested understanding of our spiritual culture and material science as interpreted in the eternal Vedas. Unprepared and unhealthy students of the Hindu literature alone will have this shameless courage. An unprejudiced study clearly shows that the ṛṣis entered the vast arena of the subjective experience of the Self only after they had walked along the unending corridors of their libraries and laboratories. Today we know not the recipes of the 12th century magicians, sorcerers and devil beaters; for, on reaching a greater knowledge through science and its experimental investigations, we have no more need to go back into witchcraft or sorcery of that barbarous age. So too, when the ṛṣis and their children came to experience this staggering truth of the inward perfection and the essential divinity of man, they came to neglect, if not totally reject, the other sciences and their conclusions and achievements.

How much they recognised the importance of the secular well-being through material knowledge, which has a great contribution to make in the development of the mind and the intellect of the successful seeker of Vedānta, is evidently clear when they assert here that the mental sheath or the psychological personality in man is rooted well upon the *Atharva-veda*. This idea, described above by the daring ṛṣis of *Taittirīya-upaniṣad,* is not the whim and fancy of that Master, but it is the truth that had been endorsed by a long line of seers, and has, therefore, come to be recognised as part of our Veda. The mantras are quoted in the following section.

Section iv – अनुवाकः ४

The Knower of Eternal Truth Fears Not – The Mental Sheath

यतो वाचो निवर्तन्ते। अप्राप्य मनसा सह।
आनन्दं ब्रह्मणो विद्वान्। न बिभेति कदाचनेति।
तस्यैष एव शारीर आत्मा यः पूर्वस्य ॥१॥

yato vāco nivartante, aprāpya manasā saha,
ānandaṁ brahmaṇo vidvān, na bibheti kadācaneti,
tasyaiṣa eva śārīra ātmā yaḥ pūrvasya. (1)

यतः – whence; **वाचः** – all speech; **निवर्तन्ते** – turns back; **अप्राप्य** – without reaching It; **मनसा सह** – along with the mind; **आनन्दम्** – bliss; **ब्रह्मणः** – of Brahman; **विद्वान्** – he who knows; **न** – not; **बिभेति** – fears; **कदाचन** – at any time; **इति** – thus; **तस्य** – of that; **एष** – this; **एव** – verily; **शारीर आत्मा** – (is) the embodied soul; **यः** – who; **पूर्वस्य** – of the former

1. Whence all the speech turns back with the mind without reaching It (the eternal Truth, the Brahman), He who knows the bliss of eternal Truth, the Brahman, fears not at any time. This mind is the embodied soul of the prāṇamaya. Of this (prāṇamaya) the manomaya is the Self.

Śaṅkarācārya, in his commentary, happens to drop this line without commenting on it since the same mantra is quoted again in the ninth section where he goes into it exhaustively. Following Śaṅkarācārya's commentary, there are a host of paṇḍitas who have dared to claim that this is an unnecessary portion worthy to be eschewed. Personally, I feel that this claim can be justified only if we accept that the critic has failed to appreciate fully the work of a teacher among a host of his disciples. If the teacher took his profession seriously and he is faithful to his duties, then he has not only to explain the theme which he is expounding in a masterly way, but he has also to prepare his grounds to guide the students to a greater state of knowledge.

This Vaidika mantra quoted, though it indicates the supreme infinite Reality, is here used by the teacher of the Upaniṣad to indicate the mind. In human life, mind plays such an all important part that to consider the mind as the very truth in the body is but a pleasant and poetic exaggeration.

The students of that age, unpardonably impatient to know and to live the perfections promised in the Vedas, cannot brook any lengthy discourses which expound theories of matter and spirit unless they directly indicate a path by which they can come to experience it.

By now, listening to the teacher's talk in the Upaniṣad, the students were getting intellectually impatient and perhaps, traces of it was evident on their faces. The description of how the five elements came, the details of the food sheath; all these endless narrations excited but the impatience in the mind of the students who were hungry to know and thirsty to live the experience of Truth. The teacher, being well tuned with all the disciples, understood implicitly the mind of the taught and therefore, in order to keep them engaged in a better spirit of thrilled joy and deep earnestness, gave a talk which would seem to us, in our hasty reading, out of place here.

Again, this mantra gives a necessary warning to those students who are not giving the necessary amount of their intellectual co-operation, but are only depending upon the Guru's words which are so far very clear and precise, in the hope that at one point in this discourse, the teacher will be able to point out the Ātman and indicate it as an object!

The theme of the Upaniṣads is the spiritual entity in ourselves. The Ātman, being the eternal subject, cannot be objectively indicated. All other sciences are, in varying degrees, objective in their scope and treatment. Therefore, an ordinary educated student would expect the teacher to conclude his discourses, ultimately holding up to their gaze, the Self as an object. To indicate that the Self is neither available for physical perception nor for mental and intellectual comprehension, is this mantra quoted here by the teacher, so that the students may sharpen and finely adjust a little more in their attunement with the teacher and this is unavoidable; the subject matter so far was relatively grosser and could be easily comprehended since they were talking about the gross body and the expressions of vitality in themselves. But the mental and the intellectual personalities, into which the theme of the discourse is now introducing to the students, are indeed subtler and therefore, this warning is quite timely and highly useful to the students.

'Whence all speech turn back' – All other themes in the world can be fully and forcibly expressed or painted in words, but when it comes to the Self, words fail. By saying so, the ṛṣis are not trying to avoid a direct demand of the student class. They are only giving expression to a fact that is accepted by the very science of language.

Though words have a mighty power and they can paint ideas, report incidents, express emotions and enunciate truths, they have their own limitations. There are occasions in life when words must necessarily fail when we try to express them. The great ṛṣis of old, with their acute intelligence, had very scientifically analysed the capacities in words and found that the entire realm of things and happenings that is expressed in terms of words, can all be conveniently grouped under four headings. Words can explain: (1) species (jāti) (2) the attributes (guṇa) (3) the activities (kriyā) (4) relationship between things (sambandha).

If a thing falls under any species, it can be expressed in terms of words such as table, chair, sugar, and so on. If it has any attribute like good, bad, black and white, it can be captured in words. If it is an activity like he cooks, eats, walks, jumps, smiles and so on, it can be conveyed in words. If it is a relationship such as wife, husband, friend, father or mother, it can also be expressed. But, if there be a factor which, like the infinite Reality, is One without a second, without jāti, without kriyā, without guṇa and without sambandha, necessarily, words cannot function in that realm of experience. Therefore, here the ṛṣi explains the Truth, as that from which all words get recoiled, declaring their failure in all their attempts at capturing the Truth in their forces of expression.

The words do not return from the Infinite all alone by themselves, but they are faithfully accompanied in their retreat by the mind. The mind cannot feel the Truth, nor can the intelligence know It, because the mind and the intellect are but inert matter and they gain their capacity to feel and know only when they are 'dynamised' by the Conscious Principle in us. Just as with a telescope we cannot see ourselves, just as a driver cannot be run over by the very car he is driving; similarly, mind, which is functioning because of the Conscious Principle behind it, cannot itself feel or know this life factor as an object other than itself.[1]

He, who has come to realise the Ātman within himself, thereafter feels no fear at any time. The state of fearlessness is here equated with a state of perfection. The lives of all great men remind us that they, after attaining perfection, lived a life of fearlessness and daring adventure. They alone had the courage at historical moments to stand against floods of criticism, and yet, break the wrong and dangerous flow of thoughts of that era, redirecting them towards better fields in man's life. The Infinite alone is the fearless harbour where threats of finitude, though howling and shrieking without, cannot penetrate and toss the ship of life.

[1] For further details refer Swāmiji's discourses on *Kenopaniṣad*.

तस्माद्वा एतस्मान्मनोमयात्-
अन्योऽन्तर आत्मा विज्ञानमयः तेनैष पूर्णः ।
स वा एष पुरुषविध एव । तस्य पुरुषविधताम्-
अन्वयं पुरुषविधः । तस्य श्रद्धैव शिरः ।
ऋतं दक्षिणः पक्षः । सत्यमुत्तरः पक्षः ।
योग आत्मा । महः पुच्छं प्रतिष्ठा ।
तदप्येष श्लोको भवति ।।२।।

tasmādvā etasmān-manomayāt-
anyo'ntara ātmā vijñānamayaḥ tenaiṣa pūrṇaḥ,
sa vā eṣa puruṣavidha eva, tasya puruṣavidhatām-
anvayaṁ puruṣavidhaḥ, tasya śraddhaiva śiraḥ,
ṛtaṁ dakṣiṇaḥ pakṣaḥ, satyamuttaraḥ pakṣaḥ,
yoga ātmā, mahaḥ puccham pratiṣṭhā,
tadapyeṣa śloko bhavati. (1)

तस्मात् वै – indeed from that very; एतस्मात् – this; मनोमयात् – consisting of mind; अन्यः अन्तरः आत्मा – another inner self; विज्ञानमयः – made up of intelligence; तेन – with that (self); एष – this; पूर्णः – (is) full; सः – he; वै – verily; एषः – this one; पुरुषविधः – in the form of a person; एव – indeed; तस्य – its; पुरुषविधताम् – human form; अनु – according to; अयम् – this one (manomaya); पुरुषविधः – of the shape of the person; तस्य – of it; श्रद्धा – faith; एव – indeed; शिरः – the head; ऋतम् – righteousness; दक्षिणः पक्षः – is the right side; सत्यम् – truth; उत्तरः पक्षः – is the left side; योगः – yogaḥ; आत्मा – is trunk; महः – mahaḥ (total intellect); पुच्छं प्रतिष्ठा – is the hind part and the support; तत् – about that; अपि – also; एषः – this; श्लोकः – verse; भवति – there is

2. Different from that made up of mind (manas) is another inner soul made up of intelligence (vijñāna) and by that this (manomaya-self) is filled. It also has the shape of man. According to the human shape of the previous, is the human shape of this one. Faith (śraddhā) is its head, righteousness (ṛtam) its right side, truth (satyam) its left side, yoga is the trunk and total intellect (mahaḥ) is the tail and the support. There is this following Vaidika verse about it.

After indicating the mental sheath in the human personality, the ṛṣi is now guiding the disciple to a still more subtler and therefore, interior sheath of matter, identifying with which the individual comes to claim his intellectual personality. This intellectual sheath, as before, pervades the entire area of the manomaya and therefore, it also is to be conceived of as having a human form.

This intellectual sheath having the form of a man, is described as having 'faith' for its head.

In this anatomy of the intellectual man in us, as described in the Upaniṣads with faith (śraddhā) as head, righteousness (ṛtam) and truth (satyam) as sides, yoga as the trunk and total intellect (mahaḥ) as the lower limbs, the attempt of the ṛṣis is to bring out at one stroke, through a clear cut caricature, the essential scientific details about the intellect (that were available then) to the memory of those vigilant students of that time. Unfortunately today we, having none of those preliminary knowledge, come to despair at the vulgarity of such rude statements that the intellectual man in us has an anatomy and a shape!!

When we approach the statement with the necessary understanding, it becomes very tame and yields its milk of satisfaction. Faith is not that ridiculous intellectual tyranny of one over a community or a caste, though such a silent and dumb following of a prophet or a revelation is now generally considered all over the world as faith: so that the priest class may conveniently trade upon the ignorant laity.

In Vedānta, faith is essentially the inward courage in us to live consistently attuning ourselves to the ideal that we have ourselves intellectually grasped. In short, we may understand faith as something like self-confidence in ourselves. It is very well known that even in our ordinary life our success depends not only upon chances or upon our qualifications, but mainly upon our confidence in ourselves. Without a certain amount of self-confidence we cannot live even an average life successfully. One who has completely lost confidence in himself, is a lunatic who is a danger to society and a sad encumbrance upon himself. Intellect can grow and assert itself therefore, only if there is an unbroken flow of self-confidence in it. The Upaniṣad rightly expresses the very head, meaning, the sacred and the most important limb of the intellectual man in us, is self-confidence, termed here as śraddhā.

Similarly, its right and left sides are the intellectually digested and appreciated essence of the great textbook (ṛtam), and the courage of conviction that propels one to live upto the ṛtam, which is called as satyam. It is evidently clear that a man can grow in his intellect only through study and training in every walk of life.

The trunk or the essence, in the sense that it is the main seat of vitality which distributes its essence and nourishes all the parts of this intellectual man, is explained here as yoga. The word yoga should not bring before your mind the picture of twisted human forms or bellowing prāṇāyāma practioners! The word yoga comes from yuj, meaning, to join; any attempt of an individual to live in life through contemplation, attuning his own imperfect being of today to the greater and nobler concept of the truth, is called yoga.

Any method by which we can live up to certain nobler and divine goal and thereby come to drop our weaknesses and imperfections under which we are today suffering – all such sacred activities, divine in concept and noble in spirit, are called yoga. Mainly the success in yoga rests upon the individual's capacity to concentrate and his ability in the deeper meditation. Therefore, to say that the very 'trunk' of the intellect is the power of concentration and its application in deeper and faithful meditation, is but expressing a fact which even modern scientists must accept without any complaint.

'This individual intellect is rooted in the Mahat-tattva', says the Upaniṣad. Mahat-tattva is the concept of the total mind or intellect. How the individual intellect is conditioned by the total intellect is very well experienced at every moment by everyone of us, although rarely are we conscious of it. Take the example of a young man sitting in the veranda of his house, rather restless because of his incapacity to visit as many movies as he wishes to or because he has not yet come to possess a radio all for himself. Compared with his grandfather's generation, we can say that this young man has started worrying for a thing over which his grandfather never thought of complaining or grudging. The young man is now thinking in terms of his age and to that extent we may say that he is a product of the thought of his times.

This idea is elaborated to include even its subtlest implications in the story of the ten great incarnations accepted by mythology in Hinduism. According to the age and the conditions, the avatāra had also changed in its physical structure, mental capacity and intellectual accomplishments. From the fish to Kṛṣṇa the entire story is revealed of how the great man-gods of each era had to prove themselves as a faithful replica of the total intellectual throbbing of their respective ages.

Mahātmā Gandhi in Italy would have been as complete a failure as Mussolini would have been in India. Not only the great leaders and the prophets are thus the product of their ages, but every one of us is guided entirely by the influence of the age. We can almost say that there is but a very meagre fraction in us which is original. This idea is expressed here by saying that the intellect is rooted in the total intellectual influence of our era.

The next section gives us the required Vaidika quotation to substantiate the statement of the *Tattirīya-upaniṣad* expounder.

Section v – अनुवाकः ५

The Intellectual Sheath – Individual Soul Is The Agent and Experiencer

विज्ञानं यज्ञं तनुते । कर्माणि तनुतेऽपि च ।
विज्ञानं देवाः सर्वे । ब्रह्म ज्येष्ठमुपासते ।
विज्ञानं ब्रह्म चेद्वेद । तस्माच्चेन्न प्रमाद्यति ।
शरीरे पाप्मनो हित्वा । सर्वान्-कामान्-समश्नुत इति ॥१॥

vijñānaṁ yajñaṁ tanute, karmāṇi tanute'pi ca,
vijñānaṁ devāḥ sarve, brahma jyeṣṭhamupāsate,
vijñānaṁ brahma cedveda, tasmāccenna pramādyati,
śarīre pāpmano hitvā, sarvān-kāmān-samaśnuta iti. (1)

विज्ञानम् – knowledge; यज्ञम् – sacrifice; तनुते – performs; कर्माणि – actions; तनुते – performs; अपि – also; च – and; विज्ञानम् – knowledge; देवाः – the gods; सर्वे – all; ब्रह्म – as Brahman; ज्येष्ठम् – the eldest; उपासते – worships; विज्ञानम् – knowledge; ब्रह्म – as Brahman; चेत् – if; वेद – knows; तस्मात् – from that; चेत् – if; न – not; प्रमाद्यति – swerve from; शरीरे – in the body; पाप्मनः – sins; हित्वा – having abandoned; सर्वान् – all; कामान् – desires; समश्नुते – attains; इति – thus

1. Knowledge performs the sacrifices and it is the real agent of all the physical activities. All the 'gods' worship Knowledge as Brahman, the eldest. If a man knows

Knowledge as Brahman and if he does not swerve from it, he attains all desires and comes to abandon all the sins in the body.

All ritualisms have deep significance and suggestiveness. One who does not know the exact implication will only be following the routine process of chanting and doing the prescribed action without benefitting himself nor feeling any sense of inspiration. The Upaniṣad is very insistent and the Vedas, with equal emphasis, roar that without a correct knowledge of not only the rules of karma but also the full significance of it, ritualism has no effect at all. Therefore, the ṛṣi here says that it is the intellectual faculty that is the true performer of all rituals.

Similarly, the mantra insists that the intellect alone is the true agent who does all actions in our transactions in our life. As soon as an external stimulus is conveyed by the sense organ to the mind, the mind informs the intellect of the impulse received and it is the determining faculty in us that issues out definite instructions as to what is to be done and how best we can make use of the external experience so gained. In short, when we analyse the theories of perception and the working of experiences as expounded by the various schools of philosophy in India and elsewhere, we find in almost all cases that the intellect is considered as the true agent in all our intelligent transactions with the world outside.

Again, intelligence is considered as Brahman or the eternal Essence by all the 'gods'. To understand this word 'deva' as a celestial being or an angel would be to confuse ourselves with ridiculous misunderstanding. The word 'deva' comes from a root which means illumination; 'deva' means illuminator. The devas in us are the five sense organs and the mind; they consider intellect as the true factor behind them; without an active intelligence, the indriyas are incapable of receiving their impulses and acting readily to meet the challenges in the outer world.

He who lives in the consciousness that every perception of sense organs is an expression of a deliberate grace of the intellect, he comes to develop his intellect more and more. Naturally, he cannot make any new mistakes and he comes to live much more happily fulfilling all his ambitions and desires. A fully awareful existence, at once intelligent and conscious, is sure to take us from success to success; to such a vigilant individual, there cannot be any sense of frustration in his desires.

The sorrows of life are all due to our misunderstanding of ourselves to be nothing but the fleshy body. This body-consciousness circumscribes our capacity and burns with terrific responsibilities and false duties. These are the sins of the body mentioned here. One who lives in the intellectual zone as a masterly intelligent being will thereby be getting himself redeemed from his bodily preoccupation and to that extent he will be feeling free and liberated.

तस्यैष एव शारीर आत्मा । यः पूर्वस्य ।
तस्माद्वा एतस्माद्विज्ञानमयात्-
अन्योऽन्तर आत्मानन्दमयः । तेनैष पूर्णः ।
स वा एष पुरुषविध एव तस्य पुरुषविधताम्-
अन्वयं पुरुषविधः । तस्य प्रियमेव शिरः ।
मोदो दक्षिणः पक्षः । प्रमोद उत्तरः पक्षः ।
आनन्द आत्मा । ब्रह्म पुच्छं प्रतिष्ठा ।
तदप्येष श्लोको भवति ॥२॥

tasyaiṣa eva śārīra ātmā, yaḥ pūrvasya,
tasmādvā etasmādvijñānamayāt-
anyo'ntara ātmānandamayaḥ, tenaiṣa pūrṇaḥ,
sa vā eṣa puruṣavidha eva, tasya puruṣavidhatām-
anvayaṁ puruṣavidhaḥ, tasya priyameva śiraḥ,
modo dakṣiṇaḥ pakṣaḥ, pramoda uttaraḥ pakṣaḥ,
ānanda ātmā, brahma pucchaṁ pratiṣṭhā,
tadapyeṣa śloko bhavati. (2)

तस्य – of that (vijñānamaya); एषः – this; एव – verily; शारीर आत्मा – (is) the embodied Ātmā; यः – who; पूर्वस्य – of the former; तस्मात् वै एतस्मात् – as already explained indeed, from that very; विज्ञानमयात् – consisting of vijñāna (Ātman); अन्यः – different from; अन्तर आत्मा – inner self; आनन्दमयः – constituted of ānandamaya; तेन – with that (self); एषः – this; पूर्णः – (is) full; सः – it; वै – verily; एषः – this; पुरुषविधः – in the form of a person; एव – only; तस्य – its; पुरुषविधताम् – human form; अनु – depending upon; अयम् – this one (vijñānamaya); पुरुषविधः – of the shape of a person; तस्य – of it; प्रियम् – joy; एव शिरः – is indeed the head; मोदः – rejoicing; दक्षिणः पक्षः – is the right side; प्रमोदः –

bliss; उत्तरः पक्षः – is the left side; आनन्द – ānanda; आत्मा – is the trunk; ब्रह्म – Brahman; पुच्छम् प्रतिष्ठा – is the hind part and the support; तत् – about that; अपि – also; एषः – this; श्लोकः – verse; भवति – there is

2. Of That, of the former, this one verily is the embodied self. Different from this self made up of intellect (vijñānamaya) is another self within, formed of bliss (ānandamaya). By this, that is filled (by ānandamaya the vijñānamaya is full). It also has the shape of man. According to the human form of that is the human form of this. Of it, joy (priya) is the right side, rejoicing (moda) is the left side, and bliss (pramoda) is the trunk. Brahman is the tail support. There is this following Vaidika verse about it.

As before, we are told that deeper within the intellectual sheath filling it up entirely and fully, is the subtlest of the matter envelopments called the bliss sheath. This is constituted of all the flickering joys that we experience in our contacts with the finite world of matter when the sense organs come to live them. All those joys put together form the subtlest of sheaths. In life, our existence is conditioned by our joys also. Just as the body and its conditions limit our personality, just as the mind and the intellect and their health, condition our egocentric existence; so too, our share of joys in life adds its colour into our individual existence.

The joys that we experience in life arise from an endless variety of sources and it would have been the despair of any people in the world to tabulate them all. But the ṛṣis of old could do so. Not only did they bring into their classification all the joys experienced by an individual but they classified under three headings all the possibilities for enjoyment of all living creatures in the universe.

This they could achieve by classifying all circumstances under three stages in the relationship between the conducive sense objects and their enjoyer. There is a kind of happiness when an individual is mentally brooding over a sense object, which to him is a source of happiness. Thus, when the object of love is absent, the lover enjoys it through contemplation. The joy thus experienced in the contemplation of the loving object is termed in Sanskrit as 'priya'; which we are compelled to translate as joy.

When the object of love is very near the lover, the enjoyment at the vicinity of the enjoyable is certainly better than that delight gained in the mere contemplation of it. This joy, which is subtler and greater than 'priya', is termed as 'moda', which we have translated as rejoicing.

When the beloved object is not only near the beloved, but he actually comes to indulge in the enjoyment of the object, the joy arising out of this actual experiencing is termed as 'pramoda' and we translate it as bliss.

As an example, a lover, when he is contemplating upon the beauty of the form, the nobility of the heart and the delicacy of sentiments of his beloved, his joys are termed as 'priya'; when he meets her in a secret arbour of love, in the actual vicinity of her throbbing heart, the joy that arises is called 'moda' and when the same loving couple comes to live in mutual embrace, living the soft joys of the betrothal the pleasure derived from that enjoyment is termed as 'pramoda'; we translate it as bliss.

Under these three classifications, all enjoyment of sense objects can be marshalled in, these three being the sources of all our joys.

In describing the ānandamaya, the ṛṣi therefore, explains that priya is its head and moda and pramoda are the two sides. In all these three sources of joy, the common vital content is but the sense of a satisfying delight and this fact is indicated when the ṛṣi declares that the trunk is ānanda.

In the above narration of joy and the bliss-personality in man, though we explained it as the joys experienced through the acquisition, possession and enjoyment of the sense objects, when we view it closely we find that all bliss springs from the same source, the supreme Self. Bliss is the essential nature of man and desire or sorrow is a condition when the flow of the Self is choked by the powerful agitation of the mind. Possession of the beloved object in its varying degrees of satisfaction calms the mind, and to the degree the mind is calmed, to that degree beams of the Self's blissful light burst upon the individual's cognition. This technique has been fully explained earlier.

Therefore, according to Vedānta, sense enjoyment is nothing but the bliss of the Self that manifests itself at certain moments, the immediate cause being the possession of the particular object. This truth is upheld when the ṛṣi declares that the bliss-personality in man is rooted in, or founded upon Brahman.

What has been said here is endorsed by the Vedas; the appropriate Veda mantra is quoted in the following section.

Section vi – अनुवाकः ६

Godhood – The Experience of Positive Existence

असन्नेव स भवति । असद्ब्रह्मेति वेद चेत् ।
अस्ति ब्रह्मेति चेद्वेद । सन्तमेनं ततो विदुरिति ।
तस्यैष एव शारीर आत्मा यः पूर्वस्य ॥१ ॥

asanneva sa bhavati, asadbrahmeti veda cet,
asti brahmeti cedveda, santamenaṁ tato viduriti,
tasyaiṣa eva śārīra ātmā yaḥ pūrvasya. (1)

असत् – non-existent; एव – truly; सः – he; भवति – becomes; असत् – non-existent; ब्रह्म – Brahman; इति – thus; वेद – knows; चेत् – if; अस्ति – as existent; ब्रह्म – Brahman: इति – thus; चेत् – if; वेद – (he) knows; सन्तम् – to be existent; एनम् – him; तत् – then; विदुः – they (the world) consider; इति – thus; तस्य – of that; एषः – this; एव – verily; शारीर आत्मा – (is) the embodied soul; यः – who; पूर्वस्य – of the former

1. If he knows Brahman as non-existent, he becomes himself non-existent. If he knows Brahman as existent, then (they) the world knows him to be existent. Of the former (ānandamaya kośa), the Self is the essence.

The theory of transcendence, as explained so far, should necessarily give the student a feeling that the Truth indicated in Vedānta is a condition to be experienced as 'non-existence.' All that we know of existence can be experienced either from the body or from the mind or from the intellect or, at least, as an inward 'glow of happiness.' But the ṛṣi was labouring all along to explain to us all these instruments in us, and he had been advising the transcendence of each one of them.

When we remove all our identification with the body, though the external sense objects become nil to us, certainly, there are the feelings of the mind that exist wherein we can live. When the mind is also transcended, there is at least a world of ideas which we can capture and live in our intellect. When we transcend the intellect also, we may still live, as the teacher explained, in the glow of happiness, in the causal body. But, when even this is transcended, the goal that we can reach must, certainly, be a complete zero, a vacuum, an emptiness, a dull and dreary non-existence in which all that we know of, is negated. When all the instruments of experiences are transcended, we must necessarily reach a void which, as far as our intellect can understand today in its calculation, must be zero – a non-existent nothingness.

That which has its own positive qualities is called an existent thing. This watch on the table exists because I see it, I touch it, I can conceive of it as my watch and I have got an idea of its make or of the company that manufactured it. The watch is existent. But when I search for my horn, it is termed as non-existent, since my sense organs cannot perceive it; neither can my mind feel it nor can my intellect conceive of its presence.

When none of the instruments of cognition can come to experience an object in the workaday world, we term it as non-existent.

The believers in asat-vāda, a group of Buddhists, have come to claim that 'non-existence' is the Truth since they pursued exclusively the path of negating everything in the cognisable or experienceable world of objects. They declared, therefore, that 'non-existence' exists. This religion of non-existence threw the generation out into an insipid animal life of atheistic values and ulcerated the society with its 'leprous sensuousness'.

This mantra clearly indicates that an individual who realises that the 'Supreme Goal' is non-existent, he, during his meditation, comes to realise only the 'non-existence'. Thereby he becomes a sad negative personality and not a positive, divine God-man.

Śaṅkarācārya, arguing against this misinterpretation, very lovingly and tenderly takes up the logic of the asat-vādins and declares that they are at the gates of the Truth refusing to go in and experience the positive dynamism of the supreme Essence in themselves. Śaṅkarācārya says that there is a palpable contradiction when they declare that non-existence exists.Their's is a cry that they had experienced non-existence in their supreme transcendental anubhava. Since they had experienced 'non-existence' there must be a positive Consciousness, an existent entity, that illumined the state of 'non existence'. That existent dynamic factor is the Truth which illumined, at that time of complete cessation of all the sheaths, the natural state of 'non-existence': meaning, the non-existence of the ordinarily known objects that are knowable only through the sheaths – which are all objects of these various sheaths.

Vedānta is not a negative philosophy. Its strength lies in its positivity, and it leads man away from his present confusions and misunderstandings and ushers him into Godhood, which is then experienced there as a positive existence. Without the assertion of the positive qualities of Godhead, with the mere negation of the delusory beliefs in ourselves, the sādhanā as explained in Vedānta is not complete. Curing the symptoms of a disease is not in itself the end of a treatment; the treatment ends only after the convalescence, when the patient positively regains his lost health and gets established in the enjoyment of his entire energy and vitality. Removing hunger is not the fulfilment of eating, but it must give to the eater the positive happiness of fullness and comfort.

Negation of our false misunderstandings about ourselves is certainly to be pursued; the false is to be negated. But Vedānta does not point out this partial method only. After the negation of the false, realisation is complete only when we come to assert and live the vital Truth in Itself. Negation of the ghost should be immediately followed by the assertion of the positive existence of the post!

This statement of the Veda therefore asserts that if a seeker overemphasises the method of negation, he may reach only a dull void which in itself is not the fulfilment of a God-man's inward divine realisation. He must not only understand that he is not a finite mortal, but must come to experience that he is the infinite eternal Truth. Without this positive understanding, Vedānta only fulfils in drawing out a melancholy caricature of a man of imperfections, rather than discover for him the celestial beauty of a perfect God that lives in him!!

The application of this Vaidika declaration can be found in life also. Unless the faithful followers of a theory or a philosophy, or even the people of a nation believe in, and come to experience the existent goal in their plans and programmes, they do not become dynamic followers who can carve out successful glory unto themselves. This is an era of planning. A plan should include not only a clear and vivid realisation of the present weaknesses and sorrows in the society, but it should also give a positive picture of what would be the goal of the nation at the fulfilment of the plan. If the people, faithfully subscribing to the plan, do not come to realise this positive goal of the plan, they can never be depended upon to fulfil that plan. Unless we have definite faith in the goal of our existence and unless we believe, work for, and actually come to experience the goal positively as an existent factor, there is no hope of any plan ever becoming successful.

So too here, in the scheme of life as per Vedānta which plans to raise man from his sensuous slavery, mental weakness, and intellectual impotency into the stature of a God upon earth, free and efficient in every field, noble and divine in every activity, peaceful and serene in every situation, cheerful and composed in every circumstance – ever a master of his own emotions and desires, never a slave of his sentiments and ideas. As such, in this subjective planning, unless the seeker has definite faith in a positive goal, unless he comes to experience it, there is no fulfilment on the spiritual path as indicated in the God-making programme of Vedānta.

This positive, existent, divine Consciousness, which is eternal and perfect, immortal and omnipotent, is the Ātman, which is the essence of the ānandamaya kośa. To know and to realise the bliss sheath is to discover the Ātman. To fix our identification with this bliss sheath entirely and completely is the last act of the conscious and deliberate human effort in his attempt at self-evolution, wherein he comes to realise his essence as nothing short of the supreme Godhood.

अथातोऽनुप्रश्नाः । उताविद्वानमुं लोकं प्रेत्य
कश्चन गच्छती३ । आहो विद्वानमुं लोकं प्रेत्य
कश्चित्समश्नुता३ उ ॥२॥

athato'nupraśnāḥ, utāvidvānamuṁ lokaṁ pretya
kaścana gacchatī3, āho vidvānamuṁ lokaṁ pretya
kaścitsamaśnutā3 u. (2)

अथ – now (thereupon); अतः – therefore; अनुप्रश्नाः – the following questions; उत – whether; अविद्वान् – the ignorant; अमुम् – there (yonder); लोकम् – world; प्रेत्य – having left (this world); कश्चन – any; गच्छति – goes; आहो – or; विद्वान् – the knower; अमुम् लोकम् – that world; प्रेत्य – having left; कश्चित् – any; समश्नुते – attains; उ – whether

2. Thereupon arise the following questions: Does the ignorant, leaving this world, go There? Or, does the knower, leaving this world, obtain That?

The diligent and daring intellectuals that they were, the children of that age, in their extreme self-integration, could not only follow faithfully the highest philosophical discourses, but they could see much beyond their classroom. The impatient enthusiasm in the students, smouldering under courageous impatience seems to take wings and voices forth these questions. The questions, in their implications, cover a greater field than the words themselves suggest in their superficial dictionary meanings. In the beginning, the teacher said that out of the Reality, defined as 'Satyam, Jñānam, Anantam,' the entire world of plurality emerged under the propelling force of a desire.

When a chain is made out of gold, whether the links in the chain know it or not, when it is melted, it cannot become anything other than gold itself. Similarly, the disciples ask: 'Will not a human being, even when he does not know anything of the Ātman; without any of the self-effort at ethical and moral living and continuous mental seeking and deep meditation, reach the Supreme on leaving from this world of existence?' This question, in its implication, raises a doubt as to what is the special benefit derived by the spiritual way of living and by following the traditional trainings of self-development when every born creature would ultimately merge back to become its cause which is the Supreme. Here the question implies the futility of any conscious spiritual endeavour.

The other question is an antithesis of the earlier one: 'Does one, who knows the Reality, reach the supreme experience after his departure from here?' Together, in their combination, both the questions indicate a doubt whether there is a Reality or not, which is to be achieved by man through a conscious effort on his part. The full implication of the question will be understood as we read more and more of the text.

सोऽकामयत। बहु स्यां प्रजायेयेति। स तपोऽतप्यत।
स तपस्तप्त्वा इदगं् सर्वमसृजत यदिदं किञ्च।
तत्सृष्ट्वा तदेवानुप्राविशत्।
तदनुप्रविश्य सच्च त्यच्चाभवत्।
निरुक्तं चानिरुक्तं च। निलयनं चानिलयनं च
विज्ञानं चाविज्ञानं च।
सत्यं चानृतं च सत्यमभवत्।
यदिदं किञ्च। तत्सत्यमित्याचक्षते।
तदप्येष श्लोको भवति ॥३॥

so'kāmayata, bahu syāṁ prajāyeyeti, sa tapo'tapyata,
sa tapastaptvā idagṁ sarvamasṛjata yadidaṁ kiñca,
tatsṛṣṭvā tadevānuprāviśat,
tadanupraviśya sacca tyaccābhavat,
niruktaṁ cānirukataṁ ca, nilayanaṁ cānilayanaṁ ca
vijñānaṁ cāvijñānaṁ ca,
satyaṁ cānṛtaṁ ca satyamabhavat,
yadidaṁ kiñca, tatsatyamityācakṣate,
tadapyeṣa śloko bhavati. (3)

सः – He; अकामयत – desired; बहु – many; स्याम् – may I become; प्रजायेय – may I be born; इति – thus; सः – He; तपः – tapas; अतप्यत – performed; सः – He; तपः – tapas; तप्त्वा – having performed; इदग्म् – thus; सर्वम् – all; असृजत – created; यत् इदम् किञ्च – whatever that is here (that we perceive); तत् – it; सृष्ट्वा – having created; तत् – it; एव – verily; अनुप्राविशत् – entered into; तत् – it; अनुप्रविश्य – having entered; सत् – the manifest; च – and; त्यत् –the beyond (the unmanifest); च – and; अभवत् – became; निरुक्तम् – the defined; च – and; अनिरुक्तम् – the undefined; च – and; निलयनम् – the housed; च – and; अनिलयनम् – the houseless; च – and; विज्ञानम् – knowledge; च – and; अविज्ञानम् – ignorance; च – and; सत्यम् – truth; च – and; अनृतम् – falsehood, untruth; च – and; सत्यम् – manifest; अभवत् – became; यत् इदम् किञ्च – whatever that is here; तत् – therefore; सत्यम् – existence; इति –thus; आचक्षते – it is called; तत् – about that; अपि – also; एषः – this; श्लोकः – verse; भवति – there is

3. He desired, 'I shall become many and be born. He performed tapas; having performed tapas, He created all this whatsoever (we perceive). Having created it, He entered

into it. Having entered it, He became the manifest and the unmanifest, the defined and undefined, the housed and the houseless, knowledge and ignorance, truth and falsehood, and all this whatsoever that exists. Therefore, it is called Existence. In this sense, there is the following Vaidika verse.'

The supreme all-pervading Consciousness, which is the substratum for the entire world, is Itself the conscious part of the life within us, called the Ātman. This has been already explained in the earlier verse of this chapter. Here in this mantra, the teacher is continuing his discourse, and is explaining how the creation has actually emerged out from the ocean of pure Consciousness which ever remains perfect, the One without a second.

There are many European critics who naturally get flabbergasted at the logic of the Master's words here. The students asked definite and pointed questions which the Master is not answering immediately and directly. From this, they conclude that the teacher was not only avoiding the questions and its implications, but was even frightening the children away by the dignity of his bearded face and the sonorous echo of his thundering words!

In fact, a closer study reveals how subtly the Master had answered all the subtle implications of the student's questions. In this dramatic situation – where the teacher was giving a discourse to a few students, who were eagerly sitting in front of him, all eyes and ears, open, with their minds surging forward to peep over ever uncovered new fields of knowledge which the Master's words seemed to open up to their view – the students, in their impatience, asked the above questions.

The teacher, appreciating the depth of understanding which is indicated in the students' questions, did not all of a sudden jump to an answer with a direct 'Yes' or 'No'. He continued his discourse covering all the fields as per his own scheme of the discourse.

There was a smile of satisfaction on the face of the teacher and he promised the children with his smile that he would be answering their questions. Thus, the teacher continued to explain how the Infinite came to play the game of the finite not by any accident, nor by the intervention of anything other than Itself, but It happened to entertain a desire to become many and play the game of life!

This description gives us a fallacious feeling that the teacher is trying to explain the 'Creation' objectively. Though the words here, 'He desired', gives the reader a wrong notion that a Creator, there among the clouds, desired and 'You and I' are all the creatures of his desire, in the tradition of the studies of Upaniṣad, the students of that age, tried to grasp the Truth in themselves subjectively. Vedānta being the science of man's subjective quest to discover the Reality in himself, at every point in the Upaniṣads, we can understand the śāstra only if we try to subjectively experience what has been objectively explained in their mantras.

The Ātman, supreme and divine, perfect and all-full, revelling in It's own omniscience and omnipotence, became aware of a desire arising in Itself. Thousands of desires do come everyday in the bosom of each one of us, but, we do not identify ourselves with them, and they immediately die away. But, at moments, we get ourselves identified with one of the desires, and then starts the endless chain of tragedies and sorrows in our effort at fulfilling the desire and regaining our mental poise.

For example, almost every day, in the afternoon, the idea of visiting some cinema show may crop up in our minds, when it is ignored, it dies away without making any stir within us. One day, suddenly, one gets a desire for a movie, and he does not keep quiet but identifies himself with the desire and then starts vitalising it with his own thoughts. He struggles hard to create that 'world of experience' by reaching the theatre, purchasing a ticket, walking in and taking the seat. Having thus created this joy, he enters it, as it were, with his enthusiasm to enjoy the 'show' and then comes to suffer the agonies of the tragedy or smiles at the comedy.

Similarly, says the ṛṣi, 'the Supreme, first desired – meaning, when a desire bumped up in that Ocean of Perfection (in It's all-fullness, desire too is in It), It identified Itself with that desire and performed tapas. Concentrated and consistent thinking in the line of a desired object is tapas. These thoughts dynamise the desire and the individual – meaning, 'the Supreme, identified with It's desire', struggles to create the necessary world in which It can fulfil It's desire. Having created the world, He enters it, meaning, He comes to live in an intimate and immediate relationship with the world of objects so created'. Thus, concludes the ṛṣi, 'the Supreme Himself became the entire world of experience in plurality!!'.

In this birth of the plurality from the Supreme, no division or change has taken place in the Infinite. The finite is only a superimposition on the Infinite. The vision of a ghost does not in any sense reduce, divide or mar the nature of the post. Rockfeller may dream that he is a beggar, roaming in the streets of New York, seeking for a lunch; but on waking up, he will not find himself even a farthing less rich for all his dream-poverty than what he was. This process of a delusory vision, which veils the real nature of the substratum and gives us an experienceable perception of something different from it, is called a superimposition. The ṛṣi here explains this all-satisfying 'theory of creation', as expounded in Vedānta.

Thereafter, the Ātman itself became the entire world of perception, manifest and unmanifest; that which has form and that which is formless; all knowledge and all ignorance; truth and falsehood; nay, in short, every object of experience came from that one substratum, divine and all-pervading, the supreme Self. The waves and the ripples, the foam and the lather, are all in real sense nothing but the one homogeneous ocean.

Whatever be the size, shape, design, colour, price or contents, all clay pots have risen up from the one mud alone.

If all these objects have risen up from the Truth, in what way can we detect something that is common to all things, both the manifest and unmanifest? In the manifest world, we have inert stones, the growing vegetable world, the sentient animal kingdom and the rational human beings. We experience the unmanifest world, such as our tendencies, likes and dislikes, love and hatred, and so on. What is that factor which is common to the stone, the plant, the animal, the man, his feelings and his ideas? If there be a common ground, which is the same for every one of these entities, certainly that factor should be an expression of the Supreme, out of which all these have arisen.

On no platform can all these pluralistic worlds be brought together and equated on the basis of one common factor except on the one idea, which is certainly common to all of them, and that is, 'Existence'. All of them exist. This fact because of which we say that they exist – as contrasted with things like a sky flower or mirage water, which we say, have no existence, that fact philosophically called 'Pure Existence', is common to all, and this is an expression of supreme Consciousness. Since the Truth is embracing all objects and giving them all a glamour of existence, it is called 'Existence'.

The declaration is not a mere intellectual hypothesis fathered by the ṛṣi of the Upaniṣads, but there is a Vaidika mantra which endorses it. It is quoted in the next section.

Section vii – अनुवाकः ७

Brahman – Bliss By Nature – Source of Fearlessness and Cause For Fear

असद्वा इदमग्र आसीत्। ततो वै सदजायत।
तदात्मानगं्‌ स्वयमकुरुत।
तस्मात्तत्सुकृतमुच्यत इति ॥१॥

asadvā idamagra āsīt, tato vai sadajāyata,
tadātmānagṁ svayamakuruta,
tasmāttatsukṛtamucyata iti. (1)

असद् – non-existence; वै – verily; इदम् – this; अग्रे – in the beginning; आसीत् – was; ततः – from that; वै – indeed; सद् – the existent being; अजायत – was born; तत् – that; आत्मानगम् स्वयम् – itself by itself; अकुरुत – created; तस्मात् – therefore; तत् – it; सुकृतम् – self-made or well-made; उच्यते – is called; इति – thus

1. In the beginning was verily this non-existence. From that the existent was born. That created Itself by Itself. Therefore, It is called the self-made or the well made.

This is a stanza often quoted by those who claim that non-existence is the eternal Truth, because, according to the Vaidika mantra as quoted here, non-existence alone existed before all creation. This mischievous misinterpretation cannot stand the scrutiny of even a moment's quiet thinking.

The very sentence, 'non-existence existed', is itself a palpable contradiction and a science or a scripture has no right to indulge in contradictions and wherever there is a seeming contradiction, it is for us to find the correct meaning and understand the statement rightly.

In the beginning, that is, before the manifested world was created, it was all in a state of non-existence, in the sense that 'existence' as we know now, conditioned by the various objects – manifest and unmanifest – did not exist, and so non-existence existed. It is only to negate the manifested world, as known to us today, in the Supreme that Vedānta says here: 'Non-existence existed'. Out of that non-existence, 'the existence was born'. Out of a piece of silver, a gold pot cannot be made, and if the effect is a gold pot, certainly the cause must have been gold. Similarly, if, out of non-existence the existent was born, then what we mean by 'non-existence' can only be 'the non-existence of the created', from Existence alone can the existent emerge.

That there is, in this creation, no intervention of a creator, is shown by the mantra by insisting that Supreme created 'Itself by Itself'. Let us take the analogy of our common dreams. I having had my food, retire to the security and warmth of my comfortable bedroom and then dream in my bed that I am starving in some unknown valley of Darjeeling. There, bitten by cold, struck by fatigue, and torn by hunger, I am roaming in the jungles, when a beast of prey pounces on me from around a bush.[1] Herein, the bush, the

[1] For a closer study of the dream world see Swāmījī's discourses on *Māṇḍūkya-upaniṣad* with Gauḍpāda's *Kārikā*.

jungle, the beast of prey, and its victim all are created from me, by myself; and the moment I withdraw again to the waking state of consciousness, the dream fades away into the nothingness from which it had come. Exactly by the same process, the Supreme, having identified Itself with a desire, creates a field out of 'Itself, by Itself'.

The pluralitistic world, therefore, is nothing but Himself and He, being perfect and divine, the created world is not to be condemned as something that is born out of sin. This is the unhappy philosophy of the Christian Bible. But here the noble cultural tradition of Hinduism considers the world as 'sukṛtam'– well done, divinely planned and perfectly executed. The Semitic religions all weep at their own imperfections when they compare themselves with the beauty and completeness of Vedānta.

Altogether this 'Theory of Creation' provides us with a complete philosophy, and not an objective theory. It is not giving us the logic of creation as much as the method of transcending it. It prescribes the secret solvent with which we can resolve the bundles of contradictions we meet with around us, and within our hearts!

The philosophy of *Taittirīya* is a brilliant idol wrapped in glorious optimism that in its shrine, the sobbing and sighing man gets revived to a godly beauty that wears an eternal smile – the smile that wells up from a satisfied, blissful heart. A man who has followed *Taittirīya-upaniṣad* properly and realised the Truth indicated by it, can no more thereafter feel any imperfection anywhere in the world since the plurality is but a superimposition upon Reality. Thus the existence wherever it be, is but the existence borrowed from the Supreme!

Thereafter, the entire world of multiplicity comes to wear a robe of divinity and an aura of perfection to one who is a true student of *Taittirīya*. There is no trace of cynicism, nor is there in the *Taittirīya*-view-of-life any hint at the futility of life or the foolishness of recognising a world. The world is no more a chain upon the soul, but is a glorious occasion to recognise the dynamism of the spirit and its perfection, both in its transcendental and immanent presence. The world is sukṛtam: well made, divinely planned and perfectly executed.

यद्-वै तत्सुकृतं रसो वै सः ।
रसगृंह्येवायं लब्ध्वानन्दी भवति ।
को ह्येवान्यात्-कः प्राण्यात्
यदेष आकाश आनन्दो न स्यात् । एष ह्येवानन्दयाति ॥२ ॥

yad-vai tatsukṛtam raso vai saḥ,
rasagṁ-hyevāyaṁ labdhvānandī bhavati.
ko hyevānyāt-kaḥ prāṇyāt
yadeṣa ākāśa ānando na syāt, eṣa hyevānandayāti. (2)

यत् – this (Brahman); वै – verily; तत् – that (which was); सुकृतम् – self-made; रसः – taste (joy); वै – verily; सः – is (He); रसगम्

– taste (joy); हि – indeed; एव – only; अयम् – this one; लब्ध्वा – having obtained; आनन्दी – blessed; भवति – (he) becomes; हि –indeed; एव – just; कः अन्यात् कः प्राण्यात् – who else can breathe out or breathe in; यत् – if; एषः – this; आकाशः – (in) the cavity of the heart (lit in the ether); आनन्दः – joy; न स्यात् – were not there; एषः – this one; हि – surely; एव – indeed; आनन्दयाति– brings us joy

2. This which was self-made ... that is taste (joy). Having obtained this taste, man becomes blessed; for who can breathe out or breathe in, if this joy were not there in the cavity of the heart? This Brahman Itself brings us joy.

The oneness of the created world and the Creator is nowhere in any other philosophy so beautifully brought out and so perfectly conceived as it is here. It says that the pluralistic world, finite in nature, pain ridden in experience, imperfect at every stage when we try to grasp it from the level of our body, mind and intellect, is itself nothing other than the Supreme, perfect – full of a vital, experienceable Bliss-essence (rasa).

There is no sense of disrespect of the finite when viewed after the experience of the Infinite! It is recognised and respected, revered and adored, worshipped and invoked, sung and glorified, as nothing but the Supreme itself. Here is a positive philosophy which roars its reverence to life: domestic, social, communal, national and international. Life itself throbs with the Reality; the pain and imperfections in it are but the ulcers that we have created by our misuse of life, in our ignorance and stupidity. Any temple can become as dirty as a dustbin if we misuse it – as we scandalously do in many of our temples. Similarly, in our irreverence to life and non-recognition of the divinity in human beings, we breed mutual hatred and enmity which 'molest' the social security and the beauty of life.

Rasa is that which is enjoyable. It is not a non-existent nothing, but an existent factor. Rasa is that which gives pleasure and joy. On realising the Self within, though we negate all objects of the body, mind and intellect in our transcendence of all the five sheaths, it is not an inert zero, an empty non-entity, but is a positive Bliss-experience. This idea is indicated here by declaring the Ātman, as full of rasa.

In the world, living in the various sheath identifications, we come to our share of happiness in contact with their conducive objects. The body is happy in contact with the beloved who satisfies all its sense organs of perception and organs of action. A beautiful piece of literature satisfies the mental zone, just as an appetising philosophy, when explained properly, satisfies our intellectual hunger. At all these levels, we enjoy when in contact with their chosen objects; while, when we have transcended all these, in the experience of the Self in the Self, it is possible that a student may doubt if there can be any joy at all. This doubt is cleared in this scripture by its declaration that the Supreme is full of rasa.

This can be observed in life when we observe a devotee closely. A Christ in rags, a Buddha under a bodhi tree, a Ramakrishna in the Kālī temple, a Vivekananda on the cold railway platform in America, a Guru Govind Singh encircled with danger and threat to his life at every moment, a Ramatirtha in the valleys of Himalayas.. none of them could, in any sense of the term, be conceived as having been provided with any reason to be happy or joyous, and yet, these are the rare ones, whom we see through the books of history, who wore their eternal smile at the perfection achieved, the contentment gained and the tranquility established!

We see on one hand a rich spendthrift seeking perfect joy through sensuous objects, sighing and weeping; while on the other hand, we see another declaring his consummate satisfaction with the limpid depths in his peaceful look and the endless smile on his loving lips, who has none of the sensuous objects around him. We have therein surely a practical demonstration of what the Upaniṣad explains: that the experience of the Self in the Self is a positive joy, so perfect in itself that all the sensuous objects put together cannot ever give even a trace of its 'Eternal Perfection!'

Having experienced this spiritual centre as one's own essential nature, that individual 'becomes blessed' in the sense that thereafter no circumstance can give him any sense of imperfection or sorrow.

When the teacher has explained this much and tried to express the glory of the spiritual experience, he, being one well established in it, he, naturally, shoots himself into that memory of lived joys, and so explodes in a general statement. In this outburst we hear echoes of the teacher's desperation at the incapacity of the language to express the Infinite Brahmānanda rasa which he wanted to convey through his students to the world at large.

This is but natural that whenever we try to narrate to someone near and dear to us an experience we had and whenever we are anxious that the other must experience the same, it must be the experience of everyone of us that our thoughts will always run faster than our words. Similarly here, when the teacher was overanxious to convey his infinite experience of the positive reality of the Spirit, his thoughts ran wild into his memory of lived joys, while his words stammer and falter at the threshold of their own incapacities!!

There is certainly a pause of breathless ecstasy on the part of the teacher at this point of delivery when the power of his memory bundles him away into the realm of his experienced spiritual ecstasy from wherein he understands that the source of all joy in the entire universe is but the Bliss of the Self and so when he tumbles down back again into his mind and intellect plane and takes up the thread of discourse, he cries out this general statement which is pregnant with suggestion.

He declares that none can breathe on the face of the globe and continue to live, if the source of all joy was not there in his heart. All joys which we gain in the sensuous world are all flashes of the brilliance of the Self emerging out through the mental agitations when they are calmed through the fleeting enjoyments of the sensuous objects, has already been thoroghly explained in the previous pages.

The psychologist, estimating the mental character and composition of a suicide, declares that a creature decides to die and raises a weapon against himself only when he, at the impact of a sudden and immediate disappointment in life, comes to feel that there is no more a chance of any happiness, nor an occasion to smile, in the future. No creature can live without joy, and every moment of life is an active seeking of a greater joy. If this motive force is removed from life, the entire existence tumbles down and permanently comes to a halt. The movement of life is continued and kept up by the dynamism of this joy hunting. Naturally, the teacher here declares quite appropriately that no creature can be there and continues to breathe in its body embodiment, if its heart is not full of this experienceable Self.

That this Brahman alone brings us all joys has already been explained when we were discussing the mechanism in the joy distilling process within the beings.

यदा ह्येवैष एतस्मिन्नदृश्येऽनात्म्येऽ
निरुक्तेऽनिलयनेऽभयं प्रतिष्ठां विन्दते ।
अथ सोऽभयं गतो भवति ।
यदा ह्येवैष एतस्मिन्नुदरमन्तरं कुरुते ।
अथ तस्य भयं भवति ।
तत्त्वेव भयं विदुषोऽमन्वानस्य ।
तदप्येष श्लोको भवति ॥३॥

yadā hyevaiṣa etasminnadṛṣye'nātmye'-
nirukte'nilayane'bhayaṁ pratiṣṭhāṁ vindate,
atha so'bhayaṁ gato bhavati,
yadā hyevaiṣa etāsminnudaramantaraṁ kurute,
atha tasya bhayaṁ bhavati,
tattveva bhayaṁ viduṣo'manvānasya,
tadapyeṣa śloko bhavati. (3)

यदा – when; हि – indeed; एव – thus; एषः – this seeker; एतस्मिन् – in this; अदृश्ये – who is invisible; अनात्म्ये – incorporeal; अनिरुक्ते – inexplicable; अनिलयने – unsupported; अभयम् – fearless; प्रतिष्ठाम् – oneness; विन्दते – attains; अथ – then; सः – He; अभयम् – fearless; गतः – attained; भवति – becomes; यदा – when; हि – however; एव – verily; एषः – this one; एतस्मिन् – in this; उ – even; दरम् – slightest; अन्तरम् – distinction; कुरुते – makes; अथ – then; तस्य – to him; भयम् – fear; भवति – is; तत् – that; तु – indeed; एव – certainly; भयम् – fear; विदुषः – the all knower (Brahman); अमन्वानस्य – for one who does not reflect, the thoughtless, proud; तत् – about that; अपि – also; एषः – this; श्लोकः – verse; भवति – there is

3. When this seeker attains the fearless oneness with Brahman who is invisible, incorporeal, inexplicable and unsupported, then he becomes free from fear. When however, he makes even the slightest distinction in Brahman, then there is danger for him. That very same Brahman Himself becomes the source of fear for him who makes a difference and who reflects not. To the same effect, there is the following Vaidika verse.

The spiritual centre which presides over the body assemblage in every living being has been explained as 'full of rasa'. This 'Blissful Centre' is not realised now by us because of its identifications with the assemblage constituted of the body, mind and other sheaths. The Ātman, when seemingly conditioned by these delusory matter envelopments, is called the ego-centre. The process of Self-discovery is the ego's rediscovery that it is the pure Self without any of its delusory identifications with It's matter vestures. On this recognition, the Self in us realises It's oneness with the Self of the universe.

In a cup of water the reflected sun entirely depends upon the condition of the water in the cup. When the water is disturbed, the reflected sun gets shattered; when the water is muddy, the reflected sun becomes muddy. The sun in the sky, conditioned by the water in the cup, stands for the Ātman conditioned by the matter sheaths. This reflected Consciousness is called ego-centre. When the cup is broken or the water thrown away, in short, when the reflecting surface is destroyed, the reflection also ends and the real sun in the sky comes to be realised as the Truth behind the reflection.

In fact, it is the sun in the sky that illumined the reflection, the water in the cup and the cup itself. Similarly, the ego-centre and the matter envelopments are all being illumined by the one pure Consciousness, but this is not realised so long as we are preoccupied with the various vicissitudes and destinies of the ego-centre. When once the seeker detaches himself from all the sheaths and thus ends the reflecting medium, thereafter the pure Consciousness, the Ātman rediscovers Itself to be nothing other than the Self in all names and forms constituting the entire universe.

The Ātman which thus rediscovers Itself, immediately understands It's oneness with Brahman.

Invisible – Here Brahman is described as invisible, meaning, It is not cognisable through the known avenues of perception, namely, the sense organs. Not only that it cannot be seen, it is equally true that Brahman cannot be heard, tasted, smelt or touched. Sense organs can function only in the world of objects and they can perceive only their respective sense objects which are other than themselves. Ātman being the subject, is not perceivable. What is visible is a modification or a phenomenon (vikāra). Brahman is not a phenomenon and therefore, It is invisible, incorporeal. That which is a vikāra or a modification alone can take a gross form. Brahman is described here as formless because it is not a modification.

By the earlier term that Brahman is invisible, if it has indicated directly that It is changeless; indirectly it also connotes that It is incorporeal (bodiless); and that which is bodiless is indescribable too. In short, Brahman is not subject to any modification, It being the cause for all modifications.

Being so, it is 'unsupported' or 'abodeless'. In this subtlest all-pervasiveness, Brahman covers all and nothing covers it. Therefore, it is abodeless. For a parrot, the cage is the abode; for the cage, the house is the abode; for the house, the roof is the abode; for the roof, we may say, the 'blue dome of the sky' is the abode; for the sky, philosophically, Brahman is the abode. For Brahman, there is no abode, since there is nothing other than That, and nothing can cover It.

All effects and their attributes have the support of the substratum, the Brahman; but there is no support for It. The Śruti says that Brahman is established in no support other than It's own glory.

An individual who thus comes to experience his oneness with the Brahman becomes free from fear. Fear can come only from something other than oneself. Nobody is afraid of himself. When a seeker successfully realises his oneness with the entire universe, the sense of distinction ends and thereafter, he has no occasion to feel the sense of fear at anything.

To convey this idea that fearlessness can come only at the realisation of the individual's oneness with the entire universe, the Upaniṣad gives here the negative statement also. The Brahman Itself becomes a source of fear for him who makes even the slightest distinction in It. The moment we recognise an objective God, other than ourselves, revelling in heaven, and we do not seek our oneness with Him, agitations and fears come to storm our bosom. Perfect tranquillity and peace comes only when we establish our unquestioned oneness with Truth. Perfect happiness is only in the fulfilment of love. Love is fulfilled only when the lover and the beloved merge to become one single mass of love experience. Similarly, when the ego-centre in us loses all its separative consciousness and comes to experience its unbroken and definite oneness with the Ātman, it comes to live the infinite state of perfection and fearlessness in itself.

The same Truth which gives fearlessness to the realised, provides occasions for fear to those who do not give enough meditative thought to the discriminative analysis of the unreal and the Real. The ego is 'Ātman playing the fool amidst the unreal'. To awaken itself to the Real is to rediscover its divine, omnipotent nature, and in this 'Self-discovery' is the state of fearlessness. Those who do not make the necessary discriminative analysis of the Real and the unreal, of the true and the false, they, in their delusory identifications, come to feel themselves different from the Real, and their realisation is never complete.

The Self in us, realisable as our own real nature full of experienceable Bliss (rasa) is by now brought within the intellectual comprehension of the students, if not fully, at least within their intuitive realisation of the seekers. In the next section we have a complete picture of the dynamism of this 'Spiritual Centre' and also a comparative statistics which gives us a certain concrete measure to divinise what is the joy experienced in the Self by the Realised Master.

Section viii – अनुवाकः ८

Brahmānanda – The Supreme Bliss

भीषास्माद्वातः पवते । भीषोदेति सूर्यः ।
भीषास्मादग्निश्चेन्द्रश्च ।
मृत्युर्धावति पञ्चम इति ॥१ ॥

bhīṣāsmādvātaḥ pavate, bhīṣodeti sūryaḥ,
bhīṣāsmādagniścendraśca,
mṛtyurdhāvati pañcama iti. (1)

भीषा – through fear; अस्मात् – of Him; वातः – wind; पवते – blows; भीषा – through fear; उदेति – rises; सूर्यः – the sun; भीषा – through fear; अस्मात् – of Him; अग्निः – fire; च – and; इन्द्रः – Indra; च – and; मृत्युः – death; धावति – proceeds; पञ्चम – the fifth; इति – thus

1. Through fear of Him blows the wind. Through fear of Him rises the sun. Through fear of Him again fire and moon and lastly, the fifth, death proceed to their respective duties.

In the phenomenal world, inspite of its confusing plurality and endless multiplicity of things, there seems to be a golden chord of uniformity inasmuch as this external jigsaw puzzle follows a definite law in its moment-to-moment existence and activity. There is, certainly, a concord that runs through the noisy discord of the world. There is a silent rhythm imperceptibly running through the endless variety of confusing movements. Seasons, similarly, follow one after another rhythmically. Each object in the universe strictly conforms itself to its own nature. There are the natural laws which strictly follow all scientific observations. The sun is never dark; the moon is never hot; fire is never cold! A cow begets no lion; a tigress begets no bird. The innumerable laws of instincts and emotions observed among the vegetables, animals and human lives are all strictly pursued everywhere in nature.

A law is always promulgated by a law giver, and wherever we find strict adherence to the law, it is always because of fear of the law giver. Similarly, if in nature we find that the natural laws are irrevocably declared and strictly followed, certainly, we have to assume that behind the phenomenon of nature there is a definite law giver who strictly executes the law. He is ever standing as it were, just behind nature with a raised whip, threatening all with total annihilation at the simplest disobedience.

This idea is brought out by the Śruti in order to establish the supremacy of the Spirit over matter and also its dynamism in it. Also, this declaration conclusively proves that this Spirit is not a non-existent nonentity, but an existent Reality which can be courted and experienced as full of bliss, omnipotence and omniscience. The Truth indicated in the beginning of the chapter as 'Satyam, Jñānam, Anantam', though invisible, incorporeal, undefined and abodeless, is the source of all dynamic life and is the Existence Principle.

Five main observations are made here by the Śruti; such as the movement of air, the rising of the sun, the heat of the fire, the light of the moon and lastly, the very principle of decay and death that sustains the perishable nature of a finite world, called death. All of these indicate that the entire phenomenal world is not a haphazard idle dream of a mad man, but it is an intelligent scheme ordered by a dynamic divine Power which executes It's will very strictly and fully through It's established laws of behaviour and reaction. This is a Vaidika hymn quoted in support of the previous mantra which declared that he who rediscovers the spiritual centre becomes fearless because he thereby becomes the very Truth, whose dictatorial sovereignty is the irrevocable sanction behind Nature's laws.

This declaration of the rule of the Spirit over matter is followed up in this section by a narration of the various joys experienced in the different realms. In this comparative study of joy, the teacher of *Taittirīya* tries to convey to the student a quantitative and a qualitative conception of the infinite joy which is the very nature of the Self.

सैषानन्दस्य मीमागूंसा भवति ।
युवा स्यात्साधुयुवाध्यायक
आशिष्ठो दृढिष्ठो बलिष्ठः
तस्येयं पृथिवी सर्वा वित्तस्य पूर्णा स्यात् ।
स एको मानुष आनन्दः ।

ते ये शतं मानुषा आनन्दाः ।
स एको मनुष्यगन्धर्वाणामानन्दः ।
श्रोत्रियस्य चाकामहतस्य ।।२ ॥

saiṣānandasya mīmāgṁsā bhavati,
yuvā syātsādhu-yuvā-dhyāyakaḥ
āṣiṣṭho dṛḍhiṣṭho baliṣṭhaḥ
tasyeyaṁ pṛthivī sarvā vittasya pūrṇā syāt,
sa eko mānuṣa ānandaḥ,
te ye śataṁ mānuṣā ānandāḥ,
sa eko manuṣyagandharvāṇāmānandaḥ,
śrotriyasya cākāmahatasya. (2)

सा – that; एषा – this; आनन्दस्य – concerning the Bliss; मीमागंसा – enquiry; भवति – is; युवा – young man; स्यात् – supposing there is; साधुः – good; युवा – youthful; अध्यायकः – well versed in scriptures; आशिष्ठः – well disciplined; दृढिष्ठः – resolute; बलिष्ठः – very strong; तस्य – to him; इयम् – this; पृथिवी – the earth; सर्वा – entire; वित्तस्य – with all its wealth; पूर्णा – laden, full; स्यात् – let there be, belongs; सः – that; एकः – (is) one; मानुष आनन्दः – human bliss; ते – those; ये – which; शतम् – hundred; मानुषा आनन्दाः – (units of) human bliss; सः – that; एकः – one; मनुष्यगन्धर्वाणाम् आनन्दः – (is) the bliss of human gandharvas; श्रोत्रियस्य – (also) one who is well versed in the Vedas; च – and; अकामहतस्य – who is free from desires

2. The following is the enquiry concerning the Bliss (Brahmānanda rasa). Suppose there be a youth, good, well versed in the scriptures, well disciplined, resolute and very strong; to him belongs all this earth full of wealth. This is one

unit of human bliss. This (unit of bliss) of man multiplied hundredfold is the bliss of human gandharvas – and this is also the bliss of one well versed in the Vedas and who is free from desires.

For any measurement, we must have a 'standard unit' with reference to which we can make all our subsequent relative measurements. In order to measure the joys of the various situations, we need a unit of measurement. The Śruti, first of all, defines here the unit very clearly.

She says that the joy of an educated, well-disciplined, mentally resolute and physically strong young man, when he comes to possess the whole world and its wealth as his own, his joy is the unit measure of 'human bliss.'

In the definition of this bliss, the scripture is also giving us indirectly the conditions necessary for true material enjoyment. Wealth in itself is no joy unless the rich man is young enough. Mere youthfulness dissipates itself with wealth unless the youth is well educated to live the healthy values of life. Mere knowledge and youthfulness cannot contribute to the enjoyment of wealth unless he is well disciplined and has a sufficiently developed willpower. One who has youthfulness, education, discipline and power of self-control and self-assertion, who is strong in body, mind and intellect, he alone is capable of enjoying the wealth. To all others wealth is an added burden weighing down their shoulders. A donkey carrying golden bricks is in no way better or luckier than one carrying mud bricks! The prārabdha of the pigs cannot be improved if they are housed in the prime minister's own drawing room!

This being the unit of the sensuous worldly joy which is to an extent within our comprehension, the teacher of the *Taittirīya-upaniṣad* is trying to indicate the various types of joys in their quantity and quality relative to this unit.

Hundred times the joy unit represented by this human bliss, he says, is the joy of human gandharvas[1]. The term 'Gandharva' indicates an artist. The joy of a human artist, in the moment of his inspiration, when he comes to forget the entire world outside and becomes one with his tune or shape or rhyme or curve, is the godly joy of a musician or a painter or a poet or a sculptor. The bliss is derived by a genius or an artist – not by a trader in art, not by an advertisement painter nor a film star or a kālakṣepam musician. The bliss of a true self-dedicated devotee at the feet of Venus is explained here quantitatively as a hundred times more than the sensuous joy of the young, self cultured man of true education when he becomes the king of a prosperous vast country.

The joy of this inspired artist which is equated with a hundred joys of the emperor is said to be, by the Śruti, the joy of one who is a deep student of the scriptures and who has come to realise the goal indicated by Vedānta. Therefore, in his conscious experience of the all-full nature, he has no more desires for the paltry things of the world.

---

[1] The time measured from the day of creation to the day of total dissolution of the universe is denoted by the term kalpa. A devotee, who during one kalpa, by his meritorious actions attains a higher plane of joy and experiences, is called as human gandharva (terrestrial angel).

ते ये शतं मनुष्यगन्धर्वाणामानन्दाः ।
स एको देवगन्धर्वाणामानन्दः ।
श्रोत्रियस्य चाकामहतस्य ॥३ ॥

te ye śataṁ manuṣyagandharvāṇāmānandāḥ,
sa eko devagandharvāṇāmānandaḥ,
śrotriyasya cākāmahatasya. (3)

ते – those; **ये** – which; **शतम्** – hundred; **मनुष्य-गन्धर्वाणाम्** – of the human gandharvas; **आनन्दाः** – bliss; **सः** – that; **एकः** – one; **देव-गन्धर्वाणाम्-आनन्दः** – bliss of celestial gandharvas (also); **श्रोत्रियस्य** – one who is well versed in the Vedas; **च** – and; **अकामहतस्य** – who is free from desires

3. A hundredfold of the bliss of the human gandharvas is the unit of measure of the bliss of the celestial gandharvas. This is the same as the bliss of one who is well versed in the Vedas and who is free from all desires.

Continuing the comparative estimate of bliss, the ṛṣi of the Upaniṣad points out how a hundred times the joy of inspiration which a mortal genius can experience in the world of art is the joy contents of an inspired moment of the heavenly artists. Traditionally, heaven is considered as that place of experience where all the joys of the world reach their climax in our imagination. The traditional belief is that life there is longer, health better, the sense organs more powerful, and the mind and the intellect more acute, so that the intensity of the enjoyments is sharper. The sense objects in heaven also have a greater potency of joy. Necessarily therefore, the artists of the heaven must have a greater joy than the artists of the world. Here, in the narration, it is said that the joys of the celestial artists are a hundred times more than the mortal artists of the world.

Does it mean that an artist's joy increases in its subtlety and tempo by living a godly life of self-control, self-sacrifice and by entertaining the divine values of the head and the heart?

Even this joy of the celestial gandharvas[1] is equated with the joy experienced by a scholar of Vedānta, who having experienced the theme of Vedānta, has come to entertain no more desires for the finite world of objects.

ते ये शतं देवगन्धर्वाणामानन्दाः ।
स एकः पितृणां चिरलोकलोकानामानन्दः ।
श्रोत्रियस्य चाकामहतस्य ॥४ ॥

te ye śataṁ deva-gandharvāṇām-ānandāḥ,
sa ekaḥ pitṛṇāṁ ciraloka-lokānām-ānandaḥ,
śrotriyasya cākāmahatasya. (4)

ते – those; ये – which; शतम् – hundred; देव-गन्धर्वाणाम् – of this deva gandharvas; आनन्दाः – bliss; सः – that; एकः – one;

[1] As a reward for the virtuous life in the previous kalpa, when one gains the joys of the gandharva world, that one born therein from the beginning of the kalpa is called the celestial angel (deva gandharva).

पितृणाम् चिरलोक लोकानाम् आनन्दः – the bliss of the manes, whose world continues for long (also); श्रोत्रियस्य – one who is well versed in the Vedas; च – and; अकामहतस्य – who is free from desires

4. A hundredfold the bliss of the celestial gandharvas is the unit of joy of the manes, whose world continues for long. The same is the joy expressed by one well versed in the Vedas and who is free from desires.

Continuing the statistics of joy, the ṛṣi says that a hundred times the joy of the celestial artist is the joy of the manes, who live in the 'world of the dead'. Pitṛloka (world of the dead) is a concept only in Hindusim. Those who have been faithfully following all the moral and religious injunctions of a true Hindu, it is declared, will on their departure from here, gain the pleasant abode of the dead and continue enjoying the subtler joys of that world for a considerably long interval of time. At the end, when they have exhausted the fruits of their righteous actions, they will again, it is traditionally believed, come back to this world to be born in divine environments, wherein they will be impelled to continue the life of a faithful devotee. Thus, having earned enough fruits, they will again return to that world of enjoyment.

It is believed that, having reached the world of the manes, the ego-centre comes to enjoy a thrill that is a hundredfold than that of the celestial gandharvas. The ṛṣi here assures, from the balcony of his own experience, that this joy is experienced equally by one who is well versed in the Vedas and who has come to experience the essence indicated by Vedānta and therefore, has come to give up all desires for the fleeting sense objects of the world.

In short, such a perfect one, on accomplishing himself in the fulfilment of Vedānta, comes to experience the diviner joys of the world of the dead even while he is among us in the mortal world!

ते ये शतं पितृणां चिरलोकलोकानामानन्दाः ।
स एक आजानजानां देवानामानन्दः ।
श्रोत्रियस्य चाकामहतस्य ॥५॥

te ye śataṁ pitṛṇām ciralokalokānāmānandāḥ,
sa eka ājānajānāṁ devānāmānandaḥ,
śrotriyasya cākāmahatasya. (5)

ते – those; ये – which; शतम् – hundred; पितृणाम् चिरलोक लोकानाम् – of the manes whose worlds are relatively immortal; आनन्दाः – bliss; सः – that worlds; एकः – (is) one; आजानजानाम् देवानाम् आनन्दः – bliss of the gods (named ājānaja) born in the deva loka; श्रोत्रियस्य च अकामहतस्य – (also of) one who is well versed in the Vedas and who is free from all desires

5. This joy of the manes[1], whose worlds are relatively immortal multiplied a hundredfold is one unit of joy of the ājānaja gods born in the deva loka and it is also the joy of a śrotriya free from desires.

ते ये शतमाजानजानां देवानामानन्दाः ।
स एकः कर्मदेवानां देवानामानन्दः ।
ये कर्मणा देवानपियन्ति ।
श्रोत्रियस्य चाकामहतस्य ॥६ ॥

te ye śataṁ-ājānajānāṁ devānām-ānandāḥ,
sa ekaḥ karma-devānāṁ devānāṁ-ānandaḥ,
ye karmaṇā devānapiyanti,
śrotriyasya cākāmahatasya. (6)

ते – those; ये – which; शतम् – hundred; आजानजानाम् देवानाम् – of the gods (named ājānaja) born in deva loka; आनन्दाः – bliss; सः – that; एकः – (is) one; कर्म देवानाम् देवानाम् आनन्दः – bliss of gods (named karma devas) who have become so by their special karmas; ये – who; कर्मणा – by special actions; देवान् – gods; अपि – also; यन्ति – attain; श्रोत्रियस्य च अकामहतस्य – one who is well versed in the Vedas and who is free from all desires

[1] As a reward for true and sincere ritualistic worship and moral living, a jīva attains the world of the manes, to enjoy therein for a time and to return again to the human womb. He is called the pitṛ.

6. This joy of the gods born in the deva loka[1] multiplied a hundredfold is a unit of joy of the gods (karma devas) who have become so by their special karmas and it is also the joy of a śrotriya, free from desires.

ते ये शतं कर्मदेवानां देवानामानन्दाः ।
स एको देवानामानन्दः । श्रोत्रियस्य चाकामहतस्य ॥७॥

te ye śataṁ karmadevānāṁ devānāmānandāḥ,
sa eko devānāmānandaḥ, śrotriyasya cākāmahatasya. (7)

ते – those; ये – which; शतम् – hundred; कर्म देवानाम् देवानाम् – of the gods who have become so by their special karmas; आनन्दाः – bliss; सः – that; एकः – one; देवानाम् आनन्दः – bliss of god; श्रोत्रियस्य च अकामहतस्य – (also) one who is well versed in the Vedas and who is free from all desires

7. A hundred times this joy of the gods (karma devas) who have become so by their special karmas is a unit of joy of the gods (office bearers) and it is also the measure of the bliss of the śrotriya who has transcended all his desires.

[1] Among them those who had performed hundred yajñas got a step higher to live as gods (deities) in charge of the heaven. Those who are thus born into this status as a result of their 'work' in the previous kalpa are 'ājānaja-devas' – the 'natives' of heaven. Those who reach there due to work of this kalpa are called terrestrial-devas i.e. 'karma-devas'.

ते ये शतं देवानामानन्दाः । स एक इन्द्रस्यानन्दः ।
श्रोत्रियस्य चाकामहतस्य ॥८ ॥

te ye śataṁ devānāmānandāḥ, sa eka indrasyānandaḥ,
śrotriyasya cākāmahatasya. (8)

ते – those; ये – which; शतम् – hundred; देवानाम् – of the gods; आनन्दाः – bliss; सः –that; एकः – (is) one; इन्द्रस्य आनन्दः – bliss of Indra; श्रोत्रियस्य च अकामहतस्य – (also of) one who is well versed in the Vedas and who is free from all desires

8. One hundred measures of the happiness of the gods (office bearers) is the simple unit of joy of Indra[1] and it is also the measure of the bliss of the śrotriya who has transcended all his desires.

ते ये शतमिन्द्रस्यानन्दाः ।
स एको बृहस्पतेरानन्दः ।
श्रोत्रियस्य चाकामहतस्य ॥९ ॥

te ye śatamindrasyānandāḥ,
sa eko bṛhaspaterānandaḥ,
śrotriyasya cākāmahatasya. (9)

ते – those; ये – which; शतम् – hundred; इन्द्रस्य – of the Indra; आनन्दाः – bliss; सः – that; एकः – (is) one; बृहस्पतेः आनन्दः – the

[1] The king of the gods, and naturally, more joy.

bliss of Bṛhaspati; श्रोत्रियस्य च अकामहतस्य – (also of) one who is well versed in the Vedas and who is free from all desires

9. A hundredfold the bliss of Indra is the unit of joy of Bṛhaspati[1] and it is also equal to the bliss of a śrotriya who is devoid of all desires.

ते ये शतं बृहस्पतेरानन्दाः ।
स एकः प्रजापतेरानन्दः ।
श्रोत्रियस्य चाकामहतस्य ॥१० ॥

te ye śataṁ bṛhaspaterānandāḥ,
sa ekaḥ prajāpaterānandaḥ,
śrotriyasya cākāmahatasya. (10)

ते – those; ये – which; शतम् – hundred; बृहस्पतेः– of Bṛhaspati; आनन्दाः – bliss; सः – that; एकः – (is) one; प्रजापतेः आनन्दः – the bliss of Prajāpati; श्रोत्रियस्य च अकामहतस्य – (also of) one who is well versed in the Vedas and who is free from all desires

10. A hundredfold the bliss of a Bṛhaspati is the unit of measure of the bliss of Prajāpati[2] and it also gives us a measure of the bliss enjoyed by a śrotriya who has no desires.

[1] The adviser and Guru of the gods.

[2] The father of all creatures. He is the Creator (sūtrātmā), and thus the greatest joy in the universe.

ते ये शतं प्रजापतेरानन्दाः ।
स एको ब्रह्मण आनन्दः ।
श्रोत्रियस्य चाकामहतस्य ॥११ ॥

te ye śataṁ prajāpaterānandāḥ,
sa eko brahmaṇa ānandaḥ,
śrotriyasya cākāmahatasya. (11)

ते – those; ये – which; शतम् – hundred; प्रजापतेः – of Prajāpati; आनन्दाः – bliss; सः – that; एकः – (is) one; ब्रह्मणः आनन्दः – Bliss of Brahman; श्रोत्रियस्य च अकामहतस्य – (also) one who is well versed in the Vedas and who is free from all desires

11. A hundredfold the bliss of Prajāpati is the unit of measure of the Bliss of Brahman, which is in no way greater than the bliss of one who is a śrotriya and who, in his experience of the Reality, is devoid of all other desires.

Continuing the entire list of comparative measurements of bliss, the teacher says, the bliss increases a hundredfold each time when we compare the manes to the 'native' gods of the heavens, the 'native' gods or karma devas to the gods (the celestial office bearers) in the heavens, and these gods of power and duty to Indra. The joy of Bṛhaspati is declared as hundredfold when it is compared to the bliss of Indra, and compared to the joy of Bṛhaspati, a hundredfold is the joy of Prajāpati. The Brahman, the Bliss Absolute, can be estimated as a hundred times the bliss of Prajāpati! The bliss of none of them is in any way more than the bliss lived by one who has truly studied the Upaniṣads at the sacred feet of a Realised

Saint and has himself experienced the theme indicated by the scripture and has, therefore, come to entertain no more any desire for the decaying finite objects of the body, mind and intellect.

It is indeed very difficult for us to understand these traditional beliefs. Especially us, who are strangers to such traditional declarations, it is impossible to swallow such ideas. We have not the faith of the olden days to believe in things because they have been handed down to us as sacred knowledge from the past. Revolt is the very essence of our life and we protest against anything that we cannot understand.

In this modern spirit, when I try to read, I can come to a certain understanding in my own which, I hope, will help you also in mentally comprehending the hierarchy of joys explained here. If we try to take a parallel from the political constitution and the social joys, I feel confident that you all will be able to understand this passage more clearly.

The joy of an Indian who is living today the active life of making history, is certainly greater than the joys of life enjoyed by an antiquated politician who lives in retirement, glorifying himself in the remembered joys of his own ancient success. They may be considered in this sample as the dead ones, living the joys after their death in their past world of activity, while enjoying today their retirement and pension. Indeed, a hundredfold more is the share of the joy of the native gods when they are compared with the manes.

We all know that the natives of a country cannot afford to live as extravagantly as a foreigner who has reached that country as an ambassador or representative of his government – a job generally given to a person by all wise governments not merely on consideration of relationships or on recommendations, but in recognition of his own achievements in his own country. The joys and comforts enjoyed by such a karmadeva is certainly hundredfold more than that of an average native of that county. This is the same, whether it is the life of the American ambassador in India or of the Indian ambassador in America.

The dignity and importance enjoyed by the cabinet ministers in a Republic are any day greater than those of the foreign ambassadors in that country. The devas meant here are the 33 great office bearers constituted of the 8 Vasus, 11 Rudras, 12 Ādityas, Indra and the Creator, the Prajāpati. Their joy is hundredfold more than those enjoyed by karma devas.

The bliss or satisfaction of the President or the Prime Minister of any country, we all know, must be greater in his own country than any of the members of the cabinet – Indra's joy is a hundredfold that enjoyed by the karma devas.

The power and satisfaction enjoyed by legislature or by the 'brain-trust' of any country that decides the policy for the Head of the State to follow strictly, must be greater than the freedom enjoyed by the Head of the State himself. This joy of Bṛhaspati, the preceptor of the devas, is a hundred times the joy of Indra himself.

The joy of Prajāpati is estimated here as hundred times the joys of Bṛhaspati. The Creator, the total mind and intellect of all living beings, celestial and terrestrial, is Prajāpati. The mind and intellect being the instruments with which we enjoy all the possible bliss in life, the total mind-intellect must at once be enjoying all the joys of all the people, at all times and in all places.

The Bliss Absolute is thus slowly and steadily indicated as hundred times more than the joy of Prajāpati.

In all these cases it has been definitely indicated that one who is well versed in the content of the scriptures, and who has, in his own personal experience, come to live the Reality pointed out by Vedānta, will come to enjoy a Bliss in no way less than that of Brahman. The chapter started, you remember, with a declaration that 'the knower of Brahman attains the Supreme' and this Supreme has been discussed as the Bliss Absolute, indicated by the definition 'Satyam, Jñānam, and Anantam.'

Again, in this chapter, in describing the cause for the creation of the world, the ṛṣi explains that the Ātman in us came to entertain a desire. Desire is the cause for the creation of the pluralistic world which gives us the agitations of the mind and the consequent individual shares unhappiness. When, even to a degree, the cause is removed, to that degree the effects are also eliminated and, naturally, the Bliss which is our essential nature manifests Itself.

Thus, the state of perfection is the state of desirelessness – a state wherein the individual is no more a victim of his desires, but a master of them. The desires in themselves cannot enslave us; in themselves they are helpless and impotent. They can chain and enslave us only when we subscribe ourselves to remain victims under their thrones. This self-redemption from our own inner desires is the self-mastery that culminates in Self-realisation. To the degree one has given up one's desires, to that degree his joys increase and in his experience he comes to attune himself with the perfect joy of the Absolute.

This is indicated when the Upaniṣad says here that the celestial joy of the gods, even of the Creator, is the same as the joys of a mortal Man of Wisdom who has come to realise his own essential divinity and has, therefore, come to drop all his sensuous desires for the finite world of objects.

स यश्चायं पुरुषे यश्चासावादित्ये स एकः ।
स य एवंवित् अस्माल्लोकात्प्रेत्य ।
एतमन्नमयमात्मानमुपसङ्क्रामति ।
एतं प्राणमयमात्मानमुपसङ्क्रामति ।
एतं मनोमयमात्मानमुपसङ्क्रामति ।
एतं विज्ञानमयमात्मानमुपसङ्क्रामति ।
एतमानन्दमयमात्मानमुपसङ्क्रामति ।
तदप्येष श्लोको भवति ॥१२ ॥

sa yaścāyaṁ puruṣe yaścāsāvāditye sa ekaḥ
sa ya evaṁvit asmāllokātpretya,
etamannamayamātmānamupasaṅkrāmati,
etaṁ prāṇamayamātmānamupasaṅkrāmati
etaṁ manomayamātmānamupasaṅkrāmati,
etaṁ vijñānamayamātmānamupasaṅkrāmati,
etamānandamayamātmānamupasaṅkrāmati,
tadapyeṣa śloko bhavati. (12)

सः – that; यः – which; च – and; अयम् – this; पुरुषे – in man; यः – which च – and; असौ – that; आदित्ये – in the sun; सः – that; एकः – is one; सः – he; यः – who; एवंवित् – knows thus; अस्मात् लोकात् – from this world; प्रेत्य – leaving; एतम् – this; अन्नमयम् आत्मानम् – Ātman made of food; उपसङ्क्रामति – next attains (crosses over); एतम् – this; प्राणमयम् आत्मानम् – Ātman made of prāṇa; उपसङ्क्रामति – next attains (crosses over); एतम् –this; मनोमयम् आत्मानम् – Ātman made of mind; उपसङ्क्रामति – attains next (crosses over); एतम् – this; विज्ञानमयम् आत्मानम् – Ātman made of knowledge; उपसङ्क्रामति – attains (crosses over); एतम् – this; आनन्दमयम् आत्मानम् – Ātman made of bliss; उपसङ्क्रामति – next attains; तत् – about that; अपि – also; एषः – this; श्लोकः – verse; भवति – there is

12. The Reality in the core of man and the Reality which is in the sun are one. He who knows this, on leaving from this world, first attains the Ātman made of food, next the Ātman made of prāṇa, next attains the Ātman made of mind , next attains Ātman made of buddhi and lastly attains the Ātman made of Bliss.... regarding this there is the following Vaidika verse.

This state of desirelessness by which an individual comes to experience the greatest sense of fulfilment and bliss is not attainable merely through an accidental windfall of Īśvara kṛpā or through any hard earned wealth of Guru's grace. Neither the number of years that one has remained in the jungle nor the amount of sacrifice one has made, nor the number of pilgrimages one has undertaken, nor even the number of yajñas one has performed – none of these has any direct bearing upon this perfect state of desirelessness and its achievement.

The only method by which one can establish oneself in this state of transcendental perfection is by experiencing for oneself this oneness with the entire universe. On realising the spiritual centre within ourselves, we come to experience immediately that the spiritual centre everywhere, in all things and beings is one and the same. There are no two Realities such as one within us and one without us. The divine Absolute is one and the same within our bosom as well as everywhere in the cosmos. This idea is nowhere so beautifully brought out as it has been done here when the ṛṣi says that the essence in us is the essence in the sun. But unless we are initiated into the secret of its suggestions, we are apt to misunderstand this statement as a philosophical exaggeration which has no real pith in it.

Each one of us is certainly the centre of our own individual world of experience. The sun, we all know, is the centre of the entire cosmos. Therefore, to say that the spiritual centre in us is the spiritual centre in the sun, is to express the oneness of the spiritual Truth everywhere in its absolute divine nature. To rediscover this 'Truth of advaita' within ourselves as our 'real Nature' is to reach the peak of evolution, the goal of our life. When we end all our futile ramblings along the by-lanes of our desires, and our swinging between the worlds of the dead and the living, comes to a halt.

Just as on reaching the evolution of 'man' our world is no more riddled with the desires of the fishes or of the birds, of the ape-man or of the barbarian, but we entertain only our own desires, and to that extent we can say that we have released ourselves from those desires; so too, on culminating our evolutionary pilgrimage and re-entering into our essential nature of Godhood, we get ourselves naturally released from all other worldly desires – desires for the acquisition or enjoyment of the sensuous objects which, in fact, can give but some temporary satisfaction for certain nervous itchings!

An individual who thus realises the Spirit in him as the spiritual centre in the sun also realises that he is himself at once the centre that controls and experiences, the 'circle' of his own world and also the centre defined by the sun that holds together, blesses and vitalises the entire 'circle of the cosmos.'

On this realisation of the Truth, the individual comes to rise above the ordinary mortal world, riddled with its own imperfections, fleshy demands for sensuous happiness and ephemeral wealth and glory. Therefore, it is said here, 'after leaving from this world'. This expression does not mean after the individual has died away, it only means, after having lifted himself from his ordinary and instinctive worldly activities and thoughts. Before the dawn of Knowledge, man, in his misunderstanding of himself, had behaved towards the world in a peculiar attitude of attachment, through which he created a life of tussles and agitations caused by the pairs of opposites such as love and hatred, heat and cold, success and failure, joys and sorrows, profit and loss, health and illness. In short, life and death in all its implications. On realising the real nature of the spiritual centre in him, the individual, as it were, has awakened to the realisation that, as the Conscious Principle, he is but the illuminator of the entire world of objects, and that the world can cause agitation only in the mind and intellect.

The Consciousness lends life to the body, mind and intellect to perceive, feel and think all its sorrows and joys. In the realisation that 'I am that Consciousness', the Man of Wisdom comes to transcend his limited small world of 'I'-ness and 'my'-ness in the physical debilities, in the mental constructions and in the intellectual limitations. It is this transcendence of the pettiness of the mortal and its evolution into the transcendental to assume its own dignity, and to live the glory of Godhood that is meant here by 'after leaving from this world'.

There are some schools of thinkers, who do not accept the state of complete Liberation while living in this body (jīvanmukti), but only accept the idea that complete and full

Liberation from the clutches of mortality can be attained and the infinite experience gained only when dead from this life (videhamukti). Śaṅkara is a staunch supporter of the former point of view and his arguments indeed weigh with anyone who is a sincere student of the śāstra, not only in the library, but also in the laboratory. More of his arguments on this point we will be giving, when we discuss the same mantra again, as it is repeated at the end of the textbook.

We have no belief in or use for the promise of a posthumous perfection, which we may, after our death, come to enjoy. Unlike the semitic religions, Vedānta is not satisfied by merely promising a post-mortem discovery of the Divine. Being practical men, the Āryans demanded and worked for redemption, a sure and certain redemption, here and now. This is clear from the words that follow in the Śruti. Following the expression, 'after leaving from this world', the Śruti, as it were, comments upon her own terms very elaborately.

She points out that a seeker, who has come to experience his oneness with the spiritual centre in the cosmos has also experienced a slow and steady transcendence of his false and delusory identifications with the five sheaths. He realises, stage by stage, the Self made of food, the Self made of prāṇa, the Self made of mind, the Self made of intellect and the Self made of Bliss, at the transcendence of which, he comes to live and experience the pure attributeless Self which has been described (in section vii) as 'the Brahman, who is invisible, incorporeal, undefined and abodeless'.

This courageous declaration is not an independent intellectual hypothesis of the ṛṣis but it is fully supported by the Vaidika declarations and entirely endorsed by the ṛṣī's own subjective experience. The Vedamantra is quoted in the following section.

Section ix – अनुवाकः ९

Knower of Brahman Is Fearless Concluding Śāntipāṭha

यतो वाचो निवर्तन्ते अप्राप्य मनसा सह ।
आनन्दं ब्रह्मणो विद्वान् न बिभेति कुतश्चनेति ॥१॥

yato vāco nivartante aprāpya manasā saha,
ānandaṁ brahmaṇo vidvān na bibheti kutaścaneti. (1)

यतः – from which; वाचः – all words; निवर्तन्ते – return; अप्राप्य – without reaching; मनसा सह – along with the mind; आनन्दम् – Bliss; ब्रह्मणः – of Brahman; विद्वान् – the one who knows; न बिभेति – is not afraid; कुतश्चन – of anything; इति – thus

1. He who knows the Bliss of Brahman, from which all words return without reaching It, together with the mind, is no more afraid of anything.

While describing the mental sheath in this chapter (Section iv) the same Vedamantra was declared by the Master, there to indicate infinite possibilities of the mind. Here, the same mantra is repeated to suggest its native import, explaining the transcendental nature of the Self, and to show how speech cannot define, nor the mind feel, nor the intellect completely comprehend the Self, which is the eternal subject.[1]

एतगूंह वाव न तपति ।
किमहगूंसाधु नाकरवम् ।
किमहं पापमकरवमिति ।
स य एवं विद्वानेते आत्मानगूं स्पृणुते ।
उभे ह्येवैष एते आत्मानगूंस्पृणुते ।
य एवं वेद । इत्युपनिषत् ॥२॥

etagṁ-ha vāva na tapati,
kimahagṁ-sādhu nākaravam,
kimahaṁ pāpam-akaravamiti,
sa ya evaṁ vidvānete ātmānagṁ spṛṇute,
ubhe hyevaiṣa ete ātmānagṁ-spṛṇute,
ya evaṁ veda, ityupaniṣat. (2)

एतगम् – such (thoughts); ह – of course; वाव – certainly; न तपति – does not distress; किम् – why; अहम् – I, साधु – good; न अकरवम् – I have not done; किम् –why; अहम् – I; पापम् –sins; अकरवम् – I have committed; इति – thus; सः – he; यः – who; एवम् – this; विद्वान् – the knower; एते – these; आत्मानगम् – the Ātman; स्पृणुते – regards; उभे – both; हि एव एषः – verily this thus; एते – these; आत्मानम् – as Ātman; स्पृणुते – knows; यः – who; एवम् – thus (ends); वेद – realises, knows; इति – thus so; उपनिषत् – Upaniṣad

[1] For details see chapter II, section iv, Pg. 176 to 180

2. Such thoughts 'Why have I not done what is good? Why have I committed a sin?' certainly do not come to distress a man of experience of the Truth. He who knows thus, regards both these as the Ātman. Verily, both these are regarded by him who knows thus, as only Ātman. Thus ends the Upaniṣad.

The joys of virtues and the sorrows of sin, are both conditions of the mind when it comes to react between specific circumstances in the outer world and the particular intellectual conditions within. The same set of circumstances in the outer world may not necessarily prove to be a sin to all people; the intellectual composition being different from person to person, the required mental structure for a tortuous sin-experience will not be created. An act which is considered as cruelty or a sin in one part of the world does not become so poignant and sinful in another part of the world, where they believe differently, since their customs and conditions have wrapped them of a different texture in their intellectual standard.

When an individual grows in his knowledge, many of his instinct motivated actions fall off the grace, and the chances are that he is rendered totally and completely incapable of doing any more sin. He is no more in his egocentric self, arrogating unto himself a false personality as body or any of the five sheaths. It is only when we come to believe ourselves to be the matter vestures that we are tempted to perpetrate immoral acts for the purposes of procuring, maintaining and preserving sense objects in the vain hope that thereby we will be able to experience a greater happiness and a fuller sense of fulfilment.

Apart from the fact that a Man of Wisdom and Perfection will not misbehave or come to act sinfully, such an entity, in his realisation of his oneness with the Conscious Principle of life within himself, comes to live fully the truth that his body, mind and intellect all belong to the outer world of objects other than his own Self. The sun is not soiled by the blood of a murder scene that he happens to illumine, nor does he become glorious and sanctified by illumining an auspicious ritual in another part of the world. The illuminator is always separate from that which he illuminates. And, the illuminated cannot condition the illuminator. The mental thoughts and intellectual conditions do not in any way limit the glory of the Conscious Principle which illuminates both these sheaths. Consciousness in us is the factor that illuminates both the concepts; of sin and virtue in our mind.

It is in this sense that it is said here that a Man of Realisation does not get flustered at any commissions or omissions in his life.

His freedom does not mean freedom from unethical and immoral acts. The Christian missionary, in his stupendous ignorance, often because of his perverted enthusiasm to misinterpret all other sacred scriptures – as if that is the only method known to him for glorifying his own scripture – has been complaining that the ideals of Vedānta takes the wind away from all initiative in living an ethical and moral life. This misunderstanding shoots high of their own ignorance, for I do not believe that they are victims of an incapacity to see eye to eye, with the great scripture.

The perfection of the Hindu religion reaches such eminence in the Upaniṣads and the ṛṣi feels so much confidence in the Man of Realisation as explained in Vedānta that he declares that such a perfect man is beyond the bounds of all rules and that he, in his perfect tuning with the Infinite, is incapable of producing even a single wrong note, when he plays upon the lyre of life. What he does is thereafter the ethical and moral standard for his generation to follow. Even the Vedas are but a compendium of how such Men of Perfection thought, felt and acted under various circumstances.

Since such a Master always lives in unison with the infinite Consciousness, thereafter, neither his external actions, nor his feelings nor his thoughts, can ever go false in their beat. No false step is possible in a dancer so long as the accompaniments are rhythmic and true. We have in our mythology many stories to illustrate this idea. Great sages like Durvāsa, though established in their own Self, now and then, as it were, propelled by some power extraneous to them, got themselves bumped into the world outside and identifying themselves with that passing saṅkalpa (willing) they cursed one or blessed another. We find in the mythology that in the long run all such curses have invariably come to bless either the individual concerned or through him, often, the entire era and its generation.

When a radio is fully tuned up to a particular station, all music that it can sing for the time being is the song that is sung at that moment in the broadcasting room of that station. Similarly, when a Man of Perfection is living in the Lord, in divine unison with the Infinite, his mind and intellect cannot come to entertain any selfish or ego-motivated false feelings. Whatever be the thought that might rise up in his mind, it can only be the reflection of the thought in the total mind. When the thought in that sage finds an expression in the outer world it may immediately bring about a positive blessing or may bring the blessing after a period of chaos and crisis.

In his total self-effacement, and therefore, of all vanities as agent or actor, enjoyer or sufferer, the sage remains ever a witness of his own thoughts, motives and actions. Such an individual is fully freed from the shackles of his thoughts, from the chains of his egoism, in short, from the prison house of his ignorance, in his effulgence and transcendental wisdom, he becomes perfectly detached both from sin and from virtue. The entire 'Dharma Śāstra', expounding and explaining, describing and enforcing moral and ethical rules for an individual life and collective existence, is a compilation of the close observations made upon the behavior of such men of studies (śrotriyas) who are well-established in the experience of the Reality (Brahmaniṣṭha).

Here ends the Upaniṣad – In the Vaidika days, Vedas were chanted and remembered and not printed and preserved. Today we see the Veda, while the children of the ṛṣis heard the Veda. They, in those days, chanted and repeated the Veda; we, today, read and forget the Veda!! Literature and its style, its sanctity and its mode of use have all been changed with the invention of the printing press. Therefore, there must be a subtle difference in the techniques of the study when the textbook is in hand and when the textbook is at hand. The method of instructions followed by the ṛṣis was the method of chanting and repeating, and therefore, the end of a chapter is to be indicated in the very closing words of the chapter. In a printed book it is sufficient if we see with our eyes that a new chapter has started or that an old chapter has ended with a short thick line.

While repeating by mouth, an end of a section or the chapter is to be clearly marked out by a direct statement of it: 'Here ends the Upaniṣad'. The philosophical portion of the entire *Taittirīya* text is contained in its second chapter and the ṛṣi here says that this important portion, where the Supreme is indicated through a definition and a plan of Realisation narrated, has come to a close.

The term Upaniṣad is here used to indicate the textbook, discussing Brahmavidyā, through which the finite mortal man comes to rediscover himself to be the spiritual infinite Reality.

The more popular and direct meaning of the word Upaniṣad has already been explained. There we said that it was a word made up of the root ṣad (to sit) prefixed by two indeclinable upa (near) and ni (in the lower seat). The word Upaniṣad gives us an idea of that literature or knowledge which is to be gained by sitting near and at the feet of a Master.

But the word sad has three different imports such as: vīśāraṇam meaning to pulverise: avasādanam or atyanta nāśam, to totally end, and gati which means to lead or to guide. Reconsidering the word Upaniṣad and its native three meanings of the suffix ṣad, we get three implied meanings in Upaniṣad.

(a) By a correct study of the Upaniṣad and by following the values of life preached and the practices of self-development prescribed therein, we can get away from our false misunderstandings in our life and consequently 'pulverise' all our fears of limitations, dreads of the finitude and sorrows of mortality.

(b) On experiencing the goal indicated in the Upaniṣad to be our real nature, we once forever get so fully redeemed from all our identifications with our finite body, mind and intellect that we come to end forever (atyantanāśa) the sorrows of life and death in us.

(c) The instructions in the text lead us or guide us through the corridors of our personality and help us to rediscover in the Sanctum Sanctorum of our life, the infinite Reality. Therefore, the textbook is called the Upaniṣad.

Śaṅkarācārya says that the knowledge in the book pulverises ignorance and ends absolutely the experiences of finitude. Since it guides us away from the plurality to the vision of the oneness, the very textbook has come to be named as the Upaniṣad.

ॐ सह नाववतु । सह नौ भुनक्तु ।
सहवीर्यं करवावहै
तेजस्विनावधीतमस्तु मा विद्विषावहै ॥
ॐ शान्तिः शान्तिः शान्तिः ॥३॥

oṁ saha nāvavatu, saha nau bhunaktu,
sahavīryaṁ karavāvahai
tejasvināvadhītamastu mā vidviṣāvahai.
oṁ śāntiḥ śāntiḥ śāntiḥ. (3)

ॐ – symbol of the Para Brahman; सह – together; नौ – us both; अवतु – may He protect; सह – together; नौ – us both; भुनक्तु – may He look after (the fruits of scriptural study); सह – together; वीर्यम् – put in effort (with enthusiasm); करवावहै – exert together (to find the true meaning of sacred texts); तेजस्वि – brilliant; नौ – of both of us; अधीतम् – study; अस्तु – may be; मा – never; विद्विषावहै – (may we two) quarrel
ॐ – om; शान्तिः – peace; शान्तिः – peace; शान्तिः – peace

Om. May He protect us both. May He help us both to enjoy the fruits of the scriptural study. May we both exert together to find the true meaning of the sacred text. May our studies make us brilliant. May we never quarrel with each other.

Om Peace! Peace! Peace!

The peace-invocation is chanted daily both by the teacher and the taught. This not only tunes up each mentally for the study and the discourse, but it also helps each to be in unison with the other.

Any constriction of heart in either of them towards the other will screen off the flow of light and love between them. Unless there are the unseen beams of mutual love and respect, the reverence and admiration connecting the thrilled heart of the inspired Saint and the thirsty head of the sincere students, no actual transaction of Truth-experience can take place. Upaniṣad being a subjective science, these adjustments are unavoidable.

In the Vedānta classroom, the teacher writes with words on the heart slabs of the boys; the students read the golden letters of knowledge in the light of kindling love and understand them with a 'head' peeping out of their 'heart'. In the still moments of its silent inspirations, in quick and brilliant flashes, the boy experiences the Truth transcendental.

Hence the chanting of peace passage both in the beginning and in the end of each chapter and each day.

Here ends Brahmānanda-vallī

Chapter III

Bhṛgu-vallī

Introduction

In the last chapter, which contains the entire philosophical discussion in this Upaniṣad, we were told in the very opening mantra that to realise and experience the supreme Brahman, 'Satyam, Jñānam, Anantam' is the goal of life, the destination of man, the fulfilment of evolution, the ascent of man to Godhood. Thereafter naturally, the teacher had to give an explanation of how from the infinite Truth, man descended, stage by stage, to become what he is; sad and sorrowful, bound and belaboured, a glorious God chained by himself to a hell created by himself! From the Supreme, the five great elements came and out of the grossest element, earth, came food and from food man was born. Analysing the various personality layers in man, we were told of five great sheaths, each subtler than the other, beneath which lies the Truth as substratum for the entire hallucination. The question whether the Reality is a non-existent, non-entity or an existent experienceable factor was also discussed. In order to show that It is an existent factor, we were told how It is the law giver, fearing whom the phenomenal world strictly obeys the laws of nature. Also we were told how that pure infinite Consciousness is 'full of rasa'. The statistics of joy emphasised here is that one who is devoid of desires comes to experience the Supreme. It was explained that out of the Supreme, five great elements came up because 'He desired'. The end of desire is the end of creation.

The philosophical ideas and ideals, however complete, would not, in themselves, give an appetising satisfaction to the serious and energetic students of the ṛṣi days when they always judged the quality of the philosophy from its practical application. Unless the philosophy could be realised, they declared it as impotent poetry fit only for old mothers to sing as a song of lullaby.

Therefore, there was an urgent need felt to indicate that the techniques of realisation suggested in philosophy were all practical and that any student can reach the same goal if only he can follow the instructions therein.

For this purpose the ṛṣi of the *Taittirīya-upaniṣad* provides us with the third and the last chapter in which a student and a teacher are brought together, face to face. We are shown how, on the instructions of the teacher, the student, through the path of correct analysis and deep meditation, is able to undress himself of his matter clothings and rediscover himself to be the Self in all Its naked glory and Godly Perfection. Here in this chapter we have Bhṛgu, a youngster approaching his own father, Varuṇa the teacher, with a humble request to initiate him into the knowledge of Brahman, the substratum for the pluralistic phenomenal world.

Peace-invocation

Śāntipātha

ॐ सह नाववतु। सह नौ भुनक्तु।
सहवीर्यं करवावहै
तेजस्विनावधीतमस्तु मा विद्विषावहै॥
ॐ शान्तिः शान्तिः शान्तिः॥१॥

om saha nāvavatu, saha nau bhunaktu,
sahavīryaṁ karavāvahai
tejasavināvadhītamastu mā vidviṣāvahai.
om śāntiḥ śāntiḥ śāntiḥ. (1)

ॐ – symbol of the Para Brahman; सह – together; नौ – us both; अवतु – may He protect; सह – together; नौ – us both; भुनक्तु – may He help us enjoy (the fruits of scriptural study); सह – together; वीर्यम् – with enthusiasm; करवावहै – exert together (to find the true meaning of sacred texts); तेजस्वि – brilliant; नौ – of both of us; अधीतम् – study; अस्तु – may be; मा – never; विद्विषावहै – may we two quarrel
ॐ – om; शान्तिः – peace; शान्तिः – peace; शान्तिः – peace

Om. May He protect us both. May He help us both to enjoy the fruits of scriptural study. May we both exert together to find the true meaning of the sacred text. May our studies make us brilliant. May we never quarrel with each other.

Om Peace! Peace! Peace!

Since we have exhaustively discussed the peace invocation earlier in the textbook, it is not proposed to repeat the same again here[1].

[1] Refer pages 142-144

Section i – अनुवाकः १

Bhṛgu Approaches His Father Varuṇa With A Request To Teach Him Brahman

भृगुर्वै वारुणिः वरुणं पितरनुपससार
अधीहि भगवो ब्रह्मेति । तस्मा एतत्प्रोवाच ।
अन्नं प्राणं चक्षुः श्रोत्रं मनो वाचमिति ॥२ ॥

bhṛgurvai vāruṇiḥ varuṇaṁ pitaramupasasāra
adhīhi bhagavo brahmeti, tasmā etatprovāca,
annaṁ prāṇaṁ cakṣuḥ śrotraṁ mano vācamiti. (2)

भृगुः – bhṛgu; वै – the well known; वारुणिः – son of Varuṇa; वरुणम् – unto Varuṇa; पितरम् – his father; उपससार – reached; अधीहि – teach me; भगवः – Bhagavān, O Revered Sir; ब्रह्म – (what is) Brahman; इति – thus; तस्मै – to him; एतत् – this; प्रोवाच – said; अन्नम् – food; प्राणम् – prāṇa; चक्षुः – the eyes; श्रोत्रम् – the ears; मनः – the mind; वाचम् – the speech; इति – thus (are all Brahman)

1. Bhṛgu, the well known son of Varuṇa, approached his father, Varuṇa and requested, "O revered Sir, teach me Brahman". Varuṇa said, thus, to him (Bhṛgu), "Food, prāṇa, the eyes, the ears, the mind and the speech – are Brahman".

The scene opens here; its narration is done in dots and dashes and has the beauty of shorthand writing; one who knows its language can read it in full. Similarly, those who have got a sympathetic intellect – an intellect that revels and works in 'love heart' – can very easily peep through the trellis of these few strokes and discover very clearly behind it all, a young boy of enthusiasm, with all humbleness and meek surrender, approaching his own father and after due prostration, in a choked voice of reverence and adoration, murmurs his great desire: 'Show me, O Lord, the nature of Reality'.

The smile of satisfaction on the face of the Guru, when he meets a sincere student, adds colour to the entire picture. The father forgets for the moment that Bhṛgu is his own son, and yet, with more than fatherly love, he embraces the disciple in his silent gaze of evaluation and 'drinks him to the bottom of the heart'! Varuṇa answers that the entire world of objects is nothing other than the 'Subject' expressing Itself.

In order to emphasise the idea that everything in the world of objects had risen from the transcendental Divine, the teacher enumerates that Brahman is 'food, prāṇa, eyes, ears, mind and speech'. In saying so, the Master means that Brahman indicates the Truth which is the common substratum for all the manifestations in the universe. The wave, the ripple, the foam, the lather – all of them are the ocean. The bangles, the chain, the ear-stud, the nose rings – all of them are nothing but gold. Similarly, here, the Master is trying to indicate the Truth through its manifestations. In order that the student may not have even a trace of doubt about what the teacher meant, he is very careful that his enumeration is exhaustive and scientifically quite appropriate.

Annam and Prāṇa: – the word 'food' indicates the entire world of matter, which can be assimilated and used for the preservation of the living creatures, and prāṇa means all the vitality that is exhibited by all the living creatures in the entire universe.

Eyes and Ears: – These two indicate all the sense organs of perception, and so, if the first two terms indicated the entire world of objects, these express the world of the subject starting with the body.

Mind and Speech: – Mind is the receiving station which absorbs the perceptions received through the five gateways of knowledge, and again, it is the mind that conveys the instructions and decisions of the intellect to the muscles concerned. And it is these transactions that really denote life. So, by the word mind, all our activities are indicated. Speech is representative of all our organs of action. Speech is specially mentioned because it is through speech that we hear and come to understand the great cultural truths of our country as explained in the Upaniṣads; and again, it is through speech that we convey the same truth to others. Study of the Truth and its dissemination are the duties of every Hindu. This has been emphasised from the beginning and, as such, speech here stands not only for the organs of action in the physical sense of the terms, but it also represents all our cultural, religious and spiritual efforts.

All these together constitute the Reality. The differentiations are all a deluded plurality that has been superimposed upon the Reality. The head, the neck, the trunk, the long legs, the thin hands, the tapering fingers, the protruding eyes, the grinning face and so on, of the ghost are nothing but the innocent post. Similarly, the entire world of phenomena that now grins at us as a belligerent army of objects, is nothing but a superimposition upon the Truth.

Having thus given this rough definition and ready estimate of Truth, the teacher observes on the face of the student a complete dissatisfaction; Bhṛgu was a seeker of erudition and scholarship; he was a true Hindu who wanted to bring about the divine transformation within himself! Practical minded as he was, the above explanation of a general scientific definition did not satisfy him and noting this look of dissatisfaction in the boy, the teacher continues:

तगुंहोवाच । यतो वा इमानि भूतानि जायन्ते ।
येन जातानि जीवन्ति । यत्प्रयन्त्यभिसंविशन्ति ।
तद्विजिज्ञासस्व । तद् ब्रह्मेति । स तपोऽतप्यत ।
स तपस्तप्त्वा ॥३॥

tagṁhovāca, yato vā imāni bhūtāni jāyante,
yena jātāni jīvanti, yatprayantyabhisaṁviśanti,
tadvijijñāsasva, tad brahmeti, sa tapo'tapyata,
sa tapastaptvā. (3)

तगुं – to him; ह – (then) indeed; उवाच – said; यतः – that from which; वै – indeed; इमानि – all these; भूतानि – beings; जायन्ते – are born; येन – that by which; जातानि – having been born; जीवन्ति – live; यत् – that into which; प्रयन्ति – departing; अभिसंविशन्ति – enter; तत् – that; विजिज्ञासस्व – seek thou to know; तत् – that (is); ब्रह्म – Brahman; इति – thus; सः – he; तपः – penance; अतप्यत – performed; सः – he; तपः – penance; तप्त्वा – having performed

2. To him (Bhṛgu) he (Varuṇa) again said: "that from which these beings are born; that by which, having been born, these beings live and continue to exist; and that into which, when departing, they all enter; that seekest thou to know. That is Brahman". He, (Bhṛgu) performed penance; and after having done penance.......

Herein we have the most scientific definition of Brahman or the ultimate Reality. The Reality behind a wave can never be more exhaustively explained than that from which it has arisen, in which it exists and into which it dissolves itself. The cause of all effects is that from which all effects arise; and during their existence, the cause continues to support the effects and into the cause, the effects merge, when they end their separate existence as effects. Thus, the fundamental cause and the support of the entire pluralistic world is indicated by Varuṇa as the Truth defined by the word Brahman.

A mere definition however philosophical it might be, would not have been accepted by the true Hindu in Bhṛgu, for, to him no philosophy was acceptable unless it is practicable. Without the technique, a mere blabbering of the highest ideals will not make a satisfactory philosophy to the Hindu mind. And at the same time, the student is not in a hurry to reject a philosophy just because the philosophic Truth is too big for him to swallow.

True to this spirit, the student retires, as it were, from the presence of the Guru and performs tapas. Tapas does not mean the kind of physical sufferings which have been popularised by the mythological literature in our country. In Vedānta, tapas is considered only as a discipline of the mind. 'Deep concentration of the mind is the highest tapas' according to the subtlest interpretation of the word. Therefore, here Bhṛgu retired to a quiet place and through his steady contemplations, meditated upon the definition and tried to discover what the Brahman could be, as per the teacher's definition.

When he had contemplated sufficiently long, Bhṛgu came to certain decisions which seemingly satisfied him for the time being. But, when his fiery intellect, purified and sharpened for the purpose, was brought in contact with his conclusions, they seemed to melt themselves away as mist at the touch of sunlight. Therefore, he felt himself confused. The next section explains his initial conclusions, and his doubts that followed. Naturally, he runs to the Guru again and again.

Section ii – अनुवाकः २

Food Is Brahman

अन्नं ब्रह्मेति व्यजानात्
अन्नाद्ध्येव खल्विमानि भूतानि जायन्ते ।
अन्नेन जातानि जीवन्ति ।
अन्नं प्रयन्त्यभिसंविशन्तीति ।
तद्विज्ञाय पुनरेव वरुणं पितरमुपससार ।
अधीहि भगवो ब्रह्मेति । तगूंहोवाच ।
तपसा ब्रह्म विजिज्ञासस्व । तपो ब्रह्मेति ।
स तपोऽतप्यत । स तपस्तप्त्वा ॥१ ॥

annaṁ brahmeti vyajānāt,
annāddhyeva khalvimāni bhūtāni jāyante,
annena jātāni jīvanti,
annaṁ prayantyabhisaṁviśantīti,
tadvijñāya punareva varuṇaṁ pitaramupasasāra,
adhīhi bhagavo brahmeti, tagṁ-hovāca,
tapasā brahma vijijñāsasva, tapo brahmeti,
sa tapo'tapyata, sa tapastaptvā. (1)

अन्नम् – food; ब्रह्म इति – as Brahman; व्यजानात् – understood; अन्नात् – indeed from food; हि – indeed; एव – alone; खलु – certainly; इमानि – all these; भूतानि – beings; जायन्ते – are born; अन्नेन – by food; जातानि – having been born; जीवन्ति – live; अन्नम् – into food; प्रयन्ति – on departing; अभिसंविशन्ति – enter; इति – thus; तत् – that;

विज्ञाय – having understood; पुनः एव – again; वरुणम् – unto Varuṇa; पितरम् – his father; उपससार – approached; अधीहि – teach me; भगवः – O! Revered Sir; ब्रह्म इति – what is Brahman; तम् – to him; ह – then; उवाच – said; तपसा – by penance; ब्रह्म – Brahman; विजिज्ञासस्व – seek thou to know; तपः – penance; ब्रह्म – is Brahman; इति – thus; सः – he; तपः – penance; अतप्यत – performed; सः – he; तपः – penance; तप्त्वा – having performed

1. Bhṛgu learnt that food is Brahman because it is from food that all these beings are born; by food, when born, do they live and having departed, into food they enter. Having known that, he approached his father Varuṇa, and said: "Revered Sir, teach me Brahman". Varuṇa told him: "By deep thinking (tapas) seek thou to know Brahman. Tapas is Brahman". He performed tapas and having performed tapas ......

As a result of his initial thoughts, he came to the conclusion that food is the material cause of the world of names and forms. To Bhṛgu food was Brahman because food has the distinctive marks of Brahman. All living creatures are born of food. They continue to exist in food and when they disintegrate at their death, whether they be the most revered and the sacred of the prophets of the age or the most insignificant of the worms, they have all to go to the world of matter made up of calcium, carbon, phosphorus and so on. The physical body made up of the five great elements have all to go back to the five elements when life and its warmth depart from the structures.

Though superficially there is for food the look of Reality, as the cause for the world of matter to exist, matter has a positive beginning and an end. It is ever changing. A changing factor cannot be the ultimate Reality. The Supreme, pointed out by the term Brahman, is the changeless substratum upon which all changes are made possible. But the world of food is ever changing and the only permanence about it is the truth that it will change on!! Therefore, Bhṛgu was not satisfied, and so he again approached his father, Varuṇa.

On being thus approached and when the student repeated the same request as before: 'Teach me Brahman', the teacher understood exactly what the trouble was. Instead of directly guiding him, which would have been an intellectual interference, he was encouraged to do more intense and poignant thinking. The teacher refused to 'bomb' the disciple with any Truth experienced in his own personal realisation. The teacher wanted the student to discover for himself the Real and the Eternal.

All that the teacher does is to encourage the student to get up again on to his feet and learn to climb a few steps higher. Thus teacher only repeats what he had already explained; 'Know the Reality through continued application of right thinking'. In order to emphasise the idea, that realisation as explained in Vedānta is the fulfilment of the path of right thinking and deep meditation, the teacher here says: 'Penance is Brahman'. The means are generally indicated as the goal itself when the means are directly connected with the goal. This is often employed in our conversation: 'Ghee is long life,' meaning, ghee (clarified butter) gives good health and assures a profitable long life.

The Bangalore Road starts verily in Madras is so called because if consistently pursued, it will directly take us to Bangalore.

Similarly, concentrated right thinking called 'Tapas', itself is called Brahman. We ordinarily say: 'We are baking bread'. Bread, as such, need not be baked, bread is the end product of baking dough yet while baking we say it is bread that we are baking.

The boy, unwhetted, in his enthusiasm, plunged again into a deeper meditation and having meditated, he came to realise that the expression of the vitality (prāṇa) in us is the Reality. But again, he discovered the hollowness of his own conclusion, and so again approached the Guru.

Section iii – अनुवाकः ३

Prāṇa Is Brahman

प्राणो ब्रह्मेति व्यजानात् ।
प्राणाद्ध्येव खल्विमानि भूतानि जायन्ते ।
प्राणेन जातानि जीवन्ति ।
प्राणं प्रयन्त्यभिसंविशन्तीति ।
तद्विज्ञाय पुनरेव वरुणं पितरमुपससार ।
अधीहि भगवो ब्रह्मेति । तगूंहोवाच ।
तपसा ब्रह्म विजिज्ञासस्व । तपो ब्रह्मेति ।
स तपोऽतप्यत । स तपस्तप्त्वा ॥१ ॥

prāṇo brahmeti vyajānāt,
prāṇāddhyeva khalvimāni bhūtāni jāyante,
prāṇena jātāni jīvanti,
prāṇaṁ prayantyabhisaṁviśantīti,
tadvijñāya punareva varuṇaṁ pitaramupasasāra,
adhīhi bhagavo brahmeti, tagṁ-hovāca,
tapasā brahma vijijñāsasva, tapo brahmeti,
sa tapo'tapyata, sa tapastaptvā. (1)

प्राणः – prāṇa; ब्रह्मेति – as Brahman; व्यजानात् – understood; प्राणात् – from prāṇa; हि – indeed; एव – alone; खलु – certainly; इमानि – all these; भूतानि – beings; जायन्ते – are born; प्राणेन – by prāṇa; जातानि – having been born; जीवन्ति – live; प्राणम् – into prāṇa; प्रयन्ति – on departing; अभिसंविशन्ति – enter; इति – thus;

तत् – that; विज्ञाय – having understood; पुनः एव – again; वरुणम् – unto Varuṇa; पितरम् – his father; उपससार – approached; अधीहि – teach me; भगवः – O! Revered Sir; ब्रह्म इति – what is Brahman; तम् – to him; ह – then; उवाच – said; तपसा – by penance; ब्रह्म – Brahman; विजिज्ञासस्व – seek thou to know; तपः – penance; ब्रह्म – Brahman; इति – thus; सः – he; तपः – penance; अतप्यत – performed; सः – he; तपः – penance; तप्त्वा – having performed

1. Bhṛgu understood that prāṇa is Brahman; because it is from prāṇa alone that all these living beings are born; having been born from it, they live by it and (in the end) on departing, they go towards prāṇa and become one with it. Having known that, he again approached his father Varuṇa saying: "O Revered Sir, instruct me about Brahman". He, (Varuṇa) told him: "Desire to know Brahman by tapas, tapas is Brahman". He performed tapas and having performed tapas...

Bhṛgu reflected over the theme of Brahman again, with a concentrated mind, when he was encouraged by his Master. He came to discover that the vitality expressed in the body, indicated by prāṇa is the Reality. Here prāṇa is not meant in the sense of only 'the air that we breathe.' We had previously explained the five great departments and activities of prāṇa that continuously go on within us. When the activities of perception, digestion, evacuation, circulation and so on are not going on, we consider that individual as dead. These activities of breathing, assimilation and so on are taking place everywhere, in the world of the plants, or animals, or humans. Wherever there is life's pulsation, in every such point, whether a unicellular being or a multiple celled organism with the highest rationality developed therein, everywhere, the activities of prāṇa represent Existence. From a dead father, no child can be born. In a vacuum no seed can germinate. In short, there is a very close relationship between prāṇa and life.

When he thought thus Bhṛgu came to the conclusion that from prāṇa life starts, in prāṇa life continues to exist and into prāṇa the life ends, when the manifested body perishes. Therefore, prāṇa is Brahman.

Though this conclusion, as it struck him at the moment of thinking, was quite obvious; when he continued his contemplation, he found that his arguments were not without their fallacies. Prāṇa is no doubt the efficient cause of the birth, sustenance and death of the body and therefore, life can be Brahman. But on a closer examination, he found that prāṇa could not be Brahman, because it is not intelligent. It is jaḍa. It is in itself, 'an effect' having a cause for it. An effect always has a beginning and an end. So, again, he approached his father after having done enough contemplation for himself.

Section iv – अनुवाकः ४

Mind Is Brahman

मनो ब्रह्मेति व्यजानात्।
मनसो ह्येव खल्विमानि भूतानि जायन्ते।
मनसा जातानि जीवन्ति।
मनः प्रयन्त्यभिसंविशन्तीति।
तद्विज्ञाय पुनरेव वरुणं पितरमुपससार।
अधीहि भगवो ब्रह्मेति। तगंूहोवाच।
तपसा ब्रह्म विजिज्ञासस्व। तपो ब्रह्मेति।
स तपोऽतप्यत। स तपस्तप्त्वा ॥१॥

mano brahmeti vyajānāt,
manaso hyeva khalvimāni bhūtāni jāyante,
manasā jātāni jīvanti,
manaḥ prayantyabhisaṁviśantīti,
tadvijñāya punareva varuṇaṁ pitaramupasasāra,
adhīhi bhagavo brahmeti, tagṁ-hovāca,
tapasā brahma vijijñāsasva, tapo brahmeti,
sa tapo'tapyata, sa tapastaptvā. (1)

मनः – mind; ब्रह्मेति – as Brahman; व्यजानात् – understood; मनसः – from mind; हि – indeed; एव – alone; खलु – certainly; इमानि – all these; भूतानि – beings; जायन्ते – are born; मनसा – by mind; जातानि – having been born; जीवन्ति – live; मनः – into mind; प्रयन्ति – on departing; अभिसंविशन्ति – enter; इति – thus; तत् – that;

विज्ञाय – having understood; पुनः एव – again; वरुणम् – unto Varuṇa; पितरम् – his father; उपससार – approached; अधीहि – teach me; भगवः – O! Revered Sir; ब्रह्म इति – what is Brahman; तम् – to him; ह – then; उवाच – said; तपसा – by penance; ब्रह्म – Brahman; विजिज्ञासस्व – seek thou to know; तपः – penance; ब्रह्म – Brahman; इति – thus; सः – he; तपः – penance; अतप्यत – performed; सः – he; तपः – penance; तप्त्वा – having performed

1. He knew that mind was Brahman; for, it is from the mind that all these living beings are produced. Being born from it, they all live by it; and on departing, they enter into the mind and become one with it. Having known that, he again approached his father, Varuṇa, saying: "O Venerable One, teach me Brahman". He, (Varuṇa) told him: "Desire to know Brahman by penance. Tapas is Brahman". Bhṛgu performed tapas and having performed tapas. ...

When he himself rejected the idea that prāṇa is Brahman, he continued his own independent reflections. When he sufficiently applied his concentrated intelligence, he came to discover in his meditations, a subtler factor. He understood that the mind which controls the prāṇa, the eternal cause of beings, is Brahman. He argued that mind colours our perceptions. A worried mind obstructs digestion, evacuation and even circulation. Thus, the intimate relationship of the mind and prāṇa, as master and slave was very evident.

Even in this very Upaniṣad, we were told that the creative activity was preceded by 'thought'. Let alone the work of an artist, even to write a note to a friend of ours, we must first of all have in our thought a definite idea of what we must write; and then alone can the activity of transcribing the thoughts into words takes place. Thus Bhṛgu decided that mind is the source of all creation, that mind feeds the continuity of existence; and that when the mind gets divorced from life, it gets released from the body and continues to exist as a mind. 'By an act of the mind alone man comes into this body' and so on are statements of the Śruti herself.[1]

But again, though this conclusion is quite appropriate, when it was brought upon the anvil of his deeper meditation, he found that it cannot stand the scrutiny of clearer thought. Mind is, at best, only an organ of cognition and as such in all its activities, it depends upon an agent who controls it and dictates to it saner conclusions. Again, mind is an effect; it has a cause other than itself. And again, it has no self-luminosity; it only shines in some borrowed light. It is very well known that no thoughts ever remain the same. Each thought has a beginning and an end, and, if at all, the mind has an existence as an entity, it is only in the continuity of its changing thoughts. In this welter of changes it is essentially finite and, therefore, cannot be the supreme Brahman, the changeless substratum upon which alone all changes are possible. Therefore, it could not be Brahman, the uncaused cause, the eternally Perfect. Therefore, Bhṛgu again approached the teacher to check up whether he had fallen away from the grand road of right thinking into the by-lanes of misunderstanding and unphilosophical confusion.

---

[1] Refer Swāmiji's discourses on *Praśnopaniṣad.*

Section v – अनुवाकः ५

Knowledge Is Brahman

विज्ञानं ब्रह्मेति व्यजानात् ।
विज्ञानाद्ध्येव खल्विमानि भूतानि जायन्ते ।
विज्ञानेन जातानि जीवन्ति ।
विज्ञानं प्रयन्त्यभिसंविशन्तीति ।
तद्विज्ञाय पुनरेव वरुणं पितरमुपससार ।
अधीहि भगवो ब्रह्मेति । तग्ंहोवाच
तपसा ब्रह्म विजिज्ञासस्व तपो ब्रह्मेति ।
स तपोऽतप्यत । स तपस्तप्त्वा ॥१ ॥

vijñānaṁ brahmeti vyajānāt,
vijñānāddhyeva khalvimāni bhūtāni jāyante,
vijñānena jātāni jīvanti,
vijñānaṁ prayantyabhisaṁviśantīti,
tadvijñāya punareva varuṇaṁ pitaramupasasāra,
adhīhi bhagavo brahmeti, tagṁ-hovāca,
tapasā brahma vijijñāsasva, tapo brahmeti,
sa tapo'tapyata, sa tapastaptvā. (1)

विज्ञानम् – knowledge; ब्रह्मेति – as Brahman; व्यजानात् – having understood; विज्ञानात् – from knowledge; हि – indeed; एव – alone; खलु – certainly; इमानि – all these; भूतानि – beings; जायन्ते – are born; विज्ञानेन – by knowledge; जातानि – the born; जीवन्ति – live; विज्ञानम् – into knowledge; प्रयन्ति – on departing; अभिसंविशन्ति

– enter; इति – thus; तत् – that; विज्ञाय – having understood; पुनः एव – again; वरुणम् – unto Varuṇa; पितरम् – his father; उपससार – approached; अधीहि – teach me; भगवः – O! Revered Sir; ब्रह्म इति – what is Brahman; तम् – to him; ह – then; उवाच – said; तपसा – by penance; ब्रह्म – Brahman; विजिज्ञासस्व – seek thou to know; तपः – penance; ब्रह्म – Brahman; इति – thus; सः – he; तपः – penance; अतप्यत – performed; सः – he; तपः – penance; तप्त्वा – having performed

1. He understood that knowledge is Brahman, because it is by knowledge that all these living beings are born; having been born, by knowledge they live, and having departed, into knowledge alone they enter. Having known that, he approached his father, Varuṇa, to know the Truth further and said, "Revered Sir, teach me Brahman". He, (Varuṇa) told him, "By tapas seek thou to know Brahman. Tapas is Brahman". He performed tapas and having performed tapas....

When Bhṛgu thus continued his contemplation, seeking for an agent under whose instructions alone the mind can really function as ably and diligently as it does now in a man's bosom, he discovered that the intellect is the true agent who does all the necessary driving of the mind.

The intellect is certainly subtler than the mind and the same Upaniṣad had declared earlier that intellect is the agent in all activities: 'Knowledge performs the sacrifices and it is the real agent in all physical activities'.[1]

---

[1] Refer page 192

This intellect, discriminating rightly or wrongly, has propelled the mind to think and act in a particular way. As a reaction to these karmas in each life, an individual takes a form and comes to live in the world. Naturally, it is from the knowledge, that we are born and every activity, subjective or objective, is propelled by the intellect in us. Not only thus life and its activities are sustained by the intellect but on departing from the physical structure, the individual goes forward seeking new venues of activities, again motivated by his own intelligence. Thus, Knowledge can be the Brahman as defined by the teacher and so the boy concludes that 'Knowledge is Brahman'.

But again, on a reconsideration, 'he was not satisfied with his own conclusions.' Therefore, by extending his thoughts a little further, he immediately discovered the obvious fallacies in these conclusions. It is helpful to note that the modern world is going through an era of a blind belief in the intellect. This intellectual era has come to believe that intellect is supreme. The generation has so blindly taken to this belief that they have not yet gained the necessary poise of mind to intelligently analyse the very intellect, since the children of this era are not trained to detach themselves from the very intellect to observe and analyse the very nature of the intellect and its knowledge.

Bhṛgu, on the other hand, could not find complete satisfaction in believing that knowledge is the supreme Brahman because he realised that the intellect is only an agent. An agent generally works for the satisfaction of the master. The agent works under the instructions of the master and the motive behind agent is the satisfaction of the master. Also, we know that an agency is marked with pain, besmeared with dependence and the agent is not perfectly pure.

Therefore, fearing lest he should 'miss the bus' in his philosophical pilgrimage to self-discovery, he continues his daring intellectual flight. In one leap he comes to understand that Bliss is the secret master behind all agencies and departments of activity within the microcosm.

Section vi – अनुवाकः ६

Bliss Is Brahman, Feels Bhṛgu

आनन्दो ब्रह्मेति व्यजानात्।
आनन्दाद्ध्येव खल्विमानि भूतानि जायन्ते।
आनन्देन जातानि जीवन्ति।
आनन्दं प्रयन्त्यभिसंविशन्तीति।
सैषा भार्गवी वारुणी विद्या परमे व्योमन् प्रतिष्ठिता।
स य एवं वेद प्रतितिष्ठति। अन्नवानन्नादो भवति।
महान् भवति प्रजया पशुभिर्ब्रह्मवर्चसेन।
महान् कीर्त्या ॥१॥

ānando brahmeti vyajānāt,
ānandāddhyeva khalvimāni bhūtāni jāyante,
ānandena jātāni jīvanti,
ānandaṁ prayantyabhisaṁviśantīti,
saiṣā bhārgavī vāruṇī vidyā parame vyoman pratiṣṭhitā,
sa ya evaṁ veda pratitiṣṭhati, annavānannādo bhavati,
mahān bhavati prajayā paśubhirbrahmavarcasena,
mahān kīrtyā. (1)

आनन्दः – happiness (bliss); ब्रह्मेति – as Brahman; व्यजानात् – understood; आनन्दात् – from bliss; हि – indeed; एव – alone; खलु – certainly; इमानि – all these; भूतानि – beings; जायन्ते – are born; आनन्देन– by bliss; जातानि – the born; जीवन्ति – live; आनन्दम् – into bliss; प्रयन्ति – on departing; अभिसंविशन्ति – enter; इति –

thus; सा एषा – is this; भार्गवी वारुणी – of Bhṛgu and Varuṇa; विद्या – knowledge; परमे – in the Supreme; व्योमन् – space (in the excellent cavity of the heart); प्रतिष्ठिता – is established; सः – he; यः – who; एवम् – thus; वेद – knows; प्रतितिष्ठति – becomes established (in Brahman); अन्नवान् – possessor of food; अन्नादः – the eater of food; भवति – he becomes; महान् – great; भवति – he becomes; प्रजया – with progeny; पशुभिः – with cattle wealth; ब्रह्म वर्चसेन – with the splendour of true brāhmaṇahood i.e. born of sacred knowledge resulting from the control of external and internal organs; महान् – great; कीर्त्या – through fame and renown (he becomes)

1. He knew that Bliss was Brahman, for, from Bliss all these beings are produced, by Bliss do these beings live. They go to Bliss on departing and become one with it – this is the knowledge learnt by Bhṛgu and taught by Varuṇa. This is established in the supreme space – in the excellent cavity of the heart. He who knows thus becomes one with Brahman. He becomes the possessor (assimilator) of food and the eater (enjoyer) of it. He becomes great in progeny, cattle and gains the splendor of true brāhmaṇa-hood. Indeed, he becomes great through fame and renown.

When Bhṛgu thus through contemplation transcended himself from annam to prāṇa, from prāṇa to mind and from mind to intellect, he was not satisfied. Therefore, he took the most daring plunge into the beyond when he left even the intellect also behind. On transcending the intellect also, he came to experience a state of Bliss which had been already described in the last chapter as ānandamayakośa. We have found there, that this bliss sheath is the enjoyer of which the intellect is an agent.

To experience the bliss sheath in itself, through a steady and awareful withdrawal of our identifications with the world outside and the outer four layers of matter, is to experience immediately the Supreme which is subtler than the very bliss sheath. He who reaches the bliss sheath, by the very momentum of his arrival there, from the outer world of his natural preoccupations, gets 'bowled out' into the infinite realms beyond it and comes to experience the transcendental glory of his own nature. To reach upto the bliss shealth is the self-effort, puruṣārtha. Having reached there, the transcendence of it and the experience of wisdom is immediate and instantaneous.

In a dark room, in the daytime, all your effort will be directed to carefully feeling your way through the objects in the room to the window and there to open its shutters. This is the last act that you have to do to flood the whole room with light. Having opened the window, you need not invite the light from outside to stream in! Similarly, our own real nature was unknown to us because of our preoccupations with the five matter envelopments and their world of objects. When we have withdrawn ourselves up to the ānandamaya kośa without any hitch or struggle, we automatically get ourselves transported to the realm of the Divine in us, which is indicated here as 'established in the supreme space – in the excellent cavity of the heart'. We have already explained what we mean by 'the cave of the heart'.[1]

[1] For elaborate explanation of the term, please refer to chapter I, Section vi – page 73

This subjective way of realisation by an intimate conscious enquiry of the different layers of personality in man is the most direct of methods available in Vedānta for Self-realisation. No other religion in the world, had ever given us such a direct method of culminating man's evolution in his discovery of the Godhood that lies concealed within himself. This method of enquiry and direct apprehension of the subtler realms of the personalities in ourselves, and ultimately to discover and realise, in an intimate personal experience that the vital source of all other existence, to be the infinite, all-pervading Reality, is called the Bhārgavī vidyā.

Just as in the modern world of science, a theory discovered by a scientist goes under his name, here the theory by which Bhṛgu realised for himself the Truth came to be called, 'Science of Bhṛgu'. Here it is interesting to note how Varuṇa, the teacher, though he enunciated this theory, had not cared to lend his name to it because, in philosophy, the touchstone is its experiencer. Bhṛgu first experienced the divine glory of his own inner Self through this technique of self-enquiry and therefore, this method is called Bhārgavī vidyā – and not Vāruṇī vidyā.

This is not an accidental coincidence that Bhṛgu heard it and came to realise this Truth. Mother Śruti guarantees that if anyone with the sincerity of Bhṛgu consistently perseveres on the path of enquiry and concentrated meditation, he too can come to experience the same fulfilment as Bhṛgu. Śruti says, 'He who knows thus becomes one with Brahman'.

Ordinarily, this portion is translated in a most impotent manner, saying that one who thus realises Brahman becomes rich in food and also very efficient in eating food. If material success and gluttony were the result of Self-perception, God forbid that philosophy and save that country! Here the word annam should be taken in the largest sense of the term as the 'entire world of experienceable objects'. In short, it means that a perfect man alone can become fully and clearly conscious of the entire world that throbs with life and joy, and also he alone is the one who can come to experience infinitely more than the dull-witted and the prejudiced.

An ordinary man of imperfections is the one who constantly keeps on running away from pains and agonies, failures and disasters, threats and despairs of life. Thus, more than half the world is, even for the best of men, a dark cave of horrid fears from which they should run away and seek a refuge and shelter! On the other hand, he who has realised the oneness of the Ātman with divine Whole, to him all circumstances and the entire world, from the simplest blade of grass to the Creator Himself, is an appetising field to revel in and dance in ecstasy. Thus, at every moment in life, at any place and in any circumstance, he is in an inspiring world, experiencing intensively the life in its totality.

Such a perfect Master, who has gained mastery over all the different limbs of his personality and has come to rule over them, must necessarily become extremely successful in the material world of secular competition, whether it be with the outer world of phenomenon or among his own fellow beings. In the Vaidika days, the wealth was cattle, and so, when the Śruti says here that he becomes great in the wealth of cattle, she means that he becomes rich. (one wonders whether the word 'purse' came from the Sanskrit word paśu!)

Again, hereafter, you will find in many places the śāstra insistently saying that such a man will have a long line of progeny. This is again translated ordinarily as 'children' – as if the father of eleven children should be a greater Man of Realisation than the father of five or three! The upper and the middle class society of today seems to take this as their watchword in their life and irresponsibly procreate children without restraint, not only within the four walls of their houses, but even outside, thus criminally creating a national problem of uncontrollable rise in population! A poor country like India, backward in her social, political and economic spheres, can ill afford such an incomprehensible pressure of population on land.

In fact, a correct understanding should be something more noble and acceptable. I, for one, believe that here the word 'children' means all those whom the revered Man of Knowledge comes to love as his own 'children' so that they learn to look up to him as more than their own 'father'.

Brahma-varcasam: – The glow of cheer and joy, peace and serenity, love and tenderness, that beams out of a person who has the mental tranquillity and the spiritual equilibrium while facing the tussle of life through all its imperfections, is what is meant here by the aura around the face of a Man of Realisation. To misunderstand it to be nothing more than physical health – a giant shape – is to eliminate some of our greatest Men of Realisation out of the Hindu fold. Śrī Rama Tirtha, Ramakrishna Paramahamsa, Bhagavan Ramana Maharshi, Yogī Aurobindo – none of them were in any sense of the term 'adipose collected in tranquillity!' In fact, such endless girth and dimension invariably indicate a buffalo constitution which has no more wisdom than that contained in the famous 'Uppu Chettiar'.[1] Such an individual well equated, developed and healthy in all his personalities must surely become a potent factor of his age and so it is said here that, 'he becomes great in fame'.

Bhṛgu, when he thus followed the instruction of Varuṇa faithfully to the last, came to feel such a consummate satisfaction that he felt no more need to come back to the Guru and enquire: 'what is Brahman'? When he reached the ānandamaya kośa and gained a glimpse of the beyond, there must have been that supreme look of contentment and divine satisfaction on his blissful face. Thereafter, there was no discussion either possible or necessary.

The Guru, rooted in his own experience, could sympathetically feel the silent experience of Bhṛgu and he feels the need to give some final advices to the boy before he left the seat at the feet of the Guru, to live the rest of his life in the glorious Consciousness of the Divine.

At the same time, the teacher was not exclusively giving audience to Bhṛgu alone. The other students, who

[1] Representation of Uppu Chettiar in status is available for drawing room decorations in India. This statue is known in foreign markets as the 'Laughing Tom.'

had not had the necessary inner purification, could not come to comprehend the entire Truth so vividly as Bhṛgu. This incapacity, on the part of some of the students, does not mean that the science is wrong or impotent. Some students of the scripture may become thus impatient and throw the book away to walk out as confirmed atheists.

In all such cases, it is only because the students had not the benefit of a true teacher to guide them. Whenever such a thing happened in the Vaidika days, the teachers never despaired but correctly understood that it was because of the student's lack of integration. Whenever such an inner maladjustment, between the psychological and intellectual personality, in a student was noted, the teachers immediately advised them some method or methods of self-integration called upāsanās.

Here, six different methods of upāsanās have been prescribed for the purpose of better integration. At the end of it all, the same Truth, of the oneness of the life spark in us and life everywhere is being repeated to bring it more clearly to the perceptions and intimate experiences of the students so integrated.

Of the six items of upāsanās, the earlier four contain, besides the instructions for meditation, a deeper message to the student of realisation in Bhṛgu. Great teachers always do have this ability of talking at once to two different levels of students in one and the same breath! We shall see how the first four of them had an obvious meaning for the ordinary student as a method of upāsanā and for Bhṛgu, the realised, a deeper message of instruction and direction as to how he should live in the world outside after his realisation.

The boy had now realised the source of the infinite Bliss within himself. These moments of experience are generally limited and broken. Until he gets himself established in this experience, there will be for him, moments of disturbances when he will be pushed out of that plane of God-experience to the consciousness of his egocentric existence. At such moments, the chances are, that he will look upon the world of plurality as inauspicious, wretched, pain-ridden and a delusion.

On realising his own divine nature, he may, by a relative estimate, come to regard his own brother creatures of the world as something undivine, as something to escape from. In order to avoid this mistaken notion and the consequent estimate of the world as undivine, the teacher had to point out to Bhṛgu, who was sitting at the feet of his Master, drowned in the intoxicating joy of Bliss, that he must consider the world outside also with as much reverence and divinity as he considers his own experienced Self. We shall see how this is most beautifully done in the following upāsanā method.

Section vii – अनुवाकः ७

Food Is Brahman. Respect Food, Gather and Distribute Food

अन्नं न निन्द्यात्। तद्व्रतम्। प्राणो वा अन्नम्।
शरीरमन्नादम्। प्राणे शरीरं प्रतिष्ठितम्।
शरीरे प्राणः प्रतिष्ठितः।
तदेतदन्नमन्ने प्रतिष्ठितम्।
स य एतदन्नमन्ने प्रतिष्ठितं वेद प्रतितिष्ठति।
अन्नवानन्नादो भवति।
महान् भवति प्रजया पशुभिर्ब्रह्मवर्चसेन।
महान् कीर्त्या ॥१॥

annaṁ na nindyāt, tad-vratam, prāṇo vā annam,
śarīramannādam, prāṇe śarīraṁ pratiṣṭhitam,
śarīre prāṇaḥ pratiṣṭhitaḥ,
tadetadannamanne pratiṣṭhitam,
sa ya etadannamanne pratiṣṭhitaṁ veda pratitiṣṭhati,
annavānannādo bhavati,
mahān bhavati prajayā paśubhirbrahmavarcasena,
mahān kīrtyā. (1)

अन्नम् – food; **न** – not; **निन्द्यात्** – one should blame; **तत्** – that; **व्रतम्** – (is your) vow; **प्राणः** – prāṇa; **वै** – indeed; **अन्नम्** – food; **शरीरम्** – body; **अन्नादम्** – (is) the eater of food; **प्राणे** – in prāṇa; **शरीरम्** – body; **प्रतिष्ठितम्** – established; **शरीरे** – in the body; प्राणः – prāṇa; प्रतिष्ठितः – is established; तत् – therefore; एतत् – this; अन्नम् – food; अन्ने – in food; प्रतिष्ठितम् – established; सः – he; यः – who; एतत् – this; अन्नम् – food; अन्ने – in food; प्रतिष्ठितम् – established; वेद – knows; प्रतितिष्ठति – becomes one with (Brahman); अन्नवान् – possessor of food (and); अन्नादः – the eater of food; भवति – he becomes; महान् – great; भवति – he becomes; प्रजया – with progeny; पशुभिः – with cattle wealth; ब्रह्मवर्चसेन – with the splendour of true brāhmaṇahood i.e. born of sacred knowledge resulting from the control of external and internal organs; महान् – great; कीर्त्या – through fame and renown (he becomes)

1. Do not blaspheme food; that shall be your vow. Prāṇa is food. Body is the eater of food. The body is fixed in prāṇa. The prāṇa is fixed in the body. Thus food is fixed in food. He who knows that food is fixed in food, becomes one with Brahman. He becomes possessed of food and he becomes the eater of the food. He becomes great in progeny, in cattle wealth and in the splendour of brāhmaṇahood. He becomes great in fame.

To the ordinary students, this is an engaging line of thinking to entertain themselves during their meditation. They are encouraged to continue their meditations with the promise of material gains, because, essentially these boys are those who have a greater share of attachment to material gains and worldly fame. Indeed, it is our attachment to the sensuous that makes us disintegrate and become incapable of great things in life. The ṛṣi here, understanding the character of his students and knowing their demands, is playing to their desires in hauling them out of their sensuous ruts! Thus, they are promised that they will become not only rich in food but equally capable of enjoying the sumptuous food; that they will have plenty of food all their lives. Besides, they are promised that they will have plenty of children to look after them in their old age and plenty of cattle wealth. Thus, they will be satisfied in their three great desires (eṣaṇās): desire for wealth (vitta eṣaṇā), desire for children (putra eṣaṇā) and desire for fame (loka eṣaṇā).

These results are promised to those who could meditate upon the food and the food-eater as one and the same. Here the śāstra says that the prāṇa is food and the physical body of man is the food-eater, meaning the body consumes the prāṇa. But at the same time, the body is established in prāṇa, and moment to moment, the prāṇa or the vitality is consuming the body; therefore, the body is the eaten and the prāṇa is the eater. Thus, the eater and the eaten is one and the same, inasmuch as there is continuous competitive eating of each by the other!

The body eats the prāṇa; and the prāṇa eats up the body too. Thus, in fact, there are two things – the eater and the eaten – but from the philosophical standpoint we can declare; 'Food is fixed in food'.

The implications of this statement are so vast that thoughts cannot exhaust all the possibilities. Therefore, there is no chance of the meditation being exhausted. One who regularly meditates, gains more and more integration within. An integrated person is ever noted for success in all spheres of activities including the material and the secular.

The above is the obvious meaning which the ordinary students comprehend when they approach this portion as a mere instruction for upāsanā. But the extremely integrated and therefore, more subtle intellect of Bhṛgu understands a deeper message from the same. This message is hammered into Bhṛgu, not so much by the force of the words as by the arresting look of depth and gravity in the eyes of the Master.

The very opening words summarise the message to Bhṛgu. 'Do not censure food'. The word 'food' to him is not the 'material supplied in the kitchen'; in its ampler meaning, it denotes food for all the sense organs. In short, the world of food constitutes the world of objects. The outer world of objects and the inner Truth of the Subject are not two distinct entities, one competing with the other; the world of objects is but the concretisation of the perceptions of the 'misunderstood Subject'. As such, the teacher instructs the students that, because of his Realisation of the divine nature of the Self, he should not entertain any undivine idea about the world outside. The world without is as divine as the world within.

When we read the appropriate meaning into this passage, we take the wind away from the false arguments that are often raised against Vedāntins. The philosophy of Vedānta does not, at any stage, laugh at and ignore the entire world as such. Wherever they say, 'the world is a dream like delusion', they only mean to point out our misunderstanding and misconception regarding the world. Vedānta requires of us to make a re-estimate of the world. A more intelligent reinterpretation of the world is all that is demanded by Vedānta.

It was probably the mischief of foreign powers in this country that encouraged this wrong notion which, by an ignorant tradition, came to be read as the philosophy of Śaṅkarācārya by successive paṇḍitas for the last 500 years. None of the great Ācāryas of Vedānta ever ignored the world and ran away from it. Certainly, their world is not the world as we recognise and experience it. We look at the world from a partial, prejudiced point of view and because of the squint in our vision, we see the world as ugly and maladjusted, abominal and undivine, a field for pain and agony, a theatre for death and destruction, a tomb of sorrows and sobs, a den of disappointments and despair! This pessimistic point of view has no place in the jubilant philosophy of the Hindu tradition. When they cried that the Ātman within is the Brahman without, the ṛṣis appealed to the people to watch for, recognise and experience the eternal divine play in and through the seemingly different names and forms.

Bhṛgu is initiated here in the vital essence of Hinduism, that a Man of Realisation has no right to censure the world of objects. He must realise that the world of names and forms experienced by the experiencer, the Ātman and the world are one and the same. Hence the world is, in its turn, as much divine as the Soul. With the newly dawned wisdom, Bhṛgu was appealed to, to walk out into the world 'without speaking ill of food'. Such a Master of Realisation really becomes a walking God upon earth, to whom the entire world becomes so many occasions to experience and enjoy the infinite Bliss.

Such a saint becomes great in progeny, meaning, a man who guides the entire generation with a devoted fatherly love and to whom the generation looks up to, as children would to their father. He indeed becomes great in fame. A hundred other Masters with the infinite experience of the Divine might be living now or might have died, unknown in the secret caves of the Himalayas like any other house rats or street dogs, but the world and the children of the present generation do not raise even a single thought of gratitude for their divine expression of Reality. On the other hand, a Vyāsa or a Vālmīki, a Yājñavalkya or a Vasiṣṭha, a Ramakrishna or Vivekananda, a Guru Govind Singh or Rama Tirtha, a Ramana or Aurobindo – they are even now remembered with grateful adorations because theirs was a realisation more complete, more perfect and more exhaustive. They realised and recognised the Divine not only in themselves but in the entire world of objects. In their perfect wisdom, they had no fears of any fall at any time in the delusory net of misunderstandings or physical appetites.

Varuṇa toeing the line with the great Masters of the Vedas, here instructs Bhṛgu to throw away his prejudices against the world of plurality and come to recognise the one supreme Self vitalising the world. Herein we have the inimitable philosophy, the like of which the world had never seen before, wherein the sacred embraces the secular. God plays with gold! Indeed, Vedānta, the paragon of philosophy, is singing here the kokila song of the descent of God into man. In the eyes of the Realised, there is nothing but perfection revelling in disorder and confusion. A little self-discipline, a few little adjustments in the valley of life will make the very same world of agitations and passions, sorrows and fights into a heaven of perfect joys.

It is a criminal misrepresentation of Vedānta to say that a Man of Realisation should run away from life into the dead jungle. Vedānta would not have been a self-surviving philosophy all these periods of history if the perfection conceived by the Hindu Upaniṣads were to make man nothing better than the rocks on the Ganga banks! To send people away from the world and its joys, from the great scheme of nature, the revelling beauty and the gorgeous extravagance of light and colour, smile and ecstasy into a dull and dreary darkness, we need no great philosophy to be profounded by any ṛṣi! Even if they could have done it, they could not have hoodwinked such a long unbroken line of a brilliant generations of Hindus and sustained it to this day. Let us not, in our overenthusiasm compliment ourselves to be the only wise generation that has come to grace the face of the globe. None of our political, economic, social and secular problems of the world today shall justify our wisdom! If greater men of bright and more steady intellect have accepted Vedānta as a philosophy of perfection, it could not be because Vedānta readily created ineffectual men out of honest seekers. On the other hand, it must have been, as we hear in the Upaniṣad, because of its appeal to the Man of Wisdom to come out into the world to recognise the divine nature of the world of plurality and to work for the redemption of man. 'Do not speak ill of food', warns Varuṇa; and he adds for purpose of emphasis; 'That shall be your vow'.

Section viii – अनुवाकः ८

'Do Not Reject Food'

अन्नं न परिचक्षीत। तद्व्रतम्। आपो वा अन्नम्।
ज्योतिरन्नादम्। अप्सु ज्योतिः प्रतिष्ठितम्।
ज्योतिष्यापः प्रतिष्ठिताः।
तदेतदन्नमन्ने प्रतिष्ठितम्।
स य एतदन्नमन्ने प्रतिष्ठितं वेद प्रतितिष्ठति।
अन्नवानन्नादो भवति।
महान्-भवति प्रजया पशुभिर्ब्रह्मवर्चसेन।
महान्-कीर्त्या ॥१॥

annaṁ na paricakṣīta, tad-vratam, āpo vā annam,
jyotirannādam, apsu jyotiḥ pratiṣṭhitam,
jyotiṣyāpaḥ pratiṣṭhitāḥ,
tadetadannamanne pratiṣṭhitam,
sa ya etadannamanne pratiṣṭhitaṁ veda pratitiṣṭhati,
annavānannādo bhavati,
mahān-bhavati prajayā paśubhirbrahmavarcasena,
mahān-kīrtyā. (1)

अन्नम् – food; न परिचक्षीत – do not reject; तत् – that; व्रतम् – (is your) duty; आपः – water; वै – indeed; अन्नम् – food; ज्योतिः – fire; अन्नादम् – (is) the eater of food; अप्सु – in water; ज्योतिः – fire; प्रतिष्ठितम् – is established; ज्योतिषि – in fire; आपः – water;

प्रतिष्ठिताः – are established; तत् – therefore; एतत् – this; अन्नम् – food; अन्ने – in food; प्रतिष्ठितम् – is established; सः – he; यः – who; एतत् – this; अन्नम् – food; अन्ने – in food; प्रतिष्ठितम् – established; वेद – knows; प्रतितिष्ठति – gets established (in Brahman); अन्नवान् – possessor of food; अन्नादः – eater of food; भवति – (he) becomes; महान् – great; भवति – (he) becomes; प्रजया – with progeny; पशुभिः – with cattle wealth; ब्रह्मवर्चसेन – with the splendour of true brāhmaṇahood i.e born of sacred knowledge resulting from the control of external and internal organs; महान् –great; कीर्त्या – through fame

1. Do not reject food. That is a duty. Water is food. Fire is the food-eater. Fire is fixed in water, water is fixed in fire. So food is fixed in food. He who knows that food is fixed in food, gets established in Brahman. He becomes the possessor of food and an eater of food. He becomes great in progeny, in cattle, and in his spiritual lustre. He becomes great in fame.

If in the previous upāsanā, the vow which the worshipper was to take be, that he 'should not censure food'; in this upāsanā the vow is that he 'should not reject any food' that comes to the table, because it is not tasty. Whatever, that comes to his table, he must be able to consume without making faces or protesting against that food. This will be respecting and revering food.

Water that is drunk is digested by the digestive 'fire' in our system. Therefore, water is regarded as food and fire is regarded as the consumer of food. Water can also be considered as food in the sense that the food grains grow with water. Heat in a living body is necessary for the food to be digested and hence the body heat can be considered as the eater of water.

Fire is fixed in water: – This is true in the sense, we all know, that the 'digestive fire' gets kindled and leaps to consume the food taken in, when we drink water an hour or so after a meal. In this sense, we can say that fire is fixed in water, inasmuch as by supplying water to the digestive system, its efficiency increases.

Water is fixed in fire: – Again, whenever the heat of the body increases, immediately we find water, in the form of perspiration, steaming out as if water is fixed in fire. Anything consumed by fire is always accompanied by moisture – let it be the driest of fuel that you can find. Completely dehydrated things cannot be burnt – they can only be charred.

Altogether the teacher wants to emphasise, in another striking analogy, how the eater and the eaten, the experiencer and the experienced are interchangeable and therefore, in fact, they are both virtually one and the same. The relationship between the subject and the object is clearly shown to be one and the same. When a glass rod is put in a trough half full of water, we find because of refraction, half of the rod outside the water is straight and the other half inside the water is bent at an angle to it. This ugly delusion is because of the medium through which we are looking at the object. Similarly, the subject and the object, though they are one and the same, the world of objects seem to be different from the subject, because of the refraction that is caused by the medium of the mind and intellect through which we are experiencing the objects.

As before, the fruits of the upāsanā are enumerated as great material success and easy satisfaction of all of the fundamental desires of life.

Turning from the ordinary students who understood this as a pure method of upāsanā, to the great student Bhṛgu, we can find that the perfect student in him had a special message in these very same words of the teacher. To a student of realisation, who has just peeped into the beyond and got divinely inspired, the message would be that he should not, on any score reject food – 'food', meaning, the world of objects that can be experienced. The manifested world of plurality is not to be rejected as a false and delusory nothingness.

The example of the waves is aptly used in this context. To misunderstand them as having independent individual existence is not to understand the ocean at all. The advice is for a reinterpretation of the world and not for its negation as a whole. With the vision of the divine that is immanent in the world of names and forms, the world presents a totally different field altogether for the Perfect Man to serve and to adore, to worship and to guide.

The main theme of *Taittirīya-upaniṣad*, apart from its philosophical theories, is the right attitude of the Man of Knowledge towards the world of multiplicity. Study of the scriptures and experience of the Truth indicated by them, is one part of the Perfect One's existence (svādhyāya). The other part is constituted of the spread of this idea among his fellow men, so that the divine culture of the land may be maintained and properly cultivated (pravacana).

Bhṛgu was advised, not to reject the world on any score but to recognise the true divine nature of the world outside and to continue his life of love and sympathetic understanding of the world. Bhṛgu was commissioned to guide the generation through the right channels of correct evaluation of life as such, and to goad the members of his generation to live the Hindu cultural way of life by themselves.

Section ix – अनुवाकः ९

Unity of Creation – Accumulate Food For Distribution

अन्नं बहु कुर्वीत । तद्व्रतम् । पृथिवी वा अन्नम् ।
आकाशोऽन्नादः । पृथिव्यामाकाशः प्रतिष्ठितः ।
आकाशे पृथिवी प्रतिष्ठिता ।
तदेतदन्नमन्ने प्रतिष्ठितम् ।
स य एतदन्नमन्ने प्रतिष्ठितं वेद प्रतितिष्ठति ।
अन्नवानन्नादो भवति ।
महान्-भवति प्रजया पशुभिर्ब्रह्मवर्चसेन ।
महान्-कीर्त्या ॥१ ॥

annaṁ bahu kurvīta, tad-vratam, pṛthivī vā annam,
ākāśo'nnādaḥ, pṛthivyāmākāśaḥ pratiṣṭhitaḥ,
ākāśe pṛthivī pratiṣṭhitā,
tadetadannamanne pratiṣṭhitam,
sa ya etadannamanne pratiṣṭhitaṁ veda pratitiṣṭhati,
annavānannādo bhavati,
mahān-bhavati prajayā paśubhirbrahmavarcasena,
mahān-kīrtyā. (1)

अन्नम् – food; बहु – plenty; कुर्वीत – accumulate; तत् – that; व्रतम् – is the duty; पृथिवी – the earth; वै – indeed; अन्नम् – is food; आकाशः – space; अन्नादः – is the eater of food; पृथिव्याम् – on the earth; आकाशः – space; प्रतिष्ठितः – is established; आकाशे

– in space; पृथिवी – the earth; प्रतिष्ठिता – is established; तत् – therefore; एतत् – this; अन्नम् – food; अन्ने – in food; प्रतिष्ठितम् – is established; सः – he; यः – who; एतत् – this; अन्नम् – food; अन्ने – in food; प्रतिष्ठितम् – is established; वेद – knows; प्रतितिष्ठति – gets established (in Brahman); अन्नवान् – possessor of food; अन्नादः – the eater of food; भवति – (he) becomes; महान् – great; भवति – (he) becomes; प्रजया – with progeny; पशुभिः – with cattle wealth; ब्रह्मवर्चसेन – with the splendour of true brāhmaṇahood i.e born of sacred Knowledge resulting from the control of external and internal organs; महान् – great; कीर्त्या – through fame (he becomes)

1. Accumulate plenty of food. That is the duty. The earth is food. Ākāśa is the food-eater. In the earth is fixed the ākāśa. In the ākāśa is fixed the earth. So food is fixed in food. He who knows that food is fixed in food, thus rests in food; and is established well for ever. He becomes rich in food and becomes the eater of food. He becomes great in progeny, in cattle and in spiritual lustre. He becomes great in fame.

That we must accumulate food in plenty for the purpose of distribution, is the vow. When one eats the food, the food is surrounded by the individual. Similarly, the earth from which all food arises is itself the food, a morsel, in the mouth space (ākāśa). It revolves on its own axis in the wide mouth of ākāśa itself! Again, in a circumscribed and limited point of view, the space of this pandal rests on the earth and so space is fixed on the earth and to that extent we may say, space is consumed by the earth. The subtle concept of space can easily be understood as interpenetrating into the very bowels of the earth. A subtler element cannot be conditioned by a grosser one. Earth, the grossest, cannot limit the ether by its bulk or substance. At every point of the earth, space is fixed up, in the sense that space penetrates into the very bowels of the earth. Here, it can be assumed, that the world (earth) is the consumer and the space is the consumed.

The usual material gains are promised here again as a reward for such a regular and deep meditation.

As far as Bhṛgu is concerned, this is yet another bit of information or instruction given to him by his teacher. He was advised: 'Accumulate plently of food. This is thy vow'. To Bhṛgu, the ideal youngster of God-realisation, it was told that he, in his universal sevā for the cultural rehabilitation of man, must not run away from the world of objects that are necessary for it, as well as from the people. 'Accumulate plenty of food', for the purpose of feeding the students of the gurukula and also for maintaining and looking after the seekers who might come to him for instruction. This is not a watchward for the material world. Under blind secular impulses, man may, at certain periods of history, try for increased production and selfish accumulation. Here, to Bhṛgu, it is not an instruction to hoard wealth and establish great monastries, and come to forget himself in the madness of power, and in the foolishness of institutionalism. On the other hand, here the boy is whipped to enthusiasm to serve and to propagate. The Master is injecting a missionary zeal into the boy, to adore and to worship the world of objects as his own Self.

The Self, which is all-pervading, 'the cause of the ether' and subtler than the ākāśa, is the eater, as it were, of the whole universe which moves in space. Even the concept of space is only at one end of pure Consciousness; it is the Awareness in us that illuminates even space. As such Consciousness is 'the eater' – the factor that makes it possible for the mind and intellect to experience the universe – of the entire world of objects. At the same time, it is to be noted that the world of objects with names and forms are necessary for the manifestation of dynamism in pure Awareness. The Supreme, clothed in matter, expresses Itself as you and I, the world and the ocean, the solar and the lunar systems, the universe and its pattern. These joyous expressions of might and glory, power and strength, beauty and music, poetry and grace of the absolute Reality can never be so conspicuously expressed in the realm of the gross but for its mirage-like delusions in its finite matter extensions.

Electricity would have been only a mathematical conception, known perhaps to a few physicists, but for the bulb and the fan, the heater and the cooler, the tram and the train and other such mechanical contrivances through which electricity is made to function and be our faithful slave to serve us and entertain us. In this sense, we may say that electricity is being consumed by the various electrical equipments! Similarly, the world, we can assume, is in a sense, the eater of the Spirit – as the gadgets consume electricity. Thus, Spirit alone becomes the eater and the eaten; the experiencer and the experienced are but one. And as such to entertain a prejudice against one is to misunderstand or misrepresent the other.

Bhṛgu understood all these implications even without a discourse. Perhaps, a lot of discourses were given by the original ṛṣis in between the mantras as some critics and commentators of the Upaniṣads have suggested. After the discourses, the great ṛṣis themselves crystallised their talks of the day into one or two mantras to facilitate the memory of their children. The students had to remember the entire talk all through their lives and these mantras helped them to do so.

However, even without the discourses, Bhṛgu was in a position to understand the implications of what the teacher said, because of his own experience of the Infinite.

Section x - अनुवाकः १०

'Don't Turn Away Anyone Who Seeks Food and Shelter' – The Hindu Code of Dharma

न कंचन वसतौ प्रत्याचक्षीत । तद्व्रतम् ।
तस्माद्यया कया च विधया बह्वन्नं प्राप्नुयात् ।
आराध्यस्मा अन्नमित्याचक्षते ।
एतद्वै मुखतोऽन्नगं्-राद्धम् ।
मुखतोऽस्मा अन्नगं्-राध्यते ।
एतद्वै मध्यतोऽन्नगं्-राद्धम् ।
मध्यतोऽस्मा अन्नगं्-राध्यते ।
एतद्वा अन्ततोऽन्नगं्-राद्धम् ।
अन्ततोऽस्मा अन्नगं्-राध्यते । य एवं वेद ॥१॥

na kañcana vasatau pratyācakṣīta, tad-vratam,
tasmādyayā kayā ca vidhayā bahvannaṁ prāpnuyāt,
ārādhyasmā annamityācakṣate,
etadvai mukhato'nnagṁ-rāddham,
mukhato'smā annagṁ-rādhyate,
etadvai madhyato'nnagṁ-rāddham,
madhyato'smā annagṁ-rādhyate,
etadvā antato'nnagṁ-rāddham,
antato'smā annagṁ-rādhyate, ya evaṁ veda. (1)

न – not; कंचन – anyone; वसतौ – (seeking) shelter; प्रत्याचक्षीत – should turn away, refuse; तत् – that; व्रतम् – (is) your duty;

तस्मात् – therefore; यया कया च – by whatever; विधया – by any means; बहु – plenty (of); अन्नम् – food; प्राप्नुयात् – let him procure; आराधि – is cooked ready; अस्मै – for this one; अन्नम् – food; इति – thus; आचक्षते – declare (the householders); एतत् – this; वै – indeed; मुखतः – in the best manner; अन्नम् – food; राद्धम् – to be prepared (and given); मुखतः – in the best manner; अस्मै – to him (the guest); अन्नम् – food; राध्यते – is offered; एतत् – this; वै – indeed; मध्यतः – in the medium manner; अन्नम् – food; राद्धम् – prepared; मध्यतः – in the medium manner; अस्मै – to him (the guest); अन्नम् – food; राध्यते – is offered; एतत् – this; वै – indeed; अन्ततः – in the lowest manner; अन्नम् – food; राद्धम् – (is) prepared; अन्ततः – in the lower manner; अस्मै – to him (the guest); अन्नम् – food; राध्यते – is offered; यः – who; एवम् – thus; वेद – knows

1. Do not turn away anybody who seeks shelter and lodging. This is the vow. Let one, therefore, acquire much food by any means whatsoever. They should say: 'Food is ready'. If the food is prepared in the best manner, the food is given to him (the guest) also in the best manner. If the food is prepared in a medium manner, food is also given to him in a medium manner. If food is prepard in the lowest manner, the same food is also given to him in a lower manner. He who knows thus, will obtain all the rewards as mentioned above.

The upāsaka, who is generally a boy who is to return back to society and live as its pillar living in working out the Hindu culture, is exhorted therefore, to live in recognition of the spiritual oneness with all, especially an intimate oneness of an indissoluble brotherhood with the Hindus. Here it is not meant in the communalistic sense. The word 'Hindu' is universal rather than communal. He who respects and reveres the noble and the ethical values of life, who lives in self-control, whose mission in life is to end the animal in him and regain the kingdom of God 'within' – all such men of cultural ambition are Hindus and there is necessarily a deep affinity of soul between such men of similar values of life.

The boy going out into the world, after his education, is instructed so completely in the spiritual communism of the ṛṣis. This was observed earlier both in the 'valedictory speech' of the teacher at the close of the initial studies, and in the 'Convocation address' deliverd at the time when the students were departing from the gurukula.[1]

The culture of Hinduism is based mainly upon duty and the Hindu code of dharma is mainly a textbook explaining one's duties. The duties of a householder instill into him the idea of charity and the spirit of hospitality. It is considered as a duty, unavoidable to a householder, that he should entertain every guest that comes to him 'without date' (atithi). Thus, the householder student, during his upāsanā, was told to consider this atithi sevā as his vow.

In order to fulfil this vow, the students will have to entertain and worship the sick, the poor and the deserving travellers, with shelter and food. This needs that the householder must have the necessary means. Therefore it is said: 'Let one acquire much food by any means whatsoever'. The latter part of the quotation may sound like a declaration of the modern lusty rich to whom procuring wealth by 'any means' seems to be the ambition and the occupation. Here it

[1] Refer chepter I, sections ix and xi, page 112-138.

only means that the one who wants to live a healthy spiritual life in the world must be able to work hard in whatever field of activity he finds himself, with all the sincerity and perseverance, so that he may get enough honest profit.

This is not a message prescribing an unethical way of living or immoral way of procuring wealth. It only insists that a boy, after education, when he goes back to his village, in the arrogance of his undigested knowledge, should not prove himself impotent in life. He is told to act diligently and sincerely in whatever field of life he finds an opening and through sincere and hard work to earn as much as he can and with that earning, keep a house warm with charity and hospitality.

As soon as a guest comes into the house, at a time which is appropriate, then a noble Hindu householder must say: 'Food is ready'. The meaning of this passage and the ardour of love and warmth it indicates cannot be better expressed than by a contrast with how we are behaving now under the influence of our 'un-Hinduistic' education. In many of the homes, we rarely hear the ready cry of 'food is ready'. On the other hand, we hear suggestive soft hissings, such as "I hope you must have come after your meals," or "perhaps you will have to return home for your lunch".

In fact, to keep a hospitable home nowadays is not very easy even for the richest man in the country because of the dire poverty and stupendous idleness that have come to curse the land of the ṛṣis. The main cause for this is certainly not the foreign rule but the foreign 'way' we live in our society, divorced from our culture, perpetrating dangerous experiments with the life and wealth of the society. The Hindu dharma alone can flourish in āryāvarta; any other weeds gathered in the jungles of other nations must necessarily die away upon this sacred soil. Thus, the modern madness for a secularism divorced from sacredness, the lunatic hurry with which we are striving to encourage the worship of gold in this land of Gods; all these are bringing about more and more confusion and instability into our midst.

Under these circumstances of poverty and the consequent privations, it is absurd to say that a Hindu should try to be as openly charitable as his forefathers were in the golden era of our civilisation. In the context of our present times, we have to add many 'buts' and 'ifs' to the statement. It would be sufficient for us if we make our home charitable enough for the near and dear ones, and also for the respected and revered members of the society who are the upholders of our sacred culture and are the champions of our national and religious progress along the right lines.

To be charitable does not mean to be foolish. To borrow, so that we may give plenty in charity, is suicide. In a vulgar and misconceived sense of vanity, to overdo charity is again an ugly mischief which none but fools would appreciate. The Śruti here says. that if you have prepared the food of a particular standard, you feed your guest with the same food. If the householder had prepared medium quality or the simplest of food, he is not asked to prepare anything extra for his guests, but the mantra commissions him only to share his food, whatever it be, with others. He who understands this meaning and practises this, comes to gain all the above mentioned fruits.

From the standpoint of Bhṛgu, the section contains another deeper message. A Man of Realisation must, by honest and sincere means, collect around him the largest number audience from all around the world, so that he may propagate the noble truths of Vedānta for the happiness of man. 'By any means whatsoever', is confusing when it is understood in its direct meaning. It reads as though it is an unequivocal scriptural sanction for the philosophy of gains preached by the modern profit-mad 'social ulcers'! But, when it is applied to a man of Self-realisation, who is attempting to create a field all around the world, to spread this universal culture of peace and love, it reads as an instruction of Varuṇa to Bhṛgu impressing upon him the fact that one must, by all means at one's command, try to attract the attention of one's age and address it in its language.

The Vaidika teacher understood that this eternal Truth cannot be preached in the same language at all times in the world. Society and patterns of living change from era to era, so that re-interpretations of the truths are needed from time to time. Bhṛgu has been instructed here: 'by any means whatsoever', to bring the generation together to listen to, to act upon to, and to live in the Perfections preached in Vedānta.

If any seeker come to a Man of Knowledge, through Bhṛgu, Varuṇa instructs the Hindu world that a teacher should not on any score 'turn away anybody who seeks shelter'. 'If food – (the seeker's inner integration) is prepared in the best manner, feed him in the best manner' – give him direct instruction of 'That' – defined in this textbook as 'Satyam, Jñānam, Anantam'. If the seeker is mediocre, give him a mediocre instruction of some upāsanā with an equal dose of philosophy. If the seeker unfortunately, happens to be of the worst type, meaning, one who is full of desires and agitation, excitements and passion, brutalities and animalism, then, even such an individual is not be turned away from the temples of Vedānta. The priest therein, the Man of Realisation, has been instructed to feed such a man with the type of spiritual food which he can easily digest and assimilate. To such a seeker, first give instructions in āsana and prāṇāyāma. When, through this haṭha-yoga, the individual has developed both his head and heart to a certain degree, he is to be initiated into the more vigorous and subtler upāsanās; and when he reacts favourably to these treatments, the highest Truth of Vedānta is to be revealed.

That the ṛṣis of old were anxious to have the largest audience when they were discoursing upon the Truths of Vedānta is evident in the very first chapter of the textbook.

क्षेम इति वाचि । योगक्षेम इति प्राणापानयोः ।
कर्मेति हस्तयोः । गतिरिति पादयोः ।
विमुक्तिरिति पायौ । इति मानुषीः समाज्ञाः ।२ ॥

kṣema iti vāci, yogakṣema iti prāṇāpānayoḥ,
karmeti hastayoḥ, gatiriti pādayoḥ,
vimuktiriti pāyau, iti mānuṣīḥ samājñāḥ. (2)

क्षेमः – well-being, safety; **इति** – thus; **वाचि** – in speech; **योगक्षेमः** – (as) acquisition and preservation; **इति** – thus; **प्राण-अपानयोः** – in prāṇa and apāna; **कर्म इति** – as a work or action; **हस्तयोः** – in hands; **गतिः इति** – as movement; **पादयोः** – in legs; **विमुक्तिः इति** – as excretion; **पायौ** – in anus; **इति** – thus; **मानुषीः** – in respect of man; **समाज्ञाः** – (is) meditation (of Brahman)

2. The Supreme resides in speech as 'well-being'; in prāṇa and apāna as acquirer and preserver; in the hands as action, in the legs as movement, in the anus as the activity of excretion. Thus, is the meditation of Brahman in respect of man.

So far the ṛṣi had been explaining the four different methods of upāsanā on food (annam), which had a double implication – an obvious one for the back benchers and a mystic meaning, subtler in import and graver in suggestion, for Bhṛgu, the young boy of experienced Realisation. Here we have two more methods of meditation prescribed, which are meant for the subjective integration of the instruments of Self-realisation, addressed here only for the back benchers in the classroom.

The analytical brain of the immortal ṛṣis of India could classify any subject, however confusing it may look to the ordinary man. Concentration can be developed by meditation upon an object, and to classify all the possible methods of meditations would be a problem almost inconceivable to any statistician. But the Hindu ṛṣis had quite successfully brought all the then existing methods of meditation, and all possible future methods of meditation – the classification being upon the basis of the condition and character of the goal of meditation – under three main headings:

1. Ādhidaivika – When the aim of meditation is upon an unmanifest idea or ideal;

2. Ādhibhautika – When the point of concentration is upon an object or a phenomenon that is manifest; and

3. Ādhyātmika – When the individual's attempts at concentration are directed towards his own physical structure and its inner world.

Under these three groups, all upāsanās can find a place. We have here the ādhyātmika and a happy combination of the other two forms of meditations. That is to say, we have a scheme of meditation described wherein ādhidaivika truths are recognised in ādhibhautika phenomenon.

The section under discussion is describing the ādhyātmika methods. Meditation upon the human personality itself, both upon its activities as well as its own structure, is described here. To superimpose a subtler and nobler idea on a grosser and ordinary object is called upāsanā. We have already seen that upāsanā is the attempt of recognising the mighty upon the meagre, as Śiva tattva upon a round stone, or the national pride and hope upon the nation's flag.

Applying this technique, the teacher instructs the student to recognise the 'Brahman in speech as well-being.' As students they are ever living in the world of sound; later on, they are to walk out into the world where also they will have to face incessantly the sound of others speaking. Thus speech is a continuous disturbance that always reaches our ears. We get disturbed by speech only when we try to understand its obvious outer meaning. The more we recognise the inner motive of every sound, made from whatever source it be, there is a unifying truth that binds them all together into a golden embrace of homogeneity. This common factor is described by the scripture here as 'kṣema' – well-being.

From the howlings of an innocent child in his mother's lap, to the thundering declarations of a politician on his platform; all sounds emerging out of any living throats are all expressions of an attempt at realising its well-being. The child weeps, seeking its well-being to be gained through some food or with some toy. The criminal and the vulgar become noisy with their foul mouths for their own well-being. The scandal monger talks ill of his neighbours, the deceiver tells a lie, the devotee sings a song, a ṛṣi gives a discourse – all of them are struggling their best to seek their own individual well-being.

Varuṇa instructs his students to recognise this fundamental factor in all sounds, wherever they are heard; may be in a jungle in the night when wild animals roar, in the daytime when the 'joy throated' birds chirp, or chirrup, where the bees buzz, or in society when men and women, young and old, make a thousand different noises in the market place, or in the temples, or in various other walks of life – all of them are, in their own way, motivated by their own conceptions of their individual well-being.

In prāṇa see Brahman as acquirer and preserver: – Prāṇa is the vitality that functions in the five sense organs which procure for the mind the new impulses for its experience. Yoga is 'procuring for ourselves that which we have not got in hand at present'. Kṣema is 'preserving that which is procured'. Thus the term yoga and kṣema together indicate a progressive growth which is constantly maintained and consistently preserved. It is by the healthy working of the vitalities in us represented by prāṇa and apāna that yoga and kṣema are maintained in ourselves.

In the hands see Brahman as the action: – Varuṇa means that if the student finds it difficult to detect and recognise well-being in all talks or cannot understand the idea of yoga kṣema in the main vital expressions of life, then he may more easily direct his meditations upon his own hand. In all hands, though they differ in shape, size, colour and strength, though they are employed in a million different activities; in all of them, the one common truth is that, at all times, however employed, all hands are doing or performing actions. Therefore, Brahman, which is common in all forms and names, can be identified as the action in all hands.

So too, 'motion in all legs', and even 'in the anus see him as the act of excretion'. One may wonder how the ṛṣis so readily jump from the sublime to the ridiculous. In the Upaniṣads this is invariably used as a very effective technique to arrest the wandering attention of the students. This is the main duty of a true teacher. Also, when we are considering the all-pervading Divine, we must be able to realise It even in the vulgar and in the filthy. Anyone who has some understanding of physiology will also admit that the action of excretion is as important for sound health and as sacred as the activity of swallowing down the food. Constipation is a threat to health and ultimately to life. In fact, apāna functioning in the anus directly determines the activities of the prāṇa on the face. There is an intimate relationship between these two forces working within us.

These are the methods of meditation that can be profitably undertaken by a student upon his own individual human personality.

अथ दैवीः । तृप्तिरिति वृष्टौ ।
बलमिति विद्युति । यश इति पशुषु
ज्योतिरिति नक्षत्रेषु । प्रजातिरमृतमानन्द इत्युपस्थे ।
सर्वमित्याकाशे ॥३॥

atha daivīḥ, tṛptiriti vṛṣṭau,
balamiti vidyuti, yaśa iti paśuṣu
jyotiriti nakṣatreṣu, prajātiramṛtamānanda ityupasthe,
sarvamityākāśe. (3)

अथ – then; दैवीः – pertaining to devas; तृप्तिः इति – as satisfaction; वृष्टौ – in the rains; बलम् इति – as strength, power; विद्युति – in lightning; यशः इति – as fame; पशुषु – in cattle (wealth); ज्योतिः इति – as light; नक्षत्रेषु – in stars; प्रजातिः – as offspring, procreation; अमृतम् – immortality, आनन्दः – (and) bliss; इति – as; उपस्थे – in the organs of procreation; सर्वम् इति – as all; आकाशे– in ākāśā

3. Now follows the meditation upon the ādhidaivika; as satisfaction in the rains, as power in the lightning; as fame in the cattle, as light in the stars, as offspring, immortality and joy in the organs of procreation and as all in the ākāśa.

In this section, we find a type of meditation wherein, though the point of meditation is upon some manifested phenomenon in nature, an unmanifested ideal or concept is superimposed upon these points of concentration. Though rains sometimes have their own nuisance value and can bring about floods in certain places and consequent misery to man and things, it generally brings satisfaction to the great majority all over the face of the globe. Plants get thrilled and 'laugh out' into tender foliage and brilliant flowers as the rains descend. Animal life becomes extremely happy as the pasture lands dress up in their green velveteen.The farmers everywhere dance in joy as the rains descend – nay, even the mill owners, if they are not merely financers, they too take an active interest in rains and feel thrilled with proper rainfall at proper seasons: since their raw materials too depend upon this benevolence of the skies.

To see satisfaction in the rain is a subtle form of meditation indeed. So too is it to recognise fame in the cattle wealth of a country which is essentially and irredeemably agricultural. The stars in the summer sky may lie scattered in a hundred directions: some small, others big; some nearer, others farther; some solitary, others in groups; and yet in all of them, there is a principle of light that knits them together into one family – a family of incandescent glory!

Even the reproductory organ is not excluded, be it in the stamen or in the pistil, in the male or in the female, in man or in woman, for purpose of meditation. The seekers being young would, naturally, at that age, be spending, in spite of themselves, a lot of thought upon the organs of procreation and this obvious sex instinct is not ignored but conscripted for the higher purpose of self-integration. To ignore it and to encourage its suppression is a sure path for self-disintegration. 'Offspring, immortality and joy can be recognised upon these genital organs'. It is obvious that 'in the concept of space we can easily recognise a substratum for all things in the universe'.

तत्प्रतिष्ठेत्युपासीत । प्रतिष्ठावान् भवति ।
तन्मह इत्युपासीत । महान् भवति ।
तन्मन इत्युपासीत । मानवान् भवति ।
तन्नम इत्युपासीत । नम्यन्तेऽस्मै कामाः ।
तद्ब्रह्मेत्युपासीत । ब्रह्मवान् भवति ।
तद्ब्रह्मणः परिमर इत्युपासीत ।
पर्येणं म्रियन्ते द्विषन्तः सपत्नाः ।
परि येऽप्रिया भ्रातृव्याः ॥४॥

tatpratiṣṭhetyupāsīta, pratiṣṭhāvān bhavati,
tanmaha ityupāsīta, mahān bhavati,
tanmana ityupāsīta, mānavān bhavati,
tannam ityupāsīta, namyante'smai kāmāḥ,
tadbrahmetyupāsīta, brahmavān bhavati,
tadbrahmaṇaḥ parimara ityupāsīta,
paryeṇaṁ mriyante dviṣantaḥ sapatnāḥ,
pari ye'priyā bhrātṛvyāḥ. (4)

तत् – that (Brahman); प्रतिष्ठा इति – as support; उपासीत – let him meditate; प्रतिष्ठावान् – well supported; भवति – he becomes; तत् – that (Brahman); महः इति – as great; उपासीत – let him meditate; महान् – great; भवति – he becomes; तत् – that (Brahman); मनः इति – as mind; उपासीत – let him meditate; मानवान् – thoughtful; भवति – becomes; तत् – that (Brahman); नमः इति – as obeisance; उपासीत – let him meditate; नम्यन्ते – they come to pay homage; अस्मै – to him; कामाः – all desires; तत् – that (Brahman); ब्रह्म इति – as Brahman; उपासीत – let him meditate; ब्रह्मवान् – wielding supremacy; भवति – he becomes; तत् – that (Brahman); ब्रह्मणः – of Brahman; परिमर – universal dissolver, destructive aspect; इति – thus; उपासीत – let him meditate; परि एणम् – around him; म्रियन्ते – die; द्विषन्तः – the hateful; सपत्नाः – enemies; परि – die; ये – those, who (are); अप्रियाः – unloving; भ्रातृव्याः – rivals

4. Let him meditate the Supreme as the support; he becomes well supported. Let one worship Brahman as great, one becomes great. Let one worship It as mind; he becomes thoughtful. Let him worship That as namaḥ (obeisance); to him all desires shall come to pay homage. Let him meditate upon That as the Supreme; he comes to supremacy in life.

Let him contemplate upon That as the 'destructive aspect' of Brahman; all those enemies who hate him and those rivals whom he does not like 'die around him'.

In this section, we find a great psychological truth enunciated and experiments are described to illustrate it. 'As you think, so you become', is a great truth recognised, accepted and declared, not only by the ṛṣis of old, but even by modern psychologists. Each one of us, at this moment, is an illustration in point. Everyone, whether he is a doctor or an engineer, a driver or an advocate, a student or a dullard, a pickpocket or a minister; whatever he be at present, is the result of his constant meditation and the resultant of his thoughts. When during concentration, if we approach the Lord with a definite attitude; we come to express that very same bhāva in our life also.

Thus, we find a lot of difference between a Christ and an Aurobindo, a Śaṅkarācārya and a Ramana, a Guru Govind Singh and Caitanya Mahāprabhu. The attitude with which you meditate determines your character, temperament, behaviour and demeanour. The courage of Napoleon, the heroism of Gandhiji, the daring of Hitler, the perseverence of Churchill, the surrender of Ramakrishna, the dynamism of Vivekananda, are all different attitudes which the great Masters expressed. This was because of the different bhāvas with which they meditated and approached the Supreme.

Here this idea is beautifully brought out when the teacher says that by meditating upon the Supreme as the support of the entire world of plurality, one becomes well supported by his fellow beings and the circumstances in life. Similarly, by meditating upon the Supreme as great, the sādhaka becomes great in life; to meditate upon the Lord as the mind is to yourself become a great thinker in your era.

The rest is all clear except the last phrase, where it is said that if the Lord is meditated upon as the 'destructive power manifested in the world' (as we have in śakti upāsanās), we develop in ourselves such might and glory, such a powerful and compelling personality that opposition withers into nothingness and even enemies become friends and allies. Here the word 'die around' is not to be construed to mean that our enemies will die away; rather, we should understand that the enmity will die away. Without the feelings of enmity, the enemy cannot maintain his belligerent attitude towards us.

स यश्चायं पुरुषे यश्चासावादित्ये स एकः ।
स य एवंवित् । अस्माल्लोकात्प्रेत्य ।
एतमन्नमयमात्मानमुपसंक्रम्य ।
एतं प्राणमयमात्मानमुपसंक्रम्य ।
एतं मनोमयमात्मानमुपसंक्रम्य ।
एतं विज्ञानमयमात्मानमुपसंक्रम्य ।
एतमानन्दमयमात्मानमुपसंक्रम्य ।
इमाँल्लोकान्कामान्नी कामरूप्यनुसंचरन् ।
एतत्साम गायन्नास्ते ॥५॥

sa yaścāyaṁ puruṣe yaścāsāvāditye sa ekaḥ,
sa ya evaṁvit, asmāllokātpretya,
etamannamayamātmānamupasaṁkramya,
etaṁ prāṇamayamātmānamupasaṁkramya,
etaṁ manomayamātmānamupasaṁkramya,
etaṁ vijñānamayamātmānamupasaṁkramya,
etamānandamayamātmānamupasaṁkramya,
imāṁllokānkāmānnī kāmarūpyanusancaran,
etatsāma gāyannāste. (5)

सः – he; **यः** – who; **च** – and; **अयम्** – this one; **पुरुषे** – in the man; **यः** – who; **च** – and; **असौ** – yonder; **आदित्ये** – in the sun; **सः** – he; **एकः** – is one; **सः** – he; **यः** – who; **एवंवित्** – know thus; **अस्मात्** – from this; **लोकात्** – world; **प्रेत्य** – on leaving; **एतम्** – this; **अन्नमयम् आत्मानम् उपसंक्रम्य** – attaining the Ātman made of food; **एतम् प्राणमयम् आत्मानम् उपसंक्रम्य** – attaining this Ātman made of prāṇa; **एतम् मनोमयम् आत्मानम् उपसंक्रम्य** – attaining this Ātman made of mind; **एतम् विज्ञानमयम् आत्मानम् उपसंक्रम्य** – attaining this Ātman made of knowledge; **एतम् आनन्दमयम् आत्मानम् उपसंक्रम्य** – attaining the Ātman made of bliss; **इमान् लोकान्** – these worlds; **कामान्नी** – having the food he likes; **कामरूपी** – having the form he wants; **अनुसंचरन्** – wandering, roaming; **एतत्** – this; **साम** – Sāman (song); **गायन्** – singing; **आस्ते**– continues, remains

5. The Reality in the core of man and the Reality which is in the sun are one. He who knows this, on leaving this world, first attains this Ātman made of food, next attains this Ātman made of prāṇa, next this Ātman made of mind, next this Ātman made of buddhi and lastly, this Ātman made of Bliss. And, thereafter, eating what he likes and assuming any form

according to his wishes, he roams upon the face of this globe and sits singing the following sāma song of joy.

The earlier part of this mantra has already been quoted in Brahmānanda Vallī, Section vi[1].

The very style of the Upaniṣads is carved in brevity and to repeat an idea twice is almost a blasphemy in the Upaniṣads. And yet, here we find an entire mantra being repeated. The justification of the teacher is that he has nothing more to add. He said these truths earlier when he had finished his 'statistics of bliss'. He had found that the students were not, at that time, ready to react to those words, because, as it were, their enthusiasm was dampened by the fear that this method, as suggested in Vedānta, of Self-enquiry into the various personality layers in man, though obviously quite direct, was not a fruitful method for Self-realisation.

Thus the teacher was forced to repeat the story of Bhṛgu's success at the feet of Varuṇa and again impart some more upāsanā methods which were intended to bring the students to the highest point of their inner integration. After having done so, he again repeats the mantra.

I want to blast some gun powder, but I find that a heap of it does not react to the naked flame of a match stick. Then I will have to understand that it is damp, and, therefore, I will have to dry it properly. After making the powder dry, I will have to again bring the naked flame to it.

---

[1] Page 200-205

Similarly the teacher brought this mantra as a spark from his own inward conflagration of knowledge earlier at the end of the second chapter, but he found that the children's minds and intellects did not get blasted off! The treatment suggested in the third chapter prepares the students better and now the Master is bringing the same spark of wisdom – declaration to them. To his satisfaction he finds that the inner world of the students burst out into a brilliant conflagration, wherein their ignorance gets blasted and the entire 'valley of darkness' is lit up at once by the blaze of Knowledge and divine Realisation.

In the later portion of the mantra, a new idea is added to declare what would be the kind of attitude taken and the type of activity undertaken by such a Man of Realisation who has left his little world of the body-mind-intellect and has become a native to a divine world of pure Knowledge and Self-realisation.

After this rediscovery of the Divine in the mortal, the awakened man thereafter comes to live in perfect freedom and godly joys. As the mantra says: 'assuming forms according to his wishes', he roams about on the face of the globe as a mighty pinnacle of joy and peace, tranquillity and poise, daring and goodness, divinity and perfection. Whether he finds himself among the lowest of the low or in the palace of a king, be he in health or in disease, in joy or in sorrow; he is at home in all situations and in all conditions.

Whether in the kingly robes of might and power or in the rags of the poor man, starving and suffering; he is the king of the situation, a Lord of circumstances, a Master of himself and a ruler of everybody. Unattached to any place or person, he roams about on the face of the globe expecting nothing, demanding nothing, wanting nothing, desiring nothing, singing the song of his own joy. Revelling in his own inward experiences of transcendental Bliss and consummate fulfilment, he sits at one place or roams about as his fancy dictates. The song of his joy is expressed here in the Sāma verse quoted below:

हा३वु हा३वु हा३वु ।
अहमन्नमहमन्नमहमन्नम् ।
अहमन्नादो३ऽहमन्नादो३ऽहमन्नादः ।
अहगंश्लोककृदहगंश्लोककृदहगंश्लोककृत् ।
अहमस्मि प्रथमजा ऋता३स्य ।
पूर्वं देवेभ्योऽमृतस्य ना३भायि ।
यो मा ददाति स इदेव मा३वाः ।
अहमन्नमन्नमदन्तमा३द्मि ।
अहं विश्वं भुवनमभ्यभवा३म् ।
सुवर्न ज्योतीः य एवं वेद । इत्युपनिषत् ॥६ ॥

hā3vu hā3vu hā3vu,
ahamannamahamannamahamannam,
ahamannādo3'ham-annādo3'hamannādaḥ,
ahagṁ-ślokakṛd-ahagṁ-ślokakṛdahagṁ-ślokakṛt,
ahamasmi prathamajā ṛtā3sya,

pūrvaṁ devebhyo'mṛtasya nā3 bhāyi,
yo mā dadāti sa ideva mā3vāḥ,
ahamannamannamadantamā3'dmi,
ahaṁ viśvaṁ bhuvanamabhyabhavā3m,
suvarna jyotīḥ ya evaṁ veda, ityupaniṣat. (6)

हावु हावु हावु – Oh, Oh, Oh; अहम् – I; अन्नम् – (am) food; अहम् अन्नम् – I am food; अहम् अन्नम् – I am food; अहम् – I; अन्नादः – (am) the eater of food; अहम् अन्नादः – I am the eater of food; अहम् =I; श्लोककृत् – (am) the author of the śloka; अहम् श्लोककृत् – I am the author of the śloka; अहम् श्लोककृत् – I am the author of the śloka[1]; अहम् – I; अस्मि – am; प्रथमजा – first-born (hiraṇyagarbha); ऋतस्य – of the True (the Eternal and the Immortal); पूर्वम् – prior, before; देवेभ्यः – the gods; अमृतस्य – of immortality; ना भायि – the navel (centre); यः – who; मा – me; ददाति – gives; सः – he; इत् – surely; एव – alone; मा – me; आवाः – protects, saves; अहम् – I; अन्नम् – food; अन्नम् – food; अदन्तम् – one who eats; अद्मि – swallow, eat; अहम् – I; विश्वम् – the whole; भुवनम् – world; अभ्यभवाम् – have conquered, overcome; सुवर्न ज्योतीः – (I am) luminous like the sun; यः – (he) who; एवम् – thus; वेद – knows; इति – thus; उपनिषत् – is the Upaniṣad

6. Oh! Oh! Oh! I am the food, I am the food, I am the food. I am the eater of food, I am the eater of food, I am the eater of food, I am the author of the śloka, I am the author of the śloka, I am the author of the śloka. I am the first born (Hiraṇyagarbha) of the True (of the Eternal and the Immortal). I am the centre of immortality, prior to the Gods. Whoever gives me, he surely does save thus. I am the food that eats him who eats food.

[1] Another meaning is 'I am unifier (of the food and the eater of the food).'

I have conquered all, in this world. I am luminous like the sun. He who knows thus (also attains the aforesaid results) This is the Upaniṣad.

On realising his real Nature to be nothing but the Spirit, the ego-centre gets struck with awe! His wonderment, choking the giddy emotions, makes language impossible. The heart stammers out seeking and searching for words to express the infinite experience of the moments of Self-realisation. The false identifications with the body, mind and intellect created the dream frankenstein within ourselves, and it is this powerful though delusory ego-centre that has suffered the feeling of many passions and sorrows, finitude and plurality, of the mortal. All these years I have lived as a helpless victim of birth, growth, disease, decay and death.

On rediscovery through the right processes of Self-realisation as narrated in Vedānta, when the same ego-centre walks out of its delusory world of the sheaths, it reaches the realm of the homogeneous, spiritual experience. On waking up from that experience, he tries to mouth his infinite discovery through finite words! Language naturally breaks, and like the music in a broken reed, halts and splashes in wrong tunes and meaningless noises!

Oh! Oh! Oh! – Wonder is a sentiment that the human heart feels when the intellect comes in contact with a problem that it cannot itself solve. The mute intellect trying to express through a choked heart its burning experiences, is the expression of surprise and wonderment. This is nowhere so well expressed as in Sanskrit, in the words 'ha-vu; ha-vu; ha-vu'; since these onomatopoetic words clearly transcribe the particular sounds a man should make during such moments of irrepressible and staggering wonder.

Limited being that he thought himself to be in his delusory relationship with his five sheaths, he suddenly shakes himself off his limitations – when he transcends them all through true discrimination – and discovers himself to be the pure spark of life, the very centre of all the activities in life. Even when a farmer is suddenly informed that he has been lucky enough to get the first prize in the Derby Sweep; at the impact of the idea that he has become a millionaire, he sometimes drops down dead. How much more then, must be the shock of Realisation when a man suddenly rediscovers that he is God! That feeling is expressed here in the words of amazement and wonder, surprise and stupor, through blabbering tones that stammer and repeat themselves in jerky confusion.

I am food, I am food: – This is the declaration of his experience that I, the subject, am myself the food, meaning, the world of objects. He realises that the pluralistic phenomenal world is but a projection of the Self in him. When pure Consciousness gets refracted at the prism made up of the body, mind and intellect, the world of objects is perceived. When a child looks at its own palm through the yellow glass pane of the window, he sees his palm yellow; similarly, when Consciousness looks out upon Itself through the spectacles of It's own matter envelopments, It seems to see the world of plurality standing mighty and powerful, to choke It and threaten It! The ghost in the post can threaten, with its fearful looks, an innocent traveller passing by on the road!

I am the eater of food, I am the eater of food: – The blabbering still continues and does not exhaust itself with the mere declarations of its experienced oneness with the entire world of objects, but in its attempts at voicing forth its experiences, it had to cry that it is not only one with the objects but, at the same time, it is the subject itself. I am the experiencer of 'food'. I am the subject that makes possible all the experiences of the objectified world. In short, the statements, by their repetition, emphatically declare and insist upon the sure and certain experience of the Perfect: he is not only one with the entire world of objects but at once he is the subject, the centre of the entire universe. In fact, the cry is an attempt at expressing the transcendental experience of the oneness of the subject and the object, the eater and the eaten, the experiencer and the experienced.

In this sense, this Sāma verse can be considered as a golden chord of a song binding together the subject and the object into one unified whole. It is the song of life sung to the music of experience, expressing the poetry of life, titled – 'I am'.

I am the first born of the Eternal and the Immortal: – Because, though born, I am the only one who is conscious of not only my person but also of the divine heritage of my transcendental glory. In the world, the first born son alone comes to live and experience the wealth inherited from his father. Out of the Infinite and the Immortal, the finite was born and when it rediscovers it's own Self, it alone can cry that it is the 'first born', in the sense that it alone has the entire right to the father's status and dignity, wealth and glory.

I am the centre of all Immortality, prior to the Gods: – The Self is immortal and the experience of the oneness of the individual Self with the universal Self is to realise the Infinite and the Eternal. All living creatures draw their share of existence only from the immortal Existence of the Truth. Gods are, relatively considered as immortal, and their immortality is also supported and fed by the immortal Self. The individual who has realised his oneness with his own Self, therefore, cries that even through the purer and the nobler equipments of the Gods, 'It is I, the Self, that revels and expresses'.

I have conquered all the world: – This is the cry of all the great souls of Self-realisation, God-consciousness. 'I am the Caesar's Caesar', cried one; 'I am the Śahenśāha,' sang another; 'I am the Rājā of Rājās,' insisted another; 'I am God' roared the ṛṣis – 'Śivoham, Śivoham'. Universally, man at this spiritual experience always feels his complete freedom from his shackling sense of dependence, limitations and bondages. When he becomes relieved from his inward slavery, he instantaneously feels that he has really become free from all his desires and wants, his misconceptions about himself and has gained his svarājya, where he knows no other God or king except his own Self. The world can no more threaten him. The entire universe thereafter exists because of his Existence; Indra's might, Viṣṇu's greatness, Śiva's prowess, Brahmā's creative ability – all have come to borrow their potency from the source of all dynamism, power and vitality, the Brahman – the Self.

I am luminous like the sun: – In the universe, the sun is the source of all light, as he is the source of all energy. This is accepted by modern physicists also. The sun being nothing but light, no other light is necessary to illumine the sun; in saying, 'like the sun', the self-effulgence of the sun is specially indicated. All other things are illumined borrowing the sun's light. Similarly, the Self being pure Knowledge, it is self-effulgent; therefore, no other knowledge is needed to know that Knowledge. Here the Saint of Realisation cries his experience of divinity which he has realised in himself.

This transcendental and superhuman experience is not the rare privilege of an exceptional individual because of some rare circumstances of the age or due to some exceptional grace of an extra godly teacher; but it shall be the experience of everyone of us, as is indicated here when the mantra concludes 'he who knows thus'. All those who come to realise the self-effulgent Ātman come to enjoy this sovereignity over the pluralistic phenomenal world and the true Bliss of Immortality.

This is the Upaniṣad: – We have already described earlier the term Upaniṣad and its significance.[1]

This announcement is necessary lest the students misunderstand that the teacher has not given out all the

[1] Refer page 262

instructions. They may doubt that there is yet some more lessons to be studied. The teacher announces that he has exhausted his discourse and that, he has nothing more to add on the subject. Especially, we can understand the need for such a definite declaration in a tradition wherein the scripture is taught and learnt orally. In memorising a passage, its conclusions have to be noted by positive statements which declare from time to time that the passage has been concluded.

Concluding Śāntipāṭha

ॐ सह नाववतु । सह नौ भुनक्तु ।
सहवीर्यं करवावहै
तेजस्वि नावधीतमस्तु । मा विद्विषावहै ॥
ॐ शान्तिः शान्तिः शान्तिः ॥७॥

om saha nāvavatu, saha nau bhunaktu,
sahavīryaṁ karavāvahai
tejasvi nāvadhītamastu, mā vidviṣāvahai.
om śāntiḥ śāntiḥ śāntiḥ.

ॐ – symbol of the Para Brahman; सह – together; नौ – us both; अवतु – may He protect; सह – together; नौ – us both; भुनक्तु – may He help us to enjoy (the fruits of scriptural study); सह – together; वीर्यम् – with enthusiasm; करवावहै – exert together (to find the true meaning of sacred texts); तेजस्वि – brilliant; नौ – of both of us; अधीतम् – study; अस्तु – may be; मा – never; विद्विषावहै – (may we two) quarrel
ॐ – Om; शान्तिः – Peace; शान्तिः – Peace; शान्तिः – Peace

Om. May He protect us both. May He help us both to enjoy the fruits of scriptural study. May we both exert together with enthusiasm to find the true meaning of the sacred text. May our studies make us brilliant. May we never quarrel with each other.

(Om Peace! Peace!! Peace!!!)

ॐ शं नो मित्रः शं वरुणः। शं नो भवत्वर्यमा।
शं न इन्द्रो बृहस्पतिः। शं नो विष्णुरुरुक्रमः।
नमो ब्रह्मणे। नमस्ते वायो।
त्वमेव प्रत्यक्षं ब्रह्मासि।
त्वामेव प्रत्यक्षं ब्रह्मावादिषम्।
ऋतमवादिषम्। सत्यमवादिषम्। तन्मामावीत्।
तद्वक्तारमावीत्। आवीन्माम्। आवीद्वक्तारम् ॥
ॐ शान्तिः शान्तिः शान्तिः ॥८ ॥

Om śaṁ no mitraḥ śaṁ varuṇaḥ, śaṁ no bavatvaryamā,
śaṁ na indro bṛhaspatiḥ, śaṁ no viṣṇururukramaḥ,
namo brahmaṇe, namaste vāyo,
tvameva pratyakṣaṁ brahmāsi,
tvāmeva pratyakṣaṁ brahmāvādiṣam,
ṛtamavādiṣam, satyamavādiṣam, tanmāmāvīt,
tadvaktāramāvīt, āvīnmām, āvīdvaktāram.
Om Śāntiḥ, Śāntiḥ, Śāntiḥ. (8)

ॐ – om; शम् – propitious; नः – to us; मित्रः – controller of day and prāṇa; शम् – propitious; वरुणः – controller of night and apāna; शम् – propitious; नः – to us; भवतु – may be; अर्यमा – controller of eyes and sun's orbit; शम् – propitious; नः – to us; इन्द्रः – controller of strength and arms; बृहस्पतिः – controller of speech and intellect; शम् – propitious; नः – to us; विष्णुः – controller of feet; उरुक्रमः – the all-pervading (wide-striding); नमः – salutation(s); ब्रह्मणः – unto Brahman; नमः – salutations; ते – unto thee; वायो – O Vayū; त्वम् – to thou; एव – alone; प्रत्यक्षम् – perceivable; ब्रह्म – Brahman; असि – art; त्वाम् – to thou; एव – alone; प्रत्यक्षम् – perceivable; ब्रह्म – Brahman; वादिषम् – I declared; ऋतम् – controller of 'right'; वादिषम् – I declared;

सत्यम् – controller of the 'good'; वादिषम् – I declared; तत् – that (Brahman); माम् – me; आवीत् – protected; तत् – that (Brahman); वक्तारम् – the speaker; आवीत् – protected; आवीत् – protected; माम् – me; आवीत् – protected; वक्तारम् – the speaker
ॐ – Om; शान्तिः – Peace; शान्तिः – Peace; शान्तिः – Peace

May Mitra (Sun) be good to us. May Varuṇa be good to us. May Aryamā be good to us. May Indra and Bṛhaspati be good to us. May the all-pervading Viṣṇu be good to us. Prostrations to Brahman. Prostrations to Thee, O Vāyu! Thou indeed art the visible Brahman. Thee I have declared the 'Good'. That has protected me. That has protected the teacher.

(Om Peace ! Peace !! Peace !!!)

For the word meanings and the implications of this invocation we may refer to the discourses reported on the same peace invocation at the opening of this Upaniṣad (ch.I and ch.II)

Exhaustive explanations have already been given upon these two Peace invocations (on Page 1 & 130) It is the sacred tradition in the study of Brahmavidyā that the teacher and the taught recite the 'Peace-Invocation' both at the beginning and at the end of each lesson.

(Thus ends Bhṛgu-vallī)

(Here ends the Taittirīya-upaniṣad)

Om Tat Sat

Alphabetical Index of Mantras

[Some of the verses are split in the commentary, the beginning alphabet of the break-up as well as other important lines/ statements although not forming the beginning of the verse are included in the index below to facilitate easy location.]

अग्निः पूर्वरूपम्	I. iii.3
अथ दैवीः	III. X. 3
अथ यदि ते	I. xi. 6
अथातोऽनुप्रश्नाः	II. vi. 2
अथातः सगुंहिताया उपनिषदम्	I. iii. 1
अथाधिज्यौतिषम्	I. iii. 3
अथाधिप्रजम्	I. iii. 5
अथाधिलोकम्	I. iii. 2
अथाधिविद्यम्	I. iii. 4
अथाध्यात्मम्	I. iii. 6
अथाभ्याख्यातेषु	I. xi. 7
अधरा हनुः पूर्वरूपम्	I. iii. 6
अन्नं न परिचक्षीत्	III. viii. I
अन्नं न निन्द्यात्	III. vii. 1
अन्नं बहु कुर्वीत	III. ix. 1
अन्नं ब्रह्मेति व्यजानात्	III. ii. 1
अन्नगुं हि भूतानां ज्येष्ठम्	II. ii. 1
अन्नाद्वै प्रजाः प्रजायन्ते	II. ii. 1
अन्नाद् भूतानि जायन्ते	II. ii. 1
असद्वा इदमग्र आसीत्	II. vii. 1
अहं वृक्षस्य रेरिवा	I.x.1
आकाशशरीरं ब्रह्म	I.vi.2
आचार्यः पूर्वरूपम्	I.iii. 4
आनन्दो ब्रह्मेति व्यजानात्	III.vi.1
आनन्दाद्ध्येव खल्विमानि	III.vi.1
आप्नोति स्वाराज्यम्	I.vi.2
आमायन्तु ब्रह्मचारिणः	I.iv.2
आवहन्ती वितन्वाना	I.iv.2
इतीमा महासगुंहिताः	I.iii.7
ऋतं च स्वाध्याय	I.ix.1
एतमानन्दमयमात्मानम्	II.viii.12
एतमानन्दमयमात्मानम्	III.x.5
एतगुं ह वाव न तपति	II.ix.2
एष आदेशः एष उपदेशः	I.xi.8
ओमिति ब्रह्म	I.viii.1
ओमित्यतद्	I.viii.2
को ह्येवान्यात् कः प्राण्यात्	II.vii.2
क्षेम इति वाचि	III.x.2
तगुं होवाच	III.i.3
तत्प्रतिष्ठेत्युपासीत	III.x.4

असन्नेव स भवति	II. vi. 1
अहमन्नमहमन्नम्	III. x. 6
अहमस्मि प्रथमजा	III. x.6
तपसा ब्रह्म विजिज्ञासस्व	III.ii. 1
तस्माद्वा एतस्मादन्नरसमयात्	II. ii. 2
तस्माद्वा एतस्मादात्मन	II. i. 3
तस्माद्वा एतस्मान्मनोमयात्	II. iv. 2
तस्यैष एव शारीर आत्मा प्राणमयात्	II. iii.2
तस्यैष एव शारीर आत्मा..... विज्ञानमयात्	II. v 2
ता वा एताः	I. v 6
ते ये शतं आजानजानां	II. viii 6
ते ये शतं इन्द्रस्य	II.viii.9
ते ये शतं कर्मदेवानाम्	II.viii.7
ते ये शतं देव	II. viii.4
ते ये शतं देवानाम्	II.viii. 8
ते ये शतं प्रजापतेः	II. viii.11
ते ये शतं पितृणां	II.viii.5
ते ये शतं मनुष्यगन्धर्वाणां	II. viii.3
ते ये शतं बृहस्पतेः	II. viii.10
देवपितृकार्याभ्यां	I. xi.2
न कंचन वसतौ प्रत्याचक्षीत	III. x.1
नो इतराणि	I.xi.3
पाङ्क्तं वा इदगं सर्वम्	I.vii.1
पृथिवी पूर्वरूपम	I.iii.2
पृथिव्यन्तरिक्षं द्यौर्दिशः	I.vii.1
प्राणं देवा अनुप्राणन्ति	II.iii.1
तत्सृष्ट्वा तदेवानुप्राविशत्	II.vi.3
तदनुप्रविश्य सच्च	II.vi.3
तन्नम् इत्युपासीत्	III.x.4
भूरिति वा ऋचः	I.v.4
भूरिति वा अग्निः	I.v.3
भूरिति वा अयम् लोकः	I.v.2
भूरिति वा प्राणः	I.v.5
भूर्भुवः सुवरिति	I.v.1
भृगुर्वै वारुणिः	III.i.2
मनो ब्रह्मेति व्यजानात्	III.iv.1
मह इति तद् ब्रह्म	I.v.1
मह इति ब्रह्म	I.v.4
मह इत्यादित्यः	I.v.2
मातृ देवो भव	I.ix.2
माता पूर्वरूपम्	I.iii.5
यतो वा इमानि भूतानि	III.i.3
यतो वाचो निवर्तन्ते.....कदाचन	II.iv.1
यतो वाचो निवर्तन्ते.....कुतश्चन	II.ix.1
यदा ह्येवैष एतस्मिन्	II.vii.3
यद्वै तत् सुकृतं	II.vii.2
यश इति पशुषु	III.x.3
यशो जनेऽसानि स्वाहा	I.iv.3
यश्छन्दसामृषभो	I.iv.1
यान्यनवद्यानि	I.xi.3
ये तत्र ब्राह्मणाः सम्मर्शिनः	I.xi.6
ये के चास्मच्छ्रेयागंसो	I.xi.4
रसो वै सः	II.vii.2
विज्ञानं ब्रह्मेति व्याजानात्	III.v.1

प्राणो व्यानोऽपान I.vii.1

प्राणो ब्रह्मेति व्यजानात् III.iii.1

ब्रह्मविदाप्नोति परम् II.i.2

भीषास्माद्वातः पवते II.viii.1

भूरित्यग्नौ प्रतितिष्ठति I.vi.2

श्रद्धया देयम् I.xi.5

श्रोत्रियस्य चाकामहतस्य II.viii.2

स एको मनुष्यगन्धर्वाणाम् II.viii.2

सत्यं ज्ञानमनन्तं ब्रह्म II.i.2

सत्यं वद धर्मं चर I.xi.1

स वा एष पुरुषः II.i.4

स य एवंवित् III.x.5

स य एषोऽन्तर्हृदय I.vi.1

विज्ञानं यज्ञं तनुते II.v.1

वेदमनूच्याचार्योऽन्तेवासिन I.xi.1

शं नो मित्रः शं वरुणः I.i.1

शं नो मित्रः शं वरुणः I.xii.1

शीक्षां व्याख्यास्यामः I.ii.1

स यश्चायं पुरुषे...उपसंक्रामति II.viii.12

स यश्चायं पुरुषे...उपसंक्रम्य III.x.5

सह नाववतु सह नौ भुनक्तु II.Śā.Pā.1

सह नौ यशः I.iii.1

सुवरित्यादित्ये I.vi.2

सैषाऽऽनन्दस्य मीमागूंसा II.viii.2

सोऽकामयत् II.vi.3

हाउ्वु हाउ्वु हाउ्वु III.x.6